AN OCEAN OF OTHERS

FIRST DANCE OF THE SIBLING SUNS

Joshua Scott Edwards

ARCHEFIRE

PUBLISHING

Archefire Publishing LLC
Lansdale, PA 19446
www.archefire.com

This is a work of fiction. Names, characters, places, and incidents are a product of the author's imagination. Any resemblance to actual people, living or dead, or to businesses, companies, events, institutions, or locales is completely coincidental.

Editing by Stacey Kucharik
Proofreading by Benjamin Grossman
Cover art by Felix Ortiz
Cover design by Shawn T. King
Map design by Jared Martin and Joshua Scott Edwards
Map illustration by Chiara Noemi Monaco

An Ocean of Others/ Joshua Scott Edwards. -- 1st ed.
ISBN 979-8-9856162-1-7 (paperback)
979-8-9856162-0-0 (ebook)
Library of Congress Control Number: 2022915867

*To the master of the game,
from whose mind this web was spun.
This one's for you, Jared.*

Table of Contents

Acknowledgments

If you'd have asked me five years ago, writing a novel would have been the last thing I expected to fall in love with. At twenty-seven, I may have been late in finding my passion, but there's no doubt I found it. Passion alone, however, cannot bring a novel to life—for that I needed plenty of help.

This story was adapted from a roleplaying campaign my friends and I played, so first I must express my gratitude toward Jared Martin for creating a world and a story that sent my life in the most unexpected of directions. The Sixty-Fourth Hand of the Agency within these pages was once called the LLAWBringers, and each member of Sixty-Four represents a close friend whose performances and decisions served as a source of inspiration in my writing. My thanks go out to Eric Alzheimer, Chris Leschak, Jeremiah Pinca (who fully embodies Sentyx in daily life), Lauren Pinca, and Tim DiIorio. I hope I did your characters the justice they deserve.

I also want to thank my writing group: Liz Leiby, my arch-nemesis who never stops killing me with kindness; Laura Wehr, who possesses seemingly endless knowledge of our craft; Katherine Parys, who is the cheerleader every author deserves; Rebecca Hane, who gave me my greatest compliment in comparing my work to Brandon Sanderson's; Marissa Priest, whom I sincerely hope to meet in person one day when the plague is behind us; and Kate Keister, who has read these chapters more than anyone else and still has not stopped providing wonderful feedback.

Other beta readers include Kelsie Olds, who will likely forever hold the record for fastest reading of this book; Jared Martin, who held me to an appropriately high bar as I adapted this story; and Rachel Keatley, who is much more than just a beta reader—she is my fiancée and the steady foundation on which my whole life has come to rest.

I would also like to extend my thanks to the ARC Team, who have so generously given their time to reading and reviewing an early version of the story: Vinamra Tripathi, Craig (Bookwyrm), Abel Montero, Michael Sugarman, NC Koussis, Conor Daley, Esmay Rosalyne, Boe Kelley, Tyra Leann, Matthew Higgins, and Andrew Mattocks. Indie authors are lucky so many amazing people like you are a part of the community.

Of course, I can't forget my mom and dad, whose love and support has never wavered in over 31 years. I love you both.

Finally, my sincerest gratitude to my editors: Benjamin Grossman for his attention paid to the smallest of details that escaped the rest of us; and Stacey Kucharik, who has been as much a mentor as an editor, and who has gone above and beyond since the day I met her; it does not go unnoticed.

N
W
E
S
CANAKO
LIWOKIN
LEPPIT
LAWIKO

Spread of the Scourge

FEAR NOT THE ERA WHEN LIGHT TURNS TO DARK,
FOR ONLY FROM DARKNESS CAN TRUE LIGHT EMERGE.

—First Proverb of the Book of Light

PART ONE

SIBLINGS

CHAPTER ONE

The Last Bounty Hunter

A bounty hunter prepares for every possibility. We feel the pulse of the city's veins, sense danger before it strikes, and ideally make a bit of coin staving off the trouble. But even I never saw the Riot coming. None of us did. It struck in an instant. I set out from the Burg one morning to track an elusive target, blinked, and found myself in the Market surrounded by blood and flames. Over six thousand deaths before the noon bell tolled, yet only the ghost of a memory remained. Of the Riot itself I could recall nothing.

Its bloody aftermath, I would never forget.

Fires shimmering in streams of blood that flowed between bodies in the streets, the sun obscured by black smoke as thick as the wailing cries that haunted our beloved city. I would never forget the way fear gripped me each time I left a vestige of safety to walk among the carnage. For weeks I'd defended myself against attempts made on my life—nothing personal, only desperate endeavors to survive by those plagued by deprivation. The city had lost thousands of hungry mouths to feed, yet food had never been scarcer. Robberies had spiked, businesses had burned, the Church even failed to ring the arrival of dawn one frightful morning. Criers had howled that the fated Dark Era of yore had returned. For a time, I'd believed they were right.

Chaos reigned in the city of Liwokin until the Agency was established. But even after the Agency's Fingers quelled the unrest with the heavy hand of the law, every passing day was a new chance for the violence to erupt once more. When an impossibility becomes real, you never let it catch you unawares again.

What started the Great Riot?

As I hunted for the answer to this question, countless Liwo gave me the same response, like students trained by an instructor. "Everyone knows what started the Riot," they'd say, as if the common answer made any sense.

"Oh? What's that?" I'd ask for the tenth, the hundredth, the thousandth time, because apparently, I never learned.

And they'd laugh, or glare, or cast a look at me like I was the one losing my mind before the same word inevitably slipped off each of their tongues.

"Nothing."

*　*　*

The warning call of the half-dusk bell rang out as I came sliding to a stop, slipping in the waste-splattered dirt alleys they called streets in the Old District.

"You don't have to run, you know," I called. "We can just talk."

Several residents of the Blight—the name most Liwo gave this district—looked up at me in surprise. A shaggy, gray-haired man snickered at me from a mound of detritus in front of the husk of a hovel lost to the Riot's fires. The wooden foundation that once kept it level on the hill had collapsed long ago. Against all odds, two walls remained standing—enough to make a home in these destitute parts. In the street ahead of me, a barefooted boy began to cry. His stone-faced mother held his hand in her own, cradling his baby sister in her arm.

I looked beyond the family, searching the shadowed path running up the steep, narrow street for any signs of movement. Nothing.

"They never want to talk," I muttered, sheathing my knife and adjusting the weight of the crossbow slung over my shoulder. "Why don't they ever want to talk?"

My target had fled the pawnbroker's shop and entered the Blight just moments earlier only to vanish without a trail. The thief had finally shown up to try and sell an expensive bauble, newly acquired, he claimed, after many measures of saving hard-earned wages. I laughed at the perpetual lack of creativity criminals possessed. It took a certain desperation to show up at all, but to do so with a lie so galling? No one in Liwokin would believe any story in which a Blightdweller saved a sum of coin. Certainly not the pawnbroker, whom I'd known since he set up shop in the Artisans District, and who was happy to help out an old friend.

It's good to have friends. With eyes all over the city, what hope did my targets have?

The old man jabbed a thumb at the alley past his hovel, then winked. I smiled my thanks and strode toward the alley's entrance. The protective mother tugged her boy's hand, yanking him behind her.

"Miss," I said, nodding kindly to the woman, who stepped back and held her baby close. The infant looked at me with bright, round, innocent eyes. She might have been a Blightdweller, but unlike me, she at least had a family; she didn't know how lucky she was.

I squeezed my way between the upper half of one home and the base of another, a narrow path, even for the Blight. Frantic footsteps sounded as I pushed through the gap, then I caught sight of a cloaked man knocking someone aside and turning the corner. My crossbow caught on a stuck-out pipe. I wriggled free of the strap and tugged the weapon loose. Freeing a quarrel from my belt, I took off in pursuit.

The setting Brightdaughter, greater of the two Sibling Suns, shone through the next street, the watchful star hovering directly ahead where the Blight ended in open air with a sudden drop. Sunlight streamed through kicked-up dust and highlighted the fleeing thief's silhouette. His undoubtedly pilfered gold-trimmed cloak billowed as he raced toward the crowded wooden structure overhanging the cliffs.

They called this man-made monstrosity the docks, as if it were comparable to the actual docks of the more reputable districts far below. No ships could be moored to them since they hung precipitously over the water, unreachable except by climbing the hill of the Old District. No one hauled cargo on them; they probably couldn't handle the excess weight if tested. They weren't flat like most docks but multi-tiered and connected by rope ladders and wooden trusses. The name made no sense except as a petty proclamation by the small men of the Blight who engineered it: "We're as capable as the rest of you."

"I hope you're more careful than my last bounty!" I shouted, then I curled my lip.

More often than not, my targets who'd risked the docks slipped on the treacherous walkways and took the long plunge down into the bay. Some of the men I chased had chosen to jump of their own volition. A swift and painless end was better than being taken alive, I supposed, but they'd cost me my reward and the comfort of a roof over my head at night. This wouldn't be one of those nights, I hoped, but there was no way I could retrieve my client's pendant if my target died and fell from the docks. I stowed my crossbow.

The splintered wood creaked and groaned as soon as I stepped on to the lowest level of the docks, and for a moment it seemed today was the day the whole structure would buckle. Several of the anchor points securing the makeshift scaffolding to the cliff face seemed shakier every time I climbed this rickety creation. I had no choice but to trust them—my target had nearly finished climbing a hanging ladder to the next tier of walkways, and I had to follow him until he got back on firm ground.

Firmer ground, at least. It was the best one could do in the Blight.

As I clambered up the rope ladder, it started swinging like a violent storm had suddenly materialized. I peered up at the thief desperately shaking the ladder, hoping to drop me into the waters. Unable to overcome my grasp, fear filled his eyes, for everyone knew what happened to those who were caught by bounty hunters. Much like the city's criminals, justice in Li-wokin had always been swift and cruel. This time, however, my client had only requested his pendant's return.

"Give me the necklace," I shouted. "I don't want to kill you!"

He didn't toss down the necklace. Instead, he hawked a glob of spit that struck me square in the eye. The wood trembled with the echoes of his flight.

"All right." I wiped my eye clear. "Now I do want to kill you."

I climbed up onto the second tier. The thief was crossing a beam that spanned two anchor points, both hands outstretched for balance, one holding the pendant dangling precariously over the water. There was no rope for him to grasp such as there were in areas designed for foot traffic. But that also meant there were no people to slow him down.

Still, I chose the safer route and climbed up to follow him from a higher tier. There was only one exit on the other side of his path—the central dock with pulley elevators to the peak of the Old District hill. If I could get to it first...

It was going to be close. On this tier, the ramshackle path was twice as wide but had three times the people. I tramped past fishing men and women dangling their legs over the edge, jumped over a bucket of dead fish, and nearly slipped in the discarded guts. I weaved my way through the dangerously dense crowd, careful to guard my pockets from picking, more careful not to push anyone over the edge, most careful not to step off the edge myself. Rushing as I was, I collided past a man carrying a basket of rice and sent it spilling out through the cracks in the wood. I only had time to shout my apologies back to him; he shouted his curses in return.

I neared the central dock one level below. But before I could climb down, I saw the thief entering the nearest elevator cage, either not trying to draw attention to himself or thinking he was free of his tail. Below, there was a gap in the crowd. Without stopping to think better of it, I backed up two steps and took a deep breath.

"Lightmother, preserve," I prayed.

Then I leapt.

I'd never been a pious man, but a bounty hunter prepared for every possibility. Sailing through the air, I felt sure the wood would buckle under my weight as soon as I struck, collapsing and taking all of the Blightdwellers on the central platform down with me. But the gods showed mercy, the platform held, and the worst I got was the wind knocked from my lungs. It was more good fortune the crossbow, loaded and drawn on my back, hadn't triggered. The crash and commotion from the crowd drew my thief's attention. He frantically closed the gate and rang the signal bell. A few pounding heartbeats later, the elevator began to rise. He was going to get away.

I rose to my feet, coughing, surrounded by wide-eyed onlookers, and searched for any way to get to the top before him or to turn the elevator around, but there was no way. The elevator and the massive stone counterweight were both out of reach. My only chance now was to make sure he was dead before he reached the top.

The elevator would catch the pendant...right?

My crossbow was armed, quarrel already locked in, string already drawn. The shot would be narrow, and I had to take it soon, before the elevator ascended out of range. I took aim, steadied my breath, and...

Another bell rang from the peak; someone was coming down in the adjacent elevator. I immediately lowered my sight and sprinted toward its counterweight. Just in time for the elevator to start moving, I vaulted over the wooden rail and landed atop the stone, grabbing hold of the heavy rope that lifted it up. The weight swung forward and clipped the cliff's wall but continued to rise, slower than usual with my weight added to the balance. The thief would still reach the top well before I did and would have plenty of time to disappear.

"All this for a useless trinket," I said, groaning at the pain in my legs and chest. But no, it wasn't useless. It was for my client, and a bounty hunter keeps his promises.

The thief's elevator reached the top. Its lock extended from the cliff while mine only crossed the halfway point. He opened the cage and exited with haste, back toward the Blight's labyrinthine streets. As my rising counterweight crested the peak, I jumped to land right in front of the elevator operator whose job

I had just made significantly harder. He looked exhausted as he extended the weight's lock and let go of his tether.

"I'm sorry, Bello," I told the operator. "But which way did he go? The cloaked man. I'll give you a cut of the reward."

"Still waiting on my cut for the last favor I did you," he said, grumbling between heavy breaths.

"You'll have double, then," I promised, "but if he gets away, we'll both have nothing!"

Come on, hurry up, old man!

Bello spat, but pointed toward the second of five streets, one that led back down toward the Artisans. Then his bell rang again, and he took up his tether with a huff.

I ran for the street, shouting back to the fed-up operator. "You're a true friend!"

"Aye? And what's that worth?" Bello muttered as I ran off. "Friendship won't put food in my belly."

Three steps after turning the corner, my own hopes of supper that night were dashed. A tall, heavily muscled man in a calf-length, grayish-green coat was holding my thief out at arm's length. I knew those colors; I saw them too often of late. The man stealing my bounty was a Finger of the Agency.

Again?

"You haven't been reporting your status," the Finger said in a bored drawl. "Makes people mighty uncomfortable when someone like you stops showing up on schedule. Now, stop squirming. I'm authorized to use lethal force if you resist." The massive two-headed axe strapped diagonally across his back gave the ring of truth to his threat. But the Agency had a different conception of justice, far less brutal than the kind commonly practiced. A kind of job security, I figured. Let the criminals go free and you'd never run out of work.

"Lethal force?" The thief scoffed. "Ulken would have your head." He narrowed his eyes. "But Ulken didn't send you, did he? Reed did." The Finger didn't deny it. The thief smiled.

Did this thief work for the Agency? I sighed. What had I gotten myself into?

"It doesn't matter which one issued the command. Ulken or Reed, those two are of one mind." The thief laughed, and the Finger turned him around to bind his wrists. Then the green-cloaked man looked up and spotted me leveling my crossbow at my target. He grinned. "A crossbow's a bit old fashioned, isn't it, bounty hunter? Lower the weapon. This one's mine. The Agency sanctioned it."

"This thief's got my client's pendant," I said. "That's all I'm after. Give it to me and I'll be out of your way." I didn't lower my aim. I would fulfill my contract, whether he agreed with me or not.

The muscular Finger laughed. "You think you can stand in my way?" He shook his head. "Bounty hunting is dead. You're one of the last in Liwokin. You know that, don't you?"

Of course I knew that. I gritted my teeth, tempted to alter my aim and pull the trigger.

The Finger searched my thief for hidden weapons but didn't do a good job and came up empty. All he had was the pendant in his hand along with some slip of paper that gave off a strange blue glow. Something was wrong. This man didn't look like a Blightdweller at all.

You're no ordinary thief, are you?

His face was shaved clean, his hair styled, if messy from our chase. With a clearer look at him I saw now the cloak he wore wasn't trimmed with silver, but with *Archemetal*. Not just anyone could afford such decadence. If it wasn't stolen, this thief must have been from the Gild. As I looked him over, he gazed back at me with keen eyes. He dropped the slip of paper to the ground.

The Finger didn't notice. He was now focused on me, and it was clear his patience was wearing thin. "When's the last time you had a real bounty, not one searching for some trinket or standing guard from dusk to dawn?"

I scowled, because he was right. Ever since Ulken convinced the city council to establish his Agency, bounties had become scarce and ill-rewarded. How could I compete with the free services the Agency provided? Surely not by letting them take the few bounties I *did* have. I was ready to fight to keep this one; my fingers hovered over the trigger.

"Fine," the Finger said, "have your trinket." He pried the thief's fingers off the pendant.

A glow of golden-red bloomed between the two men, but it was too late for warning. Archefire flowed from the thief's hand. It destroyed the pendant's chain and traveled up the Finger's arm. The Finger screamed. The thief threw his head back, skull connecting with the Finger's nose. Blood flowed. Stumbling backward, the Finger's coat sleeve burned. The thief turned to me, summoning more of the Fire between two hands.

"Too slow." I squeezed my hand, and my crossbow kicked. The quarrel punched into the thief's skull. But Archefire has a will of its own. Without the mage's control, the Fire tore its way through his body. Every visible bit of skin began to glow gold, as if the man were made of molten iron. His clothes burst into flame. His skin peeled and blackened, and he crumbled to the ground, a charred heap. I shielded my face from the radiating heat.

Burning up was a bad way to go.

I tossed my weapon down and rushed to the Finger's side, then used my coat to smother the flames on his arm. Together, we threw dirt on the flames consuming the thief until the fires were low enough to stomp out. I cringed each time my boot cracked a bone, but we couldn't let the flames spread. When we finished, chests heaving, all that remained was a smoking corpse.

"That fool nearly began another Blight Fire," I said, remembering the thousands of Blightdwellers who perished in the Riot.

The Finger grunted. "Glad you hit him in the head, or we'd have worse than fire to contend with. Reed never mentioned he was a damned Archemage."

"You should have known when you found no weapon on him," I said, retrieving my crossbow. "They've always got some way to kill you. How's the nose?"

"Not as bad as the hand," he said, grimacing as he prodded it. His clenched fist was cracked and blistered. "I can't smell anything either, but in this city that's a blessing."

I laughed. "True enough."

"I was careless. Would have been ash if you hadn't killed him. Thanks for that," the Finger said, and held out his unburnt hand. "Name's Bengard. Seems I owe you my life."

"Call me Grim," I said, shaking his hand. "And he had it coming. It was nothing."

"'Nothing' is a powerful thing, it seems." Bengard had a crooked smile. "First it starts the Riot, now it saves my life."

Nothing, or so everyone said. I refused to accept this new common sense, as uncommonly senseless as it was. After the tragedy, Liwo had longed for normalcy, but this city would never return to the state we once knew. *Something* had ravaged the city I called home. And no matter the city's evident state of mass delusion, the worst had yet to come.

"I'll take the pendant now," I said.

"Of course." I felt a twinge in my own hand when Bengard unclenched his burnt fist to drop the pendant into his other palm. He kept hold of it when I reached out to take it, said, "But you know, if you ever get tired of hunting for toy treasure, Ulken could use a fighter at the Agency." He let go of the pendant, then knelt by the dead thief and sighed. "We need mages too. Why do they all seem content to waste their talents?" He shook his head and began gathering the unburnt Archemetal, no doubt to pad the Agency's coffers.

And without leaving even a flake to me. But I had what I came for. I clutched the recovered pendant.

"Hardly anything left of this one to bring back. I'd say he'll be cleaned up eventually, but..." He stood and made to leave, looking back one last time. "Consider what I said, Grim. You'll have a friend on the inside." He strode off.

As Bengard's footsteps faded and the Blight grew quiet with dwellers taking to their homes in anticipation of the dusk bells, I examined the damaged pendant. The chain was broken, ends melted where they touched the Fire, but the frame, made of lustrous golden Archemetal and encasing a dark gem, was undamaged. Its gem inset was black as obsidian with iridescent hints of pink and gold reflecting the sky, light of the Brightdaughter fading fast. Intricate patterns were traced in the metal with expert manipulation of Archefire by the pendant's creator. It was exquisite, precious, evident of extraordinary control and talent.

But what did the thief want with it? Surely, it wasn't for the coin—his Archemetal cloak would have fetched an even better price. It must have had some other purpose. And why was the Agency interested in him? Something wasn't adding up. Then I remembered the knowing look he gave me, the glowing paper that fluttered from his hands. I searched around the charred corpse, found the note half-covered with dirt, and picked it up.

It was blank.

Did the mage make it glow with his Archefire?

That inky blue it had given off *had* appeared quite unnatural. I'd have to find a mage and see what they could make of it. But first, I had a job to do. Hopefully, the friendship I had with my client would see that he's still willing to pay the contract price with the pendant's chain destroyed. With my luck, it would be the chain he was really after. I'd never worked harder to survive than in the past year, and never been paid as poorly. If things didn't change soon, I might find myself reliving my adolescent years. Pilfering meals, sleeping in alleys, holding up honest Liwo at knife point.

That was one way to survive, but it was no way to live.

Ulken could use a fighter at the Agency. There seemed to be no room left in Liwokin for bounty hunters. I was the last holdout. Until now, I'd refused to join the Agency. I didn't like change—it always seemed to be for the worse. Bounty hunting was all I knew, and I didn't trust that organization. They quelled the chaos, but they stole my way of life. Maybe I was just stubborn. Bengard's words rang with promise, and he didn't seem a bad sort. *I'll have a friend on the inside...*

A crack of gunfire came from somewhere close behind, followed by the chilling laugh of someone who pleasured in causing pain—a common enough sort in the Old District. I tucked away the pendant and the mysterious note in the inner pocket of my coat, alongside a folded-up contract that promised a hefty reward. Then, I slung my crossbow over my back to leave.

In the streets, debris from the Riot still hadn't been cleaned up. The mess served as a reminder of what transpired that horrific dawn. Memories flashed before my eyes, and I felt myself transported back to the chaos. Fires shone through an open window, through which someone I loved had flown mere moments ago. I couldn't breathe. Blood flooded my airway. A monstrous man stood over me. But I felt no fear. I felt nothing at all.

I shook my head to clear the dying memory. The thought lingered only for a moment that despite what I remembered, somehow, I had escaped the Riot unscathed.

"Lucky me."

Sunset's light had dimmed to make room for the stars, and I heard a fading scream in the night as someone fell from the dark, wooden scaffolding below. The city's worst criminals operated in the Old District, but most Blightdwellers were simply too poor to live elsewhere. They had my sympathy. I knew how hard it was to survive the streets of Liwokin, and it only ever seemed to get harder. The Brightdaughter had remained low all day after rising in the southeast, meaning the day passed faster than most. A short day always meant a long night, and lately the nights were becoming longer and longer.

CHAPTER TWO

Lives of Luxury

Two more cracks of pistol fire echoed from the alley adjacent to mine as I hurried down the steep Old District hill. Both my blades were out to intimidate would-be attackers, but there was no telling when a desperate shooter might spot me and pull the trigger. Those that lurked in the shadows were always hungry for the treasures on a corpse. In this narrow street, chances were good the gunner would be in range of my sword before they saw me, but that wasn't a wager I would place.

Not tonight. Not when I was this close to fulfilling Inac's contract.

But killers and thieves weren't the only things to beware in the Blight. Speeding wayward down the treacherous hill, there was a danger of nicking myself on a sharp-edged roof sticking out at neck height or flattening myself against the side of a rushing-up shack. Only because I knew these streets so well could I keep control during such a rapid descent. No one survived long in my profession without learning the city inside and out.

When my old orphanage sent me out on the streets to beg for the first time, I was a scared, stick-thin boy with a dirty tangle of black hair that had never been cut and not a single possession

I could call my own. Liwokin felt like the entire world, vast and impossible to map. It only took twenty-odd years, but now the city didn't seem so big. Now, it felt like home, from the mud-slick alleys of the Blight to the paved paths of the Burg that lead beyond the Gild's guarded gates. As for belongings, I owned a knife, a sword, a crossbow, and a purse full of gold I guarded with all three. I had friends in every district, other hunters I could rely on, bounties enough to fund an extended stay in a fine inn. I had everything I needed.

Until the Riot and the Agency.

Life always changed unpredictably, in ways hard to explain, let alone reverse. Usually it was for the worse, and even if it was for the better, it could be hard to tell. The fact that something like the Great Riot could occur was undoubtedly a change for the worse; nothing that killed so many could ever be considered good. But the Riot led directly to the Agency's founding, which I would begrudgingly admit had been good for Liwokin—if not for my own well-being. Ulken's organization had swiftly calmed fears over a recurrence of the event, and the city had been able to gain its footing once more. When it seemed that the city would fall to chaos, the Agency's work made a real difference.

So why did my stomach turn at the thought of joining?

When the new enforcers of the law appropriated my contracts, the City Council clerk told me taverns would always offer independent work for bounty hunters. I was a fool to believe him. New laws required all but the pettiest of crimes to be reported to the Agency. How could I have foreseen that? Common rabble had no insight into the passage of laws. But I vowed to adapt. It was the only way to survive.

Briefly, I sought an apprenticeship in the Market, and quickly learned I had only a mind for hunting. I tried saving my coin, but they slipped through my fingers faster than I could earn them. I collected friends to help me survive, but who wants a friend who can offer nothing in return? Inac, my client, might have been my closest remaining companion, though he didn't know it. At least he was gracious enough to believe me when I kept insisting his pendant would turn up soon. Each time I visited him, my pockets had grown lighter, and my desperation had grown heavier. This was my last job; I had no other lined up. Tonight, I would finally deliver on my promise to Inac. After that, I had no choice.

I would have to join the Agency. Only they had the kind of work at which I could succeed.

Because they stole it all from me. A red heat rose behind my eyelids and nearly wrung out tears. *Liwokin couldn't just go back to normal, could it?*

After escaping the Blight intact and leaving the wreckage of the ramshackle homes behind, I slowed to a more sustainable pace. The rest of this night's journey would be on level ground, traveling through safer districts as the city gently curved around Brightcalm Bay.

First, I came to the Artisans District, which bordered the Old District. Its denizens' minds were equally disordered as the Blightdwellers, but they put them to better use here. Painted statues lined the streets outside the vibrantly colored shops of each artisan vying for business and attention. Some depicted mundane creatures. A huge, spindly crustacean lurched out to reach for passersby. A hard-edged form in the shape of a wolf howled at the empty night sky. Others were carved to portray scenes of Liwo legend. Ahead of me in an open square, an enormous sculpture of marble and Archemetal showed our forebearers' last stand against the invading armies of Paceeq, when the country expanded to conquer the northern hemisphere and unite it under the rule of the Bright Empress. I stopped to admire this masterpiece, not for the first time. Reflections of starlight shimmered in a golden Archemetal plaque that designated the artisan as anonymous.

Our ancestors fought when the world they knew was being torn away. Now no one even knew their names.

A gentle hand caressed my shoulder. "Need a break from your troubles—"

I whirled with my knife out and gave the poor courtesan a shock to equal my own. She backed up a step until I sheathed my blades. "Sorry, dear. Another time."

A friend is waiting for me, though he doesn't know it.

As I made for the next district, several other women of the night approached, making sweet-sounding offers. So too did several scammers, whose offers weren't half as sweet. I refused all requests—some more unkindly than others—and reached the Market. The central streets of the Trade District were brightly lit, torchlight flickering on the worn-smooth stone with which they had been paved. Few traversed the canopied trade rows now save for hired guards, their torches warding off darkness, their swords warding off thieves. Despite the presence of peacekeepers, I kept a grip on the hilt of my blade. This wasn't the Blight, but some of the hooded figures I passed were sure to be pickpockets who valued my coin enough to chance the guards. Not that they would protect anything but the shops that hired them. Nor was the city's old militia around to deter any cutpurse, not since Ulken convinced the City Council to cut their budget.

Just one more thing taken by the Agency.

I turned the corner onto a wide street leading toward Liwokin's Residential District, the Burg. The Agency's tower loomed in the distance, peeking over the buildings to my right, fires in the tall tower glittering like a constellation of nearby stars. But that wasn't my destination tonight. I would find my friend in another new establishment, even newer than the Agency.

Another change I'm not certain is for the better.

Though the City Council only agreed to sanction the Wistwicker for operation in the Trade District, the border between the Market and the Burg was more a suggestion than a demarcation. The poor inhabitants of the homes flanking this raucous inn surely had a few suggestions of their own. The noise of never-ending bar fights swelled as disorderly patrons stumbled out through the front door. Few topics were as divisive as the question of what to do with the inn, but, as it abided by all legal restrictions, there was little its naysayers could do. For good or for ill, the Wistwicker was part of the city now.

The front door crashed open just before I pushed my way in. I stepped aside to let two inebriated men pass, each holding onto the tunic of his foe and shouting in his face. A dozen cheering watchers streamed after them and formed a circle around the men as they brawled in the street, while the guard posted nearby pretended nothing was happening.

I shook my head and entered. The overwhelming, ever-present aroma of ale welcomed me to an establishment housing activities that made the commotion outside seem neighborly and serene. Jugs and tankards sloshed as rowdy patrons bumped the servers weaving their way through the throng. There were three different group songs happening at once, though I hadn't the slightest idea how anyone kept in time with one another over the cacophony. I scanned the room for my friend, though I guessed he wouldn't be up here. He'd be hiding in the basement, just like last time.

A long stairway led down into a wholly different environ-ment. Darker, more restrained, and with fewer people. Some seedy individuals conversed in quiet tones, inaudible over the sound from upstairs that masked their plans for misdeed. Inac sat alone at the same table as always. He was easy enough to spot. He wore the same tattered cloak, a deep ocean-blue trimmed with silver fringes, with the hood pushed back. He wore the same hair, sandy brown and curly atop his head, trimmed short at the sides. And he wore the same posture, slouched down and head hanging, sighing into his cups. If I had to guess, I would have said he was younger than me, but while the years had been hard on me, something told me they had been even harder on him. When I sat down across from Inac, he looked up at me with dark green eyes, tired and bloodshot.

Poor guy looks worse every time I see him. Good thing I'm here to make his day.

"Hope you've haven't spent everything on drink," I said, and flashed him a grin.

"Ah, Grim," he said, not smiling back. "It has for us been some time." I always met Inac in a tavern, and his manner of speaking once made me think the ale had addled his mind. But although his voice was accented and quick, he never slurred his words, despite the many empty tankards nearby. "For what have you come to me tonight?"

"Would you believe I just came to visit a good friend?"

Inac rolled his eyes.

I chuckled. "The prospect of coin of course, Inac. You know me."

"Always you say to me this." He took a long drink and swal-lowed it loudly before pushing aside another empty tankard. "Always you are hopeful, but with never a reason."

"I have to assure you I'll finish the job. The Agency certainly wouldn't do you the courtesy. And I don't want you reconsidering, thinking I've forgotten you. Have to maintain relationships, you know? Only way to survive as an independent hunter these days." I winked at Inac and took a swig from his newly delivered tankard. He frowned. "Besides, I've plenty of reason for hope tonight." I reached into my coat and held up the contract, then spread it flat on the table. "I believe the reward was specified here. 'Forty golden coins bearing the starburst sigil of the Empress,' it says."

Inac's eyebrows raised. "You brought to me…"

I reached into my pocket again, held the broken pendant and hesitated. "First, let me just say—"

"Please, Grim! Let me see it." His eyes were eager, all tiredness washed away.

I sighed and revealed the pendant's damage. "I'm sorry. The thief was an—"

He snatched it from my hand with surprising agility and examined it closely. I studied his expression as it transitioned from relief to pain, and something like…shame?

"Archemage," I finished. "He's dead now. Burned up, but not before doing some damage."

Inac wiped the start of tears from his eyes and sighed. "How long has it been…three measures? I thought to myself forever it was lost." He looked up, half grinning, then tossed a small pouch across the table. It landed in front of me with a clink. "Your stars. It seems to me I owe to you a real drink." He summoned the lone server and ordered two shots of Stinbine rum.

"Some bread to chase it for me," I said, stomach rumbling. "And crab legs, buttered. Anything for you, Inac?"

"Not for me," my friend said. "I am good."

I handed the server eight stars for the meal, a fifth of my reward already gone. For the rum, Inac handed over two more coins to the man. The server bowed deeply, then turned and darted up the steps.

"You know, not that I'm complaining," I said, "but most people wouldn't post such a bounty for a lost pendant."

Inac nodded. "Yes. I first tried the Agency, but they said to me it would be many measures before they could give to me their help. I could not wait for them. I had to have it back. It is to me...very important."

"I had a good look at it. Finely crafted," I said, then scratched the back of my head. "Sorry I couldn't return it in one piece."

Inac shook his head. "It only was this I worried about." He remained silent for a moment, rubbing his thumb over the pendant's iridescent black stone. "It reminds to me of my brother."

The way he hesitated made my chest tighten. I never had a family, but I knew loss well enough. "Your brother...how long has it been?"

His brows furrowed. "I cannot remember. Ever since I—" He flinched at his own words, then took a long breath. "I only know it was long before the Riot."

"You were here for it, then. I don't suppose you have any insight into how it started?"

Inac shrugged. "Some things are for us not meant to be known."

"You believe that? If we don't see it coming, how can we prepare? We were lucky to survive the first, but the way Liwokin's gone since then...the city can't take another."

"The years before the Riot...they only are for me a haze," Inac said. "Thinking of them only reminds to me of grief. And drink." His voice cracked, and he lifted his tankard to his lips.

"Then there was the Riot. I afterward realized I did not want for myself to die. If there is another, I at least will be awake."

A lull fell on the conversation as I stared down at the table. Hard to believe the Riot could have been good for anybody. Had the disaster truly pulled Inac back from the brink of despair? Despite meeting with him a dozen times, Inac had never been particularly talkative until this night. An air of sadness always surrounded him, but I hadn't known how heavy it hung. A server interrupted our silence to deliver two small glasses of Stinbine rum.

Not wanting to probe my friend's wounds too deeply, I changed the subject. "Tell me about the Stinbine Isles. What were they like before you left?"

Inac pulled his gaze away from his pendant. "A small isle called Sea Pot Lake was for me home. It did not back then seem to me so small." Inac picked up his shot glass and half-submerged it in a tankard. The rum sat lower than the ale, but the glass kept the two liquids from mixing. "Huge walls keep out the sea, but they also keep out most visitors. I did not know there was beyond them a whole world." He tipped the shot glass on its side and let a trickle of ale enter, then set it back on the table in a golden-brown puddle. "The great forests in Eko are like those in the Sea Pot, but I could not live with them in the treetops. So I came here. I like it here. The bay reminds to me of the lake."

"I like it here too," I said, smiling. "Liwokin's always been my home. Can't help but feel a sort of kinship with my fellow Liwo. Whether they're Blightdwellers or Gildmembers, I don't have to like them, but they're family. For good or for ill." I lifted my shot glass to my nose, wrinkling at the sharp smell of the foreign liquor.

Inac snorted. "I see you never have had Stinbine rum. I am surprised you have left any sense of smell. Have I never told to you how bad this city stinks?"

I laughed. "Makes the good smells that much sweeter."

"In Liwokin? I am not sure there *are* any good smells. The Market smells to me like rotting whale carcass."

Probably worse.

Warmth spread through my chest. Our earlier meetings had consisted of me making empty promises and an intoxicated Inac humoring me because he had no other options. After so many days searching fruitlessly for his pendant, it was good to see it had so greatly lifted his spirits.

"The Market. That's where you earn your coin then?" I asked.

"Many days I do," Inac said. "I some days work for crafters in the Artisans District. Meaningless work. Imbuing for smiths their nails. Tempering into Archemetal raw iron."

My eyes widened. "Archemetal? How've I known you this long without knowing you're a mage?"

He shrugged. "Did my robe not give to you a clue?"

I chuckled. "Thought that was a Stinbine Isle thing. Don't know much about Archemages. One tried to kill me earlier tonight, though."

"I am sure in your line of work many more than that have tried to kill you, my friend. There are many of us. You yourself could become one. The Empire teaches to all the world Archemagic, or so they believe." Inac sighed and muttered. "They do not know of Archemagic its true nature. They upset the balance, use like a crude tool the Fire."

"Its true nature?" I asked. Was he implying there was something other than Archefire?

Inac waved the question away as a server delivered my plate, overflowing with the legs of a massive, steaming crab. He set down a bowl of melted butter and a heel of fresh bread. My mouth watered—this was the first time in two measures eating anything other than dried meat and old stew.

I bet Ulken's Fingers eat this well every night.

Then I remembered something. I dug into my coat pocket and found the blank note dropped by Inac's pendant thief. The Archemage had made it glow somehow.

"Can you use your magic to light this up?" I asked, holding up the paper.

The mage snapped the fingers of his right hand and a mote of flame appeared in midair. "Easily," he said. "Why?"

I yanked the paper back. "Not like that," I said. "The mage who stole your pendant had this. It gave off a blue glow in his hand before he dropped it to the ground."

Inac cocked his head, extinguished the Fire, and took the note. "A blue glow? That does not sound to me like the Fire." Yet, as Inac held the note close to his chest, the paper began emitting the same inky blue glow I saw earlier in the Blight.

"How are you doing that?" I asked in wonder.

"This is not my doing," he said, searching the table for the culprit. He let out a curious hum when he found it. "It is the pendant." He held the pendant closer to the paper and the glow focused into letters, revealing hidden writing.

'My old friend has caught wind of more monsters abroad. No word yet whether he will make a move. Ulken thinks they remain under control, but events have outpaced him. Keep your eyes on the advisor and report back to me.'

An elaborate signature followed the cryptic message, perhaps to prove its validity to the recipient, whoever they were.

"Reed," I said. "That name mean anything to you?"

"It means to me nothing," Inac said, "but it is to me clear that this message was not meant for our eyes."

I snorted. "What gave it away, the invisible ink?"

Inac grinned wide, the gap showing between his two front teeth. "The Agency helped recover from the Riot, no? And Ulken, he created the Agency. Why would someone conspire against him, the most powerful man in the city?"

"Who else would people conspire against but the most powerful?" I broke off a chunk of bread and shoved it in my mouth. The flavor was so rich I nearly teared up. Flakes of crust spread across the table as I tore off another mouthful with my teeth. Still chewing, I said, "Maybe this Reed wants the position for himself. But what's he talking about? Monsters abroad? Only thing that comes to mind are the Skardwarves, but they're stuck in the south."

"Old tales tell to us that these were once their lands," Inac said, "before we drove them across the sea. Maybe they want to reclaim it."

I paused mid-bite and licked my lips. *The Empire wouldn't allow it.*

"Those are just stories," I said. "Ulken doesn't need to keep them under control. It doesn't fit. Peekers, perhaps? There's enough of them to take over the world."

Inac shook his head. "I have never met a Peeker Pair I did not like. There is one here now." He pointed. Two Peekers—wearing no clothes but covered head to toe in fuzzy brown hair and chitinous shells—sat at a table and conversed in their buzzing manner, sloshing their drinks and clicking with laughter. "No, I do not think these are the monsters of which this Reed writes."

My mind raced, but it was like trying to pick out a bounty from crowd while only knowing his hair color. Without some way to narrow the possibilities, the target could simply blend in. A familiar feeling came over me, the one I felt when taking on a new bounty. My skin tingled with excitement; I couldn't help but get lost in the mystery, consumed by the hunt. The way Inac's eyes darted around as he tapped his chin, I knew he felt the same. But with only this fragment, we'd get nowhere.

I caught myself. The answer was right under my nose, but I was asking the wrong questions. "We won't figure this out here," I said, "and we don't have to."

Inac narrowed his eyes. "What are you thinking, my friend?"

My pulse raced. I looked around to be sure no one paid us any attention. "I'm thinking we use this information to squeeze some reward from the most powerful man in the city."

Inac sat back in his chair and crossed his arms. "Why?"

"Because ever since Ulken created the Agency," I said with more fire than I expected, "nothing has gone my way. He's taken all my contracts and practically outlawed bounty hunting. His Finger nearly took your pendant earlier tonight. I'm sick of it. He owes me something in return."

"And me?" Inac asked. "Ulken owes to me nothing."

"No," I said. "But I do. How long did you wait for me to fulfill that contract? Whatever I get from Ulken, I want you to share in it." I tore off a leg from the crab and pointed the orange limb at Inac. "Plus, I need your help. Without your pendant, he'd never believe me."

Inac smiled. "Ah. So that is it." He swirled the remaining ale in his cup. "And how do you think it will go? We walk right up to the boss, tell to him someone is plotting against him, and he will hand to us a big bag of gold?"

I shook my head. "They don't let anyone into the Agency. We'd have to join."

Inac's hand stopped. He leveled a stare at me. "Join the Agency. Us?"

I shrugged. "It's the only way we can get to Ulken."

Inac narrowed his eyes. "And they let to join anybody who wants?"

"Don't think so. But I've got a friend on the inside. A Finger, Bengard—I saved his life. He told me they could use a fighter. And a mage. It'll be easy. He'll vouch for us."

"Then why do you not just tell to him about the note?"

"And risk losing the reward?" I chuckled. "I said I saved his life, not that I would trust him with mine. No, the information's got to come from us directly."

Inac pursed his lips and looked down. I waited for him to call the idea as crazy as it truly was. What business did I have asking him to help me extort someone as lauded as Ulken? Instead, he drank down the rest of his ale and leaned forward on his elbows. "What do you think this reward will be?" he asked.

But what he really meant was, "*Why does this mean so much to you?*"

I stared at the blank note on the table, as if my will alone would summon the secretive words. What could we get from Ulken for this? I broke open a crab leg, dipped it in the butter, and savored the delectable meat. What did I *want* from him?

To not worry about starving to death. To not only survive, but to thrive in this city... For things to return to how they used to be.

But some things were beyond the control of even the most powerful.

I ran a hand across my scalp. "I don't know. Maybe the best we can hope for is a good position in the Agency." I tossed the empty crab shell away. "Or we could burn this note in Archefire right now and go back to our lives of luxury, chasing thieves and imbuing magic nails."

Inac burst out laughing, loud enough to turn all the heads in the room. "Our lives of luxury! To that, I will drink," he said, lifting his shot glass.

"To thieves and magic nails," I said, raising my own. My voice and hand shook from the flush of adrenaline coursing through me. Were we really doing this? I was glad Inac agreed. Pulling off this plan would be much easier with a friend.

Our glasses clinked and we threw back the rum. Fire bloomed, first in my chest as I swallowed down the liquor, then in my mouth from the spices that lingered. Sweat beaded on my forehead as I panted, tongue stuck out.

Inac laughed again. "Now you see, Stinbine rum burns hotter than Archefire!"

Despite myself, I laughed as well. That, too, was always easier with friends.

CHAPTER THREE

Haze

Inac and I met the next morning at the Docks of the Burg. From there, the Agency's stone tower was barely visible as it peeked over the roofs of the dockside inns and warehouses. After a quick greeting and agreement that neither of us wanted to back out, we strode toward Ulken's headquarters fighting the flow of the crowd as thousands of Liwo filled the streets, making their way from the Residential District to the Docks. The Burg's scrunched-together houses lined wide streets, but the carts, horses, donkeys, and foot traffic made the district seem as cramped as the Blight. Still, it was nowhere near as crowded as before the Riot decimated Liwokin's population. I grimaced and tried not to think about that, focusing instead on staying close to Inac among the press of bodies.

But how could I ever forget it? Each time the houses obstructing our view gave way, the Agency tower seemed to have grown taller. The closer you lived to it, the greater a reminder you'd have of the tragedy every time you stepped out your front door. It may have seemed small from a distance, but when we reached the Agency's gates in a square bordering the Gild, it was like standing at the feet of a giant. Behind us, the City Council building was a small rock the giant could kick over.

The Agency was a concrete behemoth, plain and sensible. Evenly spaced floors with uniform rows of glass embedded in a matte gray block. A stone wall extended from its base, surrounding a courtyard only accessible through a single iron gate. All twenty-seven floors of the tower were erected in a matter of days by workers conscripted by Ulken. The courtyard took just one more day—one on which the Brightdaughter had not risen high above the horizon.

I had to give it to Ulken. The man knew how to get things done.

Inac blew an impressed whistle. "Even the Sea Pot walls do not rise this high. I hope for the sake of the city it does not fall."

"It'd take a whole lot to knock something like this over," I said, eyes following the stark tower walls toward the heavens. "Even if someone *could* do it, it'd only be a few days before they finished rebuilding it."

"Only if after this one there is stone left in the quarries."

I chuckled, then nodded toward the entrance to the courtyard. "They're stopping people at the gate. The only ones going in are wearing those uniforms."

The wide gate to the courtyard buzzed with activity. Not a half-dozen breaths passed between one person entering and another leaving. Those who came from inside trailed a wisp of the thick haze that seemed to coat the grounds of the courtyard beyond. Several different uniforms were on display, in a variety of muted colors. Most wore one comprised of different shades of gray, tightly fitted with their shirt tucked in, belt buckled, and sporting no long coat like the other colors. The sheer numbers of the gray-shirts told me they must be the lowest rank, and based on their dress, they were likely expected to stay out of the way. That would have been our uniform if we hadn't come with a gift for Ulken.

Two people wearing dark red coats entered, carrying between them some unwieldy mechanical device. Their crimson uniforms weren't half as striking as the strange, beak-like masks they wore, making them look like flightless cardinals. Shortly after the two crimson-coats disappeared, a woman in gold-and-white rushed past the guards and sprinted into the courtyard, nearly bowling over a gray-shirt who jumped out of the way.

Another five exited the gate, none of whom wore any uniform at all. I was not surprised by the two matching mages in green and blue robes, nor the brutish man with a crooked nose, nor the thin man in a tall, funny-looking hat. Yet I stood gaping at something lumbering along behind the rest. I knew the Agency recruited from all countries within the Bright Empire, but apparently, it recruited from some outside it as well.

Monsters abroad, the mysterious note had said, but it was wrong.

They were here at home as well.

I shook my head in disbelief. "Is that...?"

Inac hummed, furrowed his brows. "A Skardwarf in the north. Perhaps your first guess was not so far from the mark."

Ulken thinks they are still under control.

Stocky and shirtless, with skin like jagged stone, its body looked like rock sculpted into human form—albeit quite squat, with anchor-like feet and a bald, pockmarked head. The Skardwarf carried a quarterstaff with a gnarled, knotted end, roughly hewn from wood darker than any found in the north. It noticed me staring, bared its teeth, and raised its staff in my direction, but continued following the others, leaving deep footprints in the gravel path.

"I pictured them as being much smaller," I admitted. The stories I heard always portrayed them as short, dim-witted creatures, nothing to fear. Nonsensically, they also promised we'd be safe from them, separated as we were by a vast ocean with endlessly raging winds turning waves to knives and ships to splinters. Yet, here stood a Skardwarf, enemy of the Bright Empire in my home city. I never put much credence in stories. "How'd it survive the journey across the ocean?"

Inac shrugged as the group turned the corner and disappeared. "You should ask him sometime. Now, let us enter."

As we approached the Agency tower, a strange feeling overtook me. My unease at joining Ulken's organization was smothered, but so too was my confidence that our plan would work. I expected to feel some nerves as two armed and helmeted gray-shirts whispered something between them, then held up their hands to halt us. Instead, I felt nothing, as if my body were moved by a mind benumbed.

I noticed a gray, hazy cloud seeping out from the courtyard, slithering across the gravel until it reached my feet. The cloud seemed to crawl up my body until I couldn't help but breathe it in. When the musty wood-burning-in-a-chemical-fire scent hit my nose, I coughed and spat, but the acrid odor clung to my nostrils, until suddenly it shifted into something pleasant, a scent like flowers and honey.

One of the gray-shirt guards grunted. His stubbled chin stuck out like the toe of a boot, from a jaw that never ceased working, like he had a mouth full of gum. "Told you, just like I said. Gets everyone their first time. Now pay up."

The other guard's half-lidded eyes were topped by high brows, as if he were perpetually surprised. He grumbled and put a star into Bootjaw's open palm.

What was this stuff? I felt some of my uneasiness return and looked to Inac, wondering if he had any idea. The mage had a distracted, puzzled look on his face, but he hadn't gagged like I did.

"Didn't get him," I said, gesturing to Inac.

Both the guards' eyes went wide. Highbrow's expression turned to a look of pure elation. "Finally! One your way, one mine. Now's time *you* pay up."

Bootjaw hesitantly held out the same coin the other had just given him, clearly unwilling to give it back. He didn't let go when Highbrow tried to take it, lips pursed like he was trying to come up with some greedy excuse.

I cleared my throat, annoyed at their stalling. "We've come to join up. I know a Finger, his name's—"

Highbrow jerked the coin free. "New recruits, ah? All right then. Same question we ask everyone: What can you do?"

What can you do? It was the same question as always when offering my services to those in need... *Until after the Riot, that is.*

Ever since, the question usually came with a 'that the Agency can't?' stuck on the end.

I smiled the same way I always did when trying to convince someone they're in need of my skills. Then I recalled what Bengard said. *Ulken could use a fighter at the Agency.*

"I'm a hunter." I put my hand on the hilt of my sword, drew the iron just a palm's width. "I can handle myself in a scrape, and she's gotten her fair taste of blood. Still, I prefer the crossbow." I slammed my sword back into its scabbard, nodded toward Highbrow's holstered pistol. "More reliable than a flintlock. Quieter too. Listen, I've been at this a lot longer than the Agency has. I figure I'm doing you a favor joining up."

"We'll see about that," Bootjaw said. "And him?"

Inac looked like he hadn't heard him. He was focused on something else. I nudged him and he snapped out of it, then focused on the guard, grinning. "And me?" he said. "What I can do?"

He held up his right hand, showed it front and back, like a magician performing a coin trick. The two guards exchanged a glance, puzzled by the display. Then Inac snapped his fingers, and a molten orb of Fire appeared a few inches in front of Bootjaw's nose, hovering in midair. His eyes went wide, and he flinched back, but the orb stayed with him, like it was attached by an invisible rod. He froze, comprehending that he couldn't get away.

"Enough, stop!" he pleaded, and Inac twisted his wrist. The Fire began circling around Bootjaw's head. It went one way, then the other, before Inac swiped his hand sideways. The Archefire zipped across to circle around Highbrow's head, much to the relief of his partner.

Inac laughed and clenched his right hand into a fist. The Fire dissipated, but the sweat and fear on the guards' faces remained. "I am an Archemage," Inac said, pointing out his sea blue cloak, ragged and worn as it was. "And that was not even my good hand."

Bootjaw growled as he wiped his face dry. With angry eyes affixed to Inac, he whistled inside over his shoulder and shouted, "New recruits, Looker! One mage and one killer!"

Looker emerged from the courtyard and stopped short below the portcullis. She held a pad of paper, scribbled on it as a puff of white haze curled up and around. She wore a coat that hung down to calf length, the same style as Bengard's, but pale blue rather than green. Did the different color signify Looker held a different position than the Finger? She glanced at me and Inac, boredom in her eyes, then looked down to add some more scribbles. "Two of you? Follow me." She turned, paying little mind to the gray-shirts that scurried clear of her path.

We obeyed, following her through a busy courtyard blanketed with smoke. Several gray-shirts puffed on small cigars and chatted with one another; one sat partially submerged in the white cloud, acting as if it weren't there at all. The sweet-smelling smoke dripped from their cigars' burning ends, slowly dropping into the chaotic, hazy pool flooding the ground. Countless other gray-shirts carrying slips of paper, field supplies, weapons, and food hurried through the courtyard in all directions, disturbing the smoke in their passing and swirling it in their wake. Two stone incense pots supplied the bulk of the fumes. Near them, a man in white and gold posted a bold, black number on a lightwood signpost. It was large enough to be visible across the courtyard. 'Twenty-four', it read, and I wondered:

Twenty-four what?

"This is your assigned Hand," Looker said, stopping abruptly next to a group of four individuals. All of them were unusual, but none more so than the Skardwarf who stood among them. This one bore no weapon but was otherwise indistinguishable from the first Skardwarf I'd seen. It stared at me with an expressionless, stony face, and I realized I was staring back. I had never expected to see *one* monster from the Dark, southern hemisphere, far less two of them before the clang of the half-noon bell. I reluctantly pulled my gaze from the Skardwarf, always keeping it in my peripheral vision. Looker read off the names of the others as she pointed them out.

"Garret," she said, pointing to an Ekoan. Traders from the country of Eko were common in Liwokin, but Ekoan rangers were rare. This one stood cross-armed and regarded me with a humorless face darkened by the shadow of his raised hood. Oak-brown braids with animal bones tied into his hair hung down past his neck, and he wore a cloak of patchwork leather, bark, and bone. It was decorated with woven leaves and dyed fur in a dozen shades of green.

"Which one?" Garret asked Looker.

"Don't interrupt," she said, and continued; the ranger spat into the mist. "Lorelay." Looker pointed to a Paceeqi girl. Tall and athletic, like most from her country, she wore the crimson and gold of the Bright Empire's capital. Her long hair matched the Empire's gold near the ends and graded to blood-red up at the roots. She wore two long knives strapped across her chest, and a strange instrument hung from her belt.

Lorelay smiled at me and Inac. "Nice to meet—"

"Dunnax," Looker interrupted, pointing at another Paceeqi standing next to Lorelay.

Dunnax scowled and stepped toward Looker, but Lorelay held an arm out to hold him back. While Lorelay had the slender frame of a typical Paceeqi woman, Dunnax was big even for a Paceeqi man. He topped her by a full hand's span and carried an ornate silver glaive that was taller still.

Anyone with a weapon that big must know how to use it.

Dunnax's impressive brawn was only outmatched by his impressive look of contempt; his face only softened when Lorelay pleadingly squeezed his arm.

Looker barely reacted to the huge man's anger. Her eyes flicked up to regard him from beneath her brows, then she glanced her papers once more and said, "Sentyx."

"What?" the Skardwarf asked.

"She's not talking to you," Garret said.

Sentyx grunted.

Garret grunted back and rolled his eyes. "So," he said to Looker, "which one?"

"The killer's yours," Looker drawled. "The mage will be assigned elsewhere."

I looked at Inac and we both frowned. If we got separated, neither of us would have any evidence to give to Ulken. The pendant and the note were each useless without the other. "We need to be assigned together," I said.

Looker shrugged. "Five in a Hand," she said, and beckoned to Inac. "Follow me."

"Wait," the mage said, but the impatient escort had already moved on. Inac's shoulders slumped. "Find me tonight, my friend." I nodded and he hurried to catch Looker.

Guess I'd have to make some new friends. I looked at the odd group before me. The collection of expressions that greeted me didn't seem promising.

"So, you're a killer, eh?" The ranger, Garret, spat. "Could've used a mage. Already got plenty of killers."

"We already have a mage, too," Lorelay said. "Dunnax controls the Fire. He was a—"

"I'm no mage," Dunnax said. "The Order of Paladins teaches some practical controls. The rest are forbidden." He frowned, as if his words tasted rotten, then grunted and picked up a bulging leather pack that was hidden below the knee-deep smoke. "All five of us are here now. We should get our orders."

"Always straight to business with you," Lorelay said.

"This smoke, these...people." Dunnax narrowed his eyes at a passing trio of crimson-coats carrying a coffin overhead; their hunched backs and heavy steps told me it was full. "I'm already growing sick of it. We've been shuffled around this courtyard waiting for a fifth since dawn."

"Since dawn?" Garret barked a laugh. "You poor thing. Been coming here to wait for three days now. They let us in at dawn and kick us out at half-dusk." He threw an arm around the Skardwarf to pull him close, but only succeeded in moving himself. "Sentyx has been here even longer. You tired of waiting yet?"

"I face into the wind," Sentyx said, his rough voice loud enough to be heard beyond the walls. Two passing gray-shirts flinched at the outburst before continuing with their duties, muttering to each other.

"By the abyss, Skardwarf, we're right here." Garret pushed himself away from the Skardwarf and rubbed his ear, wincing. "*You face into the wind.* What does that even mean?"

The Paceeqis and I stared expectantly at the Skardwarf. Sentyx said nothing.

"Aye," Garret said. "That's about all you'll get out of him."

I shook my head, scowling at the Skardwarf. What did Ulken want with these dark lovers from the South in his Agency?

"You seem awfully close with the Skardwarf, Ekoan," Dunnax said. "Have your people forgotten their loyalty to the Bright Empire?"

"Dunnax, stop," Lorelay warned, but the Paceeqi stepped past her and towered over the short-statured Ekoan.

Garret spat, then looked up at Dunnax from beneath his hood. He cracked his neck, animal bones jangling in his braided hair. "Loyalty? Funny thing for a disgraced Paladin to bring up." Dunnax clenched his fists, but Garret continued. "Between us, the loyalty of 'my people' isn't worth the spit on your boots."

I put myself between Dunnax and Garret to stop them from coming to blows. "I love a good scuffle as much as anyone, but we've only just met. No need to be at each other's throats."

"He's a long way from reaching my throat," Dunnax said.

"Enough!" Lorelay strained as she picked up Dunnax's pack, then shoved it into his hands. "It's not their fault, what happened to us."

Dunnax swung the pack onto his back, nearly clobbering Sentyx with it. "To *us?*" He started for the wide-open cathedral-like doors that led to the first floor of the Agency.

I sighed. I expected some initiation procedure, some training for new recruits, an explanation of duties. Instead, I'd been separated from Inac, dumped in a smoky courtyard with a group of strangers in something called a Hand.

"Well," I said, "this isn't going as planned."

"I'm sorry," Lorelay said, her face awash with guilt. "My brother's not usually like this."

"That's your brother?" I asked, but now that she said it, the resemblance was uncanny. "What happened to you?"

"We've...had a rough year."

"Whole city has," I said.

"What's your name anyway, killer?" Lorelay asked with a grin.

"Grim."

Garret blew a sputtering laugh. "*Grim?* What, did you scowl at your mother fresh from the womb?"

I smiled. "It was the orphan keeper, actually. She never wanted me to forget what a miserable boy I was."

"Look," Sentyx said. He stared across the courtyard to where Dunnax was being questioned by a man in white and gold.

The former Paladin pointed us out to the man, who turned and stood with his hands behind his back. Dunnax said something to the man, then threw up his hands when he was ignored. Lorelay groaned and jaunted across the courtyard. The rest of us followed.

When we all gathered near the entrance to the tower, the white-and-gold cloaked man cleared his throat. "Your presence is required at once in Logistics. Please acknowledge."

"We're needed in Logistics?" I asked. "Where—"

"Acknowledgment received. Thank you." The messenger hurried off and entered the tower by a small side door.

Lorelay scoffed. "The nerve of some people..."

"It's one tower," Dunnax said, shifting his pack. "Hardly the palace in Vos. How hard can it be to find?"

* * *

Half-noon's bell clanged, and we were lost.

The ascent up the Agency's headquarters was grueling. Each flight of stairs led to a maze of hallways identical to the floor below, each with the same carpet of haze I saw in the courtyard, pouring from braziers at every corner. The dozens of gray-shirts we encountered all wore the same dull expression as they hurried past us to attend their own inscrutable business. When Lorelay asked one for directions, he told her that was the responsibility of Logistics. Apparently, putting up signs and marking each pathway was no one's responsibility, since there were none to be seen.

Bright, faintly pulsing lights hung from pipes attached to the ceiling and lit the smoke beneath our feet with a bright, nauseating glow. The subtly pulsing lights were attached to pipes on the ceiling that emitted a ceaseless whirring sound. The high-pitched squeal was soft enough that I wondered whether I imagined it. But even things that only exist in your head are enough to drive you insane.

The sooner we were out in the field, the better. A group like ours wasn't meant to be confined to such a labyrinth of monotony. Garret's face, when I chanced to glimpse it under his hood, bore lips curled in disgust. His eyes darted around suspiciously, as if around every identical corner awaited some unique danger. Dunnax looked more bored than irritated, as he had been earlier, and his sister groaned regularly as each floor failed to contain our destination. Sentyx...I didn't know how to read the Skardwarf. His face never gave any hint of emotion, and he hadn't said a dozen words. Since entering the tower, only once had he spoken to ask me if I was okay when I coughed uncontrollably after inhaling a plume of smoke. Despite my wariness at having a Skardwarf around, it was easy to forget he was there. Perhaps it was this ever-present haze sapping my will, stealing my autonomy, making me feel like all the mindless gray-shirts looked.

Noon's bell tolled before we stumbled across Logistics on the eighteenth floor of the Agency. Either the Brightdaughter hung low today, or we had been searching for far longer than I wanted to believe. But on the wall across the hallway from the door, the Sibling Sun's light filtered in through an open window. I stepped over for a breath of haze-free air. Logistics could wait another moment.

From this height, the entire city sprawled out before me and the Liwo were no more than colorful dots jostling one another in the streets. Vertigo struck me as my eyes followed the curl of the city around Brightcalm Bay, then up the hill that housed the Blight on the far side of the crescent city from the Gild. On the waters, a myriad of colorful banners marked the ships that endlessly flowed to and from the Liwokin docks. Even in the pockets of scorched darkness, grand new buildings were being erected to replace those lost to the Riot's fires.

As grand as they were, none of them matched the grandeur of the Gild. The nearby Financial District towers topped the Agency's height, behind a wall that cordoned off the moneylenders' district from the others. Solar fire reflected in the Gild's gracefully curved Archemetal, dancing with the slightest motions of my head as I took in their dizzying height. Golden metal spires twisted upward into the blue sky around a core of white marble with windows full of movement. The cluster of buildings seemed an otherworldly presence in Liwokin, imposed by the Bright Empire and matching the architecture of the capital in Paceeq. Unlike the Agency, these towers seemed more an intrusion into the city than an extension of it.

Perhaps that was unfair. Paceeqi had been welcome in Liwokin since long before I was born. But they always came for a reason. First, the Empire came for our land. Now, they stay for our wealth. I wondered why my new companions crossed the seas to Lawiko.

The door hinge squealed behind me as Dunnax, ever impatient, pushed his way into Logistics, drawing me away from my birds' eye view of the city. As I entered behind him, a woman in a bronze coat wearing circle-rimmed spectacles sat reading at her desk. A wedge-shaped plaque atop the desk read, 'Kella, Organ of Logistics.' Behind her, a half-dozen aisles of meticulously organized shelves receded toward the opposite side of the tower, stretching back so far there were windows at the aisles' ends. As we entered this boxy room, with walls painted pure white and not a speck of dust to be found, Kella looked up and raised an eyebrow. This was her domain.

The book snapped shut in her hands and she rose. "Hand Sixty-Four? Ulken's Nerve informed me of your *imminent* arrival," she said, reaching under her desk. "That was a full span ago, at half-noon." Kella pulled out an oversized, bulging envelope. Bronze string bound the envelope shut, with a silver wax seal poured and stamped on the knot.

"Sorry," Lorelay said. "We couldn't find—"

"Here. Your command package," Kella said, and shoved the package toward us before marking off some papers. "Take it." She stood and visibly composed herself, eyes shut and lips taut. Then the reprimanding began. "It isn't like the Head to hire lagabouts, you know. You won't last long lazing around like this. And on your first day?"

"Lazing around? We've been searching—" I started, but the old woman wasn't finished.

"Do you think I've no other matters to attend to? Ulken won't tolerate messy records and no other Organ will touch Logistics. I'm the only one who knows my way 'round these files, so keep me waiting again and you'll serve permanently as Heels. I'll see to it. A flick of Kella's pen, that's all it takes, I tell you."

None of us spoke. Better to let her get it out of her system, I figured.

Only now, she looked at each of us like we were a bunch of dullards, crossed her arms, and shook her head. Garret snatched the parcel and she disappeared into the rows of shelves, swearing an oath to the Darkfather under her breath. We made to leave, but her stern voice hooked us from behind.

"And where do you think you're going?"

All of us exchanged looks. Dunnax held his jaw so tight it seemed his teeth might shatter.

I spoke up, feeling vaguely like my old orphan keeper had caught me with my hand in the tithing basket. "To...open our command package and get to work."

"Hah!" The woman poked her head from the aisle, perhaps ensuring we weren't about to flee. She disappeared again. "Eager to leave me, are you? No different than my husband."

Can't imagine why.

"But I'm not through with you yet," she said. She reappeared with an appalling stack of papers and dumped them on her desk before us. When they landed with a thump, I felt the wind forced from beneath them blow across my face. "Hope you all know how to work a pen." She separated the papers into five stacks and placed one before each of us. "Elsewise we're going to be here a long time, and you've already kept the Head waiting long enough."

Ulken?

"What do you mean, kept the Head waiting?" I asked.

Kella gave an ugly cackle. "He's upstairs, expecting you for an interview. Soon as you're done signing your control agreements, silence contracts, and investigation waivers, you can go right up."

"Ulken wants to see us?" Dunnax gaped at the Organ of Logistics as if she'd just told him we had a pending meeting with the Empress. "Why?"

"Do you think we Organs question the Head's decisions?" Kella cocked her head. "I guess you lot must be special." She cracked a grin that didn't reach her eyes and slapped a pen down atop Dunnax's stack. "Now, you'd best start signing!"

CHAPTER FOUR

Sixty-Fourth Hand of the Agency

I quietly slipped out of the Logistics office, shaking my cramped hand, leaving Dunnax and Lorelay as the last to finish signing. My name now adorned several dozen documents with contents as mysterious as the reason Ulken personally wanted to interview us. In the hallway, Garret and Sentyx stood by the window looking out at the city vista.

"Ugly and gray," Garret said. "This whole city is unnatural, but this tower...humans weren't meant to build this high. And Ulken at the top? Like he's looking down on us all."

Sentyx grunted. "Skardwarf mountains are higher."

There's less air up in the mountains. That explains a lot.

"Don't you Ekoans live in trees?" I asked. "Your canopy cities are higher than this tower."

Garret turned around and his eyes lit up. "Lightwood giants, you mean. Aye, but they've fought for every drop of the Brightdaughter's sunlight, and they've stood for thousands of years." He looked out the window again. "You think this tower will last a hundred years, let alone a thousand?"

"Rock lasts millions," the Skardwarf said.

"And Archemetal?" I asked. "The Gild's towers are taller than this one."

"Paceeqi engineering, aye," Garret said. He grinned as the door to Logistics opened. "What Empire doesn't look down upon it's subjects?"

"Let's go," Dunnax said, exiting Logistics. Lorelay closed the door behind him, holding the envelope given to us by Kella. Without waiting, Dunnax tromped toward the stairs that led up to the apex of the tower.

"Shouldn't we open the command package first?" I asked. "So we know what he wants from us."

"Didn't you read the control agreement?" Lorelay asked.

"No," Garret said.

"You read the whole thing?" I asked.

She nodded, lip curling in distaste. "We're at the Head's mercy now. I don't think we should keep him waiting any longer."

"We've got nine stories of stairs," Dunnax said. "Plenty of time to review it on the way." He and his sister disappeared into the stairwell.

Garret and I glanced at each other.

"They're the ones taking their time with the snuffing paperwork," he said.

We chased after the Paceeqi siblings. Sentyx's heavy footsteps weren't far behind.

Our boots—and the Skardwarf's bare feet—pounded on seemingly endless stairs as the fragrant white smoke cascaded down from above. Dunnax charged ahead as if it were a race to the top of the tower. Half a flight ahead of us, Lorelay ripped open the envelope from Logistics.

"Coins," she said, and tossed a purse of gold stars down to us.

Garret snatched it from the air. "Advance payment?"

"Don't get too attached," I said. "Some of it's mine."

Hands freed, Lorelay pulled a small card from the package and said, "This just says 'First Eye Reed' alongside an address in the Residential District."

Reed? I remembered the slip of paper in my inner coat pocket, uselessly blank without Inac's Archemagical aid. Was our conspirator a member of the Agency?

"And there's a brief report," Lorelay said. "We're being sent to a fishing village called Leppit, on the cliffs to the south. Several villagers have gone missing, and they've asked the Agency to investigate. We've got a list here…twenty-something people, a few names. Most unknown. And listen to this: 'Be warned, we've received reports of strange occurrences in the area. Keep your wits about you, Fingers.'"

"Fingers?" My toe caught the next stair, and I nearly tripped. "Are you sure you read that right?"

Lorelay leaned over the railing above me as the stairs doubled back. "Of course I did." She looked up through the middle of the stairway toward her brother, who still kept his quick pace. "Every Paceeqi knows how to read." She started taking the stairs two at a time to catch up.

I tried picturing myself in a green coat like Bengard's. For so long, Ulken's Fingers had been causing me trouble. Now, I was one of them.

"What's so surprising?" Garret asked me.

"Not everyone at the Agency is a Finger," I said. "None of those gray-shirts we passed in the halls are. Fingers wear green coats. I don't know much about this place, but I know that."

Garret flashed a grin, then gestured to his own green cloak. "Guess I'm already in uniform then." He looked back at the trailing Skardwarf, who wore only ragged brown pants. "Hear that, Sentyx? You're finally going to have to put on some clothes."

Sentyx grunted. "Too hot."

The landing to the top floor opened before us. It contained no decorations, no furniture, no people at all, save for us. Most surprisingly, there was no brazier pouring haze onto the floor. There was only a broad, glass-paned window behind us, opposite a door of solid oak with little adornment. Stark and utilitarian, like the rest of the tower.

Dunnax sat in the corner, sweat dripping down his face, bulging pack on the stone ground beside him.

Lorelay stood over him. "Did you even hear the report?"

Dunnax looked away. "Enough of it." He pushed himself to his feet with his polearm, wiped his brow, but left his pack where it was.

I led the way across the empty room. Light from the window cast my darkening shadow on the door as I approached, until I neared enough to read a name plate nailed above the frame.

"Ulken," I said, "Head of the Liwokin Law Agency." I looked back at the rest of the group, then knocked on the door.

The door swung inward at the first knock, but no voice bid us enter. No light came from within, only darkness like a gaping maw, devouring the sunlight that filtered in from behind me. I entered the room, feeling suffocated by this shroud of black. Then, fingers snapped and a tiny spark of Archefire flickered into existence, illuminating a steady, controlling hand aloft in the void. A deep breath hissed, and fire crackled as a cigar was lit, then the Fire fragmented and darted in two directions faster than my eye could follow. All at once, light bloomed from an iron-framed glass lantern sitting on a desk cluttered with stacks of paper. Dense smoke began pouring over the lip of a brazier nestled among the paper, flowing down from the desk and filling the room. Behind the desk sat a man with a mane of black hair framing his angular face. He wore a padded black coat, collar trimmed with thick, white fur.

Ulken took a long drag from his cigar. He gestured to the front of his desk, but there were no chairs there. No chairs anywhere in the room, in fact, save for Ulken's. So, we stood silently arrayed in front of the Head's desk as he exhaled, blowing out smoke from his nostrils like a storybook dragon.

Dunnax stood at attention. "Sir, I apologize for our—"

"Don't interrupt me." Ulken pounded a fist on the desk.

He seems nice.

"Gentlemen," he said, and Lorelay coughed, to draw attention to the Head's mistake. He simply narrowed his eyes at her and continued speaking. "I've got a job for you. Do it well and you'll quickly climb the ranks of the Agency. Do it poorly and, well..." Ulken shrugged, then leaned forward on his elbows, hands clasped together. "Those fit to be Fingers are hard to find and we've got more work than Hands to carry it out. I see you received your command package, so you know what I expect of you."

Lorelay scoffed and muttered, "Obedience."

"I *said* don't interrupt." Ulken sneered at Lorelay and didn't see Dunnax staring daggers at him. "Obedience, yes. I hope that won't be a problem. The chain of command is what binds this Agency together. Without my orders, this city would once again fall to chaos." Ulken stood and turned, speaking with his back to us. He faced a map of Liwokin framed on the wall, dark with his shadow. Next to it were two more maps of increasing scope: the country of Lawiko, with Liwokin in the center, then the entire Bright Empire, with all seven of its conquered countries. "I won't lie to you. The situation is bad, getting worse by the day. Normally, you'd serve as a Heel for a year. Two, if you prove incompetent. Then, a field test. But I've got plenty of Heels. What

I need are Fingers. Strong Fingers. Survivors. I presume none of you want to die?" He paused, grinned at our silence.

Die? Looking for villagers in a fishing hamlet?

"Good," Ulken said. "As first-rank Fingers, the five of you make up the Sixty-Fourth Hand of the Agency." He sat back down in his chair, leaned back, folded his arms, and asked. "Any questions before I send you to carry out your first command?"

My mind went to the slip of paper in my pocket. Even without Inac's aid, I was tempted to tell Ulken of the conspiracy. Instead, I chose to remain quiet. Better to question Reed himself first and figure out what the mysterious note was about.

"What is the command hierarchy of the Agency?" Dunnax asked.

"Nothing like the Order you used to serve in, Paladin," Ulken barked. "As a Hand of the Agency, you execute the will of the Head. *My* will. Until the day I'm killed, my word is law, and you will carry it out faithfully, to the letter."

And on the day you're killed?

The Head continued. "In gold and white are the Nerves, my personal couriers. Treat their word as my own. Understand?" Another drag from his cigar, an exhale of smoke. "Good. Below them are the Eyes in blue, then the Fingers in green. Four ranks of Fingers. Then the Heels in gray. They're beneath you, but don't think that means you can order them around. Of course, the Organs; they keep this operation running. In red, there's..."

It's complicated. We get it.

My mind began to wander. A year of Heel work before becoming a Finger, Ulken had said. What did it take to become an Eye? What did it take to become the Head? Perhaps that's what this First Eye Reed was after.

Ulken sighed. Dunnax's question appeared to bore him as much as it did the rest of us. "Anything else?"

"Aye," Garret said. "What's the job pay?"

"What's wrong, Garret?" I asked. "That coin purse not full enough for you?"

"That depends on my command," Ulken said, ignoring me. "Prove yourself, and the Agency will provide. We've got plenty of gold for you." His eyes flicked to me. "But the coin purse with the command package is not it. The fourteenth and fifteenth floors are the Fingers' quarters if you need a bed for the night. Normally, we'd provide a uniform for you, but we're all out now." He threw his hands up, then started to rise. "Too many new recruits, but no matter. No need to waste a set of uniforms on this command. Now—"

"What about the sign outside?" I asked. "It was posted by a Nerve, wasn't it? Twenty-four what?"

Ulken glared at me for interrupting, but then a smile crept across his face. "That's classified," he said. "When you're second-rank, you'll be cleared to know. Pray to whichever god you choose that it's zero the next time you see it."

"I have some questions about the command," Lorelay said, holding up the report. "This doesn't have many details. And what do you mean by 'strange occur—'"

"Enough questions." Ulken crumpled his cigar in an ashtray atop a dusty shelf. A foul, tarry smell permeated the room. "The report has everything you need to know. Go south to Leppit and figure out what happened. Find the missing, if you can, then report back to me. That purse of stars? The good people of Leppit tried to hire us. It's their gold," Ulken said. "Give it back to them. We don't work for commission."

The Head of the Agency snuffed the lantern, plunging the room into darkness once more. "You're dismissed," he said. "Close the door on your way out."

* * *

The descent to the courtyard was more straightforward than the hunt for Logistics. That didn't make it easy.

Even the Blight has elevators, rickety as they are.

I hoped Inac's induction into the Agency was going better than mine. Otherwise, the prospect of going back to imbuing magic nails might seem rather appealing.

Stepping outside into the courtyard, I took a deep breath. The air wasn't quite *fresh*, but it was a good start.

"Can't seem to get away from this smoke," Garret complained.

"At least out here there's air mixed in," I said.

"I have no idea how the two of you tolerated it for three days," Lorelay said.

"I face into the wind," Sentyx said.

"Does he ever say anything else?" Dunnax asked rhetorically.

Sentyx grunted.

"Picked up some Skardwarf while waiting with him," Garret said. "That's either yes, no, okay, I don't know, follow me, or he's laughing. Probably at you, knowing him." The Ekoan spat into the cloud of haze. "Anything I missed?"

Sentyx grunted again.

Lorelay doubled over in laughter. Dunnax rolled his eyes, but his sister didn't notice.

I caught myself smiling. If I wasn't careful, I might find myself liking this Skardwarf. Reed's hidden words came to me unbidden.

My old friend has caught wind of more monsters abroad.

If the monsters were abroad, it seemed unlikely the note was referring to Skardwarves. They were right here at home. What, then? Without Inac, the only way to uncover more about this conspiracy was to talk to the conspirator himself.

"We should find First Eye Reed," I suggested. "To learn more about Leppit."

I expected disagreement, but the details in the command package were as meager as the bounties from the City Council once the Agency stepped in. We needed information, and Reed was our only lead. So, that was the plan.

As we crossed the courtyard to leave, a familiar figure in gray-green with a huge two-headed axe stepped through the outer gate. He was speaking to a small, timid-looking boy wearing bright Archemage's robes, newly washed and pressed. The mage flinched at the Finger's wild gestures. Bengard waved around his bandaged arm like he was telling a heavily embellished story. He made a booming noise to go along with a pantomimed explosion, then spotted me approaching, beamed, and bounded over to greet me. The mage did a double take at the sudden end to Bengard's story, then trailed closely behind him, like a lost kitten.

"Grim! You made up your mind so fast? I expected you'd spend another week or two playing games in the Blight."

"You nearly died in that *game* last night," I said, a bit annoyed. "Seemed pretty serious to me."

"Dangerous games," Bengard said, smirking, "but still just games. Now you've got real work." Bengard looked us over, standing upright with arms folded behind his back. Formal, as though he was about to give us a professional evaluation. "I see you're in a Hand already. You seem capable enough, but to be made a Finger on your first day...I didn't think Ulken did that anymore. Remember, you represent the Agency now. Try not to make us look bad out there." He relaxed, smiled broadly again, and clapped me on the shoulder. "So, what's your first command?"

"Finding some missing villagers in Leppit," I said. "Seems easy, but we're off to see First Eye Reed, to see what he knows."

"Oh, Reed?" Bengard raised one brow. "He's a strange one, but trust me, he's the best Eye we've got. He's been here since the beginning."

"From the beginning?" I asked. "He helped create the Agency?"

Bengard nodded. "The way I've heard it told, he and Ulken were the best of friends before the Riot. Both were obsessed with finding ways to improve Liwokin. Ulken used to sit on the City Council, even made a run for the Chair once."

Improving Liwokin by taking control of the city himself. I rolled my eyes. *The city would be better off with no one at the top.*

"Reed, so I've been told, was close with the Gild. The annual festival of giving, that was his idea." Bengard laughed. "Probably wasn't easy convincing those moneylenders to part with their gold for the Blight's benefit."

My eyebrows raised. The festival was Reed's doing? It had never made much difference to the average Blightdweller's opinion of the financiers in their Archemetal towers, but I'd made it a habit to sneak in for a free meal or two each year. Until recently had I never needed the charity, but I always figured the Gild could spare the expense.

"That's how they founded the Agency after the Riot. They used their connections to pool the city's resources. Ulken became the Head, and Reed his First Eye. Not sure how they decided which would be on top. I don't think I've heard them speak a single word to each other." The Finger shrugged his muscular shoulders. "Some of the old Fingers spread claims that the two hate each other now. Nothing but rumors, those. I know the First Eye just prefers to work on his own, and Ulken never seems to mind. Reed's seclusive, but in our line of work, I can't blame him. If you find him, I'm sure he'll have a detailed report from his investigation, tell you exactly what you're in for."

Seclusive, eh? Fits for someone with secrets to hide.

"What do you mean, what we're in for?" Lorelay asked.

"What you'll see," he said, "which Aura, and all that."

"Aura?" I opened my mouth to ask, but before I could get the word out, Bengard waved it aside like it wasn't important.

"It'll make sense when you get to Leppit," he said. "What number is your Hand, by the way?"

"Sixty-Four," I muttered. "But wait—"

"Sixty-Four!" Bengard whistled loud, and several Heels stopped to look. "I joined the Agency when there were only *five* Hands. Made me a Finger on day one as well, but we didn't have Heels back then. By the time I made Rank Four, five doubled to ten, but that was only two measures ago. Now Ulken's mad for new recruits. Like Muy Fuy here."

The mage hiding behind Bengard jumped at the mention of his name, then slid meekly to the Finger's side. "H-Hello," he said, then stammered out something unintelligible.

"Nice to meet you, Muy Fuy." Lorelay smiled and extended a hand in greeting.

The mageling shook it but wouldn't look her in the eye. This one was going to be a Finger?

Seems more like Heel material.

"I've got to get him up to Logistics," Bengard said. "Best of luck in Leppit. Just remember what's real and you'll be fine."

He tapped a finger to his head, then left as I stood there uncomprehending, trying to make sense of what he said.

"Come on," said Dunnax, ever impatient. "We need to be on the road south before half-dusk."

"Who put you in charge of the schedule?" Garret muttered.

But wait, Inac had told me to meet him tonight.

"I thought we might get drinks after meeting the First Eye. I know a good tavern. We can set out in the morning. Tomorrow's bound to be longer, Lightmother willing."

"Ulken didn't tell us to spend the night drinking in an inn," Dunnax snapped. "He *commanded* us to investigate Leppit." Lorelay gave a frown that Dunnax didn't acknowledge.

"He is right," Sentyx said. "We serve. To Reed."

My shoulders slumped. I didn't know much about these two, but I knew they were too stubborn to convince. "Lorelay, you have his address, right?"

The Paceeqi girl handed me the First Eye's card. "Yeah. I don't know where in the city it is, though. You lead."

"Well, let's hurry it up," Garret grumbled. "Sooner we get out of this stinking pile you call a city, the better."

I looked back at the Agency tower in silent apology to Inac.

Guess our plan will have to wait.

* * *

A short distance away in the Burg, a large, brass 718 was nailed to the door of a small home, indistinguishable from any other but for the number. In the measures following the Agency's establishment, Ulken had somehow convinced the City Council that we needed "official" names for all the streets—even little back alleys and dead ends—and every building needed a number nailed to its front door. I didn't see their purpose—any true Liwo could find their way around without them.

A shadow moved in the window to 718 as we approached the door. The door swung inward before anyone lifted a hand or knocked, and a man with a fuzzy, auburn mustache wearing a rounded, sandy-brown cap gestured for us to enter. A dark spot on the sleeve of his sky-blue Eye's coat showed me where he recently wiped the tears from his glistening, red eyes.

A vague sense came over me that I had seen this man before, and that I knew why he was crying.

I raised an eyebrow. "Bad time?"

"Who are you?" the Eye asked with a sniffle. "What do you want with me?"

"Nervous?" I asked and feigned a good-hearted chuckle. "It's not like there are monsters outside your door."

The mention of monsters ought to have gotten his attention, but Reed narrowed his eyes at me and said nothing.

"First Eye Reed, right?" Lorelay said. She took the card and report out of the command package envelope. "We got your address from Logistics."

"Logistics...you're Fingers? Yes. Five of you, of course. But no uniforms. Hmm. New recruits, then." He paused, then composed himself and gestured inside. "Come in, quickly. No one followed you?"

"Don't see why they would," Garret said. "No secret we're here though."

I looked at each of my companions as we entered. Surely, even without knowledge of the conspiracy they could tell Reed was acting suspiciously. As Sentyx entered Reed's home, the First Eye spared him no more than an unconcerned look. That was telling, but still, he was on guard. It'd be impossible to get anything from him like this.

"Other than Ulken," I said, "only Bengard knows we're here. The Finger spoke highly of you. Said you've been around since the Agency's inception, and you're one of the best."

"Ah, yes," the First Eye said, lips curling. "Bengard. I wish I could say the same of him. The man can fight, but for anything more complicated..."

So, the thief was right. Reed *had* sent Bengard to capture him.

Reed glanced at Lorelay. "Let me see that paper." He took the report and read it, muttering to himself. "Leppit? Ulken knows I haven't…" He handed it back. "Of course. What else did Ulken tell you?"

"He told us we rank below the Eyes," Dunnax said. "Other than that, sir, nothing but what was in the report."

Reed's face twisted in anger, and he let off a long string of curses, though I wasn't sure what he was mad about. Going from crying to furious in so little time? The First Eye was a man fueled by strong emotions.

"Bengard did say something about…an Aura," I added. "Said you'd have a full report for us."

Reed calmed down, ran his fingers through his mustache. "Yes, the Aura. That's what Eyes are sent to, well, see. So we know which rank of Hand is appropriate to send, and so the Fingers know what to expect. Except…" He threw up his hands. "I haven't been to Leppit."

Too busy scheming to do your job?

"So, you have no idea what we're in for," Lorelay said, concern coloring her voice.

"No," Reed said.

Sentyx grunted and made for the door, but I wasn't ready to leave just yet. I put my hand on the Skardwarf's shoulder to stop it. Its skin was like granite to the touch.

"But *he* seems to have some notion," Reed said.

I turned and flinched upon finding the Eye's gaze fixed on me. Had he already figured out what I was doing? He was sharper than I thought.

"The rest of the Hand are from abroad," Reed said to me, "but you're Liwo."

"What's that have to do with anything?" I asked.

"You were in Liwokin for the Riot. You felt it, didn't you?"

"What kind of question is that? We all—"

"Don't play dumb," Reed interrupted. "Auras, monsters...you know, don't you?" I began to speak, but Reed stopped me. "No need to answer. Even one wrong word in front of your companions would be criminal. Article fifty-eight dash B, subsection eleven: 'Disclosure of Agency secrets without Head-granted authorization. Punishable by five years minimum imprisonment.'"

And what is conspiracy to overthrow the Head punishable by?

Lorelay gave a long, impatient sigh. "Are you guys going to stop speaking in riddles, or should the rest of us just leave you alone?"

The First Eye turned to Lorelay, frowning. "I wish I could say more. Trust me, I do. But my hands are tied." Then he looked back, studied me. In his gaze there was...admiration. "You know, and you joined the Agency anyway. Not many would."

He was wrong—it was clear now he was speaking not of the conspiracy, but of something else. Still, I held my tongue. The less he knew of my intentions, the better.

Reed lifted his cap and revealed a crop of frizzy red hair. He scratched his head mindlessly while looking around, though I could tell his attention was focused inward. "The report warns of strange occurrences. The rest of you will know soon enough."

Lorelay stomped her foot. "Know *what*?"

Reed shook his head. "Just try to remember what's real."

Sentyx grunted. "Bengard said."

Dunnax saluted. "Sir, if there's nothing more, then we'll leave for Leppit right a—"

The door crashed open behind me, and Reed's eyes went wide.

"Prost is traveling to the—" The voice cut off and when I turned to look, I found a man as surprised to see us as Reed was to see him. He wore an Archemetal-trimmed, black long-coat and carried a brushed silver rod with an iridescent, obsidian stone affixed to one end—the same type of stone that was in Inac's pendant. In the other hand, he held a slip of paper. The man moved to hide the paper and silver rod behind his back, but a faint blue glow emanated from the paper. None of the others would have caught that little slip-up, but it instantly made clear what this man was.

Another conspirator.

And Prost. Is he a third?

Reed cleared his throat. "Fingers, this is Oltrov. He contracts for the Agency."

"Apologies for barging in, First Eye," Oltrov said, voice as smooth and polished as an Archemetal ingot. His chest heaved, and given the haste with which he'd entered, it was clear that he'd been running. The man's eyes held a look of urgency. "My scouts have brought some troubling news." Oltrov's gaze flicked to me and the Hand, then back to Reed.

News he doesn't want us to know.

But I was running out of time.

"Is it from abroad, by chance?" I asked. "It's so rare I hear news from outside Lawiko."

Reed's attention snapped to me, and his lips tightened. "Perhaps another time." The First Eye motioned us toward the door. "You have work to do. Be on your guard in Leppit. I'll help if I can, but remember what I said."

The First Eye ushered the five of us out, past the well-groomed man with the coat decorated with delicate Archemetal spirals.

Contractor for the Agency, eh? That's a bold lie.

The door slammed behind us.

While the rest of us left, Sentyx hesitated near Reed's home.

"Well, that was snuffing useless," Garret said, then turned and shouted to the Skardwarf. "You coming?"

Sentyx caught up to us. "Follow," he said.

"Are you going to tell us what that was all about?" Lorelay asked me.

"I'll tell you," I promised. "But not here."

We left by the Canyon Gate on the south side of the city, following the directions in our command package toward Leppit. The Hand's nervous silence left me with room to think.

Oltrov was clearly hiding something, not the least of which was an association with the Gild. Only Gildmembers could afford to wear Archemetal, and no one else would so dangerously flaunt their wealth.

Reed is close with the Gild, indeed.

A pattern was becoming clear. Both Oltrov and the dead thief wore Archemetal-trimmed cloaks and carried notes written in luminous blue ink. Perhaps the thief was a member of the conspiracy as well, gone rogue, and so Reed sent Bengard to capture him. Did that mean Bengard was a conspirator as well? My head spun.

I'd hoped Reed would provide answers, but we were left with more questions than ever.

From the distant church towers came half-dusk's soft call. From beyond the city gate, at the tree line where the road started up a gentle slope into the woods, I gazed back at my home. Excitement stirred in me, but so did fear. I'd never left the city before. All my life, I'd cultivated skills to help me survive in the city. Outside those walls, I wasn't helpless, but...well, I'd have to adapt to survive. How much will I have changed when next I laid eyes on my home? Even a simple change in perspective from the road made the city seem different. The Gild's and

Agency's towers looked massive, hulking over the rest of the city, which shrank into the distance.

The Agency and the Gild. Secrets and lies.

Garret called my name from fifty paces up the road. Against the backdrop of trees, four shadows waited for me like phantoms in the gloom.

I looked one last time at Liwokin, took a deep breath, then ventured forth into the unknown.

CHAPTER FIVE

Far From Home

It's dusk," Garret said, though there were no bells in the forest, and it had grown dark some time ago. Only once in my life did the Church of Light's mathemelodians fail to ring the five beats in the melody of time on the church tower bells, which had only added to the ensuing panic in the city. It was a relief to know someone in our Hand was capable of keeping track of the Brightdaughter without them. "We should stop and make camp. Sentyx, gather some firewood." The ranger strung his bow and ran off into the woods.

The Skardwarf nodded. Its heavy footsteps lingered long after the two of them disappeared into the gloom of the trees, leaving me with the Paceeqi brother and sister. I was glad someone in our Hand knew how to survive outside the city. South and west of the capital, dense forests sprawled across Lawiko. Apart from these woods and the Fertile Arm running along the country's eastern flank, the rocky, mountainous terrain made travel by land treacherous. But no ship would take us to Leppit, not through the Outrush Canyon with its unpredictable winds. The canyon used to be the primary route for traders seeking the Market District. Now, all but the most daring paid the Empire's toll in the Canako Canal beyond the highlands north of Liwokin. A safer route to be sure, but the Empress was likely only concerned with financing important projects, such as a bigger garden in which to take her half-noon tea.

Lorelay plucked a soft, slow melody on her instrument—a lyre, she told me it was called—and the music put me at ease, though I hadn't realized I'd been holding any tension until now. I didn't fear the dark, but the city always had some flickering source of light; here, I couldn't even see the stars, shrouded as they were by the thick canopy of trees.

"Stop that," Dunnax growled, as he unfurled the bedroll from his pack. "There could be bandits out there. They'll kill us while we sleep."

"No bandit's going to sneak up on us," Lorelay said, continuing her calming tune. "Especially once Garret's back. With an Ekoan ranger on watch, they'd have to be dark-loving stupid to think they'd win in a fight."

"They could just be desperate," I said. "Known plenty of men to do stupid things when they're desperate." *Myself among them.* "Might be worse than bandits out here, too." I remembered all the stories I'd heard of monsters beyond Liwokin's walls. "Wolves and snoutbears. Daggerclaws, even."

Lorelay laughed. "There's no daggerclaws in Lawiko. Wolves and bears, sure, but our fire will keep them at bay. You guys worry too much." Her melody sped up, seamlessly morphing to an energetic tune, plucked incredibly fast and without a single sour note. She held the harp-like instrument out, making a strange expression as she deftly traversed a soaring scale.

"I said stop!" Dunnax snapped. "*You* don't worry enough. That's why we're here in the first place, or have you already forgotten?"

The music stopped on a discordant note, which must have been on purpose. I couldn't see Lorelay's scowl, but I could hear it in her voice. "No. I haven't. You'll never let me, will you?"

"No," Dunnax said flatly, then stretched out on his bedroll, facing his back to us. He pulled his glaive as close to him as a lover.

I changed the subject, not interested in wedging myself in the middle of this sibling spat. "Where did you learn to play like that?"

It took a moment for Lorelay to respond. She put away her lyre, then sat down and sighed. "Our mother taught me, at first. Before we buried her."

I never knew my mother, but I knew loss as well as any other. "I'm sorry."

Lorelay shook her head. "It was a long time ago and we didn't get along. She would catch me play fighting with one of my friends and scold me. 'The Mother of Light arms women with song as the Father of Dark arms men with swords,' she always said. 'It's the way things must be. The way they've always been'," Lorelay said with a mocking voice. "Snuff that! I learned the Twelve Songs, but I never stopped learning to fight. I don't serve the gods or their dusty old tome."

"You don't?" I asked, taken aback. "I thought everyone in Paceeq served the gods."

"Why should I? They say some songs are worse than killing, that you deserve to *be* killed for singing them. 'It's the way things must be.'" She laughed in disdain. "Not if I can help it. People are bored of the Church's dreadful, droning dirges. Even if no one will admit it. They want to hear something new. Music they can drink and dance to without feeling the Lightmother's prying eyes. So I give the people what they want, and they love it. Of course, not everyone does..." She trailed off, looked at

Dunnax, as if to check she wasn't salting an old wound. "What about you? What's your story?"

I shrugged. "There isn't much to tell. Grew up a begging orphan in the city, poor as poor can be until I found plenty of coin in thieving. Too many hungry nights sleeping on cold cobble will turn anyone to it. I'm no exception. I got plenty of practice fighting, so figured I could make a living doing it. Worked as a bounty hunter for the City Council ever since. Then, the Agency came in and all my contracts dried up." I gave a wry laugh. "Really, bounty hunting's no way to make a living. Too many bodies; Liwokin's already got enough dead. Hope this job is better, that it's more than just killing."

Lorelay smiled.

"Don't get your hopes up," Garret said, leaning against a tree not five paces away. He held two fat rabbits skewered by arrows.

I jumped. "Darkfather! How did you sneak up on us?"

"Easily, with you two yapping away. Didn't even hear this one lumbering around, did you?" He pointed at Sentyx, who stood near the softly snoring Dunnax, carrying a bundle of branches. Garret's white teeth flashed in the darkness. "There's bandits in these woods, don't you know? Thing is, it's us. Killing for the Agency won't be any different than killing for the city or killing on your own. Sure, there's regulations and bylaws and official commands to legitimize it. Just helps you sleep at night is all. Killing is killing, in the end. There's no difference."

"You are wrong," Sentyx said.

"Aye? And why's that?" Garret asked, then waited for more from the Skardwarf. Nothing came, not even a grunt. Sentyx only dropped his branches to the ground, then kicked one away from the rest. "All right, then. Good argument. Let's get that fire lit. I'm starving." When no one moved to help, the Ekoan spat. "Got to do everything myself, eh?" Twisting a stick between his palms, he got the fire started in short time, though it felt longer for all the complaining he did.

Grey smoke rose and drifted in the wind to suffuse the wending branches of the trees. Embers flitted upward in the convection of the flames, stars flickering in the unsteady light that illumined the haze. In the smoldering glow of this celestial blaze, we sat eating morsels of roast rabbit in uncomfortable silence.

"So," Lorelay finally said, around a bite of meat, "you going to tell us what that was about with Reed?"

I stalled for a while chewing on a gamy bit of rabbit haunch, then sighed. It was unavoidable they'd find out. "I'm not sure what Reed thinks I know. All I'm sure of is that Reed's hiding something."

"You don't say," Lorelay said, then mimicked Reed's voice mockingly. "What do you want with me? No one followed you, did they?"

Sentyx looked around. "Following."

"I don't know who he expected to be following us," I said. "One of Ulken's Nerves, maybe."

Sentyx grunted, then shoved some rabbit into his mouth, and crunched into the bone.

Dunnax looked at the Skardwarf in disgust, then spat a bone into the campfire and wiped his mouth. "Reed is Ulken's First Eye. Why would he worry about Nerves?"

"I have a note signed by Reed," I said, and retrieved it from my pocket. "A bounty I was after dropped it, just before he burned up trying to kill the Finger Reed sent after him."

"Let me see that," Dunnax said, and snatched the note. He turned it over, once, twice.

I reached to take it back. "The thing is—"

"There's nothing on this..." Dunnax handed it to me.

"Right," I said. "You need something special to read it. Reed's friend, Oltrov, had a rod with a black stone attached. The thief who dropped the note had a similar stone—it was part of a stolen pendant, which Inac hired me to return."

"Inac?" Dunnax asked.

"The mage I was with," I said. "We wanted to show this note to Ulken, but then we were separated."

"And Inac has the pendant, leaving you with blank piece of paper." Lorelay laughed.

I grinned. "Not exactly the most convincing evidence."

"Evidence of what?" she asked.

"Not sure." Another bite of rabbit gave me time to think. "Conspiracy, I think. Reed's got someone spying on Ulken's advisor. Maybe Oltrov, maybe Prost, whoever that is." I shrugged.

"Who's the advisor?" Garret asked.

"Someone in the Agency?" I guessed. I had no better idea. "Anyway, the note also said there are monsters abroad, and Ulken can't control them."

"Monsters?" Garret snorted. "Things Reed doesn't understand, is all. Plenty of big animals he'd call monsters living in Eko."

"And people," Sentyx said. "Men call Skardwarves monsters."

I looked away; I was guilty of that myself. Sentyx was an odd one, but he'd done nothing to earn the label of monster.

"Aye," Garret said, and spat. "But this is all assuming we believe you, Grim. Might be you're just lying. You grew up thieving, probably learned some forgery too. Steal some special ink, sign someone's name on the note, easy enough. But why were you going to show this evidence to Ulken? As some pure act of goodness, or for some personal gain?"

"As a bounty hunter, I've done far worse than pure good for personal gain." I smirked. "But the note is real."

"I believe you," Lorelay said. "Reed *did* behave strangely."

"Everyone does in Liwokin," the Ekoan said. "Cities like that make people strange. Not enough fresh air to go around."

Dunnax tossed the last of his meager meal into the fire. "Real or not, it makes no difference now. I'll take first watch. The rest of you should sleep. We've a lot of ground to cover if we're to reach Leppit by tomorrow."

* * *

It struck me the next morning that something was missing. Many things were, really. The first thing I noticed was that I had no idea how much time had passed or even how far we'd come. We'd been walking uphill all morning, and there were no streets or buildings to use as landmarks. The melody of time was nonexistent here, far from the church bells in the city; only chirping birds and rustling leaves could be heard over the sounds of our footsteps as we tromped southward. I missed the chattering of passersby and the haggling of merchants and buyers, the pounding of blacksmiths' hammers and the tapping of chisels. The industrial fetor of blazing coal and molten metal, that I didn't miss. Nor the stink of days-old stew festering in half-empty cauldrons, still doled out to those desperate with hunger. Maybe Garret had a point about the city. The air in the woods smelled fresh and earthy. Sunbeams streamed in through breaks in the foliage above, highlighting floating pollen and lazy clouds of gnats that dispersed as we passed through. The path to Leppit was beautiful and calm and natural. Still, something nagged at me. I felt almost like we were being watched, though clearly that was ridiculous.

We're farther from anything constructed by human hands than I've ever been, that's all. There's no one in these outlands.

Except, things aren't always as they appear.

The Brightdaughter, arcing high in the sky, illuminated the road ahead where the cover of trees suddenly ceased. Though there had been no signs of civilization all morning, the trees hadn't come to a natural end at all; they had been cleared to make room for an enormous bridge that crossed the Outrush Canyon. Twin iron girders as thick as city streets sank their weight into the stony earth, shot across the chasm and anchored into the other side. Metal sheets braced by lightwood beams connected the twins and formed a roadway wide enough to fit four carriages side by side. Arched beams beneath the metal sheets bit into the cliffs of the other side to support the construction's great weight.

"The Outrush Span Bridge," I said, as we all halted before it. "Used to connect Liwokin to Sobiko on the country's southern tip."

Dunnax dropped his pack to the ground, then sat and wiped the sweat from his brow. I eyed the leather sack, wondering what was inside. Whatever it was, it must have weighed a ton. Yet the huge Paceeqi man never uttered a word of complaint about it.

"How long ago was that?" Lorelay asked.

I shrugged. "Long ago."

The bridge was stark, practical, and wholly unlike the style of engineering brought to this country by Paceeq. Only, the metal wonder, which predated the Bright Empire's expansion into Lawiko, now seemed to be falling into disrepair, with rust coloring the road and rails.

"Doesn't seem safe," Garret said. "We should go around."

"That would take too long," Dunnax said. He heaved his pack onto his shoulders and strode forth onto the bridge, his glaive clacking, metal on metal, as he used the polearm like a walking stick.

"If it can support his weight," I said to Garret, "we've got nothing to worry about." I followed the ex-Paladin. The structure felt sturdy underfoot, so I took the chance to peek over the guard rails to catch a vertiginous sight of the Outrush's waves crashing far below.

A hand landed between my shoulder blades and my entire body tensed. My knuckles clenched the guard rails to prevent me from falling to my death, but my feet never left the metal ground.

"Afraid of heights, Grim?" Garret chuckled. "What an ugly hunk of iron."

"I...why would you..." came tumbling out of my mouth. My heart still hammered but I collected myself. "That wasn't—"

"Sheath that sword!" Dunnax's voice boomed. His pack clattered to the ground.

I started, then spun around in alarm.

Dunnax had his glaive readied in a two-handed grip, his sight on a lone man standing at the far end of the bridge. Even from this distance the tip of his blade shook like a leaf in the wind and gave away the tremble in his hands.

"Let me pass, you brigands!" the man shouted back. "I've nothing of any value!"

Lorelay placed her hand on Dunnax's arm and gently lowered his weapon. "You're mistaken, friend. We're no brigands."

He hesitated but kept his sword at the ready. "No? Then what are you?"

"Fingers," Lorelay said. "We're not going to hurt you."

"Exactly what a bandit would say," Garret muttered.

The swordsman slowly approached. "Don't look like any Fingers I've seen."

"Seen many Fingers, have you?" Dunnax said.

"I have, in fact." His eyes, bright as blue sky, darted between the five of us, though they lingered longest on Sentyx. "Only one of you is wearing green," Bright Eyes said, tilting his head toward Garret, "and that don't look like an Agency uniform."

Garret grinned. "You don't like it? Made it myself."

"You'll let me pass, then?" he said, ignoring Garret.

Dunnax shrugged, then stepped aside. "If you don't do anything stupid."

"We're headed to Leppit," I said. "You know it?"

"Sure, I know it." Bright Eyes neglected to sheathe his sword. "Know not to go anywhere near it. Some darkness cropped up there."

"Darkness?" Dunnax scowled.

"Sure, Lomin said so. Been avoiding the place since."

"Who's Lomin?" I asked.

"Hunter in the Shaded Grounds, northwest of Leppit. I buy pelts off him, sell them in the city."

"Thought you didn't have anything of value," Garret said.

"Do you see any pelts? We arranged to meet at his lodge, as usual, but he wasn't there. Not like him to miss a chance to sell." The trader sighed, shaking his head. "I tell you, whole world's gone awry since the Agency showed up."

"The Agency has nothing to do with your missing fur trader," Dunnax said.

I rolled my eyes at Dunnax's loyalty. We'd only been Fingers for a day, and he already felt the need to defend the place?

Bright Eyes smiled. "Right." Then he stretched until his back cracked and said, "Well, I'm off. If you see the Net in the village, give him my regards." Once he edged past us, he finally slid his sword into his sheath and took off running.

"Odd fellow, that one," I said when he was out of earshot.

"The Net," Lorelay said. "He was on our list of the missing."

"I thought that was a mistake," I said. "What kind of name is the Net?"

"A dead man's," Dunnax said, and Garret snorted.

"You don't know that," Lorelay said, then frowned. After all, he probably was right.

I looked over to Sentyx, who seemed content in his silence. The Skardwarf nodded once, slowly, and continued across the bridge, his bare feet thumping on metal. Garret cracked his knuckles and neck, the bones tied into his hair rattling as he jerked his neck upward. Dunnax heaved up his cumbersome pack and groaned as Lorelay took out her lyre to pass the time. I followed behind the group.

Odd fellow, but no odder than us.

* * *

The cover of trees thickened on the other side of the Canyon, and the path became overgrown and rocky. After a brief reprieve from the wilds, we now walked an untamed trail. Farther and farther from the city we went, until it seemed we were the only living souls in an unbroken, lonely stretch. It came as a shock, then, that shouts of alarm and whinnying horses reached us from up ahead. Then followed shouts of dying, and the clashing of weapons.

"Bandits," Garret said. He strung his bow in a flash, nocked an arrow.

Dunnax bolted toward the danger, leaving us no choice but to follow. As we charged, Lorelay had two knives—one long, one short—in hand. I readied my crossbow with a quarrel. Only Sentyx carried no weapon.

The scene was chaos when we arrived. Two horses, frenzied and wild-eyed, had broken free of an ornate carriage and rushed past us. An equally wild-eyed man chased after the beasts. A richly dressed nobleman fought with a longsword alongside three guards to protect the carriage from bandits. He parried a wild overhand blow with his sword, then sidestepped and drove it through his attacker to the hilt. He yanked the bloody sword free, but another bandit was already on him.

"Fourteen," Garret said. His arrow took the bandit in the neck, buying the nobleman a chance to notice us. The nobleman's eyes went wide as the bandit gurgled, clutched at his throat, and collapsed. "Thirteen." Under his dark hood, rage filled Garret's eyes. He ran off in search of a new target.

Even with my Hand in the fight, we were outnumbered.

"There's too many, Vinlin!" a guard shouted. "Leave the offerings and flee!" A bandit's knife sliced the back of his knee, and he went down. The knife found his throat next.

The dead man was right. A smarter man would flee, but this Vinlin was a nobleman. He'd never leave his goods to the bandits.

Dunnax charged in toward Vinlin. His shoulder caught a bandit whose sword was overhead, knocking him to the ground. A swift strike with the butt end of his glaive caved in the man's head. "Get behind me, Your Radiance!" Dunnax shouted.

I spotted a bow-wielding woman in painted leather hiding behind a tree. Took aim. She popped out and drew her bowstring, but my trigger finger was faster. My quarrel struck her in the shoulder and the bow fell from her limp hand.

"Sentyx!" Lorelay shouted.

I turned in time to see a bandit swinging an iron sword with both hands at Sentyx's midsection. The Skardwarf didn't dodge. The sword struck its body full force and bounced off, ringing as if the man had struck a brick wall. The bandit's shock lasted long enough for Sentyx to grab him by the shoulders and drive a rock-hard forehead into the bridge of the man's nose. Sentyx tossed the broken bandit down and turned to find another. I shivered at the calm brutality of it.

Glad the Skardwarf is on our side. This one, at least.

I turned back to finish off the bandit I hit, but she was gone. Two more bandits dropped their weapons and fled from Sentyx into the woods. I counted six bodies on the forest floor, three littered with arrows. That left eight to deal with, but only one of Vinlin's guards still lived.

Dunnax swiped his glaive in a wide arc, but his target dodged backward. The Paceeqi's misstep left him open. He paid for it with a slash to his ribs. Dunnax staggered back, clutching his side. Blood seeped through his sweat-soaked white shirt between his fingers. Before the bandit's next blow found home, Vinlin stepped in to deflect it. Lorelay arrived and drove her short knife into the bandit's back.

Footsteps behind me. I tensed, then ducked, felt the wind of the blade sail over my head. I let my crossbow drop, grabbed my knife, and swiped upward. My knife caught the worn and rusted sword by the hilt, knocked it from my attacker's grip. She gasped. I pointed my knife at her. Hesitated. Her blonde hair fell to her shoulders, where a leather strap secured her makeshift armor. Red trickled down her arm from where my quarrel bit into her skin. Green paint streaked the brown leather, the same color as her eyes. Eyes filled with fear. I ground my teeth. A bounty hunter does what he must to survive.

But then a woman's words came to me.

Some choices can't be unmade.

I blinked. The adrenaline pulsed through my body; the knife shook in my hand.

"Go," I said. The bandit flinched at my words. "Go!" I drew back the knife as if to strike, and she ran.

When an arrow took her between the shoulder blades and she toppled forward, I cried out in surprise. Garret, thirty paces away, spat on the ground and nocked another arrow. I clenched my fist.

She wasn't a threat any longer...

All the fight went out of me, but it appeared to have left our attackers as well. They were routed, fleeing the carriage. Only two escaped without taking one of Garret's arrows in the back. The ranger had no mercy for bandits.

"Dunnax!" Lorelay shouted. "Help him!" She held a dying man in her arms, one of Vinlin's guards. The guard's breathing was shallow. With each tiny breath he grimaced in pain. One side of his body was entirely soaked in dark red.

Her brother threw down his weapon and scrambled toward her, still holding the wound he took. Vinlin stood nearby, looking down at the pair attempting to save his man's life. But by the time Dunnax laid hands on him, the guard had already expired. The ex-Paladin punched the ground and swore an oath. Then, he stood and bowed to Vinlin. "Apologies, Your Radiance. We failed you."

I cocked my head at that. Your Radiance? Who was this nobleman?

His eyes were like the flowers of the Brightdaughter, black pupils ringed by a bold yellow. He wore a red leather tunic with fine gold tracery. Though the garb didn't look fit for battle, it served the man well enough. Blood stained the gold and broke the symmetric patterns. As the nobleman still stood tall, it didn't seem any of the blood was his own. The way he was looking down his nose at me, I wished some of it was.

He fought well, at least. For an uppity snob.

Dunnax picked up his glaive and started walking toward his discarded pack. With a glance at his sister, he said, "Come on. We're leaving."

Vinlin slid his sword into the sheath at his hip. "No. Come here, all of you."

Four of us stood before the nobleman, but Garret was missing. Probably off hunting the last of the bandits.

With suspicious eyes, Vinlin looked us over. "A Skardwarf, here in the Bright Empire? Interesting. And you two, you're Paceeqi."

Dunnax wouldn't meet the man's eyes. His stone-faced expression resembled Sentyx's. Lorelay, on the other hand, looked positively cheery.

"We are," she said. With both hands, she grabbed his, paying little attention to the rings he wore, or his look of shock. "Thank you for saving my brother's life." She let go of the nobleman and elbowed Dunnax teasingly. "He's gotten sloppy, not enough training out of his armor."

"Armor? Uh, is that right?" The nobleman stuttered with embarrassment.

"Lorelay..." Dunnax growled, still looking at the ground.

Lorelay frowned as if recalling a bad memory. "Right...sorry we didn't arrive sooner."

Vinlin rubbed his head, mussing his crop of bright blond hair. "I'm glad you arrived at all. Without your assistance, I'm afraid my life would have been forfeit." He chuckled. "What a mess that would have caused back home."

I rolled my eyes. What nobleman didn't have an inflated opinion of himself?

"Well, we won't be around to save you again," I said. "What are you doing out here with a golden carriage like that? *Trying to attract bandits?*"

"Golden cart full of treasures," Garret said. The ranger had swept aside the velvet curtain at the back of the Vinlin's carriage to steal a peek inside. Past him, I could see the inside was as exquisitely decorated as the outside, all gold and red, and filled near to bursting with an assortment of expensive-looking objects.

"What do you think you're doing?" Vinlin demanded.

Garret hopped down and shrugged. "Old habits."

Vinlin glowered at the Ekoan. "Is this how treat your betters?"

"By saving their skins and not asking for any recompense?" Garret spat. "Better than you would have gotten from the bandits."

Garret crossed his arms and stood his ground in front of Vinlin's carriage. Dunnax tightened his grip on his glaive; I could only guess who he was getting ready to defend. I held my breath. The tension felt thicker than the schism that divided the Gild from the Blight.

There was fire in the nobleman's eyes, but then he closed them. He took a long, deep inhale, then blew it out. When he opened his eyes again, the anger had melted away. Vinlin nodded. "Right. A reward. I should be thanking you, not making any more enemies. The Lightmother knows I have plenty of those already."

"We don't require any reward, Your Radiance," Dunnax muttered. "It was my duty to protect you."

"Ah, but you'll receive one anyway," Vinlin said. "You clearly recognize me, but the rest of your companions don't. Good citizenship must never go unrewarded in the Bright Empire."

"I saw a good-looking horn in the cart," Garret said. "I'll take that."

Vinlin laughed. "Those offerings aren't mine to give. They're my mother's."

"All that for your mother?" Lorelay whistled. "She must have a taste richer than the Lightmother."

Dunnax tensed, almost imperceptibly.

But Vinlin guffawed. "The richest in the Empire, I'm sure. Sometimes I think she'd mistaken *herself* for the Lightmother."

"Your Radiance," a tired voice came, along with the clopping of hooves. "I've recovered the horses."

"Well done!" Vinlin clapped the man on the back. "Now, hitch them to the carriage so we can be on our way. I don't relish the thought of another attack before we reach the enclave." As the horse-handler led the horses toward the front of the carriage, Vinlin turned to us and produced a coin purse. "Well, I must be off. Thank you again, my friends, truly. Here, take this." Sentyx happened to be standing closest to him and took the entire purse. Vinlin laughed. "For me to pay a Skardwarf who helped save my life. Such strange times. Still, this is hardly enough. Should our paths cross in the future, I'll find a way to further repay you."

"With as much gold as you have," Garret said, "that shouldn't be too hard."

"I have much more to offer than gold, rest assured."

Garret grinned. "Oh, I'm sure."

Vinlin climbed in the back of the carriage as his man brought it around, then said, "May the Mother's Light guide you. Farewell." He banged twice on the carriage wall, closed the velvet curtain, and the ornate carriage pulled away.

When we all collected our belongings and readied to continue south, Garret said to Dunnax, "So, what does a Paladin do in Paceeq?"

The former Paladin eyed Garret warily, as if the ranger had laid a trap to ensnare him. "Whatever we're given orders to do. Upholding the law. Apprehending heretics. Protecting important property."

"Bounty hunters with a fancy name, then," I said. Dunnax ignored me.

"Hiding secrets from your Emperor doesn't make the list?" Garret asked, though it clearly wasn't a question.

This, the Paladin couldn't ignore. He growled. "There is no Emperor. Only an Empress, Ekoan."

Garret laughed. "Not anymore. I may be Ekoan, but I know the royal traditions. That was Elzia's son on pilgrimage."

Elzia. I froze. Her name was known throughout the Empire. The Empress' son? That wasn't just some self-righteous rich man.

"Wait, that was the *Bright Prince*?" Lorelay's eyes slowly widened. "And I joked about his mother... Oh, Lightmother's teats..."

"Worse than that," Garret said. "The Bright Prince collecting artifacts from across the Empire, that can only mean one thing. Empress Elzia is gone. You joked about his *dead* mother." The Ekoan snorted. "Good thing he liked you."

The Paceeqi girl burst out laughing. At the outburst, Dunnax stomped off. Lorelay followed close behind, trying to hold herself together.

Her brother may have been right. She didn't worry enough. I eyed Dunnax's glaive, sunlight glinting along its sharp edge. *Lucky our royal reward was gold. If the prince was more ill-tempered, it might have been steel instead.*

"He *is* hiding something, you know," Garret said to me as we trailed behind Sentyx and the Paceeqi siblings. He jerked his chin toward Dunnax, whose wounded side was glowing as the Paladin healed himself with Archefire.

I shrugged. "You shouldn't taunt him like that."

"I've spent too much time around bandits." Garret leveled his gaze at me. "I know an outlaw when I see one."

"Dunnax, an outlaw?"

"Why not?" Garret spat. "Everyone's got some secret."

I gave a noncommittal grunt. Those who trusted the least often had the most to hide.

CHAPTER SIX

Through the Storm

If there was one thing I could trust about Garret, it was his keen sense of direction on the forests of Lawiko. Though the run-in with Vinlin had slowed us down, according to the ranger we were now less than half a short day's walk from the village of Leppit. Night had fallen some time ago, and Dunnax could only push us to keep marching for so long. Exhausted from the fight, we stopped to make camp. The others went to sleep right away while I remained awake on first watch, keeping an eye out should any more bandits foolishly attack. But I found myself instead looking over the rest of the Hand as they slumbered.

Everyone's got some secret, Garret had said.

The more I thought about that, the more I believed he was right. The Agency itself was a mass of classified secrets, inscrutable paperwork, and suspect individuals. Who among them could I trust? Certainly not Reed, who lied to us so brazenly. Bengard? He was involved with Reed's plot, for all I knew. If no one else, I could trust Inac, right? He was a good man, and I counted him among my friends. And Ulken...the man was a strange leader, but he seemed to want the best for his Fingers.

Why, then, were there Gildmembers and people in his own organization conspiring against him?

Almost feel bad for him. Survival doesn't come easy if you have no one to rely on.

Even among my Hand, everyone seemed to be hiding something. The darkness lay so thick over my vision, I could barely see the rise and fall of Dunnax's chest. Only his soft snores told me he was asleep. Lorelay slept on her own bedroll nearby. What happened to these two Paceeqi siblings that brought them to Lawiko? Garret slept sitting upright, back against a tree trunk, as if he had to be ready at a moment's notice. Ready to kill more bandits, probably. What had they done to earn his scorn? And Sentyx...I shook my head. Sentyx slept on the hard earth, no need for comfort. Were all Skardwarves this strange, or was Sentyx unique even in the south?

Still, as strange as they all were, we'd been tested in combat. We held our own even when outnumbered. I'd been in some bad scrapes before, but that was the closest I'd experienced to a real battle. And defending the Prince of the Bright Empire, no less! Compared to that, finding some missing villagers would be as easy as making enemies in the Gild. We'd be back in Liwokin in a few days, get our reward for the job. Easy. Then I'd meet with Inac and go forward with the original plan. Until then, I figured I might as well enjoy this company while it lasted.

I nestled myself against a tree trunk, pulling my coat tight against the chill. The Bright Sibling wasn't so bright at night while it circled back east below the horizon to rise again at the start of a new dawn. None of her dim, wandering light penetrated the dense canopy of these woods. Even if someone *were* sneaking up on us, how could I have seen them coming? In this darkness, who knew what kind of beasts could surround us?

My skin crawled. Some insect zipped past my ear and bit the back of my neck; I reflexively slapped it away. Flies swarmed to the stink of Liwokin, but at least they never bit me. Out in the wild, everything was hungrier for our blood. Where I slapped my neck, a dull pain lingered. The pain faded to a numbness, then the sensation began to crackle, and bright red spots appeared in the darkness. As I stared at them, the spots grew and melded together until all the shadows in the forest had turned red and the black silhouettes of tree trunks penned us in.

The copper taste of fear filled my mouth. My heart hammered in my chest. My stomach turned at the scent of something rotting—a carcass or days-old meat. Breath came in short spurts. I looked around at the ever-brightening forest. Was it dawn already? No, the Brightdaughter never moved that fast. Yet the sky became bright as noon where it peeked through the trees. Only, it was the wrong color: fiery orange and red blazed through the gaps between dark rustling leaves.

None of the others so much as stirred. Whatever was happening, it must have been in my head, but that did nothing to stop the rising panic. I scrambled to my feet. Clutched for my knife. It wasn't there. I was defenseless. My stomach wriggled. It was filled with insects. They clawed their way up through my throat. Pried open my mouth. They tore free into the night and a horrible scream filled the void.

"Quiet," Garret said. "What's wrong with you?" But his voice trembled. When had he risen to his feet? "Listen. Something's coming."

My back was firmly planted against the tree, the only solid thing I could cling to. I tried to listen, but only my rapid heartbeat cut through the silence.

The others woke, startled out of slumber with the sudden commotion. Sentyx faced the same direction as Garret, widened his stance, and leaned slightly forward, as if preparing to be tackled to the ground.

Lorelay whimpered. "What's happening to me?"

"It's not just you," Dunnax said, picking up his pack, cradling it like a child. "It's going to be all right."

It didn't sound convincing.

I'm not the only one losing my mind, then. We all are.

"There." Garret pointed. "Who is that?"

A human figure sprinted toward us from a distance that should have made him impossible to see. He was closing fast, blue coat billowing out behind him, whipping around wildly in pursuit.

He was yelling at the top of his lungs.

"Run!" the man shouted. "Run or die!" And suddenly I recognized his voice.

Reed?

I didn't have time to question the First Eye's appearance before I was fleeing in the opposite direction, alongside all the others.

"Don't just stand there!" Reed shouted.

All except Sentyx. I looked back. The Skardwarf stood anchored in place, but I wouldn't wait for some fool who'd chosen death. I kept running...right into Dunnax, who had turned around. Whatever was in his pack nearly knocked a tooth out when I slammed into it.

Reed ran straight up to the Skardwarf and tried to turn it around. His efforts were futile.

"I face into the wind," Sentyx said, looking past Reed into the darkness.

There was nothing in the forest beyond them but the rotting scent, the painfully bright light, the taste of blood...all grew more intense with each rapid pulse of my heart. Every bit of me wanted to turn and run, or cower and hide, but the rest of the Hand had stopped, and I wasn't going off alone. The earth shook with the footsteps of some giant crashing toward us.

"Stubborn, bleeding Southerners. It's going to kill you if you don't go *now*!" Reed said, digging his heels in the dirt to push against Sentyx. The Skardwarf resisted without budging. "Your Hand is waiting. Will they all die because of you?"

Sentyx said nothing. For a moment, I thought he really would try to face this threat on his own. Then, the Skardwarf turned so suddenly, Reed nearly fell on his face. Sentyx started running toward us, slow at first but gathering momentum to catch us quickly. Reed was right beside him. Relief that we were going flooded my veins, but terror quickly swept it away. Whatever was coming, we weren't ready to fight it. A bounty hunter prepared for every possibility, but sometimes survival meant knowing when to run.

All of us were at full sprint when Reed, straining, said, "I'll lure it away. Keep going until darkness returns." Then he cut to the right and broke away from our pack.

An inhuman roar sounded behind us and I dared not look back. An unimaginable monster was right on our tails. I ran faster than I ever had. The shock wave of a nearby explosion thumped against my back and propelled me forward. I ran and ran, ignoring the ache in my chest and fire in my legs, until finally the darkness began to return. The unusual tastes, scents, and fiery night sky disappeared and left no trace that anything had ever been wrong. Pitch black silence had never been more comforting.

How did Reed know that would happen?

"Stop," Dunnax said, heaving. "Please, enough." He'd carried his heavy pack with him the entire frantic flight. Now, he let it fall to the ground with a metallic thud. He went to his knees, then toppled forward to his hands and vomited.

"What in the bleeding darkness was that?" Garret said. Impossibly, he wasn't even winded.

"A monster," I said, hands on my knees to catch my breath. I spat to try to get the taste of blood from my mouth. "Reed knew exactly what would happen when we ran."

Ulken thinks they are still under control.

Garret was still skeptical. "He also said to remember what's real. Could be the monster wasn't real, just some…" He shook his head, spat. "Some *thing* we don't understand. Plenty of that in the world."

"How could that not be real?" Lorelay asked. She rubbed Dunnax's heaving back with care, but her words were cold steel. "I felt like I was going to snuffing *die*."

No one could argue with that. We all went quiet then, for some time. She was right, it had to be real, or why would Reed have had us abandon our camp to flee? But the burning sky, the rotten scent, the copper taste, the terror…they faded as the distance grew that we put between ourselves and the monster. How? It didn't make sense.

Then Garret burst out laughing. "You really thought you were going to fight it alone?" he asked Sentyx.

Sentyx grunted. "I face into th—"

"Into the wind," Garret said. "Aye. We know. You're insane." He laughed again, mirthlessly. "We all are, if we don't tuck tail and slink away after hearing that beast."

I nodded. "Whatever that was, it would have killed us if not for the First Eye."

That fact nagged at me. Reed must have known I was in on his secret. I was a loose end. Why not just let me die?

Reed must have been more merciful than Ulken.

"We're not turning back." Dunnax opened his pack and began removing a set of oiled silver armor. "We have our command." With Lorelay's help, he began strapping into his plate.

"Can't carry out our orders if we starve to death," Garret said. "We left all our supplies at the camp. We have to turn back."

Lorelay finished tying the bevor that protected her Dunnax's throat. He pushed it up in front of his face, then put on a helmet adorned with gold and red starbursts—the sigil of the Empress. The Paladin's armor transformed the already big Paceeqi into a truly imposing figure.

Wouldn't want to be on the Empire's bad side if they've got an army of these.

"Fine," Dunnax said, voice muffled behind all the metal he wore. "We'll retrieve our equipment. If the beast is still in the area, we'll be ready for it."

"Well, if we feel it coming again, you and the Skardwarf can fight," I said. "I'm running."

"Maybe Reed killed it already," Lorelay said.

"Wouldn't count on it," Garret said. "Probably got himself killed."

If the First Eye was dead, the information I held would be useless. Then again, the man had saved our lives. Could I really expose him to Ulken?

"We can wait for dawn's light, or go back right away," I said, not dwelling on what to do about Reed. "Either way, I don't think I'll be getting any sleep tonight."

As we waited for dawn, none of us did.

* * *

The Brightdaughter's pale light filtered through the trees, casting long shadows from the east. The whole sleepless night had passed without incident, and we made our way back to the campsite to retrieve our supplies, only to discover...

"It's gone," Garret said. "All of it."

"Are you certain this is the right spot?" Lorelay asked.

Garret looked at her like she'd just asked if he's sure he knows how to read. "Of course I'm sure." Along the way, just before first light, we came across a scar on the land that led to where we now stood, a path of devastation. The ranger crouched down, examined the torn-up earth that cut through our campsite. "There are tracks here from a dozen different animals." My eye followed where he pointed, but it was just a mess of dirt. "Deer, fox, wolf, bear...deeper than they should be. Heavier."

"A stampede?" Dunnax asked, looking south where the tracks ran. Where we had run. Fully armored as he was, he looked like a metal statue with dawn's light reflecting off his plate. Minor dents and a myriad of scuffs marred the once-pristine armor. Like its owner, the armor had seen better days.

"Stampede? No." Garret shook his head. "There are human tracks too."

"Ours?" I asked.

"No."

"Then..." Lorelay furrowed her brows. "What sort of monster *is* this?"

After a sleepless night, it was beginning to feel like this was all a nightmare. Like I had only imagined that horrifying roar. Like all of it was a falsity, not just the taste of blood or the scent of rot. There mustn't have been any monster. The terror...that was real—how could emotions be anything but true? But the rest had to have been in my head. People were the only monsters that existed in this world. Everything else? Just stories to scare the children.

But we had Reed's note, and we all had heard its inhuman bellow. That revelation had contributed to our sleeplessness. The sound had been made by something unlike any animal Garret had hunted, and he'd hunted them all, to hear him tell it.

The dread that beast had elicited started creeping up again. My mind was too tired to fight it back.

I should have stayed in Liwokin.

After a long silence, Dunnax shrugged. "We're going to find out." He started south, armor jangling with every step.

Discerning the distinct tracks wasn't important. The monster left destruction in its passing, like one massive individual track, easy enough to follow. The only prints that deviated from the great bulk of the rest were our own. We took the straight path of prey on the run from a predator; there had been no time to think, only to flee. The monster's path overlapped our own often, but weaved through trees otherwise, knocking branches from high up and scraping against the thick trunks it skirted, leaving gouges in the bark.

With the help of better light, we found some supplies we missed scattered in the beast's wake, but they were all trampled, destroyed nearly beyond recognition. Sentyx had brought a bag of healing goods—salves, poultices, and sundry vials of liquid that had all been shattered. Determining that nothing was recoverable, the Skardwarf tossed the soaked bag to the ground without so much as a grunt. Dunnax had carried his armor with him last night but had left his glaive behind. He now spotted the weapon half-covered in dirt, resting near a tree. The metal haft had been bent around the trunk and now resembled the crooked handle of a scythe. With all his might, the paladin couldn't restore it. He shook with exertion trying to bend the warped metal over his knee before giving up and testing it with the new grip. The blade still cut easily enough. For everyone else, there was nothing. All that remained was what we grabbed before running: blades and bows and scarcely enough rations for two of us.

Eventually, the tracks turned west, toward the Shaded Grounds that fur trader mentioned. This must have been where Reed broke off from us, but the monster's tracks destroyed any evidence of that, so it was impossible to tell. Dunnax stopped, looked west, then south, as if trying to make up his mind.

"We're not ready for a fight," I said. "We should resupply in Leppit first."

"I agree," Lorelay said. "We can talk to the villagers, so we're not fighting it blind. The missing villagers might be unrelated to the monster anyway."

I blinked. Why hadn't I thought of that? During the night we all had assumed the monster was behind the disappearances, but Lorelay was right—its presence may have been a coincidence.

Dunnax grunted, then gave a curt nod. If fighting the monster wasn't needed to fulfill our command, he probably didn't see the point in it.

"Look," Garret said. The Ekoan bounded through the trees, following the tracks, then stopped and gestured us over. He squatted down, picked up a clump of some charred, viscous sludge, sniffed it, and recoiled in disgust. All around him, debris littered the blackened ground.

"The explosion..." I muttered. "That really happened too?"

"Real," Sentyx said.

"Apparently, everything was real," Lorelay said. "What were Reed and that Finger, Bengard, talking about?"

I disagreed. So many of the sensations were ephemeral, linked to the monster's presence, but I decided not to press the issue. "Reed tried to stop it with...what?" The blast radius only brought one thing to mind. "An Archefire bomb?"

Years ago, two dozen shops in the Artisans District were obliterated when an Archechemist's tinkering set off his entire stockpile. Carrying one around seemed like a sure way to lose a limb or three.

"Aye," Garret said. "Except..." He gestured beyond the wreckage. The tracks continued.

My heart darkened. If an Archefire bomb didn't stop the monster, what hope did we have?

Garret stood up, wiped the filth from his hands on his pant legs. "There's no body. Not that there would be, I suspect. Monster that big probably would have eaten him whole. So..."

"To Leppit?" I suggested.

Dunnax looked like he was deep in thought. He blinked, then turned to me, frowning. "We'll slay this monster. But first, we find the missing villagers."

A sinister thought crossed my mind, too dark to voice aloud. *If there are any left alive.*

* * *

The rest of our trek passed quickly. I didn't know how long we ran last night—flight from unimaginable horrors did tend to skew one's perspective of time. Our second campsite, where we passed the night doing more worrying than camping, was nearly at the edge of the village. Had Reed not drawn the monster away, it surely would have barreled right into Leppit. Maybe the monster was responsible for the disappearances after all.

The sun should have been overhead when we crossed the tree line, but something deprived us of the Bright Sibling's light. My eyes were turned down from the sky; thoughts flooded my mind trying to piece together the night's events. Step by step, I followed the others without paying attention, stomping across muddy ground until Sentyx abruptly stopped and I crashed into the Skardwarf's back like running into a wall.

"What is this?" Sentyx said, shouting over the rain.

When did it start raining?

Everyone else's confused reactions told me none of them had an answer to that question. Rain poured forth from black clouds in tremendous volume, a waterfall spilling out from the heavens. The storm raged, with gusts of whipping wind wailing like ghosts, but the clouds sat motionless in the sky. A dense fog stalked the village ahead, whose buildings could be seen as dark silhouettes in the roiling, hazy gray.

"None of us noticed this?" Lorelay said, looking around, perplexed.

A torrential downpour walloped the earth, creating a cacophony that should have caught our attention immediately. Heavy droplets rang against Dunnax's plate like a thousand miniature hammers striking an anvil, and a stream of water sloshed out from the bottom of his grieves. I held my hand out, palm up, and watched the raindrops splash against my skin. They should have been cold, but no. They weren't cold. Or warm.

They weren't anything at all.

"I can't feel it," I said. I watched recognition dawn on the Hand's faces. It wasn't just me. The drops splashed in my hand, streams trickling down my forearm, falling from my elbow like tears.

"Archemagic," Sentyx said.

Dunnax tilted his head back, watching the storm through the slit in his visor. "This isn't the Fire."

The Skardwarf grunted.

But Dunnax was trained by the Empire. Hadn't Inac said they don't know the true nature of Archemagic? I opened my mouth to say something, then shut it. There was no hope of convincing Dunnax. I'd just have to ask Inac about it when we returned to the city.

If we return to the city.

Garret looked up, opened his mouth, and stuck out his tongue. He hesitated, pondering, then tried something else. He cupped his hands to collect the falling water and tried to drink it. Garret shook his head in agitation and let the water fall to the muddy ground. I narrowed my eyes, until realization came. He was trying to figure out why this was happening.

The Ekoan bent down, dug his hands around in the brown, ankle-deep muck and came up with a twig, sopping wet and dripping. From inside his coat the ranger produced a fire striker; it sparked and the soaked twig, incomprehensibly, lit aflame. A heartbeat after catching, the flame sizzled out, then flickered alight again, then went out, over and over. All of us watched Garret's strange experiment with bewilderment. The cycle of lighting and extinguishing repeated, as if the stick couldn't decide whether it wanted to burn or not. The flame went out one last time, presumably because of the rain, and never relit. Garret threw it down, cursing, then frowned. "None of this makes sense."

"It's making my head ache," Lorelay said.

"We should leave," Dunnax said. At least *he* was finally making some sense.

"Come," Sentyx said. The Skardwarf alone seemed unfazed by the storm. "Village is just ahead."

* * *

Any hope we had of entering the village unannounced was squandered by the rain clattering against Paladin plate armor like an alarm to scare off intruders. The fact that no one responded to this alarm deepened my suspicion that everyone was already dead as we waded through the flood streaming down the main thoroughfare of Leppit village. I waddled against the strong current and the rest of the Hand did the same, sloshing and kicking up splashes in the deep water—even the Skardwarf, but it always walked that way. Moving this slowly through the decrepit town stoked an ember of fear. Anything could be waiting in the hazy darkness. The shadows lurked all around. My finger rested at the ready on the trigger of my crossbow.

None of the scattered, rundown houses we passed emitted any light from within. Nor did they show any signs of activity. I thought I saw some motion in one, but it was only the movement of fog in a gust of unfelt wind. One dwelling had a kicked-in door and a shattered window. Dunnax sidled up to it and shouted inside but received no response.

Everyone is already dead.

We continued toward the south end of the street until we saw a lone building, its hulking shadow looming, the void of light deeper in its silhouette than in the curtain of fog surrounding it. The image of a long, wooden hall with a thatch roof and two doors—one to the east, another to the west—began to emerge as we approached. By all rights, the thatching should have collapsed under the weight of the rain or blown away in a gust of the howling wind. Somehow, the storm had no bearing on the hall's structural integrity. Which was fortunate, because at that moment the shadow of a man with a spear on his back slunk through the fog and started bashing his shoulder into the west-side door. At the sounds of forced entry, a woman inside began to scream.

I leveled my crossbow and pulled the trigger as we all pushed forward as fast as the water would allow. The quarrel *plunked* into the door frame a hand's width from the door basher's head at the same time as the frame gave way. The door hinged open and let loose one final, blood-curdling scream from whomever waited within. But instead of taking cover inside, the man reacted to my bolt by spinning around and reaching for his spear in one smooth motion, bellowing a vicious war cry.

He must have noticed there were five of us. Door Basher dropped to his knees with a splash, raised his hands in surrender, and changed his tune. "Wait! Wait!" He babbled something unintelligible, probably urging us not to kill him.

"Inside. Now." Dunnax prodded Door-Basher with his pole-arm. "Keep your hands away from that weapon."

We all funneled inside, along with a rush of water that soaked the clothes of a thin, gray-haired woman cowering in the back corner of the hall. She paid no mind to the pooling water, instead praying as though she believed her death had come. A wave of rainwater rushed across the floor of the hall, crashing against the furniture, and knocking over a table. Garret slammed the door closed behind him. I blinked and the water was gone, as if it had never been there at all. The table was back where it belonged. The floor and the old woman were dry. I rubbed my eyes.

By the abyss, I need some sleep.

I scanned the room searching for other survivors, but it was clear at a glance that none were left. The building was wide open, full of musty bunk beds, overturned tables, and filthy, half-empty cabinets with flies buzzing around. Racks of barbed harpoons and fishing poles lined the long back wall. The hall appeared to be a communal abode, once home to many fishermen. Now it was abandoned, just like the praying woman. The air stank of onion and mold and rotten fish, enough to make anyone sick. Despite the sounds of whipping wind outside, none entered the broken windows from outside to whisk the nauseating stench from the room. Even the winds were unkind in this town. How long had she been living in this squalor?

Lorelay sat beside the woman and unhooked the lyre from her belt. At the sight of the instrument, her prayers grew increasingly panicked. Lorelay hesitated but began plucking a melody anyway. It was oddly soothing. Hearing the soft tune, the woman's posture relaxed almost imperceptibly, like the petals of a flower opening to the sky as the sun emerges once more from behind the clouds. The song filled the stifling room with life, something it seemed to have lacked for an exceedingly long time. But when we left and the music was gone, what would remain?

Nothing worthwhile.

While Lorelay played, Garret broke away to snoop around. The rest of us surrounded Door-Basher, who now stood by a broken window with arms raised and trembling. Wavy, sand-colored hair hung from his head, down to his neck where he wore a collar of huge, jagged teeth tight against his skin.

"Who are you?" Dunnax demanded.

I reloaded my crossbow. "Some thief or cutthroat, I'd guess."

"Cutthroat?" The man's eyes went wide. "*You* tried to kill *me*! I am the one and only Markos. A great fisherman. See?" Without taking his eyes off Dunnax's glaive, he twisted to display the gear on his back. What I mistook for a spear was only a harpoon, and in lieu of a pack he carried his supplies in a tangle of thick fishing net.

"Are you...the Net?" I asked.

A crooked smile flashed across Markos' face. "Ah, so you know of the Net. Not surprising. I am not him, but I have come to train with him."

Lorelay's song stopped, and the woman sobbed, wiping tears away with a ragged sleeve and leaving a streak of dirt running across her cheek. Lorelay placed a comforting hand on her arm. "Guys...the Net is Ciria's husband. He's been missing for...a long time."

Markos slumped down, like someone squeezed the air out of him. "I knew it...I came all this way..."

"We'll try to find out what happened to him," Lorelay said, squeezing Ciria's hand. Doubt colored her voice, but the gray widow didn't seem to notice. She sniffled and nodded, and Lorelay asked, "Is there anything else you need from us?"

Keeping my voice quiet and stepping close to the would-be apprentice, I said, "If he's been missing for that long, he's probably dead. Leave this village, Markos. There's nothing for you here."

Markos didn't react at first. He looked resigned and downcast. Then he met my eyes, and the defiance in his face was unmistakable. "If you're looking for the Net, then I am too."

"Not a good idea," Dunnax said. He looked at Ciria and lowered his voice. "There's a monster here in this village. You're just going to get yourself killed."

"Monster?" Markos said loudly, with no concern for what Ciria heard. "You think I'm afraid of some monster?" The fisherman bared his teeth, flexed his neck until the sharp fangs on his collar dug into flesh. "These came from the mouth of a bearshark in the Ayeiri strait." Markos pounded a fist against his chest. "If it's monsters you're hunting, I'm the one you want."

Why did courage always come paired with foolishness? Markos seemed more eager than most to die, but after last night, I wouldn't turn down the help of another fighter.

"Fine," I said, "but you don't know what you're signing up for."

Then again, neither did we.

Markos puffed out his chest, slammed another fist into it, and smiled at the resounding thump. "Good. Hunting sharks is only fun when the waves hide their fins. Only close to death do you truly live."

I raised an eyebrow. "That doesn't make any sense."

"There's something out there," Garret said. My spine stiffened. It had to be the monster. I crept over to join him in peering through the broken glass. In the rain, a mote of light moved through the fog. It flickered in the same strange way as Garret's twig when he set it alight.

"Another villager?" I guessed. "Or bandits?"

Garret shrugged.

"I'll stay here with Ciria," Lorelay said. "Go. I'll catch up."

"I'm not leaving you alone," Dunnax said. "I'm staying too."

That was for the best. If this was someone dangerous, I didn't want Dunnax's armor loudly announcing our arrival. Better to stay out of sight, which wouldn't be hard with the rage of the storm to obscure us. I looked back at the two Paceeqi siblings. Would this be the last I ever saw of them?

"Okay. Garret, Sentyx, let's go. You too, Markos, and you better not give us away. Stay out of sight until we know who we're dealing with."

Or *what* we were dealing with.

With one last breath to steel myself, I checked my weapons and crept out into the murk.

CHAPTER SEVEN

Memories

Slinking down the street, I could almost pretend this was the Blight and I was sneaking up on my target, except that the shacks in the Blight could never have withstood this downpour. The entire district would have slid down the hill in a slurry of mud and timber to end up in Brightcalm Bay.

We sloshed our way from house to house, peering around corners to follow the blinking light until we got close enough to see that it wasn't a pack of bandits, only a young woman carrying a torch, entirely unmindful of the storm. She didn't seem to notice that the torch kept dying out and reigniting, nor that the rain soaked her golden hair and the sheer dress she wore. The calf-high water didn't slow her graceful movements one bit. Whistling a happy tune like she was strolling to the market, she bounded right up to a dark-windowed house and rapped three times on the shuttered glass.

"Come out, Kalvin, my dear," she said, oddly jovial. "I told you I'd be back."

She continued whistling until the door opened and a leather-clad man of an age with me walked out with his head tilted down to the ground. That must have been Kalvin. A broad-chested fellow came out right behind him and grabbed at Kalvin's hand. The flex of his muscles was clear through the deep fog, but Kalvin's hand slipped free from his grip like it was slick with grease.

"Oh, Hebvek," the torchbearer said. "You're so kind to worry about your brother. But Kalvin wants to come with me, don't you dear? You know the clearing is nothing to fear. We'll be back soon."

Hebvek didn't respond. He just slumped down, a grief-stricken moan bubbling from his throat. Then he cried, his chest heaving visibly even at this distance.

I shared a look with Garret. This exchange was strange, but none of these people seemed dangerous. Maybe this was some lover's quarrel? A jealous brother? As soon as I exited cover to reveal myself, the woman turned and waved with a kindly smile. I started. Did she somehow know we were following her? Markos and Sentyx were clumsy in disguising their splashes, but the rainfall should have covered the sound. Garret, for his part, was quiet as a cat. I was impressed by how deftly he moved through the torrent, but it didn't make a difference.

Nothing ever goes as planned.

"Hello, friends. I haven't seen you around before. What brings you to our village?"

Markos spoke up from behind when I hesitated, pushing his way around Sentyx. "We're searching for the Net."

"And all the other missing villagers," I added.

"Missing villagers?" A quizzical look crossed the odd woman's face.

"Really?" Garret said. "You don't know about the disappearances? What about the monster? And what this storm is doing to your torch? Doesn't it all seem strange to you? Or are you daft?"

I tensed at Garret's mention of the monster, fearing it would only stir panic, but this fear, at least, turned out to be unfounded.

"Daft? How unkind of you, sir. The storms 'round here have always been bad. And a monster? I don't know what you're talking about. The disappearances..." She tilted her head as if considering them for the first time. "My brother and I, yes, we discuss them from time to time."

"Your brother? You discuss them?" She made it seem like a purely academic thing. I scratched the back of my head. Surprisingly, it felt dry.

"Yes, of course. Wyran and I have always been close." She giggled. "You could say we're of one mind." Her face lit up in delight just as the torch she held sputtered out, but only momentarily. "Kalvin and I were about to go visit him now. You should come along with us. I'm sure Wyran could tell you more about the villagers."

She and Kalvin stood hand in hand, though Kalvin didn't appear to be any more pleased than his own brother, Hebvek, still crying in the doorway. His leather clothes and cap were soaked, and while he meekly tugged his arm, he couldn't escape as easily as he had from his brother's grip. Eventually, he gave up and hung his head. Her words may have been gentle, but something about her was...off. People in small towns like this weren't anything like city folk.

Part of me did want to follow her. She was a beacon of light in this dark, storming town, the only one who didn't seem completely miserable. But we couldn't, not before regrouping with Dunnax and Lorelay. Finding the missing villagers was Ulken's command, but I wasn't going anywhere without backup. Not with that monster around.

"Which house is your brother's?" I asked. "We'll find you and Wyran after regrouping with the rest of our Hand. They'll be interested to hear what he has to say."

"Our house? It's on the west street, third house from the end. But—"

A reverberating sound approached: raindrops pinging off metal armor. Only the faint sound of Dunnax's muffled shouting reached me over the storm.

"We'll find you," I said to the woman. "Be careful. The monster could be close." Without a word, she strode toward the gap between houses with Kalvin, who dragged his feet and slowed her down.

I rushed to meet Dunnax with the others. Clearly, he was in a hurry.

"The monster?"

"The innkeeper," Dunnax said, nodding. "Ciria said he was with her husband. They fought it off together."

So, the villagers did know about it.

I turned around, but the torch-bearing woman was nowhere to be seen. She knew more than she was letting on.

And we'd let her get away. I hadn't even gotten her name.

I gritted my teeth as a hollow feeling filled me. "Where's the inn?"

"West of the hall. Big building, can't miss it." Dunnax turned and started running, with some difficulty, through the flooded street.

Following him, I noticed the water getting deeper the longer we stayed in Leppit village. That made no sense. Weren't we right near a cliff? The water should have been flowing down a huge waterfall, unable to collect atop...I caught myself. There was no point trying to understand it.

We'll never find the villagers. Not before that monster kills us all.

I wanted to lay down right there in the middle of the street. To stop fighting and let the waters rush over me. I slowed to a stop, ready to give in. A rough hand fell on my shoulder.

"Face the wind," Sentyx said.

"What wind?" I asked. I felt no wind, but the Skardwarf wasn't speaking literally.

"No despair," Sentyx said.

With a surprisingly gentle nudge from the Skardwarf, my feet began carrying me forward again.

"No despair."

* * *

On the other side of the village, Leppit's sole inn dwarfed the meager homes scattered all around. Without a doubt, it was the largest building in the village, as any good inn should be. Shorter than the length of the hall, but twice as tall. Who was such an establishment meant to serve? Even before some mysterious evil decimated the residents, it was hard to imagine any gathering of considerable size in a place so remote. Now, with the threat of a monster and the vanishing of villagers, not even ghosts haunted these empty streets. The six of us arrayed before the building were probably the largest crowd this inn had seen since the beginning of Leppit's nightmare.

'The Coddle Inn', a hanging sign read, below a carving of a spotted and bearded fish cresting the waves, swirling clouds overhead. Paint ran down the double-wide entrance doors. Once-bright colors streaked down into mud, pulled toward the earth by the storm's waters so convincingly I reached out to touch the wooden surface. When I interrupted the flow, the paint *snapped* back to its true position so suddenly I flinched away, and the paint dripped anew.

"You all saw that, right?" I asked.

"Aye," Garret said. "How's something like that happen?"

"Archemagic," Sentyx insisted.

"But how—"

"Save the questions for later," Dunnax said, and pushed his way through the doors.

There may not be a later.

"A man of action," Markos said, grinning somehow, despite the weight of the air. He fingered one of the teeth on his collar. "I like him."

The heavy doors slammed open, the sound echoing in the nearly empty tavern. Unlike the ragged state of the communal hall, the inn was in good condition, if one was willing to overlook the collapsed stairs. No one was accessing the second floor any time soon. Dust coated the tables, but they stood upright; most had tankards or bottles on them. The place didn't stink of rot, only of strong alcohol. Oil lanterns lit the first floor, so someone was maintaining the building. In truth, the inn was better kept than the Wistwicker in Liwokin. If I wasn't sure everyone was dead, I might have guessed everyone had simply gone home without cleaning up behind them.

Everyone but one lonesome man who remained at the bar, hunched on a stool with an open bottle of orange liqueur and a half-empty glass in front of him. He rolled his head, cheek slumping on his shoulder to look askance at the noisemakers who just entered. One humorless chuckle and he swiped the bottle, refilled his glass, and downed it in one swig. The innkeeper wiped the dribble from his chin with a clumsy hand and mumbled, "Well, well. Coddle's closed. No rooms left. No ale, neither."

Lorelay took the stool beside him. "We're not here for a room. We're here for you."

"Come to take me too, witch?" He barked a laugh. Lorelay patiently wiped the spittle from her face. "Just try it. I still got some fight in me."

Lorelay nodded. "I believe it. Ciria told us you fought the monster with her husband."

"Enh? Akun's old lady still alive? Thought she starved herself weeks ago." The innkeeper reached for the bottle, but Lorelay stayed his hand.

Akun? The way Markos' eyes lit up, that must have been the Net's real name.

"Yes," Lorelay said. "Tell us about the monster you fought with Akun. What happened? How did you get away?"

He snatched his hand away. "I didn't fight no monster. You don't know what I—" The innkeeper became inexplicably defensive. He pushed Lorelay back and she nearly lost her balance on the stool. Dunnax moved in to grab the man, but his sister stopped him.

Garret vaulted over the bar and landed with a clattering of glass. "Empty bottles back here. Dozens of them."

Lorelay frowned, then a look of understanding crossed her face. "You're...not the innkeeper, are you?"

The man laughed. "Ciria mus' of lost her mind if she thinks the innkeeper is still alive." Now it was his turn to frown. He stopped paying attention to us, looked like he was about to cry. "Perlo...I should o' been there..." The tears came.

Lorelay slapped him. Her patience lasted longer than mine had.

About time it ran out.

The man was angry. He grabbed for the bottle.

Lorelay slapped him again, harder. She snatched the bottle, threw it behind her without tearing her hard gaze from the now-dazed man.

Garret nabbed the bottle from the air and took a whiff. He sipped the orange liqueur, spat it out. "Awful."

Markos grabbed it, took a sip, shrugged, and took another.

"Now you listen to me," Lorelay said, as though she were chiding a young boy. "What's your name?"

"E-Eadrick." Anger gone, only shock remained.

"What happened to the innkeeper, Eadrick?"

"He...died." Eadrick looked away. "Like all the rest."

Lorelay looked at us, then back. "What killed them?"

Eadrick turned to us, wobbling in his seat. His eyes widened at the sight of Sentyx, who stared at him in Sentyx's usual blank way. Eadrick regained himself and looked around the room, gaze unfocused, as if watching insects flit about. "You feel it, don't you? It's all around us, sure as the storm. *She* did this."

"Feel what?" Sentyx asked.

"She did this?" I asked. "Who is 'she'?"

"Breta," Eadrick said her name like a curse. "Two of 'em came to the village a few measures ago, during the helmie migration. We needed more hands, so when a Lawi lad showed up with his sister, Akun took 'em in. Put 'em to work in boats down in the sea, hauling the helmies our divers spear out o' the water."

"So, it's true," Markos said in awe. "You really do dive from the cliffs?"

"'Course it's true," Eadrick said, trying to drink from his already-empty glass, then frowning and tossing it aside to shatter on the floor. "No other way to catch helmfish when they come 'round each year. Nasty buggers, they are. Thick skulls, but not thick enough to stop a spear from on high. Takes lots of practice, o' course. And as many prayers. That's why only our best do it. The rest work the boats, until the fall kills one o' the best. Or the helmies do. Nasty buggers, I tell you."

I tried to picture Eadrick diving from a cliff, spear in hand. The image wouldn't come.

These people are insane.

Eadrick went on. "The lad wouldn't have none of that. Wanted to prove his self, he said. Akun put a spear in his hand and walked him up to the cliffs." The drunkard cackled. "I really think he would o' done it, if Akun hadn't stopped him. We're not cruel. Or crazy. Don't give me that look. We aren't! That boy must o' been, though." He sighed, looked to Markos. "Hand me that bottle, will you?"

Markos stepped toward him.

But Lorelay shook her head. "Continue, please."

Eadrick closed his eyes, letting the silence drag on. When he continued, he was more somber, or maybe just more sober. "I was in the longhall with the rest of the fishermen when we heard screaming outside. Breta...the girl was thin as an eel, but she dragged her brother, broken and bleeding all the way up from the sea. Wouldn't have believed it if I hadn't seen it with my own eyes. That she could muster that strength, or that the lad would jump. What demon made him think he could dive in the dark?

"She saw him jump, she said. Broke his neck when he hit the water, but somehow, he was still breathing when we helped carry him to his house. Barely. The girl tried to sew him up, but he was losing too much blood. We wanted to stay, give him a proper Leppit funeral when he died. The lad was brave enough he earned that much. But no, she got real quiet instead. Even quieter than usual. Nothing like she is now. Told us to leave, so we left." Eadrick spat on the floor. "That's when she did it. Back in the hall, the mood was already sour. But I *felt* it happen. The hopelessness, then the rain... Thought we were losing our minds." Another humorless laugh. "Maybe we were. The storm's been raging ever since. Not a single day goes by that it don't."

A long silence fell as we took it all in.

Lorelay broke the spell. "How long...since that happened?"

"Long enough to drink this place near to dry. Three measures, I reckon. More?"

Markos spat out an orange mouthful. "A quarter of a year?"

"That can't be right," Garret said. "Even in the Ekoan storm-jungle, rain doesn't fall that long."

Eadrick shrugged. "What's it matter? Everyone else is gone. I'm the only one left."

"You are not," Sentyx said, but it brought Eadrick little comfort.

"Three measures." Dunnax grunted. "Ulken did say the report was from a while back."

"I don't understand," I said, rubbing my eyes. "How did this witch, Breta...how did she kill everyone?"

Eadrick grew angry, though I suspected not with me. "How should I know? Same as she killed her brother, I guess, though he would o' died in any case. Turned him into a monster, but that wasn't enough. Now she lures the rest of us, my *friends*, to die, whistling all the while. There's no stopping..."

I took an involuntary step back, no longer listening.

"The witch..." Sentyx said. "Whistling."

Kalvin...

"We need to go," I said. "*Now!*"

"Yes." Sentyx was already stomping toward the door.

"What?" Dunnax asked, raising one eyebrow. "Where?"

"To Wyran's house," I said. "No time to explain."

"Wyran!" Eadrick jolted up from the stool. He looked more clear-eyed now than during the entire telling of his tale. "That was the lad's name. You're looking to kill the witch? I know the way. I'm not sitting on my arse this time."

I wanted to object for a half-dozen reasons. It was too dangerous. He'd get in the way. I already knew where to go. But Eadrick was already out into the storm, and it was all we could do to follow him.

*   *   *

Thunder and lightning cracked the sky as we surrounded Wyran's house. It wasn't far from the inn. Even so, there was no way we had arrived in time to save Kalvin from...becoming a monster?

Once again, we had no idea what we were up against.

We all had weapons in hand, covering both entrances—one in back, one in front—to make sure there was no room to escape. The place looked inconspicuous, showing no movement inside, but through the lone window it was dark. Anything could have been happening in there. Who knew what Breta's magic looked like? Maybe the witch worked best in the dark, though I'd never heard of any Archemagic like that.

Lorelay gave the signal. She and Dunnax were in front with Sentyx and Markos. Garret, Eadrick, and I watched the back. Another crack rang out, with no lightning preceding it this time. Dunnax had smashed open the front door. Garret strung his bow with a dry string from inside his coat, nocked and aimed an arrow at the rear door just as I aimed my loaded crossbow. Eadrick ran up and clumsily kicked the back door open, then flailed to the side to get out of our way, falling into the mud with a brown splash. His head went back, and he sat up gasping for air, though I didn't see his face go underwater. The water was shallower here than on the street. Was that because Breta focused her magic on Kalvin?

We waited, ready to rush in at the sounds of violence. Only, it never came.

"Clear!" Dunnax shouted inside, then opened the back door and stepped outside.

"You're sure?" Garret said.

"Of course I'm sure. There's only one room. Nowhere to hide."

Eadrick groaned and cursed from where he sat in the muck. Dunnax offered him a hand up. Lorelay, Sentyx, and Markos came out following Dunnax.

"The place is a wreck," Markos said. "Someone put up a fight here."

"But there are no bodies," Lorelay said, "or even blood."

"No blood?" Eadrick asked. "But the lad's neck—"

"Smells like death to me," Garret said. All eyes turned to him. He shrugged. "You don't smell it?"

"Actually," I said, then nodded. I expected to smell mud and rain, but that wasn't the case. "Something does stink. It's faint."

"Old," Garret said.

The ranger began sniffing around, scanning the ground, before walking right up to Eadrick and spinning him. "What's this?" Something that looked like mud clung to his pants, from when he fell. Garret crouched, began feeling around, searching for something beneath the opaque water. "Here," he said, then stood with a human bone in his hand.

Dunnax bent down and came up with much more—a desiccated skeleton, just a bit of flesh and fabric holding it together. Its head was missing. Dunnax held it at arm's length to get a good look. An arm fell from the rags that used to be clothes the once-man wore.

"Be careful!" Lorelay said, then solemnity quelled her outburst. "This was a person. Just left here to rot..."

Eadrick dug around near Garret, then froze for a moment as his hands found something. With one item in each hand, he rose. In his right, the corpse's skull. In his left, a large, painted shell with dulled spikes around the rim. Eadrick recognized it. All the air went out of him. "This is him," he said, placing the shell atop the skull. "This is Akun. He always wore this. Crown of the largest helmfish he ever killed."

"Akun?" Markos took the skull from Eadrick's hands, trembling. The fisherman closed his eyes deferentially and bowed his head. Water poured down from the ends of his sopping hair. Markos touched the skull's forehead against his own and whispered, "I'll kill the one who did this to you."

"No justice to be found here," Garret said. "Whoever killed him's probably dead already."

"How did Akun die?" Sentyx asked. The Skardwarf's voice sounded...tender.

Garret examined the remains Dunnax held, looking for the answer. I clenched and unclenched my hands, looking around at the shadows moving deep in the fog. The wailing wind tore tree branches from their trunks. I followed one as it sailed through the air and crashed against the side of a building. At the loud crash I flinched, but the tree branch disappeared. No, it was back on the tree, where it started. I groaned. After so long in this village, it felt like I was losing my grasp on reality.

If that monster shows up again, we're all going to be joining Akun.

"We don't have time for this!" I shouted, drawing Markos' ire. "We need to finish the job and get back to Liwokin. Breta said she was bringing Kalvin to her brother, but they're not here. So where are they?"

My mind raced, trying to recall everything Breta said to coax Kalvin from his home. If she was a witch, as Eadrick said, it didn't seem to me that she cast any spell. No, she seduced Kalvin from safety with nothing but sweet words and a tender touch. There was nothing to fear, she said—a lie, that was now clear. But wait, more specifically...

The clearing is nothing to fear. Wasn't that what she'd said?

"Eadrick." I grabbed him by the shirt. "Is there a clearing near the village?"

Eadrick looked at me with confused, sad eyes. Rain streaked down his face, masking any tears that might have been there. "What's it matter? Akun is dead. I didn't dare hope, but..." He pulled free of my grasp.

My anger flared. "We need to find them!" I pushed Eadrick away. "That monster could be here any moment with all the time we wasted."

"Akun's dead, Perlo's dead..." Eadrick said, pouting. He sat down and sank into the mud. "There's no one left."

"I know where the clearing is," Markos said, as though he were admitting an embarrassing secret. "I passed it coming to the village. Felt something...drawing me toward it. Like I was being sucked down to the bottom of an undersea rift. The pressure was...terrifying. So I ran. I don't know how. I thought I'd never escape. But I ran, and I found the longhall."

So much for acting tough.

No, that was unworthy. Anger still tainted my thoughts. But... I shouldn't have been angry with Eadrick either. The man was grieving; his friends were dead. Maybe Eadrick still had some hope, despite himself, until Akun's bones stole it away. I looked at Sentyx, suffering beneath the downpour as stoically as he always had.

No despair.

Eadrick sat with his head between his knees, wracked with sobs. He'd said he *felt* it happen. The hopelessness and the rain. I didn't know how, but they were Breta's doing.

"That's where Breta is," I said. "If she summoned the storm, we can put an end to it."

Sentyx's face contorted.

Was that...a smile?

Lorelay looked at Dunnax, as if expecting him to reject the idea. "We might find the missing villagers there."

The armored Paceeqi sighed behind his visor. "I doubt it."

"Me too," Garret said, "but this rain isn't natural. We've got to stop it."

"Can you take us to the clearing, Markos?" I asked.

When Markos looked up, there was a darkness in his eyes. I thought he would be unwilling. We were strangers, after all. We had no right to ask him to risk his life. To his credit, he nodded agreement.

"Here," Dunnax said, and placed Akun's remains in Eadrick's arms. "Take care of these. Get them to Ciria." He hefted his glaive. "We'll take care of the witch."

* * *

The clearing wasn't far beyond the village's bounds. As Markos had warned, it pulled us in. The intensity of its tug grew along with the storm. The farther into the woods we went, the rougher the water became, the louder the wind howled through the trees, the heavier the feeling of despair weighed. The terrain may have remained level beneath the surging waves but going back would feel like climbing a mountain. The inexorable pull of the clearing carried me downward, dragged me into the deep. It was almost a relief when I spotted the edge of the clearing. The despair was now almost a physical sensation. We'd made it to our goal only to find that there was no way to ascend from these infinite depths. We could never return.

This is where we'll die.

The flood broke like waves on a beach. I stumbled into the clearing past bark-stripped trees into the black-sky downpour. Only the contour of flattened, brown grass told me how far the absence of trees spanned. A curtain of fog and rain veiled all else; it seemed we were alone. Then, a bolt of lightning flashed and illuminated two people standing hand-in-hand near an unnatural, irregular mound.

Their afterimage remained against the backdrop of darkness. One stood with his shoulders slumped, head down, bearing a posture of total defeat.

Defeat by the other, the witch.

Who had in her hand a knife.

I shouted wordlessly and charged, heard the others right behind me. When proximity lifted the veil of darkness, I pulled the trigger and launched a quarrel at Breta's back. Without steadying to aim, the quarrel sailed wide and struck the mound behind her. She turned with infinite grace, tilted her head, and slid the knife across Kalvin's throat.

Kalvin didn't seem to notice his own death. He swayed on his feet for a moment, then toppled forward onto the mound between two branches jutting out. The odd hill started shifting to enfold him as soon as he made contact. Kalvin's body sank into the mound as if slowly being pressed into clay. Breta, job finished, casually strolled toward Garret, who drew his bowstring back, arrow pointed at the witch's heart. From this distance he couldn't miss.

But he never loosed his arrow.

In the back of my neck, at the base of my skull, a crackling sensation started, shot lightning into my mind. All the sorrow and despair lifted. Their absence left in me a void. Sight faded, then sounds, scents, tastes, feeling. Leaving me with...

Nothing.

When awareness bloomed, I felt I had been transported to another place, another time. Emotions poured into the void. Richer, varied, deeper, and all wrong. Pinpricks of light pierced the darkness and wove into a tapestry. Vivid memories filled my consciousness. The visions were my own.

The memories were another's.

CHAPTER EIGHT

The Boy

It ended in fire, my old life.

Burning wood split and cracked, unmaking our old home; embers flitted up, glowing sparks in a black field of smoke pouring forth from the windows in plumes. We watched the blaze from afar, me and my dear sister. I had to do it, I told her. We couldn't stay here, not anymore. Not after what Father had become, after he had stolen our mother away. I stroked my sister's golden hair as she sobbed into my chest. She didn't understand. How could she?

Father brought me to the city, told me I'd become a man. I loved him; I believed him. Even as they stuck their needles in my neck, I loved him, and I believed him. I didn't know what they did to me and Father until today, when he collapsed to the floor, clutching his chest, and died. I watched it happen, watched him change. I was him; he was me. We were the same. I discovered that in that city, the two of us had become monsters.

I set the fires that ended my old life. There was nothing for us here. All we had left was each other, me and my dear sister.

The world dissolved into nothingness before reappearing as the memory jolted forward to a new place, a new time. Weeks of travel instantly passed.

The sea was close; I smelled it, salty and fresh, blowing in from the windy south. Gulls circled, diving below the cliffs, down to the waters to feed. A man wearing a strange, round cap greeted us with kindness and concern showing in his gentle smile. My sister hadn't been the same on this journey; she'd grown quiet, and the light had left her once-bright eyes. The monster who used to be Father didn't bring her with us to the city, but she had changed all the same. I had to take care of her now, even if she couldn't take care of me. She was all I had left, my dear sister.

Another jolt through time.

I'm doing it for her.

A long fall, the call of my name, then pain flashed bright white in the dark, unforgiving sea. I couldn't breathe, I couldn't swim, no matter how hard I willed my useless body to move. It was hopeless; I was broken. I gave up, letting myself sink down. Something stirred within, feeding on all that remained of me; it left me hollowed out inside, empty and waiting to die.

Instead, I awoke and through weary eyes saw my sister tearing at my neck with something sharp in her trembling, blood-slick fingers. It hurt too much, what little of myself I could feel. There was no saving me, she must have known, so what was she doing? What had I done? Who would take care of her when I was gone?

And I knew I would be gone soon. She would be all alone, and there was nothing I could do. The blood dripped from my eyes like tears before my vision blurred to black. It was the last I would ever see of her. Soon, I'd become a monster in truth, just like Father. My nightmare would end.

Hers would soon begin.

Oh, Breta. I'm so sorry.

Senses faded until all that remained was an indistinct cloud of awareness. In this tiny place I felt nothing, save for death's approach. I welcomed it; there was no hope in fighting.

But something latched on, pulled me back from the abyss.

In a rush of sensation, consciousness exploded. An infinitesimal center became an inexplicable expanse, alien in its flavor, senses unimaginable, far larger than myself. My body was as nothing, withering, helpless. Flesh fell away. But hunger grew, became insatiable, an inhuman capaciousness to consume something...not quite food, but better. More filling, more powerful; I sensed it all around. A multitude of others moved within my awareness, hoarding it all for themselves. Nearby, close enough to touch, one stood out from the rest, familiar, comforting.

Dear sister. I'm so hungry. Will you help me?

She had no say in the matter. The thing that latched onto me grabbed her too.

One final jolt, backward this time, to a memory predating the rest.

In a sterile room, bright and plain, and stinking of niter and ammonia, Father sat beside me, paying attention to the plump instructor, who spoke nonsense. I yawned, ignoring him. Two dozen or more people sat in chairs too small for them comfortably to fit, listening to the fat man while his scary friend watched from the dark corner in the shadows behind us. This place reminded me of a classroom in our town's new school, but here they allowed someone to bring with him a big dog, which looked more like a wolf with—

"Pay attention, damn you," the instructor bellowed.

Father slapped my arm and glared at me.

"If you don't want to proceed, then leave now," the instructor said, staring straight through me. "There's no room for second thoughts." All eyes were on me. I couldn't turn back now. I was more than just a boy. So I shook my head.

The fat man smiled. "Good. Now, wrinkled is *always* better than smooth. This is not a matter of opinion. It is objective fact. Keep this in mind..."

His voice faded. The classroom fell away. Something let go of my mind and left me suspended, alone with nothing but the darkness.

* * *

When the visions ended, I found myself hunched down on my hands and knees. The rain streamed to the ground from the ends of my hair. I shook my head to bring clarity.

Those were...Wyran's memories.

I clutched my head, trying to understand, but it was too much. The summoned storm, the weight of despair...and now, the agony of a dead boy had forced itself into my head like a deluge of rushing water. A Deluge of memories. A haze of forgetfulness colors dreams and distant memories, but this felt as though everything I saw had happened only a moment ago. It was real, as though I'd lived the life of another. Once, they may have been Wyran's memories, but...

Now, they're mine as well.

The boy's suffering had lasted many measures, but the vision lasted only a few breaths. My eyes snapped wide open as I realized where I was, who I was with.

And the danger we were in.

"Garret!" Lorelay shouted.

The ranger was dazed, sitting on his feet, still recovering. Breta was there. Were she two steps closer, Garret's life would have ended. The witch's knife slashed, but Garret flung himself aside. Drops of blood joined the rain as steel separated flesh; the deep wound to Garret's face would not be deadly, but the scar would last him a lifetime.

Lorelay slammed into Breta, knocking her back. The Paceeqi girl was a poet with the blade, and she had two knives, both forged for combat, to the witch's one, dull and crude. Breta stabbed at her. Lorelay parried the thrust aside with her long knife. She sliced a deep gouge up the witch's arm with the other, then rammed the short blade between Breta's ribs below the armpit. She spun, pulling the short knife free with a spurt of blood. Lorelay slammed the long knife backhand into Breta's neck. The witch crumpled to the ground with the force of the blow. Breta was dead. She never stood a chance.

I shuddered at Lorelay's angry brutality, but we finished what we came to do. I breathed a sigh of relief, tried to relax the tension in my neck...then realized the rain hadn't stopped.

An inhuman roar filled with anguish sounded in my mind. The beast lurked unseen until a bolt of lightning rent the darkness.

Wyran.

No. The monster he'd become.

All of us were on our feet. In the darkness, the silhouette of a misshapen mound approached from the other side of the clearing. It topped even Dunnax in height and was wider than the streets of the Gild at its base. An extended chain of lightning flashed and revealed a better look at the face of the enemy—if it could be said to have had a face.

Bark, stolen from the surrounding forest, covered the surface of the amorphous creature as though it were armor. Flesh and bone colored the negative spaces in-between. Around its body, large branches impaled the creature like broken spears jutting forth from a phalanx, giving the impression of a target peppered with arrows. As the monster moved, wood cracked and splintered, cutting through the sounds of the storm, until it roared again, echoing in my mind with murderous intent. Where Kalvin's body had fallen, there was only more shapeless flesh, and a patch of color that matched Kalvin's garments. The villager had been completely absorbed.

I froze, unable to act. Garret and Dunnax both broke left, circling around to attack. The monster pulsed, created a wave in its body that swung several thick branches like clubs. Small motions at their bases translated to sweeping power at their ends, granting frightening force to the attack.

Garret ducked beneath the branches then backed off. He started firing arrows into the bark armor. The monster didn't react.

Dunnax took the brunt of the creature's blow. A branch struck him and shattered against his armor. The former Paladin was flung to his back. He scrambled away before more striking branches could rain down.

Arrows were useless, heavy armor was scarcely protection at all.

What hope does that leave me?

Lorelay ran to help her brother while Markos, screaming vengeance, charged straight in. The fisherman threw his net to tangle Wyran's branches, then stabbed wildly with his harpoon. Sentyx went with him. The Skardwarf stood in the way of the myriad blows hammering down at Markos. Weathering countless strikes seemingly without care, Sentyx started ripping the bark armor from Wyran. Markos stabbed the newly exposed flesh and Wyran...started to bleed.

A bestial grin spread across my face. The monster *could* be hurt.

Wyran must have been angry. The crackling in my neck started anew and a high-pitched sound built to a roar, overpowering the winds and rain. Another Deluge of memories came, minor compared to the one following Kalvin's death. The memory overlaid itself on my senses. My mind tore in two. One half watched, uncomprehending, as Wyran struck the dazed and defenseless members of my Hand. The other half flooded with despair at a hazy memory of Wyran's—sinking, broken and bloody, into the swallowing sea. I fought to move my legs and charge, but it was as useless as trying to run with a broken spine.

When the monster's Deluge suddenly ceased, I regained control over my body. I broke into a sprint toward the monster, ripping my knife from its holster. Aiming for a spot with few branches, I forced the blade into a crack between bark. I wrenched the knife down. It felt like cutting through wet lard. The vicious gash spurted blood, covering my forearms. My blade contacted a heavy strip of bark. I twisted the knife, used it as a lever, and flung myself away. A lashing club narrowly missed my head. The bark came away with me, and I looked up. Three arrows drove deep into the vertical gouge I left. Blood continued gushing from the wound, as if Wyran were nothing more than a punctured sack of fluids.

Garret maintained distance from the monster, kept moving to find points of weakness into which he could stick arrows. Lorelay darted in and out, striking where she could, but clearly trying to avoid harm herself. Dunnax must have told her to stay away. His armor allowed him to stay close. He swung his crooked halberd in huge arcs, trimming down as many branches as he could to disarm the monster.

Was this having any effect on Wyran? It was losing blood, but did that matter? I fought to survive, but I doubted a monster like this could be beaten.

As I ran around looking for more opportunities to attack Wyran, Sentyx shouted in pain. The Skardwarf's roar was louder than the monster's. Just after, Markos started screaming. I braced for the psychic assault. None came. I circled back to do whatever I could to help, fearing it wouldn't be enough.

Sentyx appeared first. The Skardwarf was reeling backward, growling, and clawing at its rocky head. Markos' screams pitched into tortured wails. He lay on his back, legs disappearing at the knees, crushed beneath Wyran's massive bulk. His harpoon stuck out from the monster, nearly indistinguishable from nearby branches. Around it, punctures in Wyran's flesh released a bleeding torrent. Blood flowed down the beast and soaked Markos red. My stomach turned.

Desperately trying to free himself, Markos dug his palms into the dirt, failed to pull himself out. He wailed again as Wyran shifted forward, taking more of Markos' legs under.

"Help me!" I shouted, running past Sentyx, but the Skardwarf fell to one knee, ignoring me. I grabbed Markos under his arm. "I've got you," I said. Straining, I gave all I could to release him from Wyran's crushing weight. It was no use. It felt like I would sooner tear Markos' arms from their sockets than free him.

Lorelay appeared beside me, and I shifted to the side. Something clubbed me in the back, forced the breath from my lungs. I dropped Markos, gasping for air. I ducked aside as Dunnax split the monster open with an overhead cleave. Garret's arrows found their target, digging into torn-open flesh. Wyran's screams joined those of Markos. A heavy branch swung down, cracking Markos' head, silencing the fisherman's wailing for good.

The crackling in my neck started, and my body seized with fear. This close to the monster, powerless to move. I would soon join Markos in the abyss.

One by one, my senses winked out.

Then, roaring flames appeared in my mind, riding another of Wyran's Deluges.

* * *

I stood outside my home, watched a dark shape emerge from the fire. Almost human, but too massive, malformed.

Father.

He shambled toward me. A tongue of fire licked up his leg and all at once he was ablaze. He didn't even notice. It didn't slow him down...until it consumed him completely. He fell forward and began withering away. I watched Father turn to ash until I no longer could, smoke scorching my lungs, then turned and ran for my waiting sister.

* * *

When the vision ended, pain was the first thing that greeted me. Numbness came next, swelling in my left arm. My shoulder had been shattered. I laid on the ground, out of Wyran's reach. Had I been thrown back this far? Transitioning out of the vision, it was as though my drowning awareness had resurfaced from beneath a Pool of the boy's memories. The waters were still turbulent. My mind was still foggy. I looked around. Lorelay sprawled out nearby, unconscious. Dunnax worried over her, uncaring of the creeping monster behind his back. Where his fingers touched his sister's forehead, a golden light began to glow. Sentyx took heavy breaths, still on his knees, hurt mentally if not physically; flesh like stone didn't protect the mind. Quick footsteps pattered close from behind and rough hands lifted me to sit. My shoulder shot a lance of pain down my side, and I nearly blacked out again.

All the while, Wyran's body churned as it slowly, inexorably, slid toward us.

"Markos..." I started, remembering the poor fisherman; like Kalvin, he was nowhere to be seen, assimilated by the monster.

Garret grunted. "He's—"

"Don't say it," I stopped him.

Markos, Leppit, the Agency...we'd failed them all.

Despairing as I watched death draw near, Wyran's memory surfaced all on its own. My emotions matched what the boy felt as he watched his monstrous father suffer. At least the boy could act, burn down his home. He survived to salvage a kind of life with his sister. Here, there was nothing to do. Blades, bows, bleeding the monster... none of it had worked. A hopeless laugh forced its way out.

Why couldn't the boy have burned with his father?

Wyran was covered in wood. If not for the storm soaking it all, snuffing out any flames...

But the torch's flames had reignited.

My eyes widened as recognition dawned.

Remember what's real.

I cursed. Why hadn't we realized sooner? The unfelt wind and rain. The heaviness of despair. The blinking torchlight.

"This is the Aura," I muttered in disbelief. All of this was being emitted by the Benefactor, a psychic illusion so thoroughly convincing my mind that these things were real.

But they weren't.

It'll make sense when you get to Leppit, Bengard had promised. But it had taken us far too long.

I dug my fingers into the ground, paid attention to what I felt.

Dirt, not mud.

"Garret!" I shouted, turning, and wincing at the pain. "Fire! Light your arrows on fire!"

"But the storm—"

"It isn't real! You burned yourself."

Garret looked blankly at me, then the whites of his eyes showed under his hood. The ranger let off a string of curses. He pulled his fire striker and a vial of some gooey, translucent substance from his coat. His fingers moved faster than I could believe. With Wyran bearing down, they still seemed too slow. I scrambled away, hauling myself backward on one elbow, until another crackling started in the back of my neck. Just before the lightning built up in my mind and exploded to consume me for what surely would have been the last time, Garret's flaming arrow soared over my shoulder and plunged into Wyran's wooden armor.

The crackling abruptly ceased. Another of Wyran's roars resonated in my mind. This time, the sound was a scream of pure fear. The illusory rains poured down and seemed to put out the fires quickly engulfing Wyran, but each time they reappeared the flames had spread farther. Garret shot two more flaming arrows into him for good measure. Within a few breaths' span, Wyran's entire body was consumed, a smoking ruin. His cries became a piteous whine when fire began melting flesh. Where the first arrow struck, a cavity formed as Wyran withered away, stinking of rotten, roasting meat. In the center of the growing cavity, a spot of white showed through the pulsing inferno. The bright, flashing light made it hard to discern. I squinted my eyes to make it out.

A skull?

"Garret, look." I pointed with my good arm and needed say nothing more.

The ranger nocked one more arrow from his quiver, pulled the bowstring back, and loosed. The arrow pierced the flames, on target, as Garret's arrows always were. The instant Wyran's skull shattered, his cries ended in blissful silence. The rains stopped and the conflagration raged unabated with no illusion to hide the truth of the flames. As Wyran's body collapsed under its own weight, the wood that protected his vulnerable flesh became a smoldering tomb.

Relief flooded in, a blossoming euphoria that filled the void left as Wyran's influence drained away. I laid back, watched the black plumes of smoke rise into a sunlit sky, and laughed until I cried. After persevering through the depths of despair, I couldn't control it. Somehow, we'd survived. Except, not all who entered the clearing had.

Only close to death do you truly live, Markos had said.

But sometimes you just die.

Markos, Kalvin...even Breta was a victim in her own way. When that recognition came, it brought on quiet sobs. We failed everyone we came here to help. Those villagers weren't missing. They were dead, absorbed by a monster that had once been a boy. We'd survived, but what good did that do them?

I sat up when I heard Dunnax coming toward me. His helmet was under his arm, golden hair soaked with sweat. He preferred one leg, keeping his weight off the other. I didn't see the hit that gave him that limp, but the Paladin had clearly taken a beating.

"How's your sister?" I asked.

Dunnax's face softened. It was the first I'd seen him smile. "Took a blow to the head that'll leave her with a nasty bruise, but she's okay." He laughed. "I healed her with the Fire. As soon as she came to, she tried to jump right back into the fight. She's tough. Hate to admit it, but she is." Dunnax winced as he knelt beside me.

I nodded at his bad leg. "Why not heal yourself too?"

"I will. You first, though. Left shoulder?"

I'd never been healed by Archefire before. By all accounts, it was not a pleasant experience. Better to suffer through the pain and heal naturally. All the feeling in my arm stopped just below the shoulder, though. Natural healing might not have been enough this time. I nodded to Dunnax, grimacing in anticipation.

Dunnax placed his ungloved hand on my shoulder, closed his eyes, and breathed deeply. A golden-red, fiery glow blossomed, shining through the back of his palm, and began burning into my shoulder. Ten thousand tiny needles pricked my left arm, growing more intense as the Fire worked its way under my skin, mending broken bone and torn sinew. I gritted my teeth against the pain, watching as my shoulder radiated like the Brightdaughter on a cloudy day.

The Fire went out, and Dunnax sighed, shaking his hand to whisk the pain away.

"Hurts you too, doesn't it?" I asked.

"Takes a lot out of you. Don't know how mages do it all day." He grinned mischievously, then looked at Sentyx. "You may have to carry me back to Leppit."

My eyebrows raised. Was that a joke...from Dunnax?

Sentyx tilted his head, as if questioning whether he was serious. Despite fighting as hard as everyone else, Sentyx didn't appear to be particularly tired. The Skardwarf probably *would* have carried Dunnax back if he'd asked in earnest.

The apparently-not-humorless Paladin laughed once, then sat and went to work healing his own leg. Lorelay smiled; Dunnax didn't notice.

* * *

After a brief rest, we walked the short distance back to the village, only to find it was entirely different. A throng of Leppit villagers, mostly women and young children, stood in front of the long hall and listened to Ciria reassure them. She seemed as changed as the village itself—confident and hale, where before she cowered in the dark. Such was the influence of Wyran, which I was glad to see dispelled in so short a time. Eadrick stood beside the village matriarch, holding her husband's bones. When he saw us approaching behind the crowd, he interrupted Ciria and shouted, "There they are! The ones who killed the witch!" All heads turned to look.

Hebvek gently pushed his way forward and looked us over with worried eyes. "Where's Kalvin? Did you find him?"

I shook my head. "I'm sorry. We didn't make it in time."

"Why didn't you stop her from taking him?" Garret asked, with too much bite to his question.

Hebvek flinched back as if stung. "I...I did try." He looked down. "I couldn't do anything. Not after living so long like we did. Hiding inside, creeping around in the rain for food, afraid of hearing her song... She's really dead? You put a knife through her heart?"

"It's over now," Lorelay said.

At this, murmurs spread through the crowd. 'Is it true?' 'The witch is dead?' 'It must be! The storm is gone!'

All of them blamed Breta. These villagers didn't understand the monster that lurked outside Leppit.

Better that they don't.

As they rejoiced at the news of the witch's death, I felt a small rush of pride. We may not have saved the missing, but we'd made a real difference in this village. Death would have come for them all, eventually. Now, they could rebuild.

Ciria announced that her husband's funeral would begin shortly and invited us to attend. Dunnax offered to dig a grave for Akun's bones, but they had a different custom here in Leppit village. We moved with the crowd to stand near the cliffs behind the fishing hall, which offered a grand sight with the storm no longer obscuring the view. A hush fell over the crowd, silent reverence under the whispering wind. Ciria took her place beside Eadrick at the edge of the cliff.

With gulls circling overhead once again, as if nothing had been awry, Ciria spoke in praise of her fallen husband, who came here long ago and brought hope to this desperate village. She told of Akun's bravery and diligence, how he worked to ensure the village prospered. When she spoke of all those who died by Breta's hand, the tears flowed readily among the surrounding villagers. In so close-knit a place, no member of the dead was unknown to any survivor. Ciria concluded the rites and nodded to Eadrick, who tossed Akun's bones over the cliff to fall one final time into the sea far below. Finally, she thanked us, the heroes of Leppit village, and offered to provide food and fire any time we came around.

Thanks, but after this I'm not stepping foot in this village ever again.

When the crowd had dispersed and the sky turned crimson and orange with the Brightdaughter's setting, I stood atop the cliff and looked across the open vista. I imagined I could see the ever-howling winds that made the ocean crossing so dangerous. Far to the south, past the frigid island that bordered the open ocean and wilted beneath wayward winds, another sun peeked over the horizon, looking on in envy at its brighter Sibling to the north. The Shadowson had never shone on Liwokin; the city was too far north to garner the lesser Sibling's gaze. Closer to the south, the Shadowson's wan light tinged the southern sky pale blue, hinting at the dark, unfamiliar world in which those outside the Bright Empire lived.

"Sentyx," I said. The Skardwarf gazed south beside me. "That's your sun? It's so small."

Sentyx grunted. "And cold."

Sensing I'd get no more from him, I stepped tentatively forward, then looked over the edge down to the sea. A memory of Wyran's flashed, as if it were one remembrance surfacing from a Pool that contained it along with many others. The light disappeared, leaving only the waves' white spray visible in the darkness below. My breath caught. Some foreign feeling urged me to jump with harpoon in hand—desperation, or fear?

I'm doing it for her, passed through my mind as if the thought were my own.

I snapped out of it and fell back, away from the hazardous edge.

"Dizzying, isn't it?" Eadrick said. "A shame the lad didn't live through his first dive. He was brave, I'll say that for him. None of this should have happened."

No. It shouldn't have.

"Why didn't you leave when it started?" I asked.

"Leave?" Eadrick looked genuinely puzzled. "This is our home. There's nowhere else to go. That's why Akun had us pool our coin together to summon you. He alone had hope when the rest of us wanted to give up. He fought for Leppit. Died fighting the witch trying to save it."

"Markos..." I sighed. "He died fighting for Leppit too. He didn't ask for coin; he just knew it was the right thing to do." I perked up, suddenly remembering. "Oh, right. Garret. You have their coin, don't you?"

"Was hoping you'd forget about that," Garret said, grinning, then pulled the pouch from his coat. "Here."

Eadrick held up his hands in protest. "N-no. Come on, now. You earned it. Keep it, please."

"If you insist—" Garret started.

Dunnax interrupted. "Take it. The Agency doesn't need payment." He grabbed the gold from Garret and pushed it into Eadrick's hands. "You'll need it to get this village back on its feet."

Eadrick accepted the pouch with tears glistening in his eyes. "We...we can't thank you enough. If there's ever anything you need from us, you say the word and it's yours."

Just as Ciria had changed, the Eadrick we found in the tavern seemed a wholly different person to the man before us now, as if the recognition of his responsibility for the fate of this village settled like a weight on his shoulders. Some people need such a burden to bring out their best selves, to show the world what they're capable of achieving.

Lorelay's stomach let out a long growl. "Actually, there is something..."

* * *

We dined with the villagers after dusk, sharing in an overly generous meal freshly caught by some brave women who didn't wait to start diving once more. In the Coddle Inn, the empty bottles had been cleared away and Eadrick found a fresh stock of ale in the back room. As he told it, he simply hadn't thought to look, assuming that he'd drank the place dry. The tables were cleared of dust and set with plates overflowing with fresh fish and crab.

"Try the helmie," Ciria insisted. "They're a rare catch this time of year."

The fish had been gutted, but it was served with its head on the side. The creature's lifeless eyes stared at me from beneath a crown of spiked bone. After three tankards of ale, looking at it for too long started my stomach churning. I waved it away.

Lorelay stood on a table in the corner of the room, playing the lyre for a small, joyous crowd. She stomped her feet and belted raucous lyrics as her fingers danced across the strings. Even Dunnax didn't seem to mind that this wasn't one of the approved Songs from scripture.

A dozen children surrounded Sentyx and pestered him with endless questions, all of which he responded to with grunts. Perhaps it was a trick of the ale, but I was sure I could distinguish what each grunt meant. I smiled at the youngsters' fascination. They didn't see Sentyx as a monster. To them, he was just another person. A strange one, to be sure.

But then, aren't we all?

"This place is pretty nice," Garret said, picking his teeth with a splinter of wood. "For a Lawi town." He sat with his feet up on the table, leaning back on two chair legs.

I grinned. "Nice enough to sleep indoors tonight?"

"Given the circumstances," the Ekoan said, "indoors might be just what I need."

Dunnax tromped over holding two tankards and planted himself in a chair. Even without a full set of armor, the wood creaked under his weight. He slid one sloshing tankard to me. "So, you ready to tell how you killed that thing?"

I shrugged, put the drink to my lips. After what we'd been through, ale had never tasted so good. "Garret killed it. I just made a helpful suggestion, is all."

"Fire," the ranger said. "Can't believe we didn't think of it earlier." He gestured at Dunnax with his toothpick. "With your Archemagic, there wouldn't have been a fight."

Dunnax grunted, took a long sip from his own tankard. He eyed me. "And how did you figure it out? Never occurred to me to use the Fire in that storm."

He'd seen the same visions I had, hadn't he? I shrugged. "Like Reed and Bengard said, I remembered what was real."

Dunnax sat back, though he didn't seem satisfied with that answer. A loud crash filled the room, then laughing. The table Lorelay had been standing on collapsed. Dunnax rushed across the room even though the crowd had already helped Lorelay to her feet.

Garret chuckled. "He's more predictable than dawn."

Lorelay had continued playing her music. With delight in her eyes, she watched Dunnax as he danced, a jug of ale in one hand and the waist of a Leppit woman in the other. I pointed him out and Garret craned his head, tipping his chair too far back. The ranger caught himself just in time.

I laughed. "Careful, Garret. Don't think you've got us all figured out just yet."

We stayed that night in the nicest rooms on the first floor of the Coddle Inn. Ciria regretted that we couldn't access the finer suites past the broken stairs, but I was just grateful not to be sleeping on cold dirt for a change. It wasn't quite home, but I'd be back soon enough.

In the morning, we set off to Liwokin, traveling by a horse-drawn cart given to us by the villagers.

"You know," Garret said, as the cart pulled out of the village, "Wyran wasn't the monster that attacked two nights ago. He was way too slow."

Just like that, all the residual pride and relief from our victory gave way to the memory of terror. My shoulder ached as I rolled it in its socket. None of us, it seemed, wanted to discuss it any further, lest our whispers should summon the monster by ill chance. We swung the cart to the east to avoid the Shaded Grounds; best not to tempt fate. We'd have to report both monsters to Ulken, but I tried to put them out of mind for the journey back home.

Just as Wyran's had, my old life ended with fire. My old life, where monsters belonged to storybooks, and I could believe what I saw with my own eyes. The one where all the thoughts and memories in my mind could be understood as my own. Now there was something more in my head, the Pool of another left behind by the Deluges carrying Wyran's memories. He was with me now, a part of me. I glimpsed the world through his eyes.

But I couldn't shake the feeling he was watching through mine.

PART TWO

PREY

CHAPTER NINE

A Shadow of Understanding

The stink of Liwokin sat heavy in the air, so powerful it snapped me out of my snooze. I yawned, then sat up to stretch out. Garret, Lorelay, Dunnax, and I all rode in the back of our cart, while Sentyx sat at the reins, guiding the horses through the streets. The wheels rumbled on the cobblestone as we passed through the Financial District, headed for the Agency. I took a deep breath of the wafting, pungent air.

"Ahh," I exhaled loudly. "Nothing like the scent of home."

Garret snorted beside me. "There really is something wrong with you city folk."

"Can't argue with that," I said. "But spend enough time here and you get used to it. Besides, all cities stink, I'm sure."

"Not ours," Garret said.

"Only because you're used to it." Then again, Ekoans lived in cities crafted in treetop canopies; maybe he was right, and they were full of natural, sweet-smelling air. I shrugged and turned to the Paceeqi siblings. "What's it like in the capital?"

"Vos? It's a lot like this," Dunnax said, gesturing at the Empire-styled towers of the Gild. From this perspective, they looked as if they could touch the stars. "Strong. Elegant."

"Arrogant. Indulgent," Lorelay interrupted. "And it smells just as bad."

Dunnax grumbled. "It's the capital of the entire northern hemisphere. It has a right to be...excessive."

"I bet Sentyx sees things differently," Lorelay said, pushing herself up to lean her elbows on the cart-driver's bench. "What are your cities like?"

Sentyx eyed Lorelay blankly. "Our cities?"

"Yeah, you know. What are the buildings like? Does it smell as bad as the cities in the north?"

The rock-like skin on the Skardwarf's face twisted in puzzlement, as if Lorelay had asked if the world was upside-down in the south. Sentyx turned back toward the horses. Lorelay's shoulders dropped, and she moved away from the bench, sitting with an annoyed look on her face. After stewing on Sentyx's rudeness, just as she opened her mouth to say something, Sentyx spoke again. "We have no city. Not enough people."

"Oh..." Lorelay said. "A place like this must be pretty overwhelming for you."

Sentyx expertly guided the horse-drawn cart into a stall just outside the Agency's walls, then shrugged. "Squall-skar Peaks are hard. This place is soft."

Soft?

"Easy, you mean," I guessed.

Sentyx grunted. "Soft." When he hopped down from the bench, he shook the ground, gravel crunching underfoot. He handed the reins to a dull-eyed Heel, who guided our horses to the stables.

Garret laughed as we all jumped off the back of the cart and started for the gate to the Agency courtyard. "Sentyx, we really ought to have a drink. I've got to learn what life is like down there in the Peaks."

Then, the haze that poured through the gate swirled up from the ground and set us all to coughing. All except Sentyx, of course. The Skardwarf seemed impervious to any outside force. Quickly, my nose acclimated to the scent as it turned sickly-sweet. The armed and helmeted Heels at the gate didn't question us as we passed them. Perhaps they knew we were a Hand, the five of us, or maybe they didn't care enough to stop us. This haze left me feeling empty. It scarcely registered that there was a person behind each of those gray-shirts' masks.

Why did Ulken burn this stuff throughout the Agency? He probably liked his underlings meek and pliant, to prevent complaints or unrest. The stuff was like a veil that dulled the emotions. Without feeling the Aura of despair in Leppit, I wouldn't have believed such an effect was possible. That the Head relied on such a thing made me uncomfortable continuing inside, but I had no choice. Past the gate, the courtyard was as I remembered, with one major difference.

"Eighteen," I said, reading aloud the numbered sign. It had gone down by six since our last time at headquarters. "That's... good, right?"

Dunnax shrugged. "Let's just get upstairs. We still don't even know what it's counting."

Entering the main tower of the Agency, I shuddered, even through the effects of the haze. "I think I do, actually."

* * *

The rest of the way up to the top floor passed in a blur of saccharine smoke, empty eyes, and uncaring expressions plastered on Heels' faces. The farther up the tower we climbed, the more desensitized I felt. The stark, solid-oak door at the top of the tower loomed across the terrace, partly ajar and with no light to be seen through the crack. Garret pushed it open without knocking. We hurried in behind him and found the room just as we had before, pitch-black.

"Yezna..." a disembodied voice whispered in the dark. "Show me..."

"Ulken, sir," Dunnax said, saluting.

A shifting sound, then the lantern on Ulken's desk lit to reveal him sneering at Garret. "Never interrupt me again." The candlelight cast a warm glow on his face, but his words were ice-cold. His black and white-fur coat was draped over the back of his chair, and he wore a closely fitted pale shirt. It was buttoned up to his neckline, where the firm collar looked tight enough to choke him. The muscles in his forearms bunched and fought against his rolled-up sleeves as the Head balled his fists.

Garret shrugged. "Door was open."

"Open..." Ulken sighed. "No one ever listens." He lit an incense in the flame of the lantern's candle and haze poured from the burning end. Ulken breathed it in deeply, then exhaled, a puff of smoke riding the gust of breath. "Well. Have you executed my command? What happened in Leppit?"

Lorelay laughed once, shook her head. "Where should we begin? There was rain we could see and hear but couldn't feel. All the remaining villagers were devoid of hope. A witch had taken the missing villagers and lured them to be killed by...a monster. It made that storm last for several measures. Everyone believed it was real. I know...it sounds—"

"Rain you couldn't feel," Ulken said, flatly.

Lorelay met his stare. She nodded.

Even after being there, it still sounds unbelievable. I braced for a reprimanding. The Head had sent us to investigate missing villagers and we'd come back telling tales of impossible creatures. Yet, Reed had known about them. So had Bengard. I felt the conspiratorial note bulging in my inner coat pocket. It must have been crumpled in the fight with Wyran. *My old friend has caught wind of more monsters abroad. Ulken thinks they remain under control.*

The Head of the Agency dug through his desk and pulled out a paper with crisp lines and boxes. He shoved aside a bunch of clutter on his desk and laid the paper down. "Rain you couldn't feel... Huh. That's new. Several measures, you say? Imperial or local?" He found a pen in the mess of his desktop, dipped it in ink, and started writing in the boxes on the paper. "Would it have killed those villagers to date their request?"

If not for the dulling haze, I might not have been able to quell my anger in time to stop from screaming. Even with emotions deadened, I gritted my teeth. "You knew."

The Head paused his scribbling, looked up. "What? Oh, yes, of course."

"And you sent us anyway."

Ulken put down the pen, folded his hands, and his mouth curled into a smile that didn't reach his eyes. "I did. It was a risk. You were promoted to the rank of Finger straight away, but that doesn't mean you could wriggle free of a field test. I believed you would make it back alive. It appears my assessment was correct."

Reed saved our lives. Ulken tried to throw them away.

"A field test?" I was hot iron being hammered into an anvil. "We nearly died fighting that thing! Markos *did* die!" But the fires of my anger faded quickly, snuffed out by the emotion dulling haze.

Meek and pliant, just how he wants us.

At this, his eyebrows raised. "Markos? Who?" He shook his head. "That doesn't matter. You say you engaged the creature?"

"Did more than engage it," Garret said. "We killed it."

The smile crept back onto Ulken's face. "Well. I underestimated you." He picked up his pen and started writing again. "But you see, this is why the risk was worth it. The Agency has no time for weakness. Now you're prepared for what comes next."

"And what's that?" Lorelay asked, sardonically. "Off to slay a dragon?"

Dragons didn't exist. But neither did monsters, until it turned out they did.

"Patience," Ulken said. "First..." He placed the nearly completed form in front of me and handed me the pen. "Complete this report and sign, there at the bottom."

Benefactor Elimination Report (BER-11) emblazoned the top of the sheet in clean, block letters. Ulken's illegible handwriting populated most lines and boxes in the report, leaving only three fields to complete: *Finger signature*, *Victim name*, and *Benefactor designation*. I signed my name in the first, assumed the second was meant for Wyran, but the third...

"Benefactor?" I asked.

"Oh yes, the creature you killed. Just make up some name. It doesn't really matter."

The fire in Ulken's lantern drew my eye, the wax burning low on the candle inside, shying back from the flame that danced on the curling wick. A brief flash of raging infernos swept in from Wyran's pool of memories. First the burning home, Father trapped within, then the burning boy who had struck the first flame. When the candle's waver returned, I knew what to name the monster that boy had become.

Wick.

I filled in the last box and held the report out for Ulken, but he shook his head and looked over my shoulder. A woman in a well-fitting, gold-and-white coat stood with arms behind her back. The Nerve waited patiently for me to overcome my shock at her sudden appearance. Ulken's silent messenger exited the room with haste the moment I put the report in her hand.

"Excellent." Ulken clapped once. "You're second-rank Fingers now, so there are things you need to know."

"Things you couldn't tell us *before* we left?" Lorelay glared at him.

Ulken glared back. "Do you think I want to incite another Riot by letting word slip that these creatures exist? Now, interrupt me again and..." He set his jaw, got his temper under control, then continued. "Benefactors. Eliminating these creatures has been the primary purpose of our Agency since we first discovered them. There's still far too much we don't know about how the creatures work, but I'll tell you what we do. Three things," Ulken held up a finger to count off each piece of knowledge. "One. Every Benefactor was once a person. When they died, they became...well, like the creature you saw."

A memory of Wyran, shrinking down to nothing, before his awareness expanded to consume all others.

"Two. Benefactors emit Auras that force people in the area to feel the single most powerful emotion the victim experienced at the time of their death."

The despair at being unable to take care of his sister, at the life he lost when he dove from those cliffs.

"Three. Every Benefactor has an Empath, some person they shared a bond with in life, who carries out the Benefactor's will."

Breta, the witch, luring helpless Kalvin into the clearing to be consumed by her brother, the monster, Wick.

Ulken sighed. "However, we've documented every encounter. Each one is different. That storm with rain you couldn't feel? Nothing like that is on record for any prior Benefactor.

They change over time, building on each other, gaining new capabilities. Based on our reports, I'm confident those three attributes will remain, but new research is constantly emerging." He shrugged. "But that's the job. Still want it?"

We won't be leaving this tower alive if we say no.

When no one voiced any objections, Ulken said, "Well. I expect you have questions?"

Too many to count. I picked one that seemed the most important. "Is there any way to counter the effects these Benefactors have on our mind? We only killed Wyran...Wick, after we realized the storm wasn't real. Then, Garret set him on fire."

"Yes, there is a way to prevent the Aura from affecting you, to an extent," Ulken said. "But those resources are restricted to Rank Three Fingers."

"You must be joking," Lorelay said.

"I never joke about Agency work," Ulken said. "Our supplies are limited. We must preserve them for high-ranking Fingers fighting the most dangerous creatures. Fire, though. Yes, that is an effective way to eliminate them."

Surprisingly, Sentyx asked, "Do Empaths have control?"

I narrowed my eyes at the Skardwarf. Was that concern in his voice?

Feeling guilty we killed the witch, are you? There was no saving her.

Ulken frowned. "I'm not sure. All I can say is that some demonstrate more control than others. Anything else? Our time runs short."

"One more thing, sir," Dunnax said. "There was...another."

"Oh?"

"Another Benefactor, near Leppit and the Shaded Grounds."

"The Shaded Grounds... Ah, yes. We're aware of that one. An associate of the victim reported it not long ago. You encountered this creature as well?"

"It attacked us the night before we arrived at Leppit," I said. "We wouldn't have gotten away, except..."

"Except for the First Eye's intervention, yes?"

I gaped, nodded. How did he know *that*?

"I suspected as much. He followed you out of the city after you left his home."

How did he know that? Ulken must have had eyes all over the city.

The Head continued, "I didn't give him leave to follow you, and now he has yet to return." He tapped his fingers on his desk. "I've never had cause to suspect Reed's loyalty, but..."

I hid my smile from Ulken. Eyes all over the city, but he didn't know everything.

"Loyal or not," Garret said. "Reed's probably dead now."

"Unlikely," Ulken leveled a blank stare at Garret, then he sighed and buried his head in his hands. "Leave me. Hand Sixty-Four is on recess. Go. Get some rest. You'll be summoned again in a few days' time. And for the love of light, shut the door on your way out."

Ulken snuffed out the lantern and incense as we shuffled out of his office. We shut the door as he asked and left him in the dark.

*　*　*

We headed down to the Fingers' quarters on the fourteenth floor. As we descended, the dulling haze receded, and my anger began to flare. It wasn't enough to feel quite normal, but enough to leave room for indignation. Apparently, Lorelay felt the same. When we found the door labeled '64', she practically broke it down when she stormed inside. The room was plain and cramped, with five small beds with chests for personal storage at their feet, taking up the bulk of the room.

In what little space existed between the beds, Lorelay paced, ranting. "A snuffing *field test*..." she huffed. "What kind of person does that? Doesn't he care about his Fingers at all? Why does he just sit there in the dark all the time? Does he ever leave that office? And who the snuff is Yezna?"

A distant memory flashed of a dear, old friend looking at me from the doorway. His lips moved, but his voice did not reach me. With the flick of my hand, there was pain.

I jerked back. What *was* that? It felt like a memory from a Benefactor's Pool, but whose? Not Wyran's. I glanced around at my Hand. None of the others seemed to notice.

"Yezna...probably some tavern wench he bedded," Lorelay said. She stopped, then stomped her foot. "We have to tell the others. We can't let new Fingers go off to fight those things without knowing."

"Quiet," Dunnax said, claiming a bed for himself. He set his armor-laden pack at the foot of the bed and lay down. "He's probably listening in right now. We're not disobeying his orders."

He was probably right about that. Any mention of Reed or his conspiracy would have to wait until we were out of the tower. But if Ulken was spying on us even out of headquarters, what difference would it have made?

"They're *bad orders*," Lorelay said.

"That's not for us to decide," Dunnax said.

"Besides," Garret added, "if he told us what we were up against, would we really have gone? There are easier ways to make some coin."

"You're not just here for coin, Garret. I know that." I said it with a confidence I didn't feel. Garret could have joined the Agency for any number of reasons. Gold was one reason, but he had a sense of justice too. Or maybe he was just bored. The Ekoan spat on the floor.

I continued. "Look, I don't want another Riot any more than he does, but there must be some way to prepare new Fingers."

Garret shrugged. "That *is* how to prepare new Fingers. Only the tallest tree gets the light. Makes sense to me. We got lucky this time. Wouldn't count on every Benefactor being covered in kindling, ready to burn."

I grimaced. He was right about that. And if the Benefactor we fled from in the night was any indication, even Archefire bombs weren't lethal enough. We'd have to make our own luck from now on if we didn't want to end up like Reed.

"Think I've had enough talk of Benefactors tonight," Garret said. "I'm going for a drink. Anyone else?"

"Without question," Lorelay said. "Come on. I know a place, not far from here. Wistwicker, it's called…" Her voice trailed off as she and Garret left the room.

Dunnax groaned and slid off the bed. "I hate that place." Then he left too.

Sentyx stood across the room from me, staring in his usual stone slate way.

"Looks like it's just us now," I said, and sat on a bed. It was as stiff as the forest floor had been, the night we were attacked. Comfortable, as beds in the city go. "How do you feel about all of this?"

Sentyx tilted his head, then froze for an uncomfortable eternity. I was starting to get the feeling I'd never understand the ways of Skardwarves, that I would get a grunt from Sentyx and nothing more.

Instead, his face shifted into what I interpreted as a smile. "Content."

"Content. Really? After what we saw?"

"Yes. We saved Leppit. It was...good."

I sat forward, widening my eyes. Did he want to talk? My surprise must have shown, because Sentyx grunted, then waited. "I guess you're right. It was good, helping the villagers. But what about Ulken sending us down there knowing what we'd find?"

Sentyx considered. "Weakness chips away. We become strong."

"Not all of us do. Some die."

"Yes. Some are soft. If they die helping." Sentyx looked up as if he were staring straight through the building. At what, I wasn't sure. "It is good."

Harsh words, but maybe he was right. There were worse ways to die than trying to help. Trying to be a hero.

After a long pause, Sentyx sat on the bed opposite me. The wooden frame sagged and cracked, but Sentyx didn't seem to care. "Skardwarves do not have city. We have tyrant. Monster. I left the old country. Faced away from the wind." His upward expression shifted into...shame? Shortly afterward, his customary placid look returned. "But here in city. Different monsters." Sentyx looked back down and met my gaze. "We must face into the wind."

I shifted to lay back on the bed. My body relaxed. I was more tired than I knew. After some thought, I realized Sentyx must have been talking about monstrous people, not real monsters. There weren't any real monsters here in the city, thanks to the Agency.

Not yet anyway.

"So, you have tyrants," I said, thinking aloud, "and they keep your people banded together like our cities do? How?"

Sentyx let out a long, slow breath that rattled in his chest. "Anger," he said. "We have fire inside. Tyrant makes it burn."

I didn't know what a Skardwarf tyrant was like. I imagined they were like Sentyx, only tougher and angrier.

Hard to imagine.

"You crossed the ocean to escape the rule of these tyrants?"

Sentyx grunted.

"Because you want to help people."

"Yes."

The Squall-skar Peaks sounded like a brutal place. A dark sun, everlasting winds, and now a Skardwarf tyrant ruling with a stone fist... But then, the Bright Empire was brutal, too, in its own way. Every day was a struggle for survival.

Sentyx would fit right in.

"You're a good man, Sentyx."

"I am no man."

"You... you're not?" *Darkfather's balls...* "Sorry. Are you...a woman?"

"No." Sentyx explained no further.

I didn't know there *was* anything else. I figured it was as clear-cut as the light and the dark, the north and the south, the Brightdaughter and the Shadowson. But if I didn't understand, that was a problem for me to deal with, not a problem for Sentyx.

"Well, a good...person, then," I stammered. "I'm glad you're in the Hand. You're better off with us here than under some tyrant's thumb." I shook my head, feeling vaguely embarrassed, and desperately wanted to change the subject.

We have fire inside. Tyrant makes it burn.

"Do your people use Archemagic in the Old Country, Sentyx?"

Sentyx grunted again. "Not like here. Different."

"Different how?" I asked, then jolted up, remembering that there was someone else I needed to talk to about exactly the same thing. "I've got to go," I said, standing. "You really shouldn't stay in here. Can't be good breathing this haze all the time." I headed for the door.

"Goodbye, friend Grim."

Friend?

That gave me pause. I smiled. "Farewell, friend. I'll see you when we're summoned for our next command."

* * *

Wandering the labyrinthine halls of the tower, this time in search of Inac, even the deadening haze couldn't stop me from feeling satisfaction that, somehow, I had made a friend in Sentyx. The gulf between our cultures seemed wider than the ocean Sentyx had crossed to come here. Yet, just as I had been ready to accept that I would never understand him, the Skardwarf surprised me yet again. There was still so much I didn't know—a fact that became more apparent with each passing bell—but with the help of friends I might overcome that ignorance.

It was good to have another friend. As it stood, I thought I might never find the last one I'd left in this damnable tower.

Sometime after dusk chimed from the nearby church tower, I came across a door labeled "Personnel Management" and entered, expecting the room to be dark and vacant. Instead, a bronze-cloaked woman sat at a desk in front of half a dozen filing cabinets. Another Organ, one of the Agency's administrators. Her bespectacled eyes scanned each page of a thick file she was reading, and occasionally she licked her thumb to turn to the next.

I stood in front of the desk for a moment, hoping she'd notice my presence. When she didn't, I cleared my throat and blinked when she looked up. She could have been the daughter of the Organ we met down in Logistics.

If she's anything like her mother...

"Oh, hello," she said, cheerily, despite the incense that burned on her desk. "How can I help you?"

Okay, those two definitely aren't related.

I smiled reflexively at her unexpected cheer. "Hi," I said, waving like an idiot. "I'm looking for a new Finger. At least, I think he's a Finger. Inac, uh, his name is, of Sea Pot Lake." I stammered to a stop, pulse racing.

Why was my pulse racing? Was there a Benefactor around?

"Oh yes, I know Inac." The Organ smiled with her eyes closed, her cheeks rosy and full. She closed her file, returned it to its proper place in her cabinets, then found Inac's file in no time at all. It was paper-thin by the looks of it. "I just read him the other day. Early days, I know, but I think he's got a bright future in the Agency." She sat back down at her desk, looked at me over the rims of her glasses. "I've got a sense for these things. Same for you, Grim. Big things."

"Wait, you know my name?"

"Of course." She giggled. "I know every Finger's name. Your lives are more interesting than any book I've read."

"How did you know it was *me*, though? We haven't met before, have we?" No, I would have remembered this girl. She was more youthful and lovely than anyone in this tower should be.

"Every Finger has a sketch on record. See?" She flipped to the back page of Inac's file and showed me a drawing. Tattered robe, curly hair, and the pendant I retrieved hanging around his neck, just like the day we'd joined. The likeness was impeccable.

"That's him all right." I crinkled my brow. "I never posed for a drawing though."

"Oh, our artist is extraordinarily talented, Lightmother bless him. One look at you and he'll remember your face until the end of his days."

"That's...incredible," I said. "And kind of scary."

She giggled again and pushed up her glasses. "Anyway. You wanted Inac to join you?"

"Yes, if he's available." I needed to meet with him soon, but for all I knew, Inac could be off with his Hand right now, fighting for his life against some deadly Benefactor. He never should have agreed to my harebrained plan.

The Organ made a few marks in Inac's file, then retrieved three others clustered together in the cabinets. One bore the number sixty-four on its spine. She opened each of those in turn and marked them up as well. "All right, it's done," she said, distractedly, not looking up from the last one she opened. "It'll take a few days for the request to be approved, but... You killed a Benefactor already? That's even faster than Jacquin did it! I told you. Big things ahead!"

"Is that...my file? Can I see?"

The Organ snapped it shut. "No one gets to see their own file." Her eyes darted left, then right, and a mischievous grin crept onto her face. She flipped open the back page and showed me my own sketch.

"Is *that* what I look like now? I need a haircut." I pushed the oily black hair away from my eyes, feeling suddenly self-conscious. My hands hissed across the stubble on my chin and cheeks.

A shave too. And when was the last time these clothes were washed?

The Organ yanked the file away and hugged it close to her chest. "Shh, don't tell," she whispered.

I held a finger to my lips and nodded. "Our secret," I said. "And thank you...uh. I never did get your name."

"Allianne," the Organ said, prodding the nameplate right in front of me that I'd somehow missed. "But you can call me Alli."

"Thank you, Alli. For your help."

"Anything I can do," she said. "Come visit again. And be careful out there. Remember, I'm rooting for you and Hand Sixty-Four!"

I waved goodbye to Allianne and left the tower with a stupid grin that wouldn't leave my face. Not until I entered the court-yard, anyway, and saw the numbered sign. '17', it read, now that one fewer Benefactor remained in the world, slain by my Hand. Suspicions confirmed, I left the courtyard and ventured into the city with the sky dark overhead. It was time to rest, until Ulken's summons came.

That'll be soon. Unlike us, monsters don't rest.

CHAPTER TEN

Unsavory Exchange

The church rang dawn, and I wiped the sweat from my brow. The Brightdaughter might rise in the northeast one day, southeast the other, but upon its appearance the Church's mathemelodians quickly determined her course through the sky and set the day's beats in the Rhythm of Time. At dawn's light ringing, the first beat, the city awakened. The duration of time's melody was different each day, but the notes were always the same. It was the pulse of Liwokin's heart; the streets were her veins, the Liwo her blood. The same routine, day in and day out. The life of a Liwokin Docks worker never changed.

That suited me just fine. One crate, then another. A third, a fourth, a thousand. Barrels rolled down gangplanks, sloshing their contents around with every bump along the way. Sacks of grain and rice thrown over the sides of ships landed with weighty thumps atop growing piles, until someone came to move them into longer term food stores. The occasional yelp or grunt sounded as someone threw out their back trying to lift something beyond their capacity. The scent of salt melded with the city's smell wafting out over the harbor—a nauseating stench, but one I quickly got used to. Drinks after dusk, a game of cards or dice, a good night's rest in a dockside inn, then back to business at dawn. I moved with the flow of a thousand others—we were a swarm of insects, tirelessly crawling into each ship and relieving it of cargo.

Get some rest, Ulken had said. I snorted, nearly dropping a sack of grain into the bay. *Rest.*

My mind was restless with thoughts of Benefactors and Auras and the memories dredged from Wyran's Pool. Living memories that belonged to a dead boy. After the first sleepless night, I had to do something to keep my mind busy with thoughts more tolerably mundane. Taking on another bounty was out of the question; bounty hunting was a waiting game. It gave me too much time to think.

So, I found myself at the Docks—the real Docks this time, not that deathtrap hanging from the Blight cliff, thank the Lightmother—after negotiating with the dockmaster for a day's worth of wages. Fifteen stars wasn't much, but it was honest, and it felt good working up a sweat in the cool, harbor air.

Could be shoveling dung for all I care, as long as no monsters are involved.

But surviving a brush with death by a Benefactor was simply too consequential. I couldn't keep them out of my mind completely. As I hauled crates across the busy Docks, Ulken's dreadful knowledge surfaced to awareness, again and again, distracting me from my distraction. Seventeen Benefactors existed somewhere outside the city, each one a person who had fallen victim... to what? Was there an original source, some Benefactor that turned its victims into offspring? When Wick killed Kalvin and Markos, no new Benefactors appeared, so that didn't seem a likely mode of reproduction. No, the victims were...absorbed, somehow. A memory bubbled up from Wyran's Pool. The monster he'd become hungered for something not quite food. I shuddered at the idea of Markos becoming such a morsel.

I stood at the top of a gangplank, watching the workers bake under the Brightdaughter's hot glare. Everyone persisted in their daily routines, as if the world wasn't changing all around them. Steam-powered merchant vessels built from Archemetal flew Paceeqi flags in red-and-gold, the royal colors and those of the Church of Light. This new technology looked too heavy to float, lumbering low in the water beside ships crafted of the traditional lightwood; the new models outnumbered the old. Those working the Docks were a diverse mix of people from across the Empire. Just now, a crimson-coated Agency worker with a long, pointed mask made their way off a docked vessel, flanked by three Heels carrying glassware. A pair of Peekers fled together from some screaming Ayeiri man they jostled. Neither of those groups would have made sense in any context prior to the Agency's founding or the Empire's annexation of Lawiko. The shift in demographics was a change so gradual it escaped notice. That was good. It gave everyone time to adapt. When change happened fast enough to notice, hard times were surely ahead.

The sudden appearance of Benefactors carved a perpetual pit in my stomach. It joined the one that formed in the aftermath of the Riot. Only when some explosive event kicked me out of my stupor did I realize how quickly the world was falling apart.

Right as I dropped off a heavy crate in a dockside warehouse, back aching and muscles sore, dusk's somber chime signaled the slipping of the Brightdaughter past the horizon. I rubbed my tired arms and started for the dock master's office when I noticed a familiar man in a long, black coat trimmed with Archemetal casually strolling near the edge of the water. Oltrov, First Eye Reed's associate, and representative of the Gild. Immediately, suspicion washed over me. Heading to the Blight, this late in the day? I felt an urge to follow the man.

Oltrov looked to be in no hurry, unlike when he barged into Reed's home. Unfortunately for him, that made him an easy target—three footpads tailed the Gildmember. Unfortunately for me, I knew the three men.

Zeb and Fend plodded along behind the leader of their ragtag gang of robbers, a drunkard named Tipsy Tom. Tom had picked up a drinking habit early on that left him with fewer wits than friends—both friends were with him right now.

And none of his wits.

That those two still considered Tom their leader, all these years later, said everything necessary about their own lack of wits. I'd run scams with these scoundrels before turning to bounty hunting but didn't stick with these three for long precisely because Tipsy Tom would always insist on pulling reckless stunts like this. Robbing a Gild representative out in the middle of the Docks?

Even with the world falling apart, some things never change.

Oltrov was a contractor for the Agency, as Reed had put it. As a Finger, it was my duty to thwart the old gang from waylaying him. Even though the both of them had lied to my face.

Keeping the crowd of dockworkers between myself and Tom's gang, I positioned myself to intercept them without being spotted by Oltrov. A throng of workers were chatting openly about visiting a Lumeeqi fence to sell the goods they'd stolen today; I blended in with them. My intention was only to slow down the gang. I'd buy time for Oltrov to be lost in the mix, whereupon I could melt away unnoticed, quickly get paid, then catch up to stealthily follow the Gildmember into the Blight. Failing that, I could at least find a tavern, have my fill of meat and ale, then pass out in a warm, if uncomfortable, bed, too drunk to allow room for Benefactor thoughts to intrude.

But I misjudged Tom's footing. I nudged my shoulder into the gang leader after Oltrov passed and Tipsy Tom stumbled drunkenly to the side, hollering and flailing, then slipping on the wet, wooden walkway. He landed in the bay with a splash and a gurgle and didn't immediately resurface.

That could have gone better.

"Grimley? That you?" Fend's nasally voice came. I flinched. The crowd's eyes were on me now, following Fend's gaze. Needless embarrassment came with a flash of Wyran's memory, the fat instructor chiding him in the classroom.

"Get out of here," I said, glaring at Fend, not the least for using my old name.

"But Tom," Zeb protested when Fend grabbed his arm to leave. "He can't swim."

"That's his fault. I told him the Docks was a bad idea..." Fend said, dragging Zeb away.

I put my hands in my pockets to leave without a fuss, but another voice called out, smooth and polished. "You, there. Come here."

I froze, debating for just a moment whether I should run off into the city. Seeing Tom's gang was bringing my old, unlawful instincts out in full. Following Oltrov unnoticed was out of the question now, but fleeing would make it seem like I'd tried to kill Tom on purpose. Well, maybe this wouldn't be a total loss. I *had* been trying to help Oltrov, after all. I could still try to get some insight into what he was up to with Reed.

"Good to see you again," I said. "Oltrov, was it?"

"Indeed," the Gildmember said, twisting the golden Archemetal ring on his pinky finger. "I thought I recognized you. What was that all about? Old friends of yours?" Oltrov gestured to where three men hauled Tipsy Tom out of the water. The drunkard gasped for air when he breached the surface, flailing some more, and fell back in, dragging one of the men down with him, cursing. "Walk with me for a moment," Oltrov said, and began strolling once more toward the Blight. He held himself with self-assurance unsuitable for a man walking into a deathtrap. Torchlight glinted in the Archemetal swirls that decorated his expensive coat.

Won't be his for much longer, I suspect.

He glanced over his shoulder. "Coming?"

I matched his pace, if not his poise. If I wanted information, I'd have to get it quickly. "Old friends from the Old District. But I keep better company now. The Agency would urge us to avoid the lesser men of the Blight, wouldn't you say?"

Oltrov raised one eyebrow, looked at me sidelong. "I would. There are, of course, circumstances in which one must deal with the...lesser men of the Blight."

"What circumstances might those be?"

Oltrov tapped a finger to his lips, then grinned at me. "Come with me and see. You may find it enlightening."

I narrowed my eyes. Oltrov gave me plenty of cause to be suspicious, but why would he bring me along unless he truly had nothing to hide? Gildmembers weren't often the trusting type. "All right, then. I just need to collect my pay from—"

Oltrov laughed. "One day working the Docks. What's that, twenty stars? Consider this an Agency job. Escort contracts are common enough, and you'll earn thrice that, at least."

"My weapons—"

"Will be safe where they are. You won't need them."

In the Blight, after dusk? I stared at the reckless fool in disbelief. "I'd rather have—"

"Hurry along, now," Oltrov said without stopping. "We have an appointment to keep."

* * *

Entering the Blight unarmed with a rich man flaunting his wealth was worse than unwise. It was reckless. All my instincts shouted in protest as we crossed the boundary from the Artisans District, where homes turned to shanties, cobble gave way to dirt, and the streets became narrower than the rest of the city's alleys. Oltrov whistled tunelessly as we ascended the Blight hill, calling attention to himself as if he wanted to be murdered out of spite. Stars twinkled overhead, meaning the Brightdaughter was low, hidden far beyond the horizon. The dark was upon us tonight.

"Are you sure about this?" I whispered, as Oltrov stopped in front of a burned-out husk of a home. The destroyed building was a casualty claimed by the Great Riot, but I could only picture the blaze of Wyran's home. The painful memory flashed into my head. When I smelled the char, like a rot-tinged campfire, I wondered if that was another detail from the dead boy's Pool or my mind filling in the blanks with what it expected. In Leppit, Wick's Aura hadn't carried a scent. The rain could only be seen and heard. Ulken said the Benefactors were changing, but could they add new senses to my memories even without a Deluge? There was clearly much that Ulken didn't understand; the Head never mentioned anything about Pools and dredged up visions either, yet...

Oltrov slapped me between the shoulders. "Relax," he said, "I've done this a hundred times. Ulken's people worked out everything in advance."

"Oh, Ulken arranged this. That's comforting."

Wonder what kind of unspeakable monster I'll be facing this time.

Oltrov winked and went through the door, even though the wall was so crumpled he could have stepped right over it. We continued through the building to an alley out back, where three people were waiting. The alley was more spacious than most of the Blight's cramped streets, but there were five of us back here. Outnumbered and with little room to maneuver if Ulken's people weren't as amenable as Oltrov promised. My instincts howled; it took everything I had not to flee, but the Gildmember remained calm.

Which didn't mean much. The man had been courting death all night.

"You should have come alone," came a gruff voice from a figure standing with arms crossed, tapping his foot impatiently. Two others were with him. A heavyset figure, his back leaned against a shanty's slanted wall, while the other sat atop a barrel, dangling his feet in the air. The three men were merely deeper shadows in the dark, silhouettes with no detail save the whites of their eyes. Even with so little to go on, I knew these kinds of men. I'd sent plenty to the gallows.

Those that didn't get a crossbow quarrel through the heart.

"Oh, let's save the theatrics, Kilan." Oltrov waved a dismissive hand. "Hasn't the Agency's goodwill earned me a bit of trust by now?"

The heavier silhouette stopped leaning on the wall and the entire building straightened without his weight. He took a step toward Oltrov, but the figure in the center raised a hand to stop him and chuckled. In his raised hand, there was the telltale outline of a flintlock pistol. "It was for your own benefit," Kilan said, "but suit yourself. You have our stars?"

Oltrov pulled a coin purse from his coat. "Three hundred, as promised. And the Tears?"

My gut sank. We'd been transporting this much gold through the Blight, unprotected? I clenched my fists. Liwo children were starving, and the Agency was putting that kind of money into the hands of these thugs?

"You know," Kilan said, "those Druids that don't like selling to the Agency..."

"What about them?" said Oltrov. "They're still a minority, I presume?"

"They are." Kilan shrugged "A growing minority. Way I hear it, they're making to put an end to the practice. Would be easier to sway those on the fence if we had more coin to work with..."

Of course they weren't satisfied. Men like this wouldn't stop fleecing the Agency until our coffers were empty. This was when these deals typically turned violent; Oltrov would refuse, and the thugs would get angry. I started edging toward the exit, eyes on that flintlock.

Oltrov sighed. "How much are you suggesting we invest?"

"Four hundred for the next batch," Kilan said, pausing to look to his accomplices. "And one-fifty for the legwork." The heavyset man uttered a gurgling laugh. That one had been hit on the head one too many times.

"Oh, is that all?" Oltrov said. "You'll have it. Next time. Make sure the Druids stay happy until then."

I stopped myself from gaping at the ease with which the Gildmember threw around sums that I wouldn't have earned over an entire Imperial year.

Kilan nodded once. The sitting man hopped off the barrel and pried open its lid, fishing inside to retrieve a box that clinked with every sudden movement. He held it aloft next to his boss until Oltrov tossed the coin purse to land with a metallic thud at Kilan's feet, and only then delicately carried the box over to us.

"Well, gentlemen," Oltrov tipped his head forward and took the box. "I bid you—"

"One more thing," Kilan said. "Something from the First Eye." He pulled a folded note from his sleeve. "Mentions something about Ghostwriting."

Oltrov froze mid-step, breath held, his eyes sliding to me.

"Don't believe him," I said to Oltrov. This was probably another ploy to extract even more stars from the Agency. "Reed was killed five days ago. I was there."

Kilan held the note out. "Yet just two days ago he handed me this. He's in rough shape, I'll give you, but very much alive. And he's expecting a response." Kilan chuckled again. "I told you, Oltrov. You should have come alone."

Finally exhaling, Oltrov shoved the box into my hands; a distinctive shattering sounded within. He took Reed's note and said, "I told you to stop reading my messages." Then he produced the same silver rod with the iridescent, obsidian stone that I saw him holding in the First Eye's home.

When Oltrov brought the stone close to the note, words appeared on the paper, manifesting from nothing. Just like Leppit's illusions, the false light was overlaid on my true senses. The inky blue with which the text glowed was faint, but in the alley lit only by stars, it washed all five of us in a turquoise glow. Oltrov held the note so Kilan couldn't see what it said, but I got a clear view of Reed's writing.

'Injured by Benefactor. Recovering with the Druids. What news of Prost and Ulken?'

Oltrov sighed, then muttered to himself, "Your timing is terrible, my friend..." He shook his head and put away the silver tube, blue light winking out, steeping the alley in darkness once more. Then Oltrov snapped his fingers and the note burned up in his hand, turning to ash in a breath's span. I gasped. In the instant Oltrov's Fire illuminated the alley, Kilan's and his thugs' eyes went wide with surprise. They didn't know he was an Archemage either. "I need you to relay a message," Oltrov said.

"Don't have your ghost ink with you?" Kilan chuckled nervously. "It'll cost you."

"Damnation, Kilan! I don't have time for your petty ambitions!"

Kilan wilted beneath Oltrov's rage. "Fine, fine. What should I tell him?"

"Tell him..." Oltrov considered for a moment. "Ulken found his target. Cross the canyon and follow the forest road." Oltrov grabbed Kilan by the shoulder. "Repeat it to me." Kilan did, no chuckling this time. "Good. Now take two horses and make haste back to the Pinegrave. Reed will know what to do." Oltrov stormed out of the back alley.

Kilan chuckled one last time, mirthlessly. "Looks like you're in on it now."

Is it too late to get back out? I left without a word through the burnt dwelling, trying not to break anymore of whatever was in the box. Stepping through the outer door, a flintlock pistol fired inside and a moment later, a shout was cut short with the sound of steel punching through flesh. Two bodies hit the ground. *I'll take that as a yes.*

Oltrov was stomping his way down the hill, the Archemetal in his coat shimmering, reflecting what little light found its way into these streets. Was he really going to leave me here with three hundred stars worth of...whatever this was?

I undid the box's clasp and opened the lid to find out. The box was partitioned into two halves with a soft, velvety divider to match the trim around the sides. To one side, there were countless tiny glass beads shaped like teardrops. To the other side, just as many glass sticks that looked like translucent pine needles were packed in bound bundles. I reached in to pick up one of the several needles that had broken in two. It was so small and delicate that it seemed to weigh nothing, yet together the box was a considerable weight. When Oltrov yelled out to me, I flinched, dropped the needle back into the box, and snapped the lid shut. The conspirator waited for me, taking slow, deep breaths, standing in front of a pitch-black alleyway.

"Listen." Oltrov gave a false smile, then guided me into the alley so dark I couldn't see him standing in front of me. When he spoke, I smelled his minted breath. "You understand what that was, right?"

He was the only one who knew I came here, and no one would question another dead body in the Blight. My survival instincts kicked in. "Sure. I was a bounty hunter. Seen plenty of toxics deals, though usually my arrival is the end of the affair."

Oltrov sighed, blowing a warm, scented gust in my face. The whites of his teeth appeared in a grin as he took a step back. "Right. A toxics deal. That's how I've always thought of these exchanges as well." Oltrov tutted. "But Ulken can't get these materials directly. Druid's Tears are banned by Council law. He needs a middleman."

"Doesn't that put you at risk?"

"All investments are risks," the Gildmember said. "Whether they reap ruin or riches, they make life interesting."

You would have loved Markos.

"Okay, so why does he need these Druid's Tears at all?" I asked.

Oltrov lowered his voice. "You fought a Benefactor, yes? Then you know what their Auras do. These nullify the effect, or so I'm told."

So, these were the restricted resources the Head had mentioned.

"Ulken said these were in short supply, but this box is full of them. He wouldn't give them to us because we're not a high enough rank."

"Ah, yes. He claims to protect us all yet sends his Fingers into danger without the supplies they need. The Agency's Head is a strange man, is he not?"

An image of Ulken sitting alone in a dark room popped into my head. "I suppose he is."

"Reed told me you joined the Agency with noble intentions," Oltrov said, placing a hand on my shoulder. "Don't assume Ulken shares them."

"Don't worry about me," I said. "Ulken hasn't yet earned my trust."

And neither have you.

That seemed enough for Oltrov; the two of us exited the tight alley and continued down the hill. We parted ways in the Artisans District, where Oltrov took the box of Druid's Tears from me and headed back to the Agency, leaving me with nothing but time to think.

Clearly, I wasn't meant to hear the conspirator's message to Reed.

Ulken found his target.

But who was it? Oltrov mentioned Prost, and I remembered him blurting out that name in Reed's home when he'd come barging in, not expecting us. I'd considered that he was a third member of Reed's conspiracy, but was I wrong about that? Perhaps he was the target Ulken had been searching for? No, it seemed more like the two were working together. Perhaps Prost was the advisor Reed's note mentioned. But what was he advising Ulken about?

I grunted in frustration. Just the mention of that man's name *nagged* with familiarity in my mind, as though I could almost picture his face. Something was missing. What role did he play in this mess? Whose side was he on? Were there even sides, or just one man against the rest...

With a sigh, I decided I'd just have to keep my eyes open at the Agency whenever Ulken summoned my Hand for our next command. I was too tired to sort things out now, so I started for the inn I'd been sleeping at these past few days, then froze. My purse was empty of coin.

So much for a warm bed and a belly full of ale...

Not for the first time, I settled into a dark nook in the Artisans District to sleep, cold and hungry on the street. Several courtesans strolled past, peddling their own form of artisanry common in this district after dusk. Perhaps because I'd come out of the Blight, they paid me no mind. Or maybe they knew a broke fool when they saw one.

But not everyone did.

"You got my coin?" a man asked. "For that favor I did you."

I shielded my eyes against the torchlight that obscured the man's face. "Bello?"

"A true friend, right?" Bello asked. "That's what you said."

"I'm sorry," I said. "I wasn't paid for—"

"Should have known." The elevator operator squeezed his hands, his corded muscles bulging on his arms. "Keep treading on the people of the Old Hill." The Blightdweller scoffed, then spat on the ground beside me. "See what happens."

I gave a humorless laugh as Bello walked away, wrapping myself in my cloak and curling up on the ground.

Noble intentions. Right. And just look where they've gotten me.

* * *

The toe of a boot connected with my stomach, just hard enough to wake me with a gasp. Rubbing the sleep from my eyes, I squinted up at a laughing giant sporting a buttoned, gray-green coat that fell around his calves. The Brightdaughter still hid below the horizon, but judging by the pink smears in the sky, dawn's bell would soon ring.

"Time for work!" the giant said, then extended a hand to help me up.

I took it and felt my spine crack as he hauled me to my feet. "Bengard?"

"This is no way for a Finger to live," Bengard said. "We have quarters in the tower you know."

"I know. Don't like that haze though." I yawned and stretched my stiff neck. "How'd you find me here?"

Bengard shrugged. "A Nerve told me where you were. I guess Ulken has ways of tracking us."

He watches us while we sleep. Great.

Bengard grinned and jabbed me with an elbow, then started for the Agency, waving me along. As we walked, he said, "I heard you killed one, by the way. I knew you'd be a good fit. I have a good eye for new Fingers!" Bengard was a boastful sort, but if he truly had been fighting Benefactors since the Agency's early days, he'd earned the right to brag.

"Wish I was as sure as you about that," I said. Seventeen more Benefactors, and just one was nearly enough to kill us.

"Well, you could always quit. Go back to your old life. Agency could use some good competition."

Swallowed Ulken's lies, have you?

"Good to know. Maybe I'll fight some monsters on the side. Everyone needs a good pastime."

"Sure, just don't start spreading the word. Ulken will know and have you killed." Bengard laughed, as if it were a joke.

And you'd be the one sent to kill me, as you were with the thief.

I grimaced. "Does he really send every new Finger on a... field test?"

Bengard nodded. "It's the only way to be sure you're strong enough." Ulken's words came out in Bengard's voice. The Finger went oddly quiet. I sensed he wanted to say more, so I waited.

We stopped at the Docks to pick up my stored weapons, then entered the Market as the dawn bell rang the arrival of light. As always, the peddlers had gotten an early start hawking their wares. We ignored them and hurried through the district. When we rounded a corner and found the Agency headquarters towering at the end of the street, Bengard finally continued.

"You're lucky, Grim. Your whole Hand survived. Me... I was the only one who came back from my field test. It won't get any easier, you know. You need to be strong to keep your Hand alive. When it comes down to it, survival is the only thing that matters."

I pursed my lips. He was right. And it wasn't just our survival that mattered.

It was *everyone's.*

Either the Agency would defeat the Benefactors for good, or they would destroy civilization as we knew it. The reality of two hundred thousand Liwo, minds controlled by monsters, terrified me. But even that was too small a scale. A monster that powerful would be impossible to defeat, consuming everything throughout the Empire in its endless hunger. The Riot would be a minor tragedy in comparison. Even if Ulken really *would* let me go, how could I quit the Agency knowing of this potential fate? Quitting wouldn't keep me safe. It would only make me a coward, helplessly waiting to die while better men and women sacrificed themselves at my expense. I laughed, drawing a strange look from Bengard.

If I'd had a choice, it would have been an easy one.

Life had always been about survival. In that light, the Benefactors were nothing new at all. The world may have been fallen apart, but one thing hadn't changed: there were already untold ways to die.

What difference did one more make?

CHAPTER ELEVEN

Simpler Times

The Agency courtyard was quieter than usual, as if the Heels had yet to awaken and begin their bustling busyness. Two masked individuals in scarlet-red coats emerged from the main entrance carrying a cauldron full of some steaming fluid between them. A third scurried out behind the two mysterious figures, ran ahead, and opened a side door that contained wavering torchlight in a dark offshoot of the tower. All three of them disappeared down a flight of stairs before the door slammed shut behind them. One Nerve in white and gold left the courtyard with some speed—no doubt executing some vital command from Ulken—and set wisps of haze swirling in her wake. Despite the relative calm of the early morning, the burners poured their endless smoke, carpeting the ground in gray. The haze hadn't even set me to coughing as I breathed it in when arriving with Bengard. I was getting used to it.

That can't be good.

So too, it seemed, were Garret and Sentyx, who were engaged in a very one-sided conversation near the sign displaying how many Benefactors remained in the world. Fifteen, it now read. Two more had been killed during our brief recess. Maybe that hopeful fact occupied the topic of discussion between the two members of my Hand.

"...don't know how they discovered which tree I was in, but an arrow in the ass woke me faster than—" Garret broke off, following Sentyx's gaze, which had locked on to me and Bengard as we approached the duo. "Grim! Surprised to see you back. How's your sanity holding up? And you... Bendar was it? You'll make a fine replacement for Dunnax."

"It's Bengard..."

"Wait, Dunnax quit?" He'd been the hardiest of us all.

Well, except for Sentyx maybe...

"Oh no," Garret said, "he's inside right now. Wasn't too happy when he found out Lorelay was reassigned, though. Was just telling Sentyx my money's on him doing something stupid and getting the boot."

"Lorelay was reassigned?" My shoulders slumped. I had gotten used to the company of the Hand, even grown to miss them a bit during recess. I didn't want any of them to leave, especially not Lorelay. This would be a dour group without her to lighten the mood. Dunnax wasn't prone to good moods in the first place. With his sister gone...

"Five in a Hand," Bengard echoed the words spoken by the Eye called Looker on our first day. "Don't worry, you won't be sent out without a full force."

Ulken would *send us out alone then say the rules changed since our last command.*

"You replacing her?" I asked the Finger.

Bengard shrugged. "Not that I've heard."

"Ask him," Sentyx said, looking at Dunnax, who stormed out of the tower with a dark look about him. Wearing his tarnished, silver plate and hefting his crooked halberd, the former Paladin was a fearsome sight to behold.

"Might want to think twice about doing that..." Garret said.

"Did you get her back?" I asked, hopeful.

Dunnax answered by snarling, slamming the butt of his halberd on the ground. "She's already been given a new command. 'By special request,' they said."

"Who requested her?"

Dunnax let out a contemptuous laugh. "They wouldn't say." He threw up his hands, shaking his head. Bengard leaned back to escape the careless arc of Dunnax's blade. "My own sister and I'm not allowed to know? Ridiculous!" He looked Bengard up and down. "Are you here to tell us where to go next? Fifteen monsters left. Point me at the closest one."

Bengard showed his palms, a gesture of warmth, but his eyes were cold and stern. "Even veteran Fingers don't come back more often than not. Don't be so eager to lose your head."

Garret snorted. "This guy's got brains to go with his brawn. What's your excuse, Paladin?" Garret elbowed Dunnax's armored side, then winced and rubbed his elbow where it struck hard plate.

I tensed, ready for Dunnax to lash out. Instead, he just sighed and laughed at the ranger. Even Sentyx grunted what I thought might be a laugh. Maybe it wouldn't be so bad without Lorelay after all.

My eyes lit up as two more people exited from the tower. Both wore robes and pendants that marked them as Archemages. Inac had repaired his pendant with a new chain, one that didn't match the Archemetal encasing the iridescent obsidian. The other mage was the lad Bengard introduced on our first day, Muy Fuy. His pendant was inset with colorful, glowing gems. The mageling's robes weren't so crisp and new anymore, but they had a long way to go before matching the tattered state of Inac's. The Stinbine Islander ran a hand through his sandy mop of hair, looking aggravated with the younger mage, then caught sight of our group and approached.

"Please," Muy Fuy plead, "there must be something you can teach me about the Fire. Were you an Archesmith, or an Archemaker? *Something*, before this?"

"I am Arche nothing. Only Inac."

"An Arche *master* is what you are," Muy Fuy said. "I've seen the control you have. It's like no other. I bet you don't even feel pain—"

"Of course I feel pain," Inac said. "You are to me a pain *right now*."

"Please..." the boy had descended to begging.

"Please, you say? You will not tell to me why you are so desperate!" Inac looked at me, shaking his head in disbelief. I chuckled.

"It's just, well, Ulken said..." Muy Fuy stammered, looking for the right words. "I can't tell you. You're not a Rank Two Finger."

So that's what this was about. The boy had killed a Benefactor.

Apparently, the surprise showed on all our faces, because both mages turned their attention on our group. Both their eyes squinted as if we had told some joke at their expense, and I laughed; the two were so remarkably similar.

"Well, Muy Fuy," Bengard said. The young mage winced when Bengard slapped him on the back with a meaty thud. "I may not be an Archemage, but I can give you a few tips." Bengard steered Muy Fuy away from Inac and our Hand, taking him back into the tower.

"What are you not telling to me?" Inac said.

"Best get used to secrets in this place," Garret said, shrugging.

Inac glanced to each side, then kept his voice low. "Secrets here are to me no surprise."

"Please enlighten us," Dunnax said flatly.

"Not here," Inac said. "There will be for us plenty of time to talk when we are in the field."

In the field? "Inac, you were reassigned to our Hand?" I asked.

The Archemage grinned wide. "Why else would I be here?"

"The Organ," I said, "in Personnel Management. Alli. I asked her..."

You want Inac to join you? she had asked. I was too flustered to realize what she was asking. *Oh, Dunnax is going to hate me.*

"Well, uh, I asked her if you could join me." Dunnax started to react, but I rushed the rest out before he could shout his accusations. "I only meant for a meeting! I wanted to ask Inac about different kinds of magic. So he could help with...well..."

Dunnax fumed, staring right through me. I braced for the coming insults. "Why did they reassign *Lorelay*?" He gestured at Garret and Sentyx. "Why not one of *you*?"

"Oh thanks," Garret said.

"Special request," Sentyx said.

"I know that," Dunnax huffed. "But who would request her? I told her we'd stick together..."

Ah, so that's it.

"She'll be all right on her own," I reassured him. "She's tough. You said it yourself."

"No one is all right with those things out there," Dunnax said.

"What things?" Inac asked, and three of us began stammering. Sentyx simply stared at Inac.

We were saved from coming up with an excuse by the sudden appearance of a man wearing a white coat edged with gold.

Ulken's Nerve held out a folded paper. "Hand Sixty-Four. Your command."

Dunnax took the paper and the Nerve started off.

Before he got too far, I asked, "Has an Eye been sent this time?"

The Nerve stopped, turned his head, and spoke over his shoulder with his back to us. "There is no Benefactor threatening the area."

So many emotions flooded my body at hearing that. Surprise. Relief. Joy. But primarily, confusion.

Wasn't that meant to be kept from Inac?

As if he'd heard my thoughts, Inac asked, "What is a Benefactor?"

"Ask your Hand Captain," the Nerve said.

"Why does he get to know?" Garret asked. "He hasn't passed his field test." On the words 'field test,' Garret's voice dropped into a mocking impression of Ulken.

"Your Hand is Rank Two."

"Inac too?" I asked.

"Is he not in your Hand?" The Nerve strode off with the usual haste of their profession, as if helping us were an undignified use of his time.

"I don't understand this place," I said.

"The Order was nothing like this," Dunnax added.

"Who is the Hand Captain?" Inac asked.

Garret spat. "Chances are, it was Lorelay."

Sentyx gave a gravelly laugh.

* * *

Ulken's command, passed down by the Nerve, was even lighter on details than our mission to Leppit. All it said was, *Guard duty. Canako Outpost. Take a cart north.* So that was just what we did. Though none of us had been to the outpost, Ulken was generous enough to provide a map. The Heel working outside the courtyard seemed to have been expecting us. Two horses were both brushed and harnessed, attached to the cart, which waited in the street. The driver's bench even had a nice little cushion—more generosity from Ulken, though the back of the cart had no such luxury. Firm lightwood, imported from the forests of Eko, that was what the rest of us sat on while Dunnax manned the reins.

Much like the road to Leppit, our journey north began with the climbing of a steep hill. Traveling by cart was easier than going on foot, though we had to hold on tight to keep from falling out and tumbling all the way back down. Soon enough we crested the hill and Dunnax slowed the horses to take in the landscape that spread out before us. The hilltop was no summit at all, but one of many plateaus in the rolling ground that climbed unsteadily northwest toward the jagged, snow-topped mountain range called the Nobiko Peaks. On the other side of that range, the Canako Canal cut straight through the valley, all the way out to the sea that lay north of the Peeker Mounds. We wouldn't be going toward those mountains, according to our map. Instead, our path would swing east around the peaks, winding through the countryside like a serpent, where rocky outcrops provided plenty of cover for highwaymen.

At least we aren't traveling in some royal golden carriage.

Lacking any treasure, any bandits would likely leave us alone, but I still couldn't put myself at ease during the trip. Maybe we didn't have to worry about ambushes, but the chance that we could run into a Benefactor meant that I never kept my weapons far from reach. Not until we reached the outpost would I let myself relax...or try to, anyway. After accepting the reality that I needed to brave the Benefactor scourge, I was still surprised that our next command was simple guard duty, something I'd done hundreds of times before. Didn't the Agency have Heels for that? It didn't befit Ulken to waste a Hand's time. Something was amiss, but I couldn't put my finger on it.

Best to prepare for the worst.

Along the way, we filled Inac in on what happened in Leppit. The Archemage had plenty of questions, but he pondered our answers as if they had only academic significance. He seemed to believe all of us had suffered some mass delusion. I couldn't blame him, really. If I hadn't seen it for myself, I wouldn't have believed Wick was real either.

"Does that sound like any sort of magic you know?" I asked Inac after telling him about Wick's Aura.

Inac put two fingers to his lips and tapped them in thought. "No," he said. "It does not." Inac held up one finger of his right hand. "But!" A tiny flame appeared at the tip of his outstretched finger. The Fire formed into a vertical ring, tightly controlled by the expert Archemage. Inac positioned his finger and the Fire between us, then peered at me through the ring's center like he was wearing it as a monocle. "You see how the light dances, yes?"

I leaned forward. The image of his green eye shimmered and waved in the ring of Fire. "Yes."

The Fire flickered out. "This is primitive, but you see. Maybe it did to you something like this?"

"It was much more than making light dance," I said. "What about the emotion it forced on everyone?"

A sly grin slipped onto Inac's face. A moment later, bright Fire consumed my entire field of vision. Searing heat dried out my eyes. I screamed, jumped backward, and nearly fell off the moving cart. The light winked out, leaving my vision darkened. Cold beads of sweat dripped down my face.

"You feel fear now, yes?" Inac chuckled. "Manipulating emotion is not so hard to do."

"By the abyss, Inac." My heart hammered in my chest. "Warn me the next time you're going to do something like that."

"Sorry, my friend. I am showing to you how complex the world of magic is. And I showed to you only the Fire. With the Dark, even more possibilities open to us." Inac shrugged.

"The Dark?" I said, confused. "Never heard of Dark magic."

"Archedeath," Dunnax spat. "The Book of Light tells how it hastens the return of the Dark Era. The Church has forbidden it."

"Pity for the Church," Inac said, rolling his eyes. "But Fire and Dark have been here far longer than they have had these silly rules. And do not call it Archedeath. Archefire and Archedark are both necessary for life. There cannot be one without the other."

"Dark magic, eh?" Garret asked. "Reckon I'd like to see that."

"I can show this to you," Inac said, nodding.

"Don't." Dunnax looked back, a warning in his eyes.

Inac chuckled. "You remind to me of my Sage." He shrugged. "Have it as you please. But one Archemage showing the Dark will not make to the world much difference. There already are many controlling Archedark. Is this not so, Sentyx?"

Sentyx stared at Inac for an uncomfortably long time, then turned away and closed his eyes.

"The Skardwarves?" Dunnax asked. "How do you know that?"

Inac grinned. "Perhaps you should next time read to yourself the Book of Light more closely, yes?" The mage turned to me, a thoughtful look on his face. "Did you not tell to me you thought Skardwarves were monsters? You two seem to me quite friendly."

Sentyx grunted and stared at me, expecting an answer.

My face grew hot. I *had* expected Sentyx to be a monster, an enemy of the Bright Empire. "A lot's changed since last time we spoke. I was wrong about Skardwarves. Sentyx is a friend."

"Aye," Garret said. "If you can manage to pry a word or two out of him."

Sentyx's lips pulled back, showing a mouth full of flat, round teeth.

"That's a smile," Garret said, "if you can believe it."

"Something else has changed too," I said. I retrieved the crumpled note from my pocket and tossed it to Inac. "The Hand knows about Reed's conspiracy."

Inac lit the message up with his pendant to read it once more. Then he balled the paper up and tossed it off the cart. "That was a terrible plan. Ulken already knows for himself everything Reed has done."

I nodded. "There's no keeping secrets from the Head."

"Can't say the same about the Head keeping secrets from us," Garret said.

"Didn't you have something to tell us, Inac?" Dunnax asked over his shoulder.

"Ulken kept me all this time in the tower," Inac said. His faced twisted into a grimace. "He gave to me the role of Heel."

"You?" I asked. "You're an Archemage!"

Inac shrugged. "They told to me only one mage is allowed in a Hand."

"We didn't have *any* in our Hand," Garret said.

I curled my lip. "Ulken probably wanted to make our 'field test' more challenging."

Dunnax whipped the horses' reins and the cart jerked forward to crest the hill. "What were you doing in the Agency all this time?"

"Archefire is for making steam very useful," Inac said. "There are many others who all day boil water in the tower's lower levels." The mage grinned. "But I do not need for myself to be near the Fire to control it. So, I had for myself much time to wander."

Mistakenly getting Inac assigned to our Hand might have been the best thing I could have done. With such a powerful mage, we stood a much better chance in a fight against a Benefactor.

"No one told to me I should stop," Inac said. "It did not seem to me they cared what I did. It was I think the haze that fills the Agency. Something is unusual about it. It is covering something, but I do not know what it is."

"Couldn't find it?" Garret asked.

Inac shook his head. "Find it? It was everywhere. This is why also the haze must be everywhere." He sighed. "After some time, it was for me too much. It started to give to me a dull mind. I was a Heel, but I would not wear the uniform. I stayed out of the tower until a man in white said to me I would join you, Grim."

"I'm glad you're with us," I said, drawing a glance from Dunnax. "Ulken didn't know the talent he was wasting."

"Or he did," Inac said, "and he did not care. I too am glad. I have spent enough time for my taste in towers under the thumb of men who do not deserve the control they have."

* * *

The Brightdaughter danced high overhead the next day, providing us plenty of daylight to reach the Canako Outpost. Sometime after half-dusk, the outpost's gated wall crawled up into sight as we went over a rocky hill. From this vantage the city of Canako splayed out beside a crystal-blue lake, visible over the top of the outpost gate, though it sat far below at the foot of this treacherously steep final slope. The Canako Canal shot off westward from the lake, straight as an arrow, disappearing into the valley across from the city. Eastward, a natural river ran through the city and toward Liwokin. The perspective from this height cast the port city in miniature, and my eye could just make out that the tiny, colorful dots in the lake were ships flying the royal colors. I gaped at the scale of this artificial lake, hewn from the ground by the Empress' engineers.

No wonder she levies such a steep tax for passage. It probably cost a fortune to build.

I had little time to savor the awesome sight before my attention was yanked back with the tugging of the reins, which I had taken over to give Dunnax a break. The horses tried pulling away from our lumbering cart, which began accelerating on the downslope of the hill. Panic gripped me as I realized I had no idea how to slow down a horse-drawn cart. I pulled the reins, but the horses just pulled back. I yelled at them to stop, but my cries fell on deaf equine ears. Praying came to mind next but barreling down toward the outpost's gate where five figures stood shouting at us to stop, flanked on either side by sharp pikes and barricades, I decided bailing out was a better option.

Before my ill-conceived thoughts translated into action, Dunnax gripped me by the shoulder and hauled me backward, taking control of the reins for himself. I rolled heel over head and lay on the cart's floor, eyes squeezed shut, reaching around for anything I could hold on to. Clinging to a firm, solid post, I awaited the coming impact.

Praying might be just the thing after all. Never too late to prepare for a meeting with the gods.

The cart jolted and my ribs struck the lightwood sides of the rumbling cart, which lurched so treacherously it surely had nearly rolled over. With a bang and a crash, we came to a stop. I opened my eyes and found what I'd been holding onto: Sentyx's leg. I let it go. The Skardwarf stared down at me as if nothing out of the ordinary had occurred, then hopped down onto solid ground.

"Last time we let you drive," Garret said, following Sentyx.

I sat up and dusted myself off. "That's...yeah, that's for the best."

Inac offered a hand to help me up, grinning. "I would have done no better, my friend. Horses...I do not understand horses."

The four of us in the back walked around the cart, which was now completely off the road and only a few strides away from some dug-in spikes. We found Dunnax stroking a horse's mane and whispering calming words. Had he hesitated any longer, that horse would have been skewered.

Never underestimate the deadliness of a stupid mistake.

An Ekoan wearing Agency green let loose a long whistle and clapped as he approached. Between his two hands, as many fingers were missing as remained. "Some fine work there, Paceeqi. They teach you to drive horses like that in the big city? You, on the other hand," he said, pointing a three-fingered hand at me, "might consider traveling by boat."

"And you are?" Garret said.

"Neddon, I am." He pointed up to the unusually long-brimmed cap he wore. "Gate Captain of this here outpost. You must be our relief." Behind him, four morose Fingers waited impatiently for him to finish.

"Aye," Garret said.

"Good." Neddon took a step toward Dunnax, removed his strange cap, then placed it atop Dunnax's already-helmeted head, jumping up so he could reach. "You're Gate Captain now, so listen good. Just three rules." He counted them off on all the fingers he had on his left hand. "No contraband. No criminals.

No foreign persons holding neither a passport nor documentation providing express written consent by the Head of the Agency himself. Got it?"

"Uh…" Dunnax hesitantly nodded, brim of the Gate Captain's hat flopping as he did.

"Good. Let's go, boys. One of you take the reins. I'm taking a nap." The five Fingers climbed aboard our cart, one of them turned it around, and the poor, tired horses started slowly climbing back up the hill.

"Wait!" Dunnax yelled after them. "Are these fortifications for…the monsters?"

Neddon laughed. "Monsters? Only monsters you'll be seeing 'round here are from the prisoner transports. Them, and maybe a daggerclaw or two." The relieved Gate Captain cackled and gave us a curt salute, then lay down as the cart bounced away, one wheel wobbling and loose.

"A…daggerclaw?" I once heard they had one of those in the Gild's entertainment row. Rumor had it the Gild hosted all kinds of eclectic activities there—a high-stakes casino, a gallery of mechanical automata, an exotic menagerie. Even if I'd wanted to waste my coin, I wouldn't have been allowed to step foot in there.

"Ekoan joke," Garret said, shaking his head and turning toward the outpost. "Guard Captain Dunnax has a point. This place is heavily defended."

Dunnax groaned. "Don't call me that." He took off his cap and placed it on Sentyx's head. "Here, you're Guard Captain now, the perfect role for you. Threats are only going to come from one direction."

"I face into the wind." Sentyx adjusted the cap, straightening it.

"See, that's what I'm talking about. You leave your back exposed…"

The two of them started uphill together, presumably to survey the landscape that lay beyond the hill. I smiled. Even Dunnax was softening to him.

As the former Paladin lectured Sentyx about the inevitability of rear assault, I surveyed the outpost's defenses with Garret and Inac. The high wall stretched beyond sight in both directions, hugging the rolling landscape as it rose and fell. Green vines climbed up from the foot of the wall, past cracked gray stone where they joined the pale moss that clung beneath the parapets. This vast work of engineering must have been ancient, a piece of history. Perhaps it was constructed when Canako and Liwokin were two of Lawiko's many independent city-states. In any case, it had withstood the challenges of time. Lawiko was great long before the Bright Empire had arrived.

The pits dug out around the wall's base and filled with spikes were newly built, however. So too were the sharpened-lightwood barricades, and both were concentrated in the area surrounding the gate. The Nerve told us there was no Benefactor threatening this area, but clearly, they were expecting a fight.

"I'll be in the gatehouse," Garret said. "Brought plenty of incendiary arrows this time."

When he'd gone, Inac asked, "Incendiary arrows?"

I rolled my shoulder, still aching from the first fight, then sighed, regretting that I hadn't used the recess to better prepare. "Best get some rest," I told Inac. "We may need your magic before long."

CHAPTER TWELVE

Smugglers

Dunnax's incessant snoring came from the gatehouse, loud enough to keep awake some sailors down the hill in Canako. The rest of my Hand somehow slept through it, leaving me to guard this gate in the middle of the night, alone with my thoughts. Between the Paceeqi's intermittent din, it was too quiet. With no ringing bells, rustling leaves, or raucous drunks, my mind filled the silence with imagined sounds that kept me on edge.

No wonder those Fingers were so desperate for relief.

For the rest of the day, not a single traveler had passed through. It would be no different now that the sun's light had waned, leaving only a dim, pink glow peering over the hills to the southeast. On so steep a road, there was no comfortable way to stand guard throughout the night, so I wandered around the barricades beyond the light of the single torch illuminating the gate.

I ran my fingers along one of the crisscrossed spikes forming a barricade beside the road. The lightwood was sanded smooth as marble, all the way to the needle-sharp point. On its tip I pricked my thumb, drawing out a welter of blood. Even pain was preferable to boredom. I put my thumb in my mouth, tasting the metallic saltiness as I strolled aimlessly back toward the ancient wall. Staring down into the black depths of a pit at the foot of the wall, my eyes adjusted to the deeper darkness.

There was a strange shape at the bottom.

Thunder clapped and the spikes became white foam, jutting from the bay, calling for me to dive down with the rain to greet them. I had to do it. The sea was brimming with helmfish. I'd prove to Akun that I could contribute as much as any of the other men.

I'm doing it for her.

Adjusting my grip on the harpoon I'd stolen from the rack, trying to ignore the rushing of blood in my ears, I bent my knees, intoned a quiet prayer, and...

Wyran's memory released me from its grip. I fell back, away from the spike pit, tried to catch my breath.

What was wrong with me? Something was changing within my mind, and it was getting worse. It felt like losing myself, becoming someone else... One of these days it was going to happen at the wrong time and get me killed. I decided that being alone with my thoughts wasn't so bad after all.

At least those were *my* thoughts.

"Is something the matter?"

I jumped up, spinning around, almost losing balance and plunging into the pit before I caught myself with a handful of ivy hanging on the wall. A cloaked figure waited on the road outside the torch's ring of light, face obscured by a raised hood, hand guarding a satchel that hung from shoulder to waist.

A traveler, at this beat of the night? Too close for the crossbow—I'd never load it in time. My hand went to the hilt of my sword.

The traveler started. "Oh! No need for that." He pushed back his hood to reveal a head of mangy, black, shoulder-length hair that cropped a greasy face with a bulbous nose.

"Who are you?" I asked, gesturing him to come closer. Stepping into the torchlight, the man looked as if he hadn't bathed in an Imperial measure, if they even used the Imperial time system where he came from. I wrinkled my nose.

Smells like they don't.

"My name is Raylen," he said. "Will I be able to pass?"

"Depends." I shrugged. "Why are you traveling so late at night? And alone?"

"I've come a long way," Raylen said. "From the Pinegrave."

The Pinegrave? Wasn't that where Oltrov had sent Kilan?

"You're a Druid, then?"

"Well, er..." Raylen gave a nervous laugh. "Yes. You've heard of us?"

"I have. Heard you're supplying our Agency with toxics." Narrowing my eyes, I asked. "What's in the satchel?"

"Oh, just..." Raylen looked around, clutching the satchel tighter against his dingy, brown cloak. When he did, there came the muffled sound of shattering glass. "It's all perfectly natural!"

I held my hand out. "Give the satchel here. Natural or not, you can't bring Druid's Tears through the gate."

Raylen stepped back, looking offended. "Are you a guard or a brigand? The Agency hardly pays enough for us to profit, now you've stooped to stealing our harvests? The elders will hear of this."

Hardly enough to profit? Even Oltrov's lies are more believable. "Tell the elders to take it up with the Agency's Head."

Raylen slipped the satchel from his shoulder, muttering to himself. "Already lost a quarter harvest to that ungrateful Eye anyway..."

My ears pricked up. "Eye? Did he happen to be injured?"

Raylen's eye caught a glint of torchlight. He clutched his satchel tight and winced at the sound of another Tear breaking. "Might have been," he said. "Might be I know something of what he was up to. Something I'd only share with a friend."

My choice, then, was it? Learn more of Reed's conspiracy in exchange for letting Raylen smuggle his goods through the gate or confiscate the goods and send him off. Arrest him? We never did get instructions on what to do with rule breakers. Something told me the Agency wouldn't be lenient.

"Consider me a friend," I said. "Tell me."

Raylen looked around as though someone might be eavesdropping. "The First Eye came to me just before I left," he said. "Told me he needed a supply of Tears, then took enough off me to leave a man dead. We've been trading with his lackeys for some time, but now he had no gold with him. He said the Agency would pay me back in full, plus some extra for my troubles." The enterprising Druid looked me up and down. "I see now the value of an Agency promise."

"I'm letting you pass, aren't I?"

"Are you? Might be you're still planning to steal the rest of my harvest."

I shook my head. "I'm no brigand." I had been, once; now I was just someone disobeying the Head's commands. Hard to say which was more dangerous. "What else? You said you know what he was up to."

"*Might* know, I said." The Druid picked at something in his hair, looked at it, then flicked it away. "He was in a hurry. In bad shape too, though not nearly as bad as when the enclave took him in. Some of the others had been nursing him to health, but he was far from well enough to travel. Might be why he needed so many Tears. To dull the senses, you know."

"Enclave...that's the Pinegrave?" I asked. Raylen nodded. "And he was in a hurry to leave? Where?"

Raylen shrugged. "Kept muttering something about going north. Could be anywhere. May be headed this way for all I know."

Cross the canyon and follow the forest road. If the Pinegrave was south of the Outrush Canyon, Kilan had made good time delivering Oltrov's message.

"Do you know why he was in such a hurry?" I asked.

"Strangest thing. One night he's resting, barely able to get out of his bed in the Goldglass for all his injuries. The next morning he's manic, like a ghost spooked him in his sleep." Raylen laughed, gums showing where missing teeth should have been. "When he first showed up, I thought he was the ghost, looking like he did through the mists. Lucky, he made it to us in time. Some bear must have mauled him good."

"A bear, right..." I trailed off, piecing Raylen's story together with what I learned during the deal in the Blight. Reed had to head north to where Ulken found his target. He wanted to rush off, but he couldn't, not without taking a supply of Tears with him. Were they meant to stave off pain, like Raylen said...or to protect against an Aura? If so, did that mean Ulken's target was a Benefactor?

"That's all I know," Raylen said. I had nearly forgotten he was there. "Am I free to go now?"

I nodded. "Don't come through this way again. If it had been anyone but me at the gate—"

"Yes, yes," Raylen strode past me. "Chains, interrogation, all that. I've been at this a long time." With that, he took off through the open gate, leather sandals skittering down the dark slope.

I leaned against the wall below the gate. All the excitement done, I had a long night ahead and much more to think on. For once, it'd be nice to have some alone time.

"Shouldn't have let him go," came Garret's voice from the doorway of the gatehouse.

I started. *Of course that was too much to hope for.*

The ranger stepped out into the torchlight.

"What did you hear?" I muttered.

"Not much," Garret said, then spat on the ground. "Just a Finger breaking the first rule of our command to let some smuggler through the gate."

"Oh, is that all?" I asked. "Surprised you caught anything through Dunnax's snoring."

"Why did you let past a smuggler?" Inac said, following Garret outside. There was a note of disappointment in his voice.

"You're up, too?" There was no sense in lying to them. "He had information about Reed."

"Had some lies to fool a gullible gatekeeper, you mean," Garret said. "You know Reed died."

Inac rubbed his eyes. "Explain to me, please."

"Reed saved us from a Benefactor on our first command," I said. "He drew it off into the woods and allowed us to escape. We *thought* he died, but that smuggler was a Druid from the Pinegrave. That's where Reed ended up after saving us. He was injured. They helped him recover."

"And you believed him?" Garret asked.

"I wouldn't have," I said, "except during our recess I ran into Oltrov."

"Who?" Inac asked.

"One of Reed's conspirators," I said, then sighed. "You missed a lot while stuck in that tower." Inac just stared at me, his eyes ragged with sleeplessness. "Oltrov brought me with him to the

Blight, where we handed over a lot of Agency coin for some toxics called Druid's Tears. That's what the smuggler was carrying. Ulken buys them from the Druids and gives them to Fingers to help fight the Benefactors."

"Well, if Ulken says to us it is okay..." Inac said. His voice had the bite of irritation.

"What's this have to do with Reed?" Garret asked.

"The toxics seller didn't just bring Druid's Tears," I said. "He had a message from Reed. Oltrov believed it was real, and he questioned me about what I knew afterward."

Garret crossed his arms. "Putting a lot of trust in smugglers and conspirators."

I shrugged. "Believe them or not, I'm sure it was fine letting the Druid pass. For all we know, he could be meeting another Finger in Canako."

"You are a better man than this," Inac said. He shook his head and stalked into the gatehouse.

"What did I do?"

"He's just cranky from being kept awake," Garret said. The Ekoan shoved back his hood and took a deep breath. "I'll take watch from here. You're welcome to sleep under the stars like a civilized person for once. Might not have any luck in there." Dunnax's snores came to a sharp peak as if to punctuate Garret's point.

I kicked a rock that was on the road, watched it roll downhill into a spike pit. "Thanks, but I'll take my chances inside."

Dead tired as I was, even Dunnax couldn't keep me away from sleep for long after I sunk into the vacant bed in the gatehouse. Softer than any bed in Liwokin, the down mattress cradled me as I drifted off with secrets and conspiracies on my mind.

* * *

A huge shadow loomed over Liwokin, the sun blotted out by a giant figure that stood towering over the buildings of the city. The tallest reached the figure's knees. It bellowed a thunderous laugh, raised its fists overhead, and swung them down in the slow motion of giant things. Fists became great balls of fire, as though the Sibling Suns were falling from the heavens. The Liwo around me started to scream, finally noticing their imminent doom far too late for them to escape. As the impact cracked the world like an egg, the sky turned black and cold. Light was gone. The grinning teeth of the monstrous figure parted, then the shock wave swept me away. It felt like sinking into the sea.

I woke, jolting up, only to become tangled in blankets, sunken in to the soaked, too-soft bed. Was that my sweat that soaked the linens? Wrenching myself free, I rolled off the side of the bed and landed on my back with my leg still caught up in the blanket. I scanned the upside-down room, grateful to see that no one was around for my embarrassing display. Voices joined the pale sunlight and savory smells that welcomed themselves in through the open door. Still lying on the ground, I reached for my boots, slid them on, then stood and strolled out to greet the new day. Barely through the door, I stopped and groaned.

The savory smell of bacon cooking on a campfire turned out to be Inac and Dunnax burning themselves with the Fire to prove who had the greater control. The voices were the Archemage and the Paladin boasting to each other while Garret egged them on. Gate Captain Sentyx stood facing up the hill, ever diligent in his duty of watching for oncoming danger.

"At least the sunlight was as I expected." The Brightdaughter had begun her climb up from the horizon and looked to be ascending high today.

"Morning, sleep talker. About time you woke up," Garret said over his shoulder, not taking his eyes off the competition.

Sleep talker? Perhaps I hadn't completely escaped embarrassment.

"Sentyx won't place a bet," Garret continued. "My coin's on Inac, but Dunnax smells like a roasting mudpig, and he still won't quit. How's even odds sound?"

"Give it up, mage," Dunnax grunted through squeezed jaws. His helmet was off, sweat trickling down from his cropped golden hair. He wore the rest of his armor, which glowed bright with molten heat around the forearms, cooking the Paladin inside. "I endured worse than this to enter the Order."

"Hah," Inac laughed, but his face showed no mirth. He was in deep concentration, but not too deep to heckle his competition. "Does this cause to you great pain?" The Archemage's right arm seemed to be made of Fire. Flames licked up his past his shoulder as he touched each burning finger to his fiery thumb in slow sequence. He smiled nonchalantly, though the hood of his robe was beginning to smoke. "Your control is good, but this feels to me like a kiss from the Mother of Light."

"Evens?" I said to Garret. "I'm going to need better than that."

"Two to one on the mage, then. Best I can do."

They continued burning themselves. Dunnax was clearly in great pain. Inac merely looked bemused. The little wisp of smoke turned to flame as Inac's hood caught alight, but the Archemage slid his eyes over when he noticed it and raised his left hand. The light in a radius around Inac faded ever so subtly, like a cloud briefly had passed in front of the sun. A cool wind brushed my cheek, and the flame went out, leaving one more burn mark among the many that marred Inac's robe.

Dunnax's face hardened. He let his Fire burn out, his armor fading from gold, to red, back to cool silver.

Inac noticed only the latter. "You see? I win." Inac shot the Fire from his left arm up into the air where it formed a sphere, which burst into tiny embers that flitted down on us all.

"Show off," Garret muttered.

"I warned you," Dunnax said.

"No," Inac said, still gloating. "It is I who gave to you a warning. I told to you that you could not hope to compete with a true scholar of Archemagic. Consider this payback to you for keeping me up all night."

"Archedeath is no plaything," Dunnax spat. "Why are you so eager to bring about the Dark Era?"

"Ah." Inac finally caught on. "Bring to us the Dark Era? My friend, the Dark has never left. Hide from it if you like, it always will be with us."

When Dunnax balled his fists, I forced myself between the two. "It's too early for this. I haven't even had breakfast," I said. "There are plenty of Benefactors out there to kill us. No need to do their work for them."

Dunnax glared at Inac, then abruptly spun, and stomped up the hill to join Sentyx.

Inac's eyes were on the earth. "You see what they do to people, these thoughts given to them by the Church?" He sighed, turned up both palms. "Dark is not evil like they say to you." A tiny flame sparked in his right hand, beside a tiny black void in his left.

Archedark. Garret pushed me aside for a closer look at this new magic.

Motes of Archedark and Archefire moved with Inac's hands as he brought them together. The light and dark spiraled around, faster, faster, faster until they pressed into each other and became one spinning sphere that exuded, somehow, both color and its total absence. Slowly, Inac's hands closed around the sphere. He closed his right fist, brought it up, and opened it. Sitting in his open hand, a black gem struck through with hints of gold caught the Brightdaughter's light. The same material as his lost pendant.

Garret took the result of the display from Inac's hand, examined it closely.

"How can one be wrong and not the other, when together they bring to the world such beauty?" Inac asked. "Dark is not evil. No more than Light."

Dunnax screamed and my head whipped around. Sentyx was rubbing some salve into the burns on Dunnax's arm.

Inac chuckled. "If he balanced the heat of the Fire with the cold of the Dark, he would have caused to himself no pain at all."

* * *

"Listen," Sentyx said. It was the first thing he'd said all day, but there was no sound save for the singing of birds carried on gusts of wind, and the distant murmur of Canako when the blowing wind quieted. That, and the rumble of my stomach, still perversely craving bacon after this morning's events. Instead, we'd made do with a couple cooked birds that Garret shot from the sky. They were chewy and unsatisfying, but even those were better than the bread left by the previous garrison, either moldy, burnt, or both.

I joined the Skardwarf and Dunnax by the foremost barricades, careful of the treacherously steep footing. "I don't hear anyth—"

Dunnax shushed me. He turned his ear toward the peak of the hill.

I rolled my eyes, annoyed at being interrupted, but turned my head as he did. For a few breaths I heard nothing new, then my ear began to resolve the sounds. It wasn't birdsong at all. Just song. And getting louder. Soon, my ear picked apart from plucking strings a voice, which formed into lyrics. Ribald lyrics, about the Lightmother, verging on blasphemy. I looked at Dunnax, whose warped glaive was drawn.

Time to put an end to this vile sinner?

Instead, his face glowed with delight. "Lorelay?"

Indeed, as she approached the crest of the hill, his sister's voice became unmistakable, her fingering of the lyre's strings unmatched by any other hand. An ornate carriage came into view, rising above the hilltop, Lorelay sitting on the velvet, padded bench, singing loud and plucking fast. Dunnax's expression soured.

Beside the Paceeqi girl sat the Bright Prince Vinlin, heir to the Bright Throne. As Lorelay sang, he snorted and laughed in a distinctly undignified way. The Bright Prince held the reins, and despite crying from laughter, he brought his carriage to a slow stop just ahead of the barricades.

Inac and Garret joined us as Lorelay brought her tune to a crescendo. She was never one to leave a great song unfinished. At its conclusion, Vinlin hooted and applauded, then wiped a mirthful tear from his eye. "Marvelous! Simply marvelous! I do hope you will accept my invitation."

"Of course, my Prince," Lorelay said, managing a bow so deep it appeared mocking. "It would be my honor and delight to entertain your royal guests."

"You will need to entertain them with more," the Bright Prince cleared his throat, "appropriate songs, naturally. We may laugh on our travels with no one in earshot, but undoubtedly you know you cannot play any songs such as these at the event. It would cause quite a stir."

"I wouldn't dream of it, Your Radiance." Lorelay bowed again, hiding her face from Vinlin as she smiled at me and winked.

Garret coughed. "Some special request, eh Dunnax?"

Dunnax shifted, armor jangling as he looked away from the Bright Prince and his sister like he was hiding something. Except now it was in plain sight.

There was nothing Dunnax could do except hope the prince chose not to comment on his ragged Paladin's armor.

Luckily, it seemed Lorelay had put Vinlin in a good mood. "Well, well. Hello there, gentlemen. I must admit, I thought not to re-encounter your group so soon. I extend my thanks once again for that business in the woods. Dreadful, truly dreadful. A shame to deal with such senseless loss of life. This leg of my journey has been much more pleasant, as you can tell, thanks to Lorelay's exceptional talents."

"Come now, Linny," Lorelay said, "I make no exceptions when it comes to my talents. I consider it my highest duty."

I raised my eyebrows. She *did* remember that this was the Bright Prince, right?

"Indeed," Vinlin said, "and to perform your duty is to serve the Bright Throne. With that in mind, we must be off. I have my own duties, of course. My ship awaits us at Canako, and while they'll wait as long as I make them, it would be unbecoming of me to keep them in port for long."

"Hold on," I said. "We need to check the carriage for illegal goods."

"Illegal goods?" Vinlin looked almost as surprised as Lorelay beside him. The edges of their mouths both moved, Lorelay's up into a grin, Vinlin's down into a frown. "I'm the *Bright Prince*, first son of Elzia, heir to the Throne of Vos, Holy Seat of the Light."

Who are you trying to convince? Us, or yourself?

"Grim...what is this?" Dunnax growled in my ear. Garret chuckled behind me. After letting Raylen smuggle illegal goods through the gate last night, it didn't make much sense to check Vinlin's carriage.

But it wasn't every day a commoner got to lord over the Bright Prince.

"The Agency set the rules here. The crown is above the law, but you're not the emperor just yet, are you?" I spread my hands. "I'm just doing my duty, which is to say, serving your future Throne."

Vinlin grumbled as he looked down on me, good mood quickly vanishing. That was fine. Why should his mood have been any better than mine? The Bright Prince climbed down from the comfort of his high bench, then bid me follow him up the hill to the back of his opulent carriage.

Lorelay stretched out to relax, then started strumming her lyre.

Quiet but incredulous, Dunnax said, "*Linny*? And those songs... Lorelay, he's going to find out who you are." Lorelay only laughed and told Dunnax he worried too much.

Vinlin glared at me as he pulled the velvet curtain aside, revealing the golden, scarlet-trimmed interior of his carriage. "Go on, then. Quickly. I have a schedule to keep."

Ducking under his arm, I clambered into the carriage to find an interior that was better furnished than the finest room of any tavern in which I'd stayed. I moved toward a small bed along one side of the carriage, and Vinlin climbed aboard behind me. I reached out to touch the silky sheets, curious to feel the comforts of traveling royalty.

Vinlin tutted. "Do not touch anything. You may look, but if I find anything is broken or missing, all of Paceeq will raise arms against you."

Yes, I'm sure all your subjects will be upset over my ruffling of their prince's bed.

I pulled my hand back, turned to look over the hoard of treasure Vinlin had accumulated in his travels. The standard fare of silver plates, gold goblets, and jeweled baubles were of course present, but mixed in were artifacts whose origins I couldn't fathom. Ivory in the shape of a horn, banded with three steel brackets. A curling skeleton of some small creature with no legs but jaws large enough to compensate. A glass box with tiny holes cut out, next to a box draped with red fabric. I peered inside the empty box, and a reptile suddenly appeared, its tongue snapping out to catch an unfortunate fly that crawled in through a hole in the glass. The creature looked at me with an absurdly bulging eye before its skin changed to match the red fabric behind it. What use anyone possibly could have for these useless treasures escaped me. They were like a stash of stolen gems hidden in the den of a bandit I once hunted down. *Has the Bright Prince paid for these artifacts or stolen them by royal decree?*

Light filled the room with the sigh of velvet as Dunnax peeked inside. "Hurry up, Grim. His Radiance has better things to do than make sure you don't break his belongings."

Ignoring him, I turned toward the front of the trove, where stood a small, jagged branch, potted in a ceramic vase. Its roots had clawed their way out of the dirt and began drooping over the pot's edge like parasitic worms. Something about the tree stood out as different from the rest of the treasures. The unnatural way those tendrils writhed filled me with disgust. For all that the plant seemed eager to grow, there were no leaves or flowers budding from the thin needles it had for branches. No, there seemed to be no life in this plant, if such a thing could be called a plant at all.

This is no treasure...

Vinlin huffed with impatience, but as the Bright Prince's shadow rolled across the potted stalk, something glimmered on the side of the stem.

I knelt. The plant was leaking a translucent drop of sap, just below one of the protruding glassy needles. It formed into a teardrop shape, then, unable to bear its weight any longer, dropped into the vase and landed with a clink.

"Explain yourself, Prince."

"Grim!" Dunnax could take my insults to his future Emperor no longer. "Has the abyss swallowed your senses?"

Vinlin responded more coolly. "You recognize the branches of the Grieving Pine, do you?" The Bright Prince was calm, but a cold anger radiated from him.

"No," I said, pulling a sticky half-formed bead from the branch. It trailed a wisp of sap, thin as spider's silk, back to its origin. "But I recognize these. Why are you smuggling Druid's Tears out of Lawiko?"

"Smuggling..." Dunnax's mouth hung open. His brow was a knot of confusion.

"I will not be lectured by some common Finger, nor an oath breaking Paladin. Oh yes." Vinlin turned and scowled at Dunnax. "I know who you are. I had my suspicions in the forest but now there can be no doubt." Vinlin reached into his coat and produced a purse full of stars. "I will pass through this gate whether you like it or not. Take these and hold your tongue. Now, get out of my carriage."

It seems royalty is no different than banditry after all.

Vinlin shoved his bribe into my hands. I had no room to judge the man, but I resented Vinlin's betrayal of my friend's faith. The pouch I held stank like bile, as though its purpose had tainted it with a foul stench. I looked at Vinlin with disgust, and the way he looked back at me told me the feeling was mutual. Then, he wrinkled his nose, as if he smelled something too.

The carriage was suddenly swarming with insects, tiny gnats buzzing in a cloud, and crawling all over the coin purse and my hand. I instinctively flinched back, dropping the stars. I pushed past the Bright Prince and knocked him onto his royal bed. Beside Dunnax, I jumped out into the open air. The air smelled like death, as though I had landed in a pile of rotting bodies left out in the blazing sun. But the Brightdaughter was nowhere to be seen overhead. She was shaded by coagulated, murky clouds that flowed and swirled in a viscid dance, turning the sky a sickly green. Flies swarmed in ephemeral pillars of light that pierced the overcast display. Their ceaseless buzzing filled the air. My stomach roiled and struggled to keep down my meager breakfast. This sudden, rotten scene could mean only one thing...

A shape crested the hilltop, not a great beast, but a cart. One pulled not by horses but by a single, ragged man. It wasn't slowing down. I turned back to the carriage, drawing my sword.

Dunnax donned his helmet and shouted. "Lorelay! Get the Prince out of here!"

Lorelay snapped the reins and set the carriage rolling down to Canako. Vinlin's bewildered face peered out between two insect-covered curtains. A few landed on his cheeks and lips. One crawled up his nose. The Bright Prince didn't seem to notice. In a few rapid heartbeats, they were through the gate and Garret strained, groaned, pulled the lever to close it shut behind them. The portcullis squealed and protested as if the rust had been building up since the day it was built. Maybe it had, because it didn't come down any farther than the tangled vines already hung.

"I must not stop!" yelled the cart-puller behind me. "Get out of the way!"

Sentyx strode forward, not a hint of fear or worry on his face despite Archefire shooting out and licking his stone-hard flesh, burning up a cloud of insects that harried the Skardwarf.

The blast of heat from the Fire reached me as I turned around. The stench was unbearable. My throat constricted to keep from retching. I blinked and the cart was right on top of me, barreling down. I flung myself aside, diving off the road, nearly landing on my own sword. Someone shouted, then there was a deafening crash. Before I could turn to look, a jolt of lightning crackled at the base of my skull.

All my senses went dark.

CHAPTER THIRTEEN

A Mother's Curse

Mama's going to be okay," a woman's voice came, like an echoed promise from a disembodied spirit. The voice was my own; the promise was a lie. For just a moment, the voice sounded like it belonged to someone with hope, but that facade wouldn't last. This curse had taken too much from me. My body, my faith, my future. *But not my children, my beautiful children. Don't you worry, my loves.* Blinking away the feeling of tears in my eyes—as if my body had any fluid left to spare—I turned my head with what little energy I had to face them.

It was there on their faces.

Not worry, or fear, or even sadness. No. The same emotion marred their faces as I felt when I looked down on my own rotten body, scarcely more than a corpse already. Disgust. I looked down in shame; I couldn't face them, couldn't bear that look in their eyes. Where flesh remained it was discolored, like my whole body had been badly bruised or burned in sickening fire. It felt even worse. My limbs ended in poorly stitched stumps that dribbled blackened blood, but taking my limbs hadn't stopped the pain. *Damn this curse. It eats at me even when I've nothing left to give.* I lay on this stone slab, stained with the filth that leaked out from me. It pooled and dripped to the ground, filling the room with a sewer smell. This curse would plague me beyond death, tormenting me in dark eternity.

An unbearable lance of pain shot down my crooked spine, sent my vision spinning. I screamed, the tearing sensation in my throat inconsequential compared everything else I had endured. All light faded away.

I dreamed that I could overcome this, even traveling from our homestead in the foothills away to the far-off city, where Egren assured me the best healers practiced. *So good, those healers were, he abandoned me with them.* What a loving husband I have. The healers had a fitting name: morticians. They prodded and cut until they gave up and sent me off to some stone tower. An experimental treatment, they'd called it. A needle in the neck was all it would take, the big man said. He had been working with his brooding companion on just the thing. It wouldn't reverse the damage, but it would stop my body from falling apart, grant me time to spend with my family. *What use is faith when the world's gone to the abyss?* For a time, the injections had worked, but the Darkfather's curse had returned with renewed vigor to drag me down to a freezing afterlife.

Through closed lids, a diffused light stirred, but I was so cold I could do nothing but lie on my back. The hard surface bit into my skin. Eyes struggled to open. Head lolled to the side. Beyond blurred vision there was my boy, lying on another slab. Pallid. Still. *Dead.* Tears would have come if I had any left. My eyes remained dry as death.

"Is Mama going to get better?" my little girl said.

No...Lightmother, please. No. Not her too. I tore my eyes from my boy and dragged my head to the other side. She stood wrinkling her tiny nose at the edge of my slab. Behind her, Egren, my witless husband, rubbed his eyes.

"Yes, bright one, I'm sure she will," he said, not putting the least effort into making it convincing. My little girl furrowed her brow. The useless oaf couldn't even comfort his own daughter. "Now give your Mama a kiss and wake your brother. We'll see her again soon."

"No," I croaked, but even the simplest of words was beyond my reach now. I had one foot in the abyss already, and I'd be damned if my children were coming with me. "Don't," came from my mouth like the whisper of wind. "Stop."

But she didn't hear, my baby girl. She climbed up onto the slab, unmindful of the filth, leaned over the wreckage that I'd become and gave me a kiss on the forehead.

"I love you, Mama," she said. Then she jumped over me. My heart stuttered when she almost slipped off the edge. She threw her arms out and waved them around to keep her balance, hopped down, and ran to her brother to wake him. He stirred. *Alive.* I hadn't the energy to feel relief.

After shepherding my children from the room, Egren stopped at the door, turned back, and whispered, "Mother's light, Andya. Won't you die already?" He sighed and left the room.

Worthless husband, I should have taken the children away from you long ago. But we were meant for each other. Our fates were intertwined. *The only thing more worthless than him...is me.* I closed my eyes and let the chills of fever sweep me into oblivion.

I woke to a violent shake of the room. It rumbled beneath me. Everything was dark, with just a thin line of light shining from above, through a crack. I strained to focus my eyes. Blue skies soared beyond the crevice. The world shuddered and rocked again. *I'm in a cart. Where am I going?* My head tipped to the side and landed on something soft. *Another limb, another piece of me gone?* My eyes adjusted again to perceive the soft, illuminated thing. Clothes, skin, a red line, a lifeless face. My little girl, her neck cut. The weakest of breaths caught in my throat. My hand, the last extremity remaining to me, stretched out to the other side, felt something else soft. All strength left me. What little I'd had couldn't have turned my head, but I didn't have to look. My baby boy. Compared to this agony, the pain of the curse was nothing.

My beautiful children, defiled, the three of us riding in a coffin, no doubt pulled by Egren himself. He sought to hurry me to the abyss, but to send our beautiful, sweet, innocent children ahead of me...it was too much. When the curse could take no more, Egren had taken the rest. With nothing left to cling to, I finally gave up. One final thought murmured in my mind.

There's only one thing more disgusting than the rotting corpse I am. At least now the pain will end.

Only, it didn't.

Of course it didn't.

The curse latched on to me, kept me from joining my children in the deep. They were all alone, without a mother to keep them safe in the abyss. My pain amplified a thousandfold. A shrill sound ripped from my ruined throat, like the distant shrieking of a tortured ghost. I felt a strange satisfaction at Egren nearly jumping out of his skin. A surge of energy flowed through me, beyond me. I felt everything my husband did. Fear, confusion, guilt, grief.

Disgust.

The feeling is mutual. I sent the curse out to grab him too. The afterlife was nothing like I expected, but at least I could haunt this disgusting man until the end of time. *You had better start running, dear husband, and never stop. If I catch you, even the Darkfather will pity you.*

Like a distant tremor, the cart jolted into motion, and darkness consumed all.

* * *

As the crackling of the Deluge faded, my senses returned. With them came the sickness. My gorge rose as I writhed on the ground, only a hand's width away from the edge of a pit full of sharpened pikes. A cloud of dirt and dust billowed up into the green sky. I struggled to my feet, barely holding in the half-digested bird that sloshed around in my stomach. Maggots crawled all over my hands as I pushed myself up from the ground. When I wiped them away, they disappeared, only to be replaced the next time I looked. I didn't feel them, so I forced myself to ignore them and looked downhill toward Andya's cart.

The concealing cloud of dirt blew toward the gate, slowly uncovering the scene. A body lay face down in the middle of the road, the back of its head a ruined mess. That must have been Egren. Beyond the blood that pooled under his corpse, two deep grooves led underneath the stopped cart and into the dust. The tilted cart occasionally shook. Muffled moaning emanated from within. When the dust finally cleared, Sentyx, gate captain's hat flopping and covered in flies, stood anchored at the end of the grooves, where he'd brought the cart to a sudden halt. Through the open gate, Vinlin's carriage barreled down the hill, carrying Lorelay and the prince to Canako.

I staggered toward the cart and pointed at a smear of blood running down Sentyx's chest. "You're hurt."

The Skardwarf looked down, then shrugged. "Not mine."

"Inac, stop!" Garret yelled.

"For the love of light, mage," Dunnax cried, "you'll burn us all!"

Swarms of insects burst into flames as Fire bloomed around the Archemage. Inac incinerated the illusions flitting through the air and crawling on his skin, apparently incapable of distinguishing what was real. He wasn't in Leppit. Even if he had been, why should he have done any better than I had when faced with Wyran's Aura? Inac kept torching the phantom bugs, unmindful of Garret's and Dunnax's shouts. Garret jumped aside as an arc of Fire shot dangerously close to him and scorched the ground.

Only one way to stop this.

Somehow, I'd retained my grip on my sword. I jammed the blade into the crack between the casket and its lid. When I levered the hilt up, the wood warped and bent, weakened by moisture. I gave one final heave, and with a crack the lid swung open, releasing a noxious plume of gas into the air.

I peered inside at the Benefactor, Andya, a physical embodiment of the plague. A churning, amorphous mass oozed pus that mixed with mucous leaking from a dozen or more orifices. The flesh was as green as the churning sky, though it was bruised in places, purple and black. In other spots bone white poked through the bloody, pulpy red. A putrid slime in which it bathed soaked into wood that decayed and folded around the creature. I managed only a brief look before the smell struck me like a fist and knocked me away from the cart. No longer able to hold back, I retched my breakfast onto the trampled dirt.

Garret stepped over me, took one look inside the cart, face twisting, then stepped back and lifted me up. "Smells worse than Liwokin," the Ekoan said, "and that's saying something."

Pops of flame bursting in midair punctuated Inac's grunts. The mage would tire out if we didn't end this soon. Even for someone with Inac's control, using the Fire when exhausted could be deadly.

"Garret, you have your—"

"No need," Dunnax interrupted. He raised his hand and splayed his fingers. The heavy gas hovering above the open cart ignited. Dunnax drove his hand downward and the flame trailed down to the cart to consume the Benefactor with a roar.

In my mind, laughing, sobbing, and screaming all echoed as one. A pang of regret shot through me, but there was also a strange satisfaction. Andya hadn't killed anyone like Wyran and Greta had. She'd committed no crimes, hadn't deserved such a gruesome fate.

But at least her pain would end.

As if it had never been there at all, the rotten stench disappeared. Andya's cries ceased, leaving quiet in my mind. The Brightdaughter shone overhead, as if looking down with a questioning eye, wondering why she couldn't see us for a time. Inac collapsed onto his knees, drawing heaving breaths now that he'd spent all his reserves. The Archemage looked around with dazed eyes. What was going on in his head?

Inside the cart, the fires had snuffed themselves out before the moist wood dried out and caught flame. Burned bones were all that remained in the cart. None belonged to skeletons fully adult and unbroken, only to a tortured mother and her children. My stomach clenched as if they had been close friends of mine.

They were more than that, though, weren't they? Andya's experiences were mine now, in my head alongside Wyran's, another Pool of memories. Her children felt like my children, even though that was ridiculous. I could never be a father. The Darkfather was the only one I ever knew. The corpse of Egren— Andya's husband and Empath—surfaced some residual disgust, no Aura required. With fathers like that, it was no wonder this world had gone to the abyss.

"I thought it would put up more of a fight," Garret said.

"Me too," Dunnax said. "Disappointing." He lifted his glaive and prodded the bones with its crooked end. I suppressed an urge to yell at him. After experiencing the pain Andya endured, how could he be so callous? The Paladin treated his own armor with more reverence. He kept prodding the remains, knocking Andya's charred skull and sending it rolling into the corner of the mucky cart. It rattled as it came to a stop.

"Never heard brains sound like that," Garret said.

Dunnax bent over the cart's edge with a groan and fished for the skull blind, face turned aside to avoid the lingering stench. The Aura may have amplified the smell to extend beyond the makeshift casket, but the cart had still been full of dead bodies until the Fire burned them away. With the blackened skull in hand, Dunnax shook it to produce the rattling sound once again. He held it up with the empty eye sockets facing down and shook it a few times until one of the sockets was no longer empty.

Something resembling a walnut poked out from the hole, dripping some viscous liquid onto Dunnax's pauldron. It may not have sounded like brains, but it sure looked like them.

Wrinkles textured the mysterious walnut-like object, but it was too big to fit through the socket so we couldn't get a better look.

"Any idea what this is?" Dunnax asked, but none of us had any answers.

"Give to me the skull," Inac said, and swiped it. The Archemage closed his eyes. His eyebrows played on his forehead. His lips pursed and relaxed. He tilted his head and his eyes snapped open. "It is as I thought. Dark magic is resonant in this skull."

"Darkfather's breath..." Dunnax muttered. "The Aura is Dark magic?"

"The Aura it is called? Yes," Inac said, then grinned. "You are not surprised. But also, I sensed Fire. Together. Ah, now you are surprised. As am I. This is unlike the balance I used to create my pendant." Inac tossed the skull back to Dunnax, who quickly handed it off to me, no longer something he was willing to touch.

"Well, what do we do with this?" I asked. "This thing must be related to the Benefactor somehow. We should tell the Agency, right?"

"Think Ulken doesn't already know about them?" Garret said, shrugging. "But sure. Maybe we'll get some new secret out of him."

"I will take it," Sentyx said.

"What, now?" I asked. "We don't have a cart to get back."

"I will walk." Sentyx took the skull from me and started up the hill.

"Wait," I said. "Why not just wait until we're relieved?"

But it was too late. Sentyx didn't even look back. He crested the hill and was gone.

*　*　*

Inac shut the door to the gatehouse behind him as he entered. Dunnax took first watch and Garret went...wherever Garret went. The ranger tended to disappear for long spans of time. Was he hunting? Communing with nature? Who knew? Maybe he just needed a break after all we'd been through. After the two of us had finished cleaning up the mess of the Empath's remains in the road, I was exhausted too. Red streaks in the brown dirt were all that now remained, only discernible by the most scrutinizing of eyes. It wouldn't have done to have travelers come through, asking prying questions about a dead body out in the open. A cart full of bones and diseased slime would have raised further suspicions, but Inac and Dunnax took care of that. I doubted Inac needed help burning the cart to ash, but it was good to see him working alongside Dunnax. As long as the mage kept from using Archedark, the Paladin seemed willing to overlook their religious disagreements.

"Will you tell to me what that was?" Inac asked.

"That was a Benefactor," I said, sitting up in the bed. "Like Wick in Leppit."

"Not that," Inac said. "I mean to say...did you see the sick woman too?"

"Andya..." I nodded. "The Deluge hit you too?"

"A Deluge you call it? Yes..." Inac scowled, as if trying to make sense of a complicated mathemelodical equation. "I was not myself. I was Andya."

"That happened with Wyran too. I think it's their memories. We see what happens to them before they...turn into monsters."

"And after. Is that how it feels to them, becoming a Benefactor?"

"Not something I'd ever want to experience," I said. Inac raised an eyebrow. "For real, I mean. No wonder all their Aura's are so awful."

"This Aura, it is to me like no magic I have practiced. It is to me something new."

I gave a wry chuckle. "Get used to it. Seems like every day since I joined the Agency, the world flips on its head."

"The others. They saw these Deluges too?"

"Yeah," I said, nodding, then stopped. "At least, I assumed they did. Now that I think about it, maybe not..."

Was that why Dunnax treated Andya's remains that way? As if they were nothing more than dead bones, rather than once belonging to a living, breathing person who had suffered so greatly. The gods had asked too much of her.

"Is the feeling to you like buzzing in your neck?" Inac asked.

"Buzzing?" I nodded, rubbed the spot where I always felt the Deluge coming on.

"And Andya had put in her neck a needle. Do you think that is significant?"

Another memory from Wyran's Pool flashed before my eyes. Beyond the double-vision of Inac looking puzzled, the gray walls of a stone room appeared. It was a cold, empty space, save for me, the chair I sat in, and a big man with a delicate glass needle. The rotund, masked man leaned over and said in a deep, muffled voice, "You'll feel a small prick. Nothing a man like you can't handle." I winced as it went in, but he was right. It was nothing I couldn't handle, just a small pinch in my neck. If this is what I had to do to prove to Father I was a man, then I'd do it. I smiled. He'd be so proud of me.

"Are you okay?" Inac asked.

"Yeah." I shook the memory off, touching the base of my skull where the needle had entered Wyran's and Andya's necks. "I think it's significant, Inac. Someone is creating these Benefactors."

Inac grunted, sounding almost like Sentyx, not surprised. "Who?"

"I have no idea. But I intend to find out."

* * *

This will never end.

Guard duty, once so familiar, had become as strange as the rest of the world beyond Liwokin turned out to be. I'd done this job countless times, and the worst I ever dealt with were some unruly drunks and one scoundrel who tried to pull a knife on me but ended up with it jammed instead into his own belly. Nothing ever came close to plague-ridden monsters that blotted out the sun with clouds that clumped like coagulated blood. One constant that remained, however, was the boredom that came with such trivial work. For four days, no travelers came from the south. On the fifth day, only one cart rolled through, but it came from the north, leaving Canako and heading back toward Liwokin. By the time we'd finished debating whether we were meant to guard that direction, the cart had already passed.

After the relative excitement of the first two days of duty, my mind began to fray with memories of Andya and Wyran roiling around beneath the surface and occasionally, unexpectedly coming into full focus. With nothing else to distract me, I let the visions play out, hoping to learn something new about how the two others that shared my mind became the monsters we met. I learned little of importance, and even that came at a cost. The more I let myself become them, the less I felt like my own individual self.

A foolhardy boy and a diseased mother have taken up residence in my head. Not exactly how I pictured making new friends in this Agency.

I snorted.

"You okay?" Dunnax asked. How long had he been standing there?

I gave him a weary smile, then shook my head.

The Paceeqi grunted, crossed his arms, waiting for more. Inac and I had shared our revelation of a Benefactor creator with Garret and Dunnax, but no one could guess who it might have been. The only clues to work with came from Deluges, which it turned out Garret and Dunnax never had. We had no idea why that was the case, but after explaining to them what Deluges were, they considered the memories to be reliable information. Given that I had experienced more of the mysterious visions than anyone else, I became our expert on the subject.

Lot of good that does us, having an expert who's losing his mind.

"These Benefactors," I said. "They're changing me. Believe it or not, I liked who I was before. Now...I don't know."

Dunnax sighed. For once, he wasn't wearing his armor. "If it's any consolation, you don't seem much different to me. You're just as sarcastic and cynical as the day we met."

"Sarcastic? Me?" I grinned. "Sounds more like Garret."

The Paceeqi couldn't help but smile. "Yeah, well...you're not so bad as the Ekoan. And at least you respond with more than a grunt when I talk to you."

"Sentyx is all right. Must be hard for him, in a strange land with no one he knows in the Hand."

I winced as the words came out of my mouth. I could have said the same about Dunnax.

"I'm sorry," I said. "For getting Lorelay reassigned."

Dunnax closed his eyes, let the silence drag on. Then, he blew out a breath and smiled, shaking his head. "She called him *Linny*. The Bright Prince, our Kindling Emperor. Linny." He laughed. "She hasn't changed at all."

Is that...apology accepted?

"She's one of a kind," I said.

"Always has been," Dunnax said. "She never was one to blend in with a crowd."

"And what about you?" I asked, looking up at the huge Paceeqi. "Seems like it'd be easy for you to stand out."

"Too easy," he said. "With everyone's eyes on me, there was no room for mistakes. I played my part perfectly. Father allowed no less. I joined the Order, trained hard, always obeyed the rules. In a few years, I would have served in the Radiant Palace." A wistful smile crossed his face. "Sacrificing everything for the royal family, patrolling the gardens beneath those golden spires. It's the highest honor a Paladin can earn. It would have been mine..." He trailed off, looked toward the setting Brightdaughter.

"What happened?"

His lips twitched, the briefest flash of remorse. "Lorelay happened." He clenched his fists, bones showing through the skin of his knuckles. His jaw muscles worked. When he looked me in the eye, there was fear. "We fled from Paceeq. Now she's with the Bright Prince. If he realizes who she is, he won't let her out of his grasp."

The prince? He'd sooner claim her as his bride than harm her.

"She'll be safe," I said.

"She'd better be," Dunnax warned. "Because I'd still be able to protect her if not for you."

If she were with us instead of the prince, she'd be stuck killing monsters.

"Lorelay doesn't need your protection," I said. "Sounds more like you need her."

Dunnax started to protest but shut his mouth and turned away. He glanced toward the top of the hill, beyond which the sun had set. The Brightdaughter's light caught the sides of the Nobiko Peaks. Their long shadow lay across the valley and the canal. Ships flying colors bright and dark skirted that passage toward the ocean, setting out for the other countries of the Bright Empire. Lorelay might have been traveling home on one of those ships right now.

If she's lucky.

Just as the sky faded to a deep purple, the bells of dusk rolled up the hills from Canako. From the other direction came the sound of clacking horseshoes and rumbling wheels. A cart full of green-cloaked Fingers crested the steep hill, drawing Garret and Inac out from the gatehouse.

A young man disembarked, stood at attention in front of me, and saluted, his lanky arm swinging up to his ginger hair, above his pointed, acned face. "Hand Seventy-Two, reporting for duty." His voice cracked on the word 'duty,' and the Fingers with whom he'd arrived snickered at his embarrassment. The lot of them couldn't have had a year of combat experience between them. I flashed a blank look at Garret, who returned an equally blank stare.

The youth faltered in his salute and looked worryingly between each of us, staring back at him in silence. "Are you...are you the captain here?" he asked me.

"Me? No. Our captain ran off with the skull of some monster we stopped going through the gate."

The lad took a step back at that. Was the Agency so desperate for manpower that they were bringing on kids like this? It was a wonder they had passed Ulken's field test.

Or maybe this was supposed to be their test, and the Benefactor arrived too early.

"We were told to report to the captain," the boy Finger said.

"You're the captain now, kid," I said, walking past him to join Inac and Garret, already climbing aboard the cart the children arrived in. "Don't let any monsters through the gate."

Dunnax's armor clanged in his gathered pack with each of his tired stomps. "Three rules," he said. "Stop anyone who breaks them. No contraband, no criminals, no foreign persons without express written passports or...something like that. You'll figure it out."

The group of fresh Fingers started mumbling to one another as the cart shifted under the weight of the Paladin taking the driver's bench. He took hold of the reins, turned the cart around.

"How will we know if there's a monster?" the red-haired Finger shouted, voice cracking when the word 'monster' escaped his lips.

I gave him a hard look from the back of the cart. "You'll know," I said. "Remember what's real. Only that can kill you."

The reins snapped and the cart lurched into motion.

"Think you scared those boys half to death," Garret said, chuckling.

"Good," I said. "Being afraid is the first step to finding some courage."

CHAPTER FOURTEEN

The Price of Knowledge

We'd ridden throughout the night, not stopping even as Garret loosed a stream of piss off the back of the cart. After the endless tedium of guard duty, another command from Ulken would have been welcome, except that it'd mean killing another Benefactor. Who would be the next victim we slew? Some spurned lover who threw himself into the canyon? A Blightdweller who starved to death in their shanty?

I didn't have room for any more miserable memories.

I sighed, rubbed at my eyes trying to recall more details from Wyran's and Andya's Pools. Occasional visions surfaced, but I had no way to trigger them. When they did come, they were random flashes of their lives that made little sense out of context. What thread connected these two strangers? Trying to answer that by searching disjointed fragments was impossible. Recalling their memories was as hard as recalling my own—the more effort I put into the attempt, the more elusive they seemed.

"Any luck?" Garret asked.

I blinked, surfacing from the murky Pools. No warmth came today from the Brightdaughter, hiding as she was behind the cover of heavy clouds. Beneath the gray, the rolling stone hills of Lawiko splayed out before me. Far to the south, columns of dark smoke rose into the overcast sky. We were almost home.

"You hear me?" Garret asked.

"What?" It was hard to focus on the present when the past had become so much deeper.

"You two always get that faraway look when you do it," Garret said. "Find anything in those dead memories?"

I shrugged. "Andya came from a town west of Canako that was devastated by plague. Most died quickly, but she held on long."

"Too long," Inac said, and I couldn't say I disagreed.

"And Wyran was from the southern tip of Lawiko's Fertile Arm," I said. "About as far away as you can get from Andya's town. It doesn't make sense. How were both of them turned into Benefactors?"

"Andya was not turned to a Benefactor in her town," Inac said. "It was in the city."

"Liwokin?" My eyes widened as a memory of the boy's bubbled up. "Wyran was in the city too. His father took him there. But the person who stuck him with a needle wasn't the same one who stuck Andya."

Dunnax grunted. "Whoever created these monsters is working with someone?"

"Already knew there's a conspiracy," Garret said. "Reed, Oltrov, and that smuggler you let through the gate."

"What smuggler?" Dunnax whirled around from the driver's bench. The horses started to swerve before he stopped them from running off the road. "You disobeyed a command from Ulken?"

"I had a good reason," I said. Dunnax shook his head, as if doubting there could ever be a good enough reason for insubordination. "You think Reed helped create them? He works for the Agency."

Garret shrugged. "He's keeping his enemies within reach."

"Maybe his enemy created the Benefactors," Inac muttered. "Maybe it was Ulken."

"Ulken?" I asked. "I don't like him either, but he's trying to keep the Benefactors under control. If he helped create these monsters, why form the Agency to fight them?"

"I do not know." Inac fingered the bauble hanging from his neck. "But I think I felt an Aura in the Agency."

"That makes as much sense as a sabrederm riding a snout-bear," Garret said.

All our faces twisted in confusion.

Garret threw up his hands. "Makes no sense! How could Ulken be hiding a Benefactor in the Agency? Wouldn't we feel an Aura?"

"No," I said. "We wouldn't. The haze is covering it up."

Inac nodded. "No one knows like I do Archedark. That is how I sensed it."

"Dark magic all throughout the tower?" Dunnax asked. He spun around, grimacing. "We have to end that."

I chuckled. Finally, he had a good enough reason to disobey a superior.

"What?" Dunnax narrowed his eyes at me.

"Nothing," I said, smirking. "So, there's two conspiracies within the Agency. One group against another. Ulken's against Reed's." I gave a humorless laugh. "Think there's a third?"

"Aye," Garret said. He spat off the back of the cart and grinned. "Us."

* * *

"We are Rank Three," Sentyx said, by way of greeting us in the courtyard of the Agency.

"Great," Garret said. "Bigger, badder monsters to kill."

"How long have you been waiting here?" Dunnax asked.

The Skardwarf slowly turned toward the Paceeqi before answering. "Not long."

That told me nothing. Not long for a Skardwarf could mean days.

"You let Ulken know we killed another one?" I asked.

Sentyx grunted. "The Stink Cart."

Garret snorted. "Should have expected some name like that."

Sentyx eyed him in apparent confusion. "Smelled bad."

"I would have gone with the Plagued," I said, but he didn't know Andya's story. Really, it was more fitting to use their human names. That way, we wouldn't forget they were the victims in all this.

"What about the skull?" Dunnax asked.

Sentyx grunted again, then turned and began walking toward the tower's entrance.

"He means for us to follow him?" Inac asked, under his breath. "How rude he is to us."

Sentyx grunted a third time.

Garret smiled. "Skardwarves have good ears, Sentyx told me. Only way they can hear over the wind."

"That's not good," Dunnax said.

"Good ears?" I asked absently, distracted by the haze swirling around my feet, covering up what I now recognized as a Benefactor's Aura. An Aura that numbed the minds of everyone within these walls. I said nothing aloud. There was no telling who might overhear me. "Good ears. Useful for scouting."

Or listening for secrets.

"Not that," Dunnax said. "*That.*" He pointed at the count of remaining Benefactors.

Twenty. I grimaced. "Two more in one week?"

"Not counting any that were killed while we wasted our time guarding that outpost," Garret added.

"What was that about keeping them under control?" Inac asked. He gave me a knowing look. What had Reed's note said? *Ulken thinks they remain under control, but events have outpaced him.*

Two conspiracies among the Agency leadership and these monsters were multiplying faster than we can kill them. *But at least we've gotten a promotion.*

Sentyx led us up sixteen flights of stairs, down three separate corridors, and then to the fifth door on the left, which read, Evidence. Just before Sentyx reached the door, it flung back toward the Skardwarf and crashed into him, stopping as surely as if he had been a stone wall. Something broke with a crunch and several things hit the ground, followed by a loud groan on the other side. If a cart barreling down a hill carrying a Benefactor couldn't knock Sentyx over, no human could hope to do better. Sentyx grabbed the door's edge and stepped back, swinging it open.

One Heel awkwardly sat on the hazy floor, a broken box in his hands, while strange, chirping insects hopped in and out of the cloud around him. A second Heel frantically tried to capture the insects, but several had already leaped past Sentyx and out into the hallway to...well, not freedom, exactly.

"I am sorry," Sentyx said.

"Ulken will have me flayed for this," the sitting Heel said before an insect hopped onto his face and he let out a loud squeal.

We edged around the two gray-coats into the evidence lockup, careful not to tread on any hapless creatures while the Heels flailed their hands around beneath the haze, fruitlessly trying to catch them. All of this occurred while a disinterested-looking Organ watched with his elbows propped up on his desk, fists balled under his chin.

"That was the most entertainment I've had all measure," the Evidence administrator said to Sentyx. "I suppose you'll be wanting that skull back?"

Sentyx grunted.

"Follow me," he said, then stood and disappeared into a row of shelves that extended behind him so far it didn't seem like it should fit within the tower. Each shelf was packed with assortments of evidence, meticulously grouped by the number assigned to each Hand. We walked past two rows, the first of which contained bins marked with low numbers, overflowing with items. Blood-crusted knives, rusted chains, canvas sacks with who-knows-what inside. Among the rest were vials of blood, bundles of hair, utensils with dried saliva and bits of moldy food still affixed, and more. What did the Agency need with so many bodily fluids? The second row held emptier bins with the same kinds of items, and the third row, which we now followed the Organ through, was populated by bins that were all empty, save for one. Ours, marked with a big, black and white 64 contained the sole item in the row: the blackened skull of Andya.

The Organ picked it up and asked, "Whose skull was this anyway?"

"Benefactor," Sentyx said, and the Organ flinched and tossed the skull at the Skardwarf as if it had suddenly caught on fire. Sentyx's hand shot out and effortlessly nabbed it from the air, pulling it close as the mystery object inside produced its telltale rattle.

"You know what the thing inside it is?" Garret asked.

"Do I look like a mortician to you?" The Organ said.

A mortician? Why did that sound familiar?

"Ask Tak, or one of his technicians."

"Who?" Dunnax asked.

"Tak, our lead mortician. He's in the mortuary, naturally."

"Which is where?"

"Well...I don't know," the Organ looked surprised by this. "Check with the Organ in the Directory."

Silence for a moment, then I spoke. "Which is...where?"

"You don't know where the Directory is?" he said, laughing. "Well, it's...um...next to Navigation." The Organ tapped his chin thoughtfully. "I suppose you don't know where that is either." I shook my head. "Well, best of luck, gentlemen. I have urgent business to attend to." He squeezed past us, straightening a bin he knocked out of alignment, and shuffled back to his desk. When we left the room, he refused to look me in the eye, choosing instead to stare down at his desk, which was conspicuously empty.

*　*　*

Finding the Directory proved easy once we found Navigation. Unfortunately, finding Navigation took the better part of the span between noon and half-dusk. Nevertheless, we found our way down to the mortuary, which involved leaving the tower, entering a side door, and descending a dark, twisting staircase. The tower delved underground nearly as far as it rose over Liwokin. In spots, Dunnax's bulging armor scraped the uneven stone walls, which closed in tighter and tighter the deeper and deeper we went. The spiral depths seemed never-ending, until a sour smell permeated the air and announced the nearing of our destination.

When the stairs bottomed out, the ceiling of the passageway that stretched before us hung so low we needed to proceed at a crouch. We trod forward slowly, until the sound of unmelodious humming leaked from the crack under a closed door marked by a crooked, fading sign that read, Mortuary. At Garret's touch, the door creaked open to reveal a vast, sweltering chamber, one wall stacked to the ceiling with urns, the other pocked by open mouths of fire. Between the two was a stone slab attended by a half-lit man, hunched over at work. Two of the red-cloaks who wore masks like birds' beaks hovered over his shoulder. The orange glow illuminating the three radiated from the flames of cremation, the only source of light in the room.

The hunched and humming man had been probing a bloody corpse, but at our sudden intrusion he ceased. Lifting his goggles to his shock of gray hair revealed thick spectacles. He turned and studied us for a moment, then wiped his hands on his heavy black apron and clasped them together with a clap. "Visitors," he said, "it's so rare to see another face. Apart from those of the dead, of course." He chuckled, then paused, waiting for one of us to speak.

"What about them?" Garret asked. The masked red-cloaks turned toward each other, expressionless eyes showing through fogging goggles.

"My technicians? I've forgotten what they look like beneath those masks." One technician's head drooped, pointed mask aiming at the ground.

"You must be Tak then," Dunnax said.

"Ah," the man tutted and shook his head, wild gray hair flinging off beads of moisture. "Apologies for my lack of manners. As I said, I don't receive many visitors. Allow me to introduce myself. I am Taktus, lead mortician of the Agency, but as you have already discerned, most refer to me simply as Tak." The mortician bowed, caught the spectacles that fell from his face, and replaced them in front of his eyes with a bright smile. "What brings you to my dark domain, here in the bowels of the Agency?"

"Show him the skull, Sentyx," I said.

Sentyx held out Andya's skull, and Tak took it in hand. The lead mortician turned it over, shook it and listened to the rattling, nodding and humming while his technicians scribbled notes behind him.

"I see, I see," Tak said, wiping the skull's char on his apron and producing a hollow knock with the rap of his knuckle. "This is indeed a skull. Human, I surmise, but you know that. Nothing out of the ordinary as far as I can tell. Why come down all those steps only to show me this?"

"Nothing out of the ordinary?" Garret asked. "What about that walnut bouncing around inside?"

"The seedling?" Tak said, taken aback. "What's odd about that? All civilized beings possess them." The mortician placed two fingers on his head, just above and behind his left ear. "It rests right here, nestled snugly within the folds of brain matter."

Upon learning this, it seemed I could feel the seedling inside my own head. *Funny how the mind plays tricks on the body.*

"Never heard of it," Garret said. "What does it do?"

A broad smile lit up Tak's face and he held out his hand to the side, palm up, as if expecting something. His technician started, then flipped rapidly through his book of notes before landing on a page and slapping the book into Tak's hand. The mortician adjusted his spectacles with Andya's skull and began to read. "Seedling. Found in all civilized beings, not Peekers." Tak whipped to face his technician. "Why is 'not Peekers' written here? You already noted 'all civilized beings'. No need to repeat yourself." He sighed, turned to Sentyx. "Meaning no offense."

"I am no Peeker," the Skardwarf said.

"Right, I only meant that Skardwarves too...well, never mind. Where was I? Oh yes. Located in the left temporal lobe. Good, good. Multiple functions. Negates Aura. Regulates human pattern. Yes, ah! You forgot to note that it amplifies the Aura of an Emergent Benefactor." Tak tossed the book over his shoulder, pages flailing in the air as the book came apart at the seams. The technician grumbled and stooped to pick up his notes. "Er, sorry about that." The mortician cleared his throat. "Anyway, quite how any of these functions are accomplished remains unknown to us."

I glanced around to see if anyone else understood what Tak was talking about. If we were to defeat these Benefactors, we'd need to extract as much knowledge as we could from this expert. "So, this seedling," I said, "it protects us from Benefactor Auras? Why did that skull have one then? It came from a dead Benefactor."

"Oh, my!" Tak tossed the skull into the air just as the Organ upstairs had, only this time we had learned our lesson, and no one deigned to catch it.

Brittle from Dunnax's Fire, the skull shattered as it hit the stone floor, spilling out the seedling for us to look upon. It really did look like a walnut, or perhaps a dried out, miniature version of a brain. A technician hurried away, then quickly returned with long metal tongs and a glass container, used the utensil to pick up the seedling, and sealed it inside, screwing the lid on tight. He held out the sample for Tak to take, extended arm trembling while the mortician ignored him.

"Thank you, very good," Tak said as the other technician began sweeping the pieces of bone into a dark hole in the wall. "As

I said, the Emergent Benefactor uses this seedling to strengthen its own Aura. I have proposed that it can do this because of the seedling's function in preserving the human pattern." Tak frowned, fuzzy gray eyebrows closing to a near-touch above his spectacles. "I see that you're confused. Think of the human pattern as an Aura that each of us has, much weaker than an Emergent Benefactor's, but which preserve the normal functioning of our minds."

"We all have our own Auras?" Dunnax asked. "Why don't we feel them like we do a Benefactor's?"

"An excellent question. That is because the human pattern has an aspect of Archefire." Dunnax looked somewhat proud upon learning this. "Conversely, the Emergent Benefactor produces an Aura attuned to Archedark. In fact, the discovery of the human pattern is thanks to the sudden appearance of Benefactors. Only by finding a phenomenon that breaks our expectations can we learn something new." Now Inac nodded, flashed a grin at Dunnax. "I must say, while this ordeal with the Benefactors has been terrible, it has certainly advanced our understanding of how the human mind works, quite considerably so." Garret, for his part, seemed to find this convincing. Sentyx did as Sentyx always did and grunted.

"What about animals?" Garret asked. "None of Eko's biotists have ever noted an animal Aura."

Tak considered this. "As far as I'm aware, no animals contain a seedling. But perhaps some of the more intelligent species produce an Aura by a different means, such as Peekers and Skardwarves do to preserve their patterns."

Meaning Peekers and Skardwarves weren't safe from Benefactors either. I eyed Sentyx, an uncomfortable weight settling on me. This scourge really could take over the whole world.

"Skardwarf pattern?" Sentyx asked.

"Indeed," Tak said. "All living creatures have patterns, with some more closely aligned than others."

"Might explain why certain animals have affinities for one another," Garret said.

One of Tak's morticians nodded vigorously. "I proposed that same theory!" she blurted out from behind her mask. "Over time, as species interact, their patterns could become more closely aligned, such as happened with horses and dogs." Garret nodded along, as excited by the theory as the mortician. "That was, of course, because of humans bringing them together more of—"

"Arza, please," Tak said, waving her idea away. "These Fingers have no time for wild ideas. They need information backed by evidence. We have yet to discover any creature but a human that has become an Emergent Benefactor."

"Why do you keep calling them *Emergent* Benefactors?" I asked.

"Simply to distinguish them from Incubating Benefactors," Tak said. "Ulken only commands Fingers to eliminate Emergent Benefactors, so I can see why the distinction might escape you. But where do you think those Emergent Benefactors come from? Incubating Benefactors, of course! The humans who are poised to become Emergent Benefactors when they die. Now, the next question is logical. Where do Incubating Benefactors come from? This," and Tak chuckled, "is a question to which I have no answer. I fear that too is quite a mystery."

Finally, something I know more about than the expert.

I scratched my neck. A phantom sensation of being pricked with a needle surfaced from someone's Pool of memories. I froze, suddenly remembering why 'mortician' sounded familiar. Andya's injections were performed by a mortician. I narrowed my eyes at Tak. "How did you learn all this?"

"The Agency has produced plenty of work for me, which I can't complain about, though I daresay my subjects might voice some complaints. If they still had voices to complain with, that is." I grimaced at the notion of becoming one of his subjects myself. "Ulken commanded me to learn about Benefactors, presumably so that we may find a way to stop them."

Or Ulken sees Benefactors as useful tools and needs you to tell him how to use them.

"I must confess, however, that my research has hit a rather... dead end." The mortician chuckled. "I fear I have learned all there is to learn from these deceased subjects." I looked over at the wall where stacked urns reached the ceiling of this vast room. The Benefactors provided him with no end of subjects, and the mortician had been hard at work in his research, indeed. "What I need is a *living* specimen. Meaning, a live, Incubating Benefactor."

"You want for your research a living person to torture?" Inac asked, looking at the mortician's latest subject, face twisting as if Andya had returned. The corpse had been dissected and taken apart, organs and entrails lying beside it on the messy stone slab.

"Torture?" Tak laughed nervously. "Who said anything about torture? I assure you my research would be quite humane." The mortician lowered his voice in a conspiratorial tone. "Of course, the Agency would not view this in a favorable light, but I would be willing to pay you handsomely if you—"

"We're not even discussing this," Dunnax said.

"Yeah," Garret said. "Too risky. You want us to sneak an Incubating Benefactor into the Agency under Ulken's watch?"

"Oh, certainly not," Tak said, faking offense. Then, he lowered his voice again. "I have a private laboratory in the Burg." Tak retrieved a dirty slip of paper from his apron pocket and found a pen on the stone slab. Lacking ink, he dipped it in the blood that pooled upon the slab, scrawled an address, and handed the slip to me.

"You're lucky if we don't report this to the Head right now," Dunnax said, and stormed out. Inac followed, but only after giving me a transparently pleading look.

"Go ahead," Tak muttered as they left. "Tell Ulken. The Head knows I am essential to the Agency's work." He waved to dismiss them, though they had already gone. "You three seem willing, at least. Consider how freely I've given you the knowledge discovered through my research. Would a small favor be such an unfair trade?"

"Favor doesn't seem so small to me," Garret said, "but fair's fair."

I fidgeted with Tak's note. Anyone we brought to Tak likely would meet a grisly end. But if the Benefactors continued to spread, we all would meet that grisly end. What was one Incubating Benefactor compared to tens of thousands of Liwo? The man was practically dead already. If Tak could pry some decisive new secret of the Benefactors from him, wouldn't that sacrifice be worth it?

"How would we find an Incubating Benefactor anyway?" I asked.

Tak smiled. "I happen to have received word of a certain highwayman who arrived just yesterday in the city."

*　*　*

When the door to the morbid room shut behind us, Dunnax's clanking armor came echoing from the end of the cramped hallway. We hurried to catch up to the Paladin and the mage. When we reached them, halfway up the stairwell, the argument began.

"Grim," Inac demanded, "tell to me you are not considering this."

I looked away from my friend, but I'd made my decision.

Sorry to disappoint you, but disappointment is a small price to pay for saving Liwokin.

"He doesn't have to tell you anything," Dunnax said. "He has no say. We're not handing over an innocent person for this guy to kill."

"Innocent?" Garret snorted. "He wants us to bring him a bandit. World's better off with him dead, I say."

Better off dead.

Memories washed through me, surfacing new understanding from Andya's and Wyran's Pools. Their pain at the end was immense. Both were simply waiting to die, for their nightmares to end. Instead, their deaths unleashed a new nightmare on the world. That was how it happened.

Benefactors became Emergent when the Incubating died.

I caught myself holding my breath. I'd stopped and been left behind, so I raced up the spiral stairs to catch up to the shouting. "He wouldn't kill him," I said. "He can't kill an Incubating Benefactor. Otherwise, it would become Emergent, a monster in the city. He knows that."

I hope.

Everyone went quiet, perhaps trying to understand what I meant without their own Pools of the dead to draw from.

"I do not trust him," Inac said. "He works for Ulken."

"Don't trust him either," Garret said, "but so do you."

Inac huffed.

"What do you think?" Dunnax asked Sentyx.

The Skardwarf grunted and waited a long time before responding with another cryptic southern saying. "Winds shift. Shards fly."

We soon reached the top of the stairs and emerged into the courtyard where someone could have overhead us, so the argument ended with that. Dunnax sullenly turned away from us.

"What are we to do now?" Inac asked. "Can we leave this place? It reminds to me too much of my apprenticeship with the Sage. It is hard to say whose tower is more unpleasant."

"We'll be out in the field soon enough," I said. "But first we need to get a new command from Ulken." I started toward the entrance, then stopped when a Nerve jaunted down the steps to alter the Benefactor count. The white-and-gold coat obscured my sight of the sign as I approached. When she stepped away and ran back inside, I froze in place. "Six?" A chill ran down my back, tingling like the onset of a Deluge.

"Unlikely," Sentyx said of the new Benefactor count, and I agreed. Even this basic information was a lie. Was there nothing we could trust?

"More or less likely than hiding a Benefactor in there?" Garret asked.

"You see?" Inac said, folding his arms. "Ulken cannot be—"

"Keep quiet," Dunnax said, leaning in close. "Both of you. The Head has ears all over this place."

I scanned the courtyard. Heels swarmed all around, busy as flies on corpses.

"These unmindful Heels hear from us nothing we say," Inac said. "The Aura has sapped their will like the Brightdaughter saps the Sea Pot waters."

Maybe he was right, but at that very moment a group composed not of Heels, but of Fingers entered the courtyard. Muy Fuy, Lorelay, and two brutish looking fighters—identical twins save for the number of hideous scars they bore across their faces—trailed behind Bengard. An unlikely Hand, all things considered. Were we the only ones who didn't get shuffled around repeatedly?

"...not the first Aura of panic I've ever encountered," Bengard said, "and you'll have Tears this time, but don't think that means it isn't serious. Tears only mask so much, and I don't aim to lose any more Fingers because you can't stop from breaking formation and running."

Muy Fuy looked like he was about to run away just hearing about this monster. "You'll tell us what to do though, right?" The young Archemage's voice quavered. "You've more experience than the rest of us combined."

Bengard laughed. "That's true, but I need you thinking on your feet. A good Finger knows when to act even without commands. Looker said this one's small, but it could still be the one that kills any of us. Even me."

Muy Fuy didn't seem reassured by that, but Bengard failed to notice. Lorelay slapped the boy on his back and whispered something that made the Archemage laugh. Bengard paid no attention, instead bounding over to greet us.

His eyes went wide at the nearby sign. "Six to go! Can you believe it?"

No.

"There's hope we'll win this fight yet. Can you feel it? Something big is going on. I haven't seen the Agency alive like this since the early days."

"Seems normal to me," I said. "What's going on, you think?"

"Beats me," Bengard said, stretching his huge arms out above him and leaning back until his spine gave a satisfying crack. "But the Heels have more urgency in their step, can't you see it? The Head knows how to whip them into action. I only hope we don't miss it. Just ran into Jacquin and Ulken in the Burg and got a command the Head said to handle quickly. We're only here to requisition some Tears before heading out."

"You're taking Lorelay with you?" Dunnax asked and regarded his sister. "How did you even get back here? We didn't see you go through the gate."

"Took a boat," Lorelay said, shrugging. "I couldn't very well take a *normal* carriage like you lesser lot, not after traveling in style with the prince." A playful smile spread across the Paceeqi girl's face.

"See," I said to Dunnax. "Told you she'd be fine."

The scarred twins looked completely bored by this conversation. The uglier one played with the haft of his broad axe as if he wanted to start the killing right away. His twin—still ugly, but at least this one's nose remained intact—had a finger up his nostril, deep in concentration, as if searching for his brain.

Not that it takes one of those to become a Finger.

"Ulken's not in his office?" I asked.

Bengard shook his head. "They were heading toward Reed's place, I think." I resisted the urge to shoot a suspicious glance at my companions. "Not sure where the First Eye's been lately. Maybe they're looking for him."

"Thanks," I said. "We'll see if we can catch up with him. Good luck with the Benefactor. Small one, you said?"

"According to our Eye."

"Good luck anyway."

Dunnax wrapped his sister in a metal embrace. "Be careful."

"You worry too much," Lorelay said, but there was worry on her face too.

* * *

The door to Reed's home hung loose on the hinges. Someone had kicked it in. The house seemed abandoned, until there was movement inside the window. I led the Hand through the open door, careful not to make too much noise. There was no telling whether the silhouette inside was Ulken, one of his lackeys, or some random thief who'd chanced upon a good opportunity. Of course, our element of surprise was doomed to be spoiled before long, since we had a Paladin clad in heavy armor with us.

Dunnax bumped into a table and knocked a potted flower to the ground, vase shattering and sending dirt across the floor.

"Who's there?" an angry voice shouted from the other room. A short man in a blue Eye's coat stepped out, orange-red hair poking out beneath his rounded cap. A well-groomed beard framed his face, matching the thin mustache that sat over lips pressed tight. His hand gripped the hilt of his sword, partly drawn, showing a fraction of his steel. "Identify yourselves."

I showed him my palms. "We're no threat, Eye. We're Hand Sixty-Four."

The Eye narrowed his gaze. The guard on his hilt snapped back against the scabbard, and he smiled, no trace of suspicion remaining on his face. "My apologies. I should have recognized you. What brings you here?"

"Looking for Ulken," I said.

"He's out in the field," the Eye said.

Inac snorted. "Out in the field? The old man has decided to get himself killed by a monster?"

"Watch your tongue, Finger, or it will see you debarred from this institution." The Eye's face was back to hard rage. "And never underestimate Ulken. He's shepherded this city through unspeakable turmoil. One Benefactor won't be enough to do him in." His posture relaxed and his face became neutral once more. It seemed the Eye had only two modes: calm neutrality or flaring emotions. Perhaps such emotional turbulence was the mark of too much time spent in a Benefactor's Aura. "In any case, I can speak for him. I'm First Eye Jacquin, so speak your—"

"Uh," Garret said, the ranger's eyes narrowing as if lining up a distant shot. "Isn't Reed the First Eye?"

Jacquin eyes glistened, lips curled down, as if he were about to cry. "You haven't heard? I...I'm sorry to tell you this. Reed is dead."

Curious that a man who so plainly wore his emotions on his face could tell such a lie without breaking character. The liar looked infinitely confused by our disbelieving silence. He decided digging a deeper hole was the right approach.

"Yes, I see you're as shocked by this news as I was. Three Peekers, highwaymen on the western road, killed the poor fellow. Ulken got there in time to help Reed fight them off and together they killed two of the villains, but the First Eye suffered grievous injuries. There was nothing the Head could do to prevent his friend from perishing, but Ulken managed to capture the last surviving Peeker and bring him back to the city for questioning."

"Right," Garret said. "Highwaymen. Three Peekers, even though they always come in pairs. Makes sense."

"You don't believe me." Jacquin's eyes went wide with such shock as would fit the Brightdaughter not rising at dawn. "It is... quite difficult to believe, I understand. But Ulken explained the situation himself when he chose me to replace Reed. If you're suggesting that Ulken lied to me—"

"Wouldn't dream of it," Garret said. "Never met anyone more trustworthy than our Head." Garret's tone had the edge of sarcasm, but it slipped past Jacquin. Some Eye he was.

"Good," Jacquin said. "Well then, take the rest of the day to gather yourselves then return to the Agency at noon tomorrow for your next command. You're dismissed."

The five of us stalked away without returning the crisp salute Jacquin gave. I held out a hand to slow Garret down until we lagged far enough behind the other three to speak privately.

I kept my voice down. "That highwayman Ulken brought back is the same as Tak told us about. I'd bet my life on it."

"If he exists," Garret said.

"What say we pay him a visit tonight, just the two of us? We'll find out if he's real, get some answers, and do that mortician a favor."

"Just the two of us," Garret said, nodding.

"Three," Sentyx said. The Skardwarf had stopped and turned around while Dunnax and Inac walked on.

Garret chuckled. "He did warn us he had good ears."

CHAPTER FIFTEEN

Mental War

The three of us arrived in a seedy part of the Artisans District well after the somber chime of dusk. An occasional pair of guards patrolled the cramped streets, casually conversing. Their torchlight announced their arrival like a herald and sent pickpockets scurrying like rats. So long as they took their time meandering around the district, they would never find any crime; it would hover at the periphery of their vision. After all, this wasn't the Old District, where crime found you like an old acquaintance whom you disliked, but who always seemed eager to make up for lost time. The distant cracks of flintlock pistols made sure most steered clear from this part of the city; no one sane wanted to be caught in this area after dark. But those confined to our destination were not sane.

And when did what we want ever matter?

In a desolate plaza, a shallow staircase led up to a boxy, behemoth structure. Grimy limestone bricks and mortar, piled one upon the other, jutted toward the dark heavens as though the building were trying to claw its way free from the city. On the dim frontal exterior, a hanging wooden sign swung in some ethereal breeze. Liwokin Mental Ward, it read, though the last letter and most of the city's name had been scratched out to near illegibility. Where the stone met shale at the lid of the building, a greasy black mold crept down like weeping blood. Dirt streaks marred the entire surface. Chunks of stone here and there had eroded away entirely. From barred windows on the second and third stories drifted the dull moans of dazed patients, crying out wordlessly in their medicated misery.

If someone were to become a Benefactor here... I shuddered at the thought.

We climbed the stairs to the entrance, where torchlight cut through the grainy shadow to reveal a rusted double-door with equally rusted hinges. I pushed hard and the door gave a loud wail; its echoes filled an empty lobby. Once inside, the door began to close on its own, struggling against its own hinges, which screamed like one of the patients of the ward. The piercing sound grew louder and higher pitched, digging into my skull. I slammed the door shut and the thump reverberated down the long, barren halls.

A lone receptionist's desk sat unattended with no one there to greet us. Garret vaulted over the desk and began rifling through the drawers.

"Listen," Sentyx said, and Garret looked up, tilted his head, then slammed the desk shut. He vaulted back across the desk to rejoin us just as clicking footsteps began descending from the second floor. A woman's voice followed, muttering to herself. She appeared, clothed in stained white, with a rumpled brown cap on her head. She brushed the creases from the front of her dress as she reached ground level, quickly made her way behind the desk, and flopped ignominiously into the chair, grumbling all the while.

"Which one of you's getting checked in?" the nurse said. She looked at Garret. "You? Ekoans never last long in this city before going mad."

"And Liwo never last long in Graln," Garret said. "Don't go mad, though. Just fall straight to the forest floor."

"No one's getting checked in," I said. We had hoped to sneak in here undetected—if Ulken found out we were here, he'd kill us all, and the receptionist too, most likely—but that door had been a more effective alarm than any bell-wielding guard.

"You all must be mad then, coming here in this beat. Not that that wailing gets any better by day. I've got rounds to make. So kindly tell me why you're here or get out." The nurse tried to make an angry face, but her trembling lip gave away what she really felt. Exhaustion.

"Are you okay?" Sentyx asked.

"Am I—" a strange expression crossed the nurse's face, as though she were about to shout. "No, I'm not okay. These patients wail and wail all day until they get their medication. Some don't stop even then, but I can't give them any more." She waved her hands, rolled her eyes. "Council regulations. Like they know better than me what our patients need." She scoffed. "By the time I get to the end of a wing, the beginning is back to wailing again, and I just have to move on to the next, because there's no one else to help and they need my care too." The nurse rubbed her eyes. "My feet hurt. My head hurts. My back hurts. But after all the wings are tended to, there's no time to rest before starting again. One day I'm going to check *myself* in to a room."

"I can help," Sentyx said.

The nurse's eyes widened, glistened with the start of tears. "No one's ever offered to help before." She wiped her eyes, shook her head. "No, I can't let you. You don't have medical training."

"I do," Sentyx said.

Garret and I glanced at each other. If Sentyx was lying, neither of us could tell.

The nurse let out a short laugh. "Really? Well, all right then. Wait, what did you come here for again?"

I shook my head. "It can wait. Sentyx, meet us later." I walked to the door with Garret.

The Skardwarf grunted and let himself be pulled by the elbow up the stairs, one happy nurse chattering in his ear about doses and procedures and some other jargon. I pulled the door open so the nurse would think we'd gone, let it go through the effort of pulling itself shut, grating my teeth against the aural assault. Before it finished closing, Garret was already back behind the desk, searching through the nurse's papers. He laid a thick, leather-bound book atop the flat desk and opened it up, leafing through the pages, starting at the back.

"You can read?" I asked.

"'Course I can read," Garret said, scanning the pages with frightening speed. "It's writing I can't do."

"You can skewer a hare at five hundred paces, but you can't scratch letters on the page?"

"You aim a bow with your arm. My wrist won't do the motions right." His finger poked at the book. "Here, got him. Name is Pinch. First floor, H wing, room two-thirty-one."

"Come on. The quicker we're out of this madhouse the better."

"You go," Garret said, still searching the book. "I'll catch up."

* * *

The hallway I started down was marked by a moldy sign that read, 'Wings A - J', but beyond that the place was nearly as confusing to navigate as the Agency, with room numbers smudged or rusted over. The ward was so full it seemed every mad Liwo resided within these halls. Striding down the dimly lit hallways, I peered inside several rooms. Most contained motionless figures lying on beds—impossible to tell whether they were dead or peacefully slumbering. A couple writhed in their beds, slumbering, but definitely not peacefully. The rooms that weren't pitch black were candlelit, the dancing flames casting distorted shadows of shambling patients on the walls' flaking paint. Many patients rambled incoherently, perhaps replaying in their minds a part of their lives that immersed them in better times, before they wound up in this cold, forgotten place. Worst were the patients who screamed incessantly, as if possessed by some demon of the abyss. Their chilling cries filled these fetid halls.

At last, I came to the room with our target. The door was unlocked. Ulken wasn't concerned with his prisoner escaping. Entering the room, it was clear why. A long metal board with lightwood wheels at one end and handles at the other stood propped up at an angle against the back wall. Rope so thoroughly bound a Peeker to this device that, apart from his rounded triangular head, only his three-toed feet were visible, poking out near the wheels. He took notice of me when I entered the room, but he looked on with glassy eyes and didn't seem to comprehend anything.

Peeker pairs were common in Liwokin—their city in the Mound was the most populous city in the Empire, after all— but this was my first time seeing one up close. Their ubiquitous almond-hued skin was actually a thick crop of stiff hairs, which I imagined would feel bristly to the touch. I reached forward to test the theory, then stopped. With those over-sized eyes locked on me, it didn't feel right. This was a person, not a piece of furniture, despite the callousness with which most Liwo treated them.

"You didn't kill him, did you?" I asked. "The First Eye. Blue coat. Fuzzy mustache. Sound familiar?"

It tilted its head like a curious puppy. Perhaps it didn't speak my language, or maybe the Head had already had it lobotomized.

"You don't look like a bandit." Maybe I had the wrong Peeker, but how many could there have been in this place?

"Pinch? That you?" I sighed. "Anyone in there?"

The Peeker's eyelids closed from the sides in a slow blink. It made a quiet, chittering sound with its crescent-like mandibles that sounded like a purring cat.

"This is a dead end," I said, but as soon as I turned to make for the door, the Peeker began straining against the rope that bound it.

It let out a phlegmy cough and shouted, "This one will give its a snuffing dead end! This one didn't kill that blue-coated, mustached bastard, but wishes to have had the pleasure."

I whirled. The Peeker's eyes had filled with life, as if its spirit had just entered its body—a murderous spirit indeed. Its mandibles clicked as its head snapped out, trying to bite me. I flinched away, then spun again as the door crashed open and Garret rolled in another Peeker on a gurney. It was restrained in the same way as Pinch but didn't fight for freedom. It shivered as Garret lay the second stretcher on the floor, kicking the door shut behind him.

"Heard it yelling out in the hall," Garret said, laughing. "That's one mean Peeker. I saw two in the book, wasn't sure which it'd be. Guess we know now."

I looked down at the second Peeker. It began whimpering, whipping its head around as if trying to prevent someone from spooning food into its mouth. Bubbles foamed around its mandibles as it groaned. Was just entering this room bringing it pain?

"It didn't say anything until you got here," I said.

Garret grunted. "A lone Peeker is more useless than an arrow without feathers. Need to pair them up to get their brains working right."

"When this one is through with it, *its* brain won't be working right!" Pinch yelled, then went back to chewing at its restraints.

"They're...connected?" I asked.

"One brain in two bodies," Garret said. "How I've always heard it."

That made sense of the other Peeker's gurgling. A murdering psychopath had become half of their shared mind. If connecting with another Peeker felt anything like receiving a Benefactor's Deluge, it must have been terrified.

"It can't keep this one here," Pinch said around the rope in its mandibles. "It's dead when this one gets free." But its resolve faded fast. Mad or not, you could only struggle for so long without accomplishment before giving up. Garret and I looked on at the Peeker's piteous attempts at escape.

I crossed my arms. "Is 'this one' done yet?"

Pinch stared at me, breathing heavy.

"Tell us what happened to Reed," I said. "The First Eye. If he's not dead, where is he?"

Pinch growled. "This one wishes to have killed it. But the human died by its own hand."

"What?"

"Liar." Garret spat.

"That one is not lying," the whimpering Peeker said. Its eyes were wide open, but I couldn't quite place the expression. The Peeker's face moved more freely than a Skardwarf's, but its anatomy was far less human.

"Killed itself," Pinch said, clicking noises coming from its throat that might have been laughs. "Why doesn't it untie this one and do the same to itself? That's the best it can hope for once this one escapes. This one will not show mercy."

"Think we'll take our chances," Garret said.

Trading insults with Pinch wasn't getting us anywhere. "You're right," I said. "He deserved to die. But why did you want to kill him? What did he do to you?"

Pinch's expression shifted, and it loosed a spray of spittle that hit me square in the chest.

"This is useless, Grim. Let's just get him to Tak. He'll dig some answers out of his head."

It was hard to feel sorry for what was going to happen to Pinch. Whatever evils Tak was about to perform, the Peeker probably deserved them.

"The human killed that one's brothers," the second Peeker said. "A pair of pairs called itself brothers. Ridiculous. All ones come from the same mother."

I smiled at Garret. "It's drawing from the other Peeker's memories."

"Shut up!" Pinch snarled.

I crouched down to the other Peeker. After the initial terrifying connection, it had calmed down. "What's your name?"

"One's name is not important. Only the collective. But other humans have called this one Tunnel."

"Tunnel." I nodded. "What else do you know?"

"Only what that one remembers clearly. Bandit brothers, those were. But no more. That one is the only remaining."

"How did that happen?"

Tunnel hummed and his head twitched. "Those attacked the blue coated one." Tunnel looked up at Pinch. "Foolish. Those deserve what those got. The collective has no room for anger."

Pinch growled and fought its restraints with renewed vigor.

"Jacquin said Reed and Ulken both fought off the bandits," I said. "Were there any other humans in the fight?"

"No. One human."

So Jacquin had lied. Or he'd believed Ulken's lies.

Tunnel twitched again. "But wait. One more human, later. Not fighting. Pleading."

"Who could that be?" I asked.

"Doesn't sound like Ulken," Garret said.

"That is when the blue-coat did it," Tunnel said. "A knife to its own heart. This one sees it clearly. Like it's happening right—"

Someone had been pleading with Reed before he took his own life? Something wasn't adding up.

"Uh, Grim."

Pinch went still, but Tunnel started squirming, panicking, screaming at the top of its lungs. It started shouting for help, shouting that it was going to be eaten, shouting that it would kill everyone in this room. Pinch cackled with chittering laughter. Any more of this and the nurse would be here in moments.

"Think we're done here," Garret said, grabbing Tunnel's gurney.

"Meet me at Tak's," I said, avoiding Pinch's snapping mandibles as I went for the handles to wheel him out.

We left the room and ran in separate directions. As Tunnel's screaming faded, Pinch quieted down as if drifting off to sleep.

* * *

"It's dead, human! Dead!" Pinch shouted in my ear.

I jumped at the sudden noise. The Peeker had been quiet for some time now, and I'd started to doze off while waiting for Garret to arrive. I glanced at each end of the dark alley to make sure no one else heard Pinch. Two figures were striding toward me, wheeling another ahead of them.

"What took you so long?" I asked.

"Wouldn't be easy sneaking a Peeker through the city in this darkness if I knew how to find an address," Garret said. "I got lost. Sentyx spotted me darting from alley to alley. Not sure how you know how to navigate this place."

Sentyx grunted. "I studied city maps."

Garret scoffed. "Who needs maps?" The irony was lost on him.

"Why'd you bring Tunnel?" I asked.

"That one will suffer with the humans," Pinch snarled. "Does that one hear?"

Garret ignored him. "Already edited both their records. Figured, why not?"

"You edited their records?" I asked. "I thought you couldn't write."

Garret shrugged. "Can't, but it was easy enough to splash ink across the page."

"Its bones will adorn this one's hearth," Pinch said. "Its skull will be mounted over this one's door."

"We need to shut it up," I said. "Get Tunnel out of those restraints, Sentyx. Tak doesn't need two for his experiment."

Sentyx snapped the ropes binding Tunnel with little effort. Tunnel slumped forward onto Sentyx. The Peeker was unconscious, but that didn't stop Pinch's mind from working. The Skardwarf lifted the little Peeker up as easily as if he were holding a baby. "I will take this one."

"Where?"

"The colony," Sentyx said, and walked away. I didn't bother shouting after him. Once the Skardwarf's mind was made up, there was little hope in changing it.

"The colony? He's not going all the way to the Peeker Mound, is he?" Garret asked, as Pinch's growling and thrashing mercifully ceased.

I shrugged. "Let's see if Tak is still awake." I poked my head out of the alley to check for guards. There weren't likely to be any in the Burg this long after dusk, but it wouldn't do to have Ulken learning what we'd done by finding his Fingers in the stockades. The long street was clear, so I rolled the gurney up to Tak's door and propped it against the wall, then knocked.

In no time at all, the mortician opened the door wide, standing against a backdrop of strange lab equipment. I leaned to the side for a look at the eccentric furniture filling the house. Bulging glass containers, metal pipes spewing hot steam, a variety of polished utensils—many with serrated edges—and a technician sitting asleep in the corner.

Asleep? Or had Tak worked him to death?

Tak looked delighted. "Come in, come in." The mortician gestured into his abode. "I didn't expect you to arrive so soon. The lab is a bit of a mess, but I just brewed a kettle of tea." I followed him inside, pulling his test subject behind me. Tak lifted a kettle from his fireplace, which burned with bright green fire, casting Tak's shadow in a ghostly tinge on the matte stone walls. "Would you care for a cup?" The green flame sputtered and shot up ashes into the fireplace. The mortician sipped at his own cup, wincing at the heat.

"Don't think so," I said, stomach churning at the mixed scents of spiced tea and acrid chemicals. "We're not staying long. Here's your test subject. What will—"

"A Peeker!" Tak said, nearly spilling his tea as he bounded over to look him over from all angles. "How marvelous! Most unexpected. And you're sure this is the Incubating Benefactor?"

I nodded. "What will you be able to tell us from this..." My eyes flicked to his cutting instruments. *Torture? Dissection?* "Research?"

Tak turned his bespectacled face from the emerald fire and studied the senseless Peeker. His shifting expression bespoke the puzzles and possibilities that must have raced through the mortician's mind. "What will I learn from him? That depends on what I do to him." Tak rubbed Pinch's head as though petting a dog. "Now you ask, what will I do to him? That depends on what I learn from him. In matters such as these, you can never predict what new knowledge will emerge. You can only follow the path that lays itself before you, step by step. Only one man I ever met had a knack for predicting the path of knowledge. To state it simply, I don't know what I don't know, and I don't know how I will come to know it."

"Simply," I muttered. "Right..."

"With hope, what I learn will be useful to the Agency," Tak continued, "but until I learn it, I cannot say. I can assure you, however, that I do not intend for this Peeker to die. I need a *living* specimen, as I told you, to learn as much as I can."

Garret spat on the floor, and Tak frowned. "He's a bandit and a murderer. Whatever happens to him, good riddance."

"No," I said. Regardless of how much I hated Pinch, there was a good reason to keep him alive. "If he dies, he'll become an Emergent. That can't happen, not in the city."

"Yes," Tak said, distracted as he prodded at the unresponsive Peeker. "That too."

CHAPTER SIXTEEN

Just Desserts

Despite it being closer to dawn than to dusk, the Glisten Inn still bustled with the activity of the wealthy patrons. But as soon as I stepped through the door to this fine establishment, a hush fell over the room, and all eyes turned to me.

I grinned, wobbling a bit, and reveling in all these rich folks' surprise. "Didn't expect to see me, did you? What you waiting for? Call the guards. They'll drag me out to the Burg gate. Go on."

I'd just sneak back in. No one could stop me from drinking in the Gild tonight.

"Go back where I belong, right?" I hiccupped. "Whoops, what's this?" I fumbled for the pouch of stars. The guilt of the Peeker heist had been weighing on me, but not as heavily as Tak's coined weighed in my pocket.

The owner of the Glisten Inn placed himself in my path after only one step toward an empty seat at the bar, nose crinkling as if he could smell poverty from a thousand paces away. He put his hands on my shoulders, and the world spun.

I wriggled free and stumbled backward. "What's the matter? My coin not good enough for you, sir?"

Shouting started all around me.

"Get him out of here!"

"This is a disgrace!"

"He's filthy!"

"Can't hardly blame *me*," I said, looking down at my dirt-stained clothes. The same ones I'd worn through guard duty—the same I'd been wearing since joining the Agency for that matter. "Still never gave us uniforms." I shrugged away from another set of grabbing hands and gave them my coin to hold onto instead.

The owner's eyes went wide as he hefted the purse. As promised, Tak had paid us well, a good, heavy purse of stars each for Garret and me. 'In consideration of the risks your actions carried,' he'd said. Great risks, indeed, for justice in Liwokin was as cruel as Ulken.

But what the Head didn't know couldn't hurt us.

I lurched forward. Someone caught me and urged me to follow him. Not toward the exit, but up an endless set of staircases to an ornate room.

"The dawn suite has been prepared for you, sir."

"Dawn?" I asked. "Pretty dark, isn't it?"

Hot water splashed over my head and snapped me out of a stupor. I was in a bath. Gentle hands began scrubbing my hair, my neck, my back. I closed my eyes.

"Cheat!" someone shouted. He threw down his cards and stood, flinging his chair back, then stomping away.

I looked down. In front of me were a set of six matching cards with pictures of Peekers on them. All the loser's coins made their way into my pile. "Another shot!" I announced, to cheers from around the table. Two men with shaggy gray beards wore chains of gold. One woman flaunted her figure in a flowing blue dress; bands of Archemetal adorned her wrists.

Who were these people? When cups of clear liquor arrived, all eyes were on me. Someone snapped their fingers, and the liquid alighted. I flinched back, spilling a flaming drop, and singeing the edge of a Peeker card before the Archefire extinguished. "To Peekers!" I shouted and tilted my head back to drink.

When I opened my eyes, my head was on a soft, down pillow. I sat up in a plush bed at the center of the Glisten Inn's dawn suite, leaned forward, and groaned. My bones ached. Someone was pounding my head like a drum. On the table across the room, a beam of light glinted on a solitary gold star. The coin rested next to my purse, which was appallingly thin.

Never been one for saving, have I?

The one time a bounty had paid well enough for me to dare venturing into a bank, I'd been laughed out of the lobby before I made it to the teller. Banks weren't meant for bounty hunters, only those rich enough to put bounties on heads.

I tossed aside the heavy blanket, hopped down from the high bed, and padded barefoot across the room to the window. Throwing open the dark curtains let the Brightdaughter gaze into my suite. Her light scattered off the polished Archemetal, painting the whole room in gold.

Glittering furniture. That's all that gold had bought me. But I had no need to save my stars today. I'd be off on a new command to fight some monster soon enough, and a heavy purse would only slow me down. The real reward for delivering a live subject to Tak was what we would learn from his research. With that edge, the Agency could defeat the Benefactors. No amount of gold compared to that prize.

I turned my gaze outward toward Liwokin. My home. A beauty, despite her blemishes. From this tower in the Gild, even the Agency tower looked squat. I had never been higher above the city.

So why did I feel so low?

A tightness gripped my chest. I'd have to explain yesterday's events to Dunnax and Inac. Assuming they didn't request a new Hand right away, the best I could hope for was an erosion of trust after going behind their backs. Their faces flashed in my mind's eye—Inac's disappointment, Dunnax's anger. Bringing Tak the Peeker was necessary, but was it right?

A single, hard knock at the door startled me from my rumination. A firm voice said, "Grim, the Head commands you open the door."

Ulken was here? My stomach rolled. What the Head didn't know couldn't hurt us, true, but the Head had eyes everywhere. I shuffled to the door like a man walking to the gallows, not bothering to put on any clothes. The elegantly curved silver handle was cold in my hands.

At least my final night of freedom was well spent.

I took a deep breath and pulled open the double doors. Not Ulken, but a towering man wearing a white coat trimmed with gold waited on the other side.

A Nerve.

"Finger," he said. "Your Hand awaits at headquarters. Best hurry to join them."

"First Eye told us noon."

"Change of plans." The Nerve raised one eyebrow, looked me up and down. "Best put on your uniform first."

"We didn't get uniforms..." I muttered, but the Nerve had already turned the corner down the hall. The tail of his coat fluttered out behind him, inlays glistening in the dawn light, then disappeared. It was clear where Ulken's priorities lay.

* * *

For the first time, the portcullis in the Agency's gatehouse barred the entrance to the courtyard. Only after arguing with a Heel on the other side did the gate raise to let me in. I hesitated. It might have been safer to remain outside.

The Heels within all buzzed with activity, as if the courtyard were a burning beehive. Agency coats of all colors swarmed in and out of the doors on the inner walls. Most avoided collision, though one accident produced shouts of pain. Every door inside stood open to ease the flow of traffic, in contrast to the way outside. Only the flowing haze escaped beyond the porous gates.

My name came shouted above the din. Garret waved me over. Making my way through the flurry of bodies, nearly being bowled over by one particularly hurried and brutish Heel, I managed to rejoin the Hand.

"Didn't know we had this many Heels," I said. "What's going on here?" The Benefactor count remained at six, but that didn't mean much. That number was as real as an Aura, just a trick.

Dunnax glared at me and turned his back. Inac wouldn't meet my eyes.

That secret didn't last long.

At least they both were smart enough not to open their mouths about the heist while at Headquarters, else we would all have lost our heads in these quarters.

"Some big operation's got everyone excited as wolves on the scent of blood," Garret said. "Wonder what part we'll play."

"The bleeding bait," Dunnax said over his shoulder, "after what you've done."

"The gale comes," Sentyx said, turning. "Soon."

Very soon. A Nerve with long brown hair strode toward us, the crowd seeming to part at her passing. She stopped with a stomp on one foot, then folded her arms behind her back and looked at each of us in turn. Her stern eyes lingered on me a moment longer than the others, gaze narrowing, but when she spoke her focus was distant, as if she were looking right through us. "Hand Sixty-Four," she said. "Ulken commands you cease your dealings with Tak. Will you comply?"

Silence, for three slow breaths.

"Comply?" Garret asked, chuckling.

"Yes," the Nerve snapped. "Comply. Obey his commands. Do your duties."

"We know what it means," Dunnax cut in. "Yes, they'll comply."

"The Head commands the *entire* Hand," the Nerve said. "Now, take this. Your next assignment." She handed me a rolled-up paper, sealed with a wax stamp. Before I slipped a finger under the seal, she had already disappeared among the crowd.

"This is all?" Inac asked, shaking his head. "Where is for us the punishment?"

"A light gust," Sentyx said, nodding slowly.

"Told you," Garret said, and spat on the ground. "Agency doesn't mind us getting our hands dirty."

The Hand started arguing again while I unrolled the paper and read through it, corners of my mouth dropping with each line. A description of the path to the Pinegrave, directions to head southwest to the Shaded Grounds, and a list of Fingers who had gone before us—two Hands of the highest rank. Neither returned.

"Grim?" Sentyx asked, and the argument ceased.

"This isn't an assignment," I said. "It's a death sentence."

* * *

Under the cloudy-gray, half-noon sky, our wagon departed for the Pinegrave, where our instructions commanded us to stop for help. We left by the Span Gate, just as we had on the way to Leppit village. Indeed, the first leg of the journey matched that of our first command—the so-called field test, run by Ulken to determine our mettle. Once again, the Head sent us to die without saying as much in so many words.

But this time we'd be ready for a fight.

The road was the same, but we had become so vastly different. The landmarks we passed now seemed unrecognizable despite less than a measure elapsing. We crossed the Outrush Span Bridge, but it no longer seemed so grand. Beyond it waited nothing but misery. Memories resurfaced of the storm that haunted Leppit and the monster that stalked within. Worse, there was the monster that roamed outside the village, the Benefactor we now hunted—if it didn't end up hunting us instead.

That night, we fled to survive. Now, we kill or die.

Before we came upon the part of the road where we saved the Bright Prince, we angled our cart westward toward the Druids' hidden enclave, following a map provided by the Agency. Unlike the rest of the details in the command we received, those pertaining to the nature of the assistance we could expect proved sparse, but my previous interactions with the Druids had given me some idea. What excuse Ulken made up for why the Agency couldn't provide us with Tears directly, I didn't know. Perhaps he claimed they needed to hoard them for some great coming battle. Either way, their toxics wouldn't help us any more than they had the last Hand, but the Head couldn't afford the appearance of impropriety as he sent us to die.

An unnatural quiet fell in the forest, followed by the rising of a thick gray fog. Carried on the fog was a waft of something musty, but oddly pleasant—familiar, though I couldn't place it. A worry we might lose our way in this murk tickled the back of my mind, but it too was quiet. What did I have to fear? Garret's natural sense of direction kept us true to the course laid out on the map, though the ranger never once looked at it. Dunnax snoozed in the back, using his helmet as a hard pillow. The Paladin didn't seem to mind, snoring softly with a slight grin on his scarred lips. Motes of Fire danced between Inac's fingers, darting back and forth with practiced control. Even Sentyx let out a long, relaxed sigh.

I was alive and surrounded by good company, and that wouldn't be changing any time soon. We were survivors, this Hand. My thoughts drifted back to the Organ named Alli. She rooted for Sixty-Four, said we had a bright future in the Agency. What was I so worried about?

Lights faded into view so gradually I wasn't sure how long I had been seeing them. No one spoke as we approached the Druids' enclave. There was only the rhythmic sound of a hoof beat, the clatter of wheels on rock and soil, the occasional crunch of a snapping stick. When our wagon came to a halt, several Druids attended us. They shuffled close in deep-green hooded robes that appeared to have been crafted of the forest around us. One near the center drew back her hood and the fog seemed to lessen. She spoke in a calming, gentle voice. Her words whisked away what little darkness hung in the air.

"We greet you, guests from the Agency." She bowed, one hand extended out to her side in a flourish, the other placed over her heart.

"You know we're from the Agency?" Dunnax asked, yawning.

"A Paceeqi, an Ekoan, a Liwo, a Skardwarf, and...a Stinbine Islander, if I'm not mistaken." Inac smiled and nodded vigorously; his curly hair bobbed back and forth. "Only a Hand can be so diverse. My, but the Agency does bring the people of the world together. You'll find that our enclave does the same. You are welcome to stay here, as are all people."

"Are you the leader of this enclave?" I asked.

She shook her head. "We have no leaders among us. Each of us contributes however we can and receives as much in return from the others. I am Pyra." She gestured to the group. "And these are the Druids of the Pine."

"No leader," Garret said, "but you speak for the group now?"

"Any one of us would extend the same greeting," Pyra said, and her smile broadened. "There is no need for suspicion, Ekoan."

"Generally find the most need for suspicion is when someone says that," Garret muttered.

One of the Druids was looking down, kicking at the dirt—the only one not greeting us with a lifted face and easy eyes. "Are we making you uncomfortable?" I asked.

It took a moment for him to realize who I was talking to, but the realization hit him with a start. "Er, me?" He croaked, head still down. "No, no, not at all."

Ah, the smuggler.

I laughed. "Good to see you again, Raylen. How was Canako? Manage to offload your whole harvest?"

Raylen pulled back his hood. His hair and face were no less greasy for being in the enclave. His grime mustn't have come from the road. "What are you talking about?" the smuggler said, playing dumb.

One of the older Druids huffed and tutted, blowing out a flowing gray mustache that hung below his chin. He walked away and a small, grumbling contingent followed him off.

Pyra still smiled, but her lips tightened. "Raylen, please explain. These Fingers know you?"

Raylen sputtered. "You can't arrest me here!" he shouted in a shrill voice. "These are protected lands! We are a sovereign people!"

"Control yourself!" Pyra snapped, her expression finally breaking. "These Fingers are not here for your head." Two Druids took Raylen by the arms, and another three moved toward our wagon, apologizing profusely for their colleague's behavior. "If I were to guess," Pyra continued, "they are following in the footsteps of the last Hand to pass through."

"Can you tell to us what happened to them?" Inac asked.

"The same thing that will happen to you if you don't turn back." Pyra shook her head.

"I know," I said, then scratched at my chin.

Do I?

I supposed that deep down I did, but on the surface I didn't *feel* like anything was wrong.

"Ulken sent us to you for assistance," Dunnax said. "Can you help us?"

Pyra pleaded with her eyes. "What would help you most is to follow my advice. Leave. Go back to the city and tell your Agency that there was nothing you could do. You may lose your jobs, but you'll keep your lives. Which is more important?"

"We can't do that," Dunnax said, then looked right at me. "We follow our Head's commands. We'll see it through."

The gaggle of Druids grew quiet. Pyra scanned our faces and apparently saw nothing but resolve. That broke hers. "If you won't accept my advice," she said, sighing, "then we can provide only one other resource. If you are familiar with Raylen, then I am sure you know what it is." She gestured toward the toxics smuggler, who shrugged off the hands restraining him. "Allow him to make amends for his outburst by joining him at his home. He will give you everything you need."

* * *

Before arriving, I'd expected the Druids to live in makeshift tents of haggard hides and strewn-about sticks, a class of home hardly fit for the Old District. But Raylen's house proved once again how little I knew of the world. Though modest in size, it was built in a surprisingly modern Liwo style, modified with exterior decoration as if to blend into the surrounding woodlands. The fog lay thick around the house, making it seem alone in the middle of the forest rather than part of a community. Far from belonging in the Blight, it would have been the envy of every neighbor in the Burg.

Stepping through the threshold to the interior, the air smelled fragrant with burning incense. Wisps of smoke trailed up, concealing the wooden ceiling, gathering and flowing like some otherworldly ichor. Along the walls inside this toxics operation disguised as a cozy cottage, various symbols painted on hide canvases glowed in vibrant colors, pulsating slowly in the drifting haze. Assorted plants filled the room wherever there was a space between furniture, making it seem—despite the smoke and lack of windows—that we remained outdoors.

Breathing deeply, a wave of tranquility spread out from my chest, down through my limbs, then up to my head. It was a curious feeling, but pleasant enough, so I let it settle in. Raylen seemed to have relaxed as well, after maintaining a wariness for the duration of his escort, checking over his shoulder as if I were about to pounce on him. Dunnax's hard face softened, and Garret sat down on a cushioned chair, kicking his feet up on a nearby table as if it were his own house. Sentyx stood by the doorway, unreadable as always, in contrast to Inac who was clearly hesitant to breath in so much haze.

"If I am to breathe this, you must tell to me what it is," Inac said, waving a hand through the air. Smoke flowed around it like water.

"Huh? Oh, that's just for me," Raylen said, voice slurring as he turned away from his work at a cabinet in the corner of the room. You came for these." He cast a sidelong glance at me. "Should look familiar." The Druid swung around, wobbling, and holding a woven basket in his arms. One Druid's Tear rolled down from the mound inside the basket, clinking as it bumped its way to the wicker edge. Raylen placed the basket of toxics on the table in the center of his room, pushing Garret's feet off the furniture.

"Glass beads?" Dunnax said. "That's what we came for?"

"Looks can be to the eyes deceiving," Inac said, taking one of the Tears between his fingers, examining it with one brow raised. "There is in this bead a trace of Archefire."

"Indeed, there is," Raylen said. "Very pure, they are. The finest of elixirs."

"Toxics," I said, "is what you meant to say."

"An ugly term," the Druid said, "and unworthy of our product. I assure you, once you experience the effects of these Tears, there will be no doubt as to which term better applies." Raylen dug around in his pocket and produced a thumb-sized vial of dark red liquid. He cleared his throat, unstopped the vial, and launched into a clearly rehearsed speech with perfect enunciation. "Observe! Druid's Tears. They calm you but leave your head clear and ready for battle. With the help of this elixir, you can overcome your fear and set your enemies to fright. With a dose of Archefire, you will achieve your true might." He passed a set to each of us. "Here's how they're used. The first one is free, now follow along. Two simple steps are enough to grow strong."

We gathered close to watch Raylen pour a drop from the vial onto his outstretched forearm. It clung to his skin like a welling of blood. Then, he mimicked jabbing himself with one of the translucent needles that came paired with the glass bead. The Druid frowned when none of us moved to repeat the action, but composed himself and said, "First, prick the skin." He retrieved the glass bead from his palm. "Then, drop it in." He dropped it into the liquid, where it dissolved almost instantly. Raylen wiped his arm clean. "That's all there is to it. You'll feel the effects shortly. Er, well, you would have if you followed along."

"Why should we take these?" Dunnax asked. "Archefire in them or not, there's a reason the Empire banned them."

"I do not know this reason," Inac said. Dunnax opened his mouth to enlighten us, but then closed it and scratched his head in thought.

"The last Hand to pass through neglected to purchase any," Raylen said, "and well, you know what became of them."

"I do not know this, either," Inac said, frowning, "but I take from you your meaning."

"Purchase?" I scoffed, remembering the purse Oltrov threw at Kilan's feet. "After what the Agency already paid?"

"They previously purchased a quantity of our harvest in good faith, yes. A fair trade," Raylen said. "I'm offering you another. This is an honest operation."

"Liar," Dunnax said. "This place is no more than a toxics smuggling ring."

Garret shrugged. "Fair is fair. I've still got plenty of stars after last night. I'll buy some for you Dunnax. Marching to our deaths in these woods. Might as well live a little."

At Garret's words, a spike of alarm jabbed me in the stomach, but quickly subsided. I glanced at the others, but no one reacted. Something strange was happening in this enclave.

"This man knows his business," the greasy smuggler said. A broad smile crept toward his ears. "So, what do you say?"

Inac, Dunnax, and I all looked at one another. Dunnax was right, they were called toxics for a reason, even if the Paladin couldn't name it. Raylen spoke of elixirs and purity, but what was so pure about adding tree sap to your blood? Something about it felt wrong—

But I worked for the Agency buying these toxics in bulk, let Raylen smuggle them through the gate. I had done much worse, both before and since joining the Agency. What need did I have to worry about purity? I eyed Dunnax and Inac; something on their faces told me similar thoughts crossed their minds.

Before any of us could protest, Garret slapped his purse down on the table and said, "How many will this get us?" He turned questioningly to each of us. "Some for all of us, right?"

Sentyx grunted. "No."

Garret laughed. "Doubt you need them anyway, Skardwarf. You're tougher than an apsidon defending its roost." The Ekoan rapped his knuckles on Sentyx's shoulder, producing a dull thud. Sentyx slowly turned his head and looked down at his shoulder.

Raylen finished counting Garret's coin and cleared his throat. "This is sufficient to purchase...four."

"Four baskets?"

"Four Druid's Tears."

Garret spat. "Fair is *not* fair. This is deep woods robbery."

Raylen shrugged. "That's the price. You'll need these if you want to slay your monster."

I started. "You know about them?"

"Of course. It's vital to understand our customer's needs. In any case, the Grieving Pine keeps them away, but we've lost several harvests sent in caravans going south."

"The Grieving Pine?" Inac asked, twisting his pendant around in his fingers. "Can you show to us this pine?"

"Is that a tree?" Dunnax whispered to Garret. The Ekoan nodded.

"Sure," Raylen said. A sly half-grin crossed his face, lingering just long enough to notice. "After we close our deal, of course."

* * *

The tree stood alone in a forest, an alien thing. If Raylen hadn't named it a pine, I might not have believed it a living thing. The green grass turned to brown and then black as we approached. Shriveled and broken stumps bespoke the presence of trees that stood here before this visitor arrived, pity for them. Overhead no boughs or branches hung, exposing the decay to the drying sun. Underfoot, it crunched and wilted, and the ground moved as though displaced by something writhing below, hidden from the eyes. In the center of this swath of death shone a brilliant sight—a tree of glittering glass, infinite iridescence, a marvelous pillar staked deep in the plane of rot. Reaching up and out from the trunk, great luminous limbs caught the sunlight and cast it on the dark ground as ten thousand swimming rainbows.

"Well, here it is," Raylen said, gesturing as if he hadn't just shown us a wonder of the world.

"I am speechless," Inac said, though clearly not. "Can you feel the power of the Archefire emanating from this artifact?"

"Oh, that?" Raylen said. "That's what keeps the monsters away. It's the Pine's Aura."

An Aura...one that felt strangely familiar. Without Inac's attunement, I could discern no Archefire, but the Pine's Aura was unmistakable. Without realizing, I'd been feeling it since we arrived in this enclave. Now that I was aware of its presence, my mind compensated for it, and thoughts of imminent danger began to reassert themselves. I set my jaw. If we didn't face the danger head on, death would be certain.

Remember what's real. Especially when it's painful.

"What are they doing?" Garret asked.

Around the base of the tree, two Druids moved slowly, donning helms like sprouted mushrooms and walking with immaculate posture. They stopped only when lowering themselves straight down to retrieve something from the ground. Raylen bid us follow him and brought us forward to where the longest of the Pine's branches nearly reached overhead. He held out his arm to prevent us from taking another step, but Sentyx pressed on, ignoring the Druid's restriction. Something shattered atop the Skardwarf's head, but Sentyx continued without noticing.

"No!" Raylen shouted, then turned to us with pleading eyes. "Stop him! He's ruining our harvest."

A small crunch drew my attention down to where a glassy bead was nestled in the bone-dry earth with a small spray of dust floating just above. A small whistle sounded as I crouched to pick it up, and before my mind could tell my body to move, a needle plunged into the ground less than a hand's width from my own.

I jerked my hand back. "I'm not going over there."

The Brightdaughter glinted in another needle as it dropped, then another, like raindrops of light. Beautiful, but deadly—to all but a Skardwarf. Again, they were the exception to the dangers of life.

It's a miracle they haven't conquered the world.

Sentyx kept walking all the way to the base of the Grieving Pine, then rested one hand on the trunk and lowered his head. The two Druids collecting their harvest tried to pull him away from the tree, but nothing could break the Skardwarf out of his apparent reverence.

Garret laughed. "He's fine."

"It's not *him* I'm worried about," Raylen said, stomping his foot and wincing at the sound of another accidentally destroyed source of profit.

"Serves you right," a voice came from behind.

I turned to find the Druid who sported an elaborate, flowing mustache—the one who had stormed off earlier. He crossed his arms and cast a wicked smile at Raylen.

"That Skardwarf ruining the harvest doesn't serve your purpose either, Ingwid." Raylen glared at his rival.

"I'd rather the Pine die than see you leeches make another copper off her fruits." Ingwid breathed hard and blew out his mustache.

"Die?" Inac said. "I do not understand."

"The Pine drops her fruits into the ground, rejuvenating the earth with reserved Fire," the old Druid said. "You don't think the ground has always been like this, do you? The Aura has grown so weak, almost no Fire remains." Ingwid shook his head, then jabbed an accusing finger at Raylen. "This is your doing. Desecrating the Pine, stealing her fruits to sell them for personal gain."

"The *enclave's* gain," Raylen countered. "I don't see you and your stingy old friends swearing off the new tavern. You're benefiting too, remember."

"Oh, I never forget it," Ingwid said, flaring his nostrils. "It makes me sick to my stomach."

My Hand awkwardly stood by, as if we'd just walked in on a spousal feud. A memory surfaced from Andya's Pool; in her husband's eyes was the same look of absolute disgust that tainted both Druids' gazes.

Garret spat on the ground between them, redirecting four violent eyes toward him. "If you two are going to fight, just get on with it. What do you think, Grim? I would put my money on the young one, but the old one's got some ferocity. He believes in something. The other's only purpose is greed."

"Fight, eh? We just may, at that," Ingwid said, pinching his lips. "But not now. You've worn my patience thin, Raylen. Allowing that princeling to steal a branch of the Pine was going too far."

"It was a *royal decree*, and besides that, an investme—"

"Your dream of profits will come to nothing," Ingwid snapped. "When the Grieving Pine dies, we shall all share in the misery you sowed. I won't let it come to that." With that, Ingwid looked at each of us in turn, then stormed off. If looks were Archemagic, we all would have burned.

"I believe he means to kill you," Inac said to Raylen. The smuggler only sighed and walked away, running his fingers through his greasy hair.

Dunnax had his gauntlet off, fingers rubbing at his eyes. "We shouldn't have come here," he said.

I frowned at Garret. "I know you were joking, but stoking that fire wasn't a good idea."

Garret's laugh was drier than the ground we stood upon. "Look at the bright side. We won't live long enough to feel its burn."

CHAPTER SEVENTEEN

Shaded Grounds

I felt strangely at peace waking up on the day Ulken expected me to die. I kicked off the sweat-sodden blankets then swung my legs over and sat up from the bed, rubbing my forehead with my palm. Darkness filled this windowless room; it could have been dawn or dusk, for all I knew. As I lit the room's dim lantern and dressed, a slight unease buzzed within me. Though I pushed the feeling down, lingering impressions of violent nightmares kept creeping back up.

But were they nightmares? Or simply memories from the Pools of the others? The line between dreams and reality became blurred when even my memories were not my own. How, then, could I remember what's real?

A shudder swept through my body. For me, these visions were merely nightmares, but for Wyran and Andya, the nightmare was real. I couldn't turn away. Despite witnessing their deaths and monstrous rebirths firsthand, nothing I expected to face compared to the suffering they had experienced. My stomach was in knots, but I was prepared for the pain. On this day, there would be plenty of it. My Hand had to fight not just to survive, but to rid the world of another Benefactor. If we had the chance to release even one more victim from their torture, we had to take it. It wouldn't be easy, but nothing worth doing ever was.

Best get on with it.

The Brightdaughter's unmistakable dawn light bathed the room when I opened the door to leave. The wooden stairs creaked beneath my feet as I stepped down into the Goldglass Tavern's common room. It seemed to have transformed over-night. We had come here from the Grieving Pine and found intoxicated patrons slouching at tables, joined only by their empty cups. Languid smoke filled had the room, bestowing a drunken, tired malaise. Now each table hosted a lively conver-sation, bringing the noise level at times up to a rowdy crest. Behind the ebb and flow of discourse, a young Druid stood on a small stage in the corner and entertained with a trilling flute performance. Still, a vaporous mist suffused the air, but the mist of the morning energized and swept away the remnants of sleep. It filled me with an optimism I shouldn't have rightfully felt. But when I spotted my Hand at a table off to the side of the long room, my breath came easy.

Ulken thinks to rid himself of us. I can't wait to see his face when we return to report our success.

I stole an empty chair from a nearby table and dragged it over, sitting reversed with my arms over its tall back. "So, what's the plan?"

"Plan?" Garret asked. "Do corpses need plans?"

"No," Sentyx said, standing while the rest of us sat. At the Skardwarf's feet were littered fragments of a broken chair. "We will not die."

Dunnax, already donning his Paladin armor, gave a curt nod. "We've faced worse."

"Have we?" Inac's fingers were fidgeting at the cup of tea in his hands. "I have not."

"The monster we're hunting nearly killed us outside Leppit," Garret said.

"But we escaped," I said. "And so did Reed. After the First Eye's Archefire bomb, it might still be licking its wounds."

"And we've fought two of these monsters," Dunnax said. "We know what we're up against now."

Sentyx grunted his agreement.

"So did the other Fingers," Inac said. "If I were you, I would not be so confident."

Garret spat on the ground, drawing a disgusted look from a passing Druid. "Aye. I'm expecting a fight. Don't expect it to be a slaughter like it was with Andya."

Unless we weren't the ones doing the slaughtering.

I shifted in my chair. My shoulder still ached from our fight with Wyran. It had been healed with Archefire, but the pain from that one blow still flared up from time to time. I'd been lucky to get away from that fight alive. Lucky Wyran's club didn't come down on my head, like the one that had killed Markos. This time, we'd have to make our own luck. I ordered a big breakfast for all of us. We'd need the energy. And too many of my old friends had already died on empty stomachs.

"Let's look at the map," Dunnax said. "Figure out where we're going." He unrolled it and laid it flat on the table, using empty plates and cups to hold down the corners—metal dishware, not wooden. The Druids flaunted the wealth they had gained exploiting the Pine. "The Shaded Grounds," the Paladin said, pointing a gauntleted finger at a malformed, red circle that lay to the south of the Pinegrave and northwest of Leppit. Deep in the woods, far from civilization. A quiet place to disappear. "How do we find the Benefactor once we're there?"

"You already know how it feels to you, yes?" Inac asked. "We follow to it the Aura."

My hands trembled at the memory of the beast's Aura. A fiery sky, blood in my mouth, pounding in my chest, nose full of the heady scent of prey. Only, we were the prey, and it was the hunter. The Aura was more likely to scare us off than to lead us to it.

"Place is too big," Garret said, shaking his head. "Aura only affects us when they're close."

"Any other ideas?" Dunnax asked.

"There's a hunter in the Shaded Grounds," I said. "Didn't we meet a guy who said he bought furs from him?"

Dunnax thought for a moment, then grunted. "The one with blue eyes who thought we were bandits."

I chuckled. "He probably fled from the bandits attacking the Bright Prince's carriage and thought we were coming to join the plunder. Probably thought he'd die on that bridge. What did he say the hunter's name was? Lomin?"

"Aye," Garret said. "Told us the hunter was missing, though. Probably tried to fight the beast off on his own, but the predator became prey." The ranger shrugged. "Happens all the time in Eko."

"Maybe," I said, "but if his lodge is marked anywhere on the map..." I leaned over to get a better look. "That would give us a place to start, at least."

"Won't be on the map," Garret said, "but it doesn't matter. If there was someone hunting in these woods, there'll be trails, tracks, traps. Let's just go, we'll find the man. If the beast doesn't find us first."

"Not until we're done eating," I said as a Druid placed my order on the table. Two plates full of bacon, eggs, a loaf of bread, and a mug full of some drink they called "mud." Deep brown and piping hot, it steamed up and smelled strongly, though not of mud.

"You paying for all that?" Garret asked.

"Figured you'd cover it for us," I said with a grin. Garret raised an eyebrow. "What? Do corpses need coin?"

* * *

At the edge of the enclave, Pyra stopped us—the only Druid who cared enough to do so after the sale of their toxics had fallen through—and made one final attempt to save our lives.

"Don't be foolish," she said. "There is no reason you can't stay here and remain safely within the Pine's Aura."

"We are bringing with us the Pine's Aura, no?" Inac said, gesturing at his bundle that held a Druid's Tear. Each of us had one after refusing to give back the free samples Raylen handed out. Each of us save for Sentyx, of course, who returned his, claiming he didn't need it.

Pyra gave a sad laugh. "Other Hands have passed through to fight this monster. Some have accepted our aid. Others refused. In the end it made no difference. What makes you think your Hand will fare any better?" At that, none of us had anything to say, but Pyra knew we would not be swayed. "I will grieve for you, then," she said, turning to leave, "as I have grieved for all the others."

"She's got a point," Garret said. "Some beasts are too big to slay. We could just go tell Ulken the job's done."

Dunnax scoffed. "Trying to get us all executed?" He stomped off without waiting for a reply.

Sentyx looked at me and Garret, then gave a slow shrug. The Skardwarf followed the Paladin.

"He blames you both for this," Inac said. "If you had not assisted Tak, we would not be here."

"Maybe," Garret said. "But if it wasn't this Benefactor, it'd be another." The ranger spat, then set off into the woods behind the others.

"We had to help him," I said. "We need to learn more about these monsters. Tak was our best chance." I smiled, hoping Inac would return it. "Plus, we were bound to get on Ulken's bad side eventually."

The mage sighed. "My friend, I am starting to think we should have stayed with our old lives of luxury."

I chuckled, slapped him across the shoulder blades. "You're only now starting to think that? Come on, let's catch up to the others."

No border or precipice marked the transition to the Shaded Grounds. We walked until the trees clustered together, and darkness encroached on the sunlight cast on the ground. The shadows of the shaking, angular leaves of the canopy became dominant, spots of dancing light shrinking until they separated, then were snuffed out entirely. Though the Brightdaughter's rays did not survive the journey to the ground, the trees above gleamed, like some translucent bundle of green-gold fire. Despite that, the world beneath the trees remained dark, as though my eyes refused to adjust to the shadows, preferring the light overhead. The farther we traveled, the brighter the leaves glowed. But for all their radiance they afforded no better vision.

The Pine's Aura had faded long before the sun, and the calming presence of the Grieving Pine had given way to a fear that slowed our march. I expected the fears to multiply, expected someone to suggest turning back, expected better sense to win out.

Instead, some nascent desire awakened within me—an urge to track my prey, to sink in teeth, to gnash its flesh in my jaws. The sweet smell of blood drew me into the hunt. We drove forward together, no longer a Hand, but a pack of wolves. Garret caught some scent and hastened us through the gloom until a scene began to take shape, a tableau of inhuman violence.

Black-red blood, sticky wet, dripped from broken boughs into a gore-soaked mud of viscera and death. Shattered sticks and splintered bones jutted from a gelatinous mixture, coated in the same pungent fluid. There were so many body parts I couldn't tell how many people they belonged to. That they belonged to *people* I never doubted. A tattered green uniform, spattered with brown and red, decorated the gouged trunk of a nearby tree.

Garret plunged wrist-deep into the muck, felt around, and came back up with another scrap of stained fabric. "Whole Hand was wiped out here."

Inac looked up into the canopy, holding in his hand a stick with clinging globs of blood. "How tall are these trees?"

"Lightwood dwarfs," Garret said, digging again in the viscous mire. "Not as tall as the giants in Eko, but big for this region."

"Dwarfs?" Sentyx said.

"Short things," Garret said, wiping his hands on his thighs, leaving dark red smears. "No offense."

"You are taller than I expected any of your kind to be," Inac said to Sentyx, nodding.

The Skardwarf grunted.

Dunnax swiped at the canopy with his long glaive, severing one of the lowest branches—the only ones he could reach. The glow in the leaves dissipated as the branch crashed to the soiled ground with a squelch. "How *big* is this Benefactor?"

"Big enough to leave these tracks," Garret said. Sure enough, the beast's tracks led away from this gruesome scene. They were the same as we had seen before Leppit—a chaotic tangle of animal prints forming one unmistakable trail that would lead directly to our quarry.

Impatience clawed at me. The taste of blood graced my tongue. "The bigger the prey, the more glorious our kill."

Sentyx looked at me with an expression I had never seen on the Skardwarf's stony face. "Are you okay?"

That was an odd question. My steel was sharp and oiled. My crossbow was waxed, with quarrels mounted. The scent of prey filled my nostrils. The time for killing was near. But we were taking too long. The faster we finished this hunt, the sooner we could get back to the Agency, where a Head needed lopping off.

"Never better," I said. "What are we waiting for? Even I can follow these tracks."

I sped into the dark woods, leading the hunt, satisfied to hear that the rest of the pack followed close behind.

* * *

We came to a point in the trail where the tracks lurched in one direction for no obvious reason, tracing a semicircle before quickly continuing on the same course. Ignoring the detour, I almost stepped into a rope trap that lay hidden under a scattering of leaves. But our prey had seen it, swerved to avoid it. I bared my teeth in an animal grin. The beast was perceptive, maybe even intelligent.

This is getting more interesting by the moment.

But like Garret had said, predator often became prey.

Something unseen struck me, like a changing of the scents on the wind. My hackles raised. Shoulders tensed. I was shaking and couldn't stop. Perhaps it was watching us even now, hiding in the distant shadows. I sensed its eyes on my back and turned—

There was nothing. Only darkness below, fiery light above, and the rest of my Hand between them.

Inac flinched at my sudden movement. "What?" He and Garret were both twitching.

"Is it near?" Dunnax's hands repeatedly tensed and relaxed on the grip of his axe.

My obsession with hunting this monster suddenly struck me as insanity. Had I really been running headlong into the beast's jaws? A copper taste still filled my mouth, and a sour odor filled my nostrils. The glow of the canopy had grown so bright I could hardly look at it. It appeared the whole forest was burning above us—the crackling and popping of flame filled the void around us. Only...

There was no heat.

Oh.

"Grim?" Sentyx asked.

Digging carelessly into my pack, a prick of pain shot through my hand as the end of a Druid's needle jabbed my thumb. My fingers found the smooth form of the Tear and grasped it. By the time I pulled it out, the toxic had already dissolved into my hungry blood. Relief washed through my body, tearing away the veil of fear, cleansing me of the Benefactor's Aura. The illusory sensations of the Aura remained, but subdued, easy to put out of mind, like the crack of a Blightdweller's flintlock heard from the Gild.

The others looked on, faces contorted into expressions I had never seen. How much of what these faces betrayed was their own, and how much was imposed by the Benefactor?

"Take the Tears," I said, and they all did, save Sentyx. His face remained impassive. Did he even feel the effects of the Aura?

Dunnax clawed off his gauntlet, apparently eager to escape the Benefactor's influence as soon as he could.

Garret's eyes widened as soon as the toxic dissolved from his fingers. "Feels like I'm free again. Benefactor doesn't have control anymore."

"Yes," Inac said, "but how much of this feeling is the Tears taking from us control?"

Dunnax sighed in relief. "Can't you just accept anything for what it is?"

"If I did this," Inac said, "I would not have discovered for myself an entire form of Archemagic."

"That would have been for the best..." Dunnax muttered, replacing his gauntlet. He slammed down his helmet's visor. "Now, we've got a command to see through."

I chuckled. The Hand was back to themselves. But we still had to kill a deadly monster before the day was through. My smiled faded.

Why do I feel so calm?

As we continued following Garret toward the hunter's lodge, I couldn't help but linger on Inac's comment. I paid closer attention to what the toxic was doing to my body and my mind. It hadn't merely washed away tainted emotions or cleansed my thoughts. It had replaced them with a different falsehood. Maybe it protected us from surges of fear cast out by the Benefactor's Aura, but it also took away feelings with utility—vigilance and courage, confidence and aggression. The Tears allowed us to think clearly, but it only clarified how vulnerable we were.

We had to be ready for anything, or Ulken would get his wish after all.

A thousand quiet paces later, the trail came to a clearing of sorts, where the trees clustered less tightly. The Benefactor evidently traveled through here often—the whole area was pounded down into flat earth, with tracks leaving in multiple directions.

"Are we close to the lodge?" I asked Garret, fearing the worst for our missing hunter.

"Aye," the ranger said, "should be just a few hundred paces in that dir—" Garret stopped mid-sentence, allowed his pointing finger to fall, and tilted his head. "You see that?"

Sentyx grunted. Were his eyes as good as his ears? Following Garret's gaze, I stared into the darkness, but that's all there was—darkness.

"Do we see what?" Inac asked, and looked at Dunnax, who shrugged. "Hmm..." The clearing lit up as a spear of Fire formed over the Archemage's raised right hand. It shot off without so much as a twitch of Inac's muscles, flashing out like a bolt of lightning. The Archefire froze in mid-air as a mote of bright light and traced the outline of the biggest wolf I had ever seen.

Garret had his bow out, arrow nocked, string drawn before the breath had fully caught in my lungs.

"Wait," Inac said, holding out his hand, which didn't affect the behavior of the Fire in the least.

"Am I crazy," Dunnax said, lifting his helmet's visor and squinting, "or is that wolf wearing a collar?"

The wolf ambled right up to Inac's hanging Archemagic, sniffed at it, then carried on as if it hadn't a care in the world. Its metal collar jangled with each slow step. As it passed underneath the Fire, the tip of its shaggy gray tail began to singe, but it didn't react at all, and Inac quickly put out the flame.

Garret laughed, sticking the arrow back in his quiver. "Biggest dog I ever seen." He held out his hand to let the wolf sniff him.

Forcing myself to think of this creature as a huge dog took some effort. What would a dog have been doing this deep in the woods anyway?

"It could be the hunter's," I guessed.

"Or it may be under the Benefactor's control," Dunnax said. "Careful."

"Seems harmless enough. Besides, animals like me," Garret said, frowning as the dog came to a stop in front of him. "Makes 'em easier to kill." The ranger drew his knife faster than my eye could follow and stabbed down at the dog's neck.

Inac shrieked. "What are you—"

The knife stopped, its sharp point grazing the dog's skin beneath its mangy fur. "Thought so." Garret put the knife away and spat. "Something off with this thing. Smells like death and look." He parted the fur at the side of the dog's neck, revealing a gaping wound, crusted with dry blood.

I observed the dog more closely. Its eyes were lifeless, staring blankly into space. The creature walked but did not breathe. Only now did I realize how quiet it had been, silent except for the chain around its neck.

"Archedark," Sentyx said.

"Yes," Inac said, "I too feel this."

"I knew it," Dunnax said, preparing his glaive to strike. "Move aside, Garret."

The dog barked once, and I jumped back, expecting an attack. But it only turned and ambled back the way it came.

"No need to kill it a second time," Garret said, and shouldered his bow. He pursed his lips. "Not yet, anyway." He started after the creature.

"You're following it?" I asked. "The Benefactor's tracks don't lead off that way."

"No, but it's going the right way," Garret said. The ranger pointed out a less noticeable trail that had been cleared through the woods. "Back home."

* * *

We weaved around more hidden traps, following in the dog's curiously knowing footsteps. It was obvious it had traveled this path before, untold times. What I didn't understand was why there were so many traps in these woods to begin with, when we had yet to spot any other animals. Was this hunter incredibly unlucky, or had the Benefactor driven them all away?

As we continued, the sky began to show again, the westering Brightdaughter casting a pale orange warmth through the trees. Though the Druid's Tears still dulled my senses, some tension I didn't know I held began to evaporate. Soon, a scattering of buildings came into view as we neared the exit to the forest. A wood cabin with an ivy green roof, flanked by several minor structures; beyond them all was a lake, shimmering in the waning sunlight with birds circling overhead. If the lake hadn't been marked on our map, I would have mistaken it for the sea, waters extending to the horizon. The dog loped to the cabin's door and pushed his way inside.

"You were right," Inac said. "It is the hunter's dog."

"Not anymore," Dunnax said, tightening his grip on his weapon. "It's the Benefactor's dog now. Has to be. You ready for a fight?"

"Can you feel it?" I asked.

"Feel what?" Dunnax said.

"There is nothing to feel," Inac said.

"Exactly," I said. "There's no Aura here. The Benefactor's far off."

"Then how do you explain its dog walking around here like it hasn't got a cut throat?" Dunnax asked.

I shrugged. "I can't. We can trust Ulken on one thing at least: we know too little about how these things work. But the Benefactor isn't here."

Still, a bounty hunter prepared for every possibility, and Ulken said the Benefactors were changing in unpredictable ways. Could this one have gained the ability to mask its Aura? I pushed open the door to Lomin's lodge with my crossbow leveled, but there was no need for alarm. The big, shaggy dog lay with its head rested on crossed paws, tucked into the corner of the cabin. Its golden eyes did not track us as a living dog's eyes would but stared off aimlessly. The interior of the cabin was spacious but bare. Along the back wall, near a window that looked out on the lake, a worn leather journal rested on an unadorned desk. There was a simple kitchen area for preparing food, well stocked, though the vegetables had rotted and filled the air with a pungent odor. One wall cordoned off the only other room, which contained an unmade bed and a wooden chest.

"Looks abandoned," I said.

"Looks like this hunter preferred being out in the woods," Garret said, poking around the place, following his nose as though he were a dog himself.

"This reminds to me of my home," Inac said, looking out the window. "But the Sea Pot was not half this size even when the sea spilled into the island." He let his gaze linger a while longer, then picked up the open journal. Turning the pages, he said, "It is a logbook. The hunter tracked in this his prey. So much killing." Grimacing, he flipped to a spot near the end. "The last entry he wrote to this page has with it a note." Inac slowly read the hunter's note, which sounded clumsy on his tongue. "'They're getting more aggressive even as they become harder to find. Darkfather, I've nearly hunted them to extinction. I should start charging higher rates, earn me enough to let the population recover some.'"

"Aggressive?" I asked. "Maybe the Benefactor's Aura affected them."

"Could be it got to the hunter too," Dunnax said.

"Aye." Garret was still sniffing around. The ranger grunted in frustration. "Where's that coming from?" He broke the glass in the window at the back of the lodge, then jumped outside.

"Wait—" I began, but Garret was no easier to stop than Sentyx once he made up his mind. Heading for the door, I noticed the Skardwarf crouched down by the dog, staring into its lifeless eyes. "That's a staring contest even you can't win," I said, but Sentyx only grunted.

Outside, I turned the corner of the cabin to find Garret standing before an open-air barn, the legs of which had broken beneath a collapsed roof. The Benefactor's tracks ended right at the rubble. As I got closer, a reek like sour, rotten meat struck me. Fighting my urge to gag, I buried my nose in the crook of my arm and ducked under the partially caved-in entrance, following Garret into the barn. There was no way to hide from the stench of death. Spatters of dried blood coated the ground. Flies buzzed incessantly in my ears. A piece of torn flesh hung from a splintered crossbar above broken wooden supports that pointed out toward the woods. Seeing the mutilated scrap conjured a memory from Andya's Pool, of the dying woman staring down at her plague-ridden body.

I escaped from that foul barn, coughing, and spitting on the ground as the rest of the Hand rejoined us. Garret strolled out from the destroyed structure and slapped me on the back as I hunched over, hands on my knees, still trying to get the rotten taste from my mouth. It seemed to coat the inside of my nose and mouth no matter how much I spat.

"Bad in there," Garret said, "but I've seen worse."

I let out a laugh between gagging and coughing. "Of course you have."

"Only once, inside a daggerclaw den. Butchered just as many animals as our missing hunter but left their remains to rot. That's what I don't get. Plenty of blood in there, but where are the carcasses?"

"The barn was broken open," Dunnax said, surveying the destruction. "These tracks lead *out*, not in."

Inac pursed his lips. "This is where the Benefactor was created, yes?"

I considered, nodding. It made sense. "It was created in the Liwokin, like all the rest. But this is where the victim became Emergent."

"Hunter wasn't killed by the Benefactor, then," Garret said. "He *is* the—"

A loud bark interrupted him. The dog had snuck out of the lodge, quiet as the dark, and slunk up to the Hand unnoticed. He sniffed at Garret, then wagged his tail enthusiastically and barked three times. Then the dog hopped back, snapped at the air as though catching a piece of meat someone had thrown. He chewed on nothing for a few breaths while I looked on, perplexed, then spun in a tight circle sniffing the ground, stopped, looked up, and bolted off into the woods.

Right where the tracks from the barn led.

"Dead dog's got some life back in him," Garret said.

Seeing the animal behave like a living dog rather than a sad ghost of one surfaced something from Wyran's Pool. "I've *seen* that dog," I said. "It was there when Wyran's dad brought him to the city."

"That's perfect," Dunnax said, without a hint of irony. "He'll lead us right to the Benefactor." The Paladin trudged ahead ready for battle.

I glanced at the others. "I was afraid he'd say that."

* * *

We followed the dog, which repeatedly bolted ahead into the darkness, waited for us to arrive, then barked and wagged its tail before taking off again. Knowing what lay ahead, fear began to creep in behind the veil of the Druid's Tears. The dog led us toward the hunter, Lomin, just as Wyran's Empath had led Kalvin to him.

And look how well it ended for Kalvin.

Was it possible for a Benefactor to have an animal Empath, let alone one that was dead? I didn't know much about Empaths, but Benefactors had been reborn after death. Why not this animal too? And it wasn't too far-fetched that a solitary hunter had found his best friend in a canine companion. The dog certainly knew the travel-worn deer trail well enough to avoid the hidden snares the human hunter had lain. The Benefactor's tracks lay parallel to one of those trails, visible at the edge of shadow, a straight line through the dense forest. The beast hadn't navigated around the trees but had knocked them aside with a momentum that did not falter against the barrage of the overgrown woods. We broke away from that path, following the Empath dog instead.

Light bloomed overhead. The trees glowed a golden-honey hue in the light of the westering sun. The copper taste of fear filled my mouth and tightened my throat. The closer we got, the more powerful Lomin's Aura became, until it seemed like the toxics had no effect at all. If indeed the Tears *were* working, the undiminished Aura would have driven any creature insane. I glanced at Sentyx, tromping along as if everything were normal. How did the Skardwarf's mind fend off this assault?

Inac, on the other hand, shook and panicked. He slowed down. "The hunter is ahead," the mage said. "I can feel on me its eyes. It knows we come."

"Doesn't change what we've got to do," Dunnax said, pushing Inac forward.

The Archemage resisted the Paladin's push, but I didn't think of him as a coward. The rest of us were reckless. Why were we doing this?

I clenched my fists to still the tremors in my fingers. "Dunnax, we shouldn't—"

Something unseen pulsed through the forest. I straightened, as though the heavy air had stopped pressing down on me. Copper turned to iron in my mouth, no longer the taste of fear but of blood. Funny how they tasted so alike. The touch of blood on a predator's tongue is the fear that fills the prey's mouth. The luminescent trees seeped from gold to a murky red. The Brightdaughter's light left us in darkness, but my eyes saw more clearly than ever, as though I'd been granted the eyes of a wolf. The glow of the leaves tinted all I could see in scarlet, perfect for the coming bloodshed.

And the creature we sought came into view.

At two hundred paces it was still just an ill-formed shadow, a deeper negation of light in the distant void. We approached steadily, quietly, as a single unit, a pack. The slightest mistake would be deadly. Any noise would alert our prey. At one hundred paces, Sentyx held Dunnax back. Any closer and the rustling of his armor would give away the game. Inac remained with them, while Garret took to the trees. Silent movements thrust the ranger up into the dense growth of branches. I approached on foot, padding from trunk to trunk, trusting darkness to conceal my motion. At fifty paces, my steps instinctively slowed as my ear acutely picked up each delicate footfall. The creature's details began to resolve. The animal's back was turned, but my hackles were still up.

This was like nothing I had ever hunted.

I struggled to comprehend the shape of the Benefactor Lomin had become. Its bloated mass balanced precariously upon its base like a bulging waterskin, its hide shifting and sloshing with the monster's slightest movements. A tattered patchwork of animal parts comprised its flesh, like the skins of dozens of creatures had been stitched together. The gruesome tapestry was coming apart at the seams, oozing coagulated blood. The scruffy mange of a wolf, the bristly coat of a deer, a trailing wisp of horsehair, even the smooth gray skin of a shark; all slowly dripped red from vicious tears in the flesh. Muscular legs sheared from animals I could only guess at—several with long, sharp blades for claws—bore the bulk of Lomin's weight, thick pillars sunk into a ground that writhed with something unseen. The other limbs slapped ineffectually at the dirt, vestigial forms that seemed to serve no purpose but to unnerve me with the sight of twitching, alien motions. The body of this abomination bespoke the fate of all the animals missing from these woods.

It had hunted them all itself.

This Benefactor was the apex predator of these Shaded Grounds, the king whom we had come to dethrone.

It turned, a myriad of legs working in coherence to bring the beast to bear. Its face—such as it was—came into view, a grotesque creation from the mouth and jaws of every creature it had killed. Each one gnashed and clamped its teeth individually, yet they worked together to form a single, gaping mouth. Razor fangs protruded out in every direction, cutting into the creature's own flesh as it snapped its jaws. It extended a slithering neck, craning it around to look back toward where stood Dunnax, Sentyx, and Inac.

The exposed mage yelped, causing the Benefactor to...perk up. Its head lifted and pulled back like a coiled serpent ready to strike. And where its gaze had been searching before, now it was focused. Directly on Inac, who stood frozen in place. But a single heartbeat later, one flaming arrow, followed by a second, came soaring from the trees, plunging directly into the Benefactor's back. When the flames licked it, the beast *roared*, and the trees shook in resonant reverberation. Its long neck retracted, and the menagerie of legs all swarmed in one direction.

Lomin was fleeing.

Nothing more quickly heats the blood of a predator than seeing its prey in flight. I dropped all pretense of stealth, drawing my blade. It sang to me leaving its scabbard. My boots pounded the earth to close on the hunted before it could escape. A latent feeling drove me forward, one that accompanied me often on the hunts for my bounties, but it had been a long time since I felt this thrill.

The taste of blood filled my mouth, but I thirsted for so much more.

CHAPTER EIGHTEEN

Predator and Prey

The Benefactor's bulk slowed it down at first, but once it got going, its countless limbs clawed in unison and churned the ground more effectively than I could believe. The wind whipping past Lomin put out Garret's fires before they could take hold. Soon my prey kept pace ahead of me, then began gaining distance. I growled and ran harder, calling to mind the memory of our flight outside Leppit. If we'd gotten away from it then, I could catch it now.

"Help!" Inac's shout echoed from the dark void behind me, but I ignored it. The hunt was on, and—

Garret dropped down from the trees ahead of me, blocking my path.

I snarled at him. "It's getting away!"

He put his hand on my chest to stop me. "Won't be hard to track. Come on, let's regroup."

"The beast must die," I opened my mouth to say, but the objection died in my throat. As Lomin gained distance from the Hand, its Aura slowly faded. The urge to hunt still lurked in the back of my mind, but the animal was caged. For now. What was I doing chasing the Benefactor on my own? Even with the

Druid's Tears in my blood, I'd nearly succumbed to the blood-lust. Was that Lomin's Aura?

Or is this just who I am?

The shaggy, undead dog shot past me, following the Benefactor's trail. I jumped back, startled. I had forgotten about the Empath; the Aura's influence had narrowed my gaze to focus solely on the Benefactor. Garret's arrow flew silently into the darkness but drew no canine yelp. Another shout sounded behind us, this time from Dunnax. Garret and I exchanged a quick glance then took off at a run.

Just as we arrived, the broad blade of the Paladin's glaive slammed deep into the ground. On either side of the iron axe head, half of a grey-brown worm flailed, spurting black fluid into the air. It was as thick as my arm and had no mouth, but sharp teeth and claws dotted its flesh. A few strides away, the worm's vice-like grip on Inac's lower leg slackened, and the mage pulled himself free. He pulled back his tattered robe to examine his leg, which bled where the worm's teeth had dug in.

"Fitting that a hunter would leave behind snares," I said.

"Thank you, my friend," Inac said to Dunnax, standing and wincing as he put weight on his injured leg. Dunnax grinned, until Inac destroyed both halves of the worm with two quick bursts of Archedark. The worms liquified in an instant, splashing to the ground in a puddle of grey-brown soup that seeped into the dirt.

"Don't mention it," Dunnax said. The Paladin frowned but didn't mention something himself: Inac's use of Dark magic. Even he recognized how desperate our situation was. "Let's go. It's getting away."

Desperate, but not enough to interfere with duty.

* * *

We followed the Benefactor's trail, killing snare worms as we went. The attacks were rare but sudden. Painful when successful. A quick shake of the ground, a slight movement in my peripheral, then teeth and claws lashed out like flying knives. Each of us felt the bite of their grip—even Sentyx, whose rocky skin protected him from laceration. The worms could still immobilize him, a deadly prospect while fighting the monster. For once, even the Skardwarf was vulnerable.

I grew more apprehensive with each fallen worm, the last of which wrapped around my thigh tight enough to bruise. I still felt the cold touch of Inac's magic as I walked favoring one leg. I rolled my injured shoulder, which began to ache with renewed fire.

"At this rate, we're going to be too injured to fight when we find it," I said.

"Or when it finds us," Garret said.

I froze. The urge to hunt had left me entirely. Fear grew quickly. The Aura intensified. I held my sword white-knuckle tight and cursed myself for not better preparing for combat. What good was a sword and crossbow going to do me in a fight with Lomin? Somehow, the possibility of dying to another Benefactor had always been a remote concern. Other, more important matters had taken precedence. But I couldn't unravel conspiracies, help my friends, or protect Liwokin if I was dead. How foolish I had been. Nothing helps one sort their priorities faster than looking death in the eye. As always, the basest instinct won out.

First, I had to survive. Everything else was secondary.

"The ground," Sentyx said.

"No snare here," Dunnax muttered, but Sentyx wasn't talking about a worm.

The sensation was slight at first but ramped up quickly. The ground quaked beneath my feet, growing in ferocity. It came from every direction, echoing throughout the Shaded Grounds. Only a faint blood-red light kept us from fighting blind. The five of us formed a defensive circle, ready for the beast to arrive with the force of a stampede.

The sound of crackling Fire whipped from Inac's hand. I spun and watched the blazing bolt strike the charging Benefactor's head. With a flash, the rotten, hairy flesh of the beast went up in flames. The forest filled with inky, reddish black smoke. The Benefactor roared as melting hide dripped from its extended neck, but it continued coming right for us. Its amorphous mass twisted around the trees with surprising grace. As the flames crept up its neck, closer to its bloated body, it lurched forward and skidded along the ground, smothering the flames but also bringing the beast to a halt. When it lifted itself again, the damage dealt by Inac's Archefire was plain.

But only momentarily.

Flesh knitted itself together; the creature's marred body re-formed. Only the material that burned off remained on the forest floor, strewn across the ground in an ember-ridden lump of hide and bone. The ruined neck retracted with a snap into Lomin's body. Its mass rippled like the surface of a lake struck by a falling stone. The animal parts that faced us rearranged themselves, too many moving parts for the eye to track, until they formed into three dense clusters. From the center of each cluster, a tendril emerged. They thickened and extended toward us, dragging black eyes and yellow teeth in its flesh like flies caught in dripping honey. Bile burned in my throat as three new gaping maws formed, dribbling blood and thick saliva from a grotesque, threefold smile. Its jaws wrenched open to let out a howl that sounded like a thousand demons breaking free from the bounds of the abyss.

The Benefactor began its charge anew. A snare worm burst from the ground in the center of our circle. I lashed out with my sword. Garret moved at the same time, the both of us chopping the worm into three parts before we all scattered. I took cover behind the thickest tree I could reach. My heart pounded, and my muscles seized up as Lomin's stomping closed in. It wouldn't be enough to stop the beast's charge. Far from the confident predator I judged myself earlier, abject terror pulsed through my entire body.

I hid behind the lightwood dwarf until a crunch filled the forest. The Benefactor had slammed into a different tree. Cracking and rustling continued as Lomin pushed against that tree, tearing its roots from the ground. In the swinging branches, Garret tried maintaining his balance, but the Benefactor's strength prevailed, and the trunk snapped at its base. The ranger jumped from the tree, rolling maladroitly as he hit the ground. As he came to a stop, one of Lomin's snares lunged at Garret and burrowed into the ground on the other side of him. He was pinned.

The felled tree crashed to the forest floor, and Lomin disengaged from the broken wood. The Benefactor turned its three heads toward Garret, who struggled against his writhing bonds, lips moving but silent. I willed my feet to move, to help my friend, but something inside me fought back, a little voice that paralyzed me with the truth.

If it sees me, I'm dead.

One of the three jagged-toothed heads lashed out toward the grounded ranger. Dunnax appeared, throwing himself in front of Lomin's strike. He blocked the blow with heavy armor and sturdy footing. The Paladin spun and chopped down with his polearm, blade cleaving through flesh. Its severed neck spurted black blood, but the Benefactor was not fazed. Another head swung round and bit into Dunnax's side, immobilizing his arm as teeth gouged into plate armor. The Paladin cried out in pain, but if that had been me, there would have been no crying out. I would have been torn apart in an instant, guts showering my friends as they stared on in horror.

If it sees me, I'm dead. My breaths came in rasps. My feet seemed to weigh a thousand pounds.

Sentyx freed Garret. He tore the snare worm off the ranger with his bare hands. The both of them moved away from the beast. Garret winced as he loosed several well-placed but ineffective arrows in their retreat.

While Dunnax was still ensnared, Lomin's severed head twitched. The jaws of its third head opened wide and wrapped around the twitching flesh like a snake swallowing a dying toad. Reclaimed animal parts bubbled up through the cracks in the Benefactor's flesh as it began to regrow its lost head. Normal weaponry would not work against this foe.

Luckily, not all of us used normal weaponry.

The shadows darkened. Inac cried out with a rage to match Lomin's howling. The mage's eyes trailed golden Fire, and dark veins traced his skin as though his blood had run black. In his left hand, a growing void appeared like a puncture in reality. A gust of icy wind blew toward the mage, freezing cold on my sweat-covered skin. A narrow beam of Archedark shot forth from Inac's outstretched hand, cutting through the necrotic flesh of the head that was assaulting Dunnax. Lomin roared and reeled back, leaving its severed head to fall lifeless to the ground. For some reason, this time it did not reanimate. It lost its form and became a mess of sludge.

The Paladin staggered back and pried himself free from Lomin's jaws. He began tearing off his pauldron, dragging his weapon on the ground as he retreated. Blood dripped from several of the holes punched in his armor by Lomin's fangs. Dunnax took cover behind a fallen tree, and the glow of Archefire healing radiated from his position.

When the Benefactor's churning regrowth completed, a pulse went through the air, like a sudden drop in air pressure. My ears rang. I grew short of breath and fell to my knees. My heart raced faster, faster, until a familiar sensation crackled at the base of my skull. A Deluge began with the red light of the Shaded Grounds fading to black.

* * *

The cave stank of snoutbear. Even the mildest of them were territorial creatures that would kill to protect their cubs, but this one was the most aggressive I'd hunted. Vicious, like the existence of every animal he came across was a grave insult. He ranged far beyond his territory, feasting on the Grounds' deer and squirrels, foxes and wolves, even the occasional terrorbeak, judging by the bright feathers at the mouth of the cave.

It's like he's trying to put me out of business.

I almost laughed, suppressed it just in time. The crunch of bone told me the snoutbear was enjoying his meal well enough, but if he heard me, he wouldn't mind adding another course. I peeked around the stalagmite. The great beast's back faced me, muscles flexing as he tore meat from bone. What unlucky creature comprised his supper this time?

He shifted to reveal a human head, blonde hair matted with blood, no body attached at the neck. Dead eyes stared at me, wide with surprise. The Shaded Grounds were so dark, she had probably walked right into her killer. But what was she doing here in the first place?

In these woods, you're either predator or prey.

The snoutbear's head suddenly turned up, long snout sniffing at the air.

Got too close. Knew I shouldn't have washed earlier.

I ducked behind the rock and readied myself to run, but if he turned this way, chances were slim I'd see daylight ever again. My mouth dried out then filled with a metallic taste. My heart hammered in my ears.

If it sees me, I'm dead.

I almost missed the growling coming from another direction. My stomach dropped. Fear for myself transmuted into fear for another. Val's eyes glinted green in the dim light. Her gray fur bristled as she padded toward the beast, fangs bared at the bear. He growled right back at her, then stood on his hind legs to let Val know who would come away from this fight the victor.

Lucky these animals never realize. It's what you don't see that kills you.

My canines showed in a wolfish grin. My heart beat fast, but time slowed, the moment of the kill drawing out to a savory length. Val barked and distracted the snoutbear while I snuck toward him, knives drawn, quiet as death. Chances were good I'd still die in this cave, but how could I live with myself if I turned tail and let Val die instead? What kind of man would I be?

I pounced and felt my steel sink deep into the snoutbear's back. Holding on tight as he screamed and whipped around, I prayed to the Darkfather for strength. In places like this, he was the only one listening.

* * *

If it sees me, I'm dead.

When I regained control of my body, I was lying on my back in the dirt. I searched for my friends and found Garret lying flat on the ground. Sentyx was trying to shake him awake. Dunnax's healing glow had gone dark, but the Paladin's armor stuck out from behind the fallen tree trunk. The Benefactor's two heads slithered around toward Inac, who struggled to his feet, chest heaving, eyes dark with seething rage, a deeper darkness surrounding him.

If it sees me, I'm dead. The thought ran endlessly through my head and kept me anchored in place, out of sight like the hunter cowering behind the stalagmite.

I clenched my teeth so hard I thought they'd crack. My fingernails dug into my palms. My entire body trembled. I *hated* myself. Hiding like a coward, I was useless. My Hand—no, my *friends*—struggled to survive. But I listened to the voice that told me to fight was inevitably to die.

If it sees me, I'm dead.

I hated it. Hated myself for obeying it. But a moment of hatred can change a man. And it wasn't myself I despised.

It was the Benefactor.

Remember what's real.

Its Aura of fear had gripped me. It separated me from the pack, made sure I wouldn't help. We would each die alone, one by one. Ulken would get his wish. No. It was time to act.

Clenching my fist around my sword's hilt, I took a deep breath. *I won't let it see me.*

I skirted the periphery of the combat. Sentyx held down one of the Benefactor's extended necks, gnashing teeth incapable of penetrating the Skardwarf's hardened skin. Dunnax had risen with his shoulder healed. He passed a hand over his blade, and it glowed white-hot along the edge, imbued with the Paladin's Archefire. The glowing glaive raised and swung down in a blur of burning light, cleanly severing Lomin's neck. Dunnax plunged his weapon into the fallen head and flesh ignited once more. The head was lost to the beast. Only one remained. Lomin roared and retracted its cauterized stump of a neck to save what little it could.

I peered out of cover near the Benefactor's rear flank. Coagulated blood seeped from between a torn patchwork of fur, but there were no eyes watching its back. I rushed in, sword drawn, and quickly severed four or five flailing limbs. I retreated to a nearby tree to conceal myself once more, but I needn't have done so. The Benefactor hardly concerned itself with me hacking off its legs.

Its fallen appendages started twitching and deforming, then folded into one another, becoming a single piece of twisting flesh. It writhed and stretched, merging into a uniform, brownish creature. A snare worm. The worm burrowed and popped out near Sentyx, who quickly turned, caught it in the air, and crushed it in his grip. I growled in frustration. If anything, my attack seemed to help the beast, giving him more snares with which to attack my Hand.

Another bolt of Dark magic shot toward the beast and traveled through Lomin's back before hitting the trunk of another tree. The tree began to wither. Its weight compressed the trunk where the magic struck it. The tree fell, crashing near the Benefactor. Inac yelled once more, another blast of magic building in the air around him, but two snare worms burst from the ground by the mage's feet, breaking his sorcerous concentration and disrupting the spell. I cringed and my stomach lurched, but Inac wasn't consumed by whatever the Archedark equivalent of burning up was. Instead, he gracefully spun away from the worms and turned them to brown soup with two touches of Dark.

As Sentyx rushed to aid Inac and Dunnax dealt with his own worms, I ran alongside the Benefactor, slicing through the bones of a snoutbear's leg that the lumbering beast used to support its weight—it buckled. Without stopping, I cut through several other limbs. They turned into snare worms behind me as I rounded a tree to hide.

I could immobilize it, but there were many limbs left to go, and the most important were hardest to get to, surrounded by the flailing claws that protected Lomin's flanks.

A fire arrow shot from the branches above me. I looked up, surprised. Garret was there. A second arrow flashed out and joined the first in Lomin's side. Around both arrows, flames took hold of hide. Abyssal howls filled the air as the Benefactor burned. The beast kicked and bucked like a huge, disfigured horse. My nose rankled when the burning stench reached me. The ground underfoot shook with the creature's furious dance.

Lomin flipped itself ignominiously onto its side, smothering all the flames. When it returned to its feet it revealed the huge craters in flesh left by Garret's fire. This time, when the Benefactor mended itself, something became apparent—with every lost crater of flesh, the creature shrank.

If we kept this up, we would win this fight.

But Garret's attack also caused Lomin to turn, and now it gazed right at me with its one remaining head.

My whole body seized once more. I could think to do nothing more than stay behind the tree and pray to the Lightmother for mercy. But like Lomin had said, in places like this only the Darkfather listened. With my back to the tree, grasping my sword in trembling hands, I closed my eyes and waited. The thunderous rumble of the Benefactor's charge closed in.

Something hammered me in the back. The breath left my lungs, and my feet left the ground. There was no pain, not yet. In midair, something massive struck my side. I hit the ground, rolled several times, and skidded to a stop. My head pounded.

The world spun. Through dazed eyes I saw the Benefactor, outstretched neck creeping around the side of a huge, leaning tree.

Now the pain bloomed. I sucked in a gasping breath, which only confirmed I had broken some ribs. I struggled to one elbow with the one arm I could still feel, but the effort was denied by a snare worm. It sprung from the ground and wrapped around my chest. Tightening. Crushing. My head felt like it was about to pop. As if from a distance I heard myself screaming in agony.

But with mortal threat came clarity; thoughts faded as my mind drifted toward primeval. My sword had landed out of reach. The hilts of my knives dug into my back, uselessly pinned. I had nothing but one hand to use; it clawed viciously at the snare worm. I craned my neck to bite at the worm, but it was out of reach. Sentyx had made it look so easy, but my strength quickly waned. I couldn't grasp the slippery worm. At the edge of sight, darkness crept in. Breaths grew shallower. All feeling below my chest left me.

Thunk.

The worm uncoiled, slithered into the ground with a squeal. Sensation came rushing back and I drew another painful breath, deep as I could before coughing and sputtering. My arm grazed the shaft of an arrow sticking from the ground, and I followed its pointing feathers back to where Garret hunched in the boughs of a tree.

"Thanks," I rasped, and immediately regretted it. But Garret had already gone, jumping through the trees.

Lomin paid no further attention to me. Instead, it focused on Inac and the danger the Archemage's Dark magic posed. Countless worms sprang from the ground, trying to ensnare and crush the life from Inac. He danced between them, killing each snare that came, his every defense seeming just-in-time, the pace of fighting too frenetic for recovery. He couldn't keep it up for much longer. Sentyx protected Inac, but the enemy's numbers would soon overwhelm them both. More and more limbs detached from Lomin's body to become worms.

With the Benefactor's attention on Garret who evaded in the trees, Dunnax landed a powerful blow to its taut neck and cleaved fully through it with his Fire-imbued glaive. The head fell to the ground on fire, but a thick claw batted the Paladin to the side, sending him crashing into a tree. The glow on his axe head fizzled out as the Benefactor smothered the fire and reclaimed its head.

I pushed myself up, but before taking a single step my knee buckled. Pain lanced up my side on impact with the rocky ground. Vision dizzied and blurred as I collapsed to the ground, nearly losing consciousness. I wanted to help but could only listen to the pulse of Inac's magic and the heavy rumble of the Benefactor's movement. Then, behind me, a dog growled and barked. My eyes snapped open. A memory surfaced from Lomin's Pool. Apparently, those formed in my mind even after minor Deluges.

It's what you don't see that kills you.

I rolled over and sat up, ignoring the nauseating lurch in my vision. Lomin's Empath padded toward me, bearing sharp teeth in its slavering mouth, the same way it had approached the snoutbear in that cave.

"Val," I croaked, remembering her name, but she only snarled louder.

The Empath sprang forward. I flinched, waiting for teeth to close around my neck. A small yelp, a brush of wind, and something landed on the ground in front of me.

I stared at Val's severed head in confusion, before spinning around. A billowing green coat ran toward the Benefactor, brandishing a huge axe.

Bengard? Is this another vision?

That axe looked immovably heavy. Nonetheless, Bengard *jumped* with his weapon in hand. He twisted in midair to bring the massive blade down on Lomin like a guillotine. Severed head and neck fell to the ground and began to twitch, but the Finger jumped back and threw down a flask that burst into flame, incinerating the odious lump of flesh. As copious gray-red smoke erupted, Lomin roared and lashed out with its claws. Bengard dove to dodge the blow, which cut a gash in his long coat. With one more thunderous bellow that came directly into my mind, the headless Benefactor turned and charged away. With impressive speed, now that it no longer had such bulk to carry around, the beast disappeared into the darkness of the Shaded Grounds.

The valence of Lomin's Aura changed from terror to bloodlust once more, but I felt no urge to chase our fleeing prey. A predator knew when to stay back and lick his wounds.

"Quickly, Hand Sixty-Four!" Bengard shouted, turning to continue the hunt. When no one moved to follow—out of exhaustion more than anything else, judging by the state of the Hand—Bengard slowed. "Tak is in these woods! He's brought urgent news!" The Finger took off in pursuit of the beast.

Barely capable of remaining on two feet, I shouted after him, "Then why aren't we going to him?"

"We are!" He called back over his shoulder, and the darkness swallowed him from sight. The rest of the Hand followed close behind, leaving me alone in a rising red mist that swirled with the light of the dying sun.

CHAPTER NINETEEN

Survival

My chest ached with every choked-on breath as I fought to keep pace with the others. My knee and hip ached each time the forest floor jolted against my left foot. Nausea and dizziness came in unpleasant waves. My sword arm barely responded when I tried to move it. I was in no condition to continue fighting, yet the others rushed headlong into battle. I had painfully loaded my crossbow with only one functioning hand—even that proved nearly too much to handle. The weapon tugged at my fingers, willing me to drop it and leave it behind, as the others had left me.

But maybe one quarrel would be enough. One arrow was all it had taken to kill Wyran.

A surge of flame lit up through the mists ahead and told me I was getting close. The nagging pull of Lomin's Aura inexorably drew me toward the chaotic combat, even as the murky darkness swallowed up my friends and left me alone. I stumbled over the torn body of some Finger bleeding out into the earth, his tattered green coat stained red and brown. His lifeless eyes stared up into the trees. I didn't recognize him, but I sympathized.

If I'm not careful, I'm looking at my near future.

Inac's Dark magic pulsed as a sphere of darkness around the mage. Worms melted into brown liquid by the dozens at the touch of his sorcery. Still more came. They fell from the Benefactor like writhing drops of sweat, burrowing into the ground to strike at the Hand from below.

Slowly, the shedding of worms and the impacts of Bengard's bombs ate away at the Benefactor's mass. No longer did its body slosh around with each swipe of its claws. It had transformed again. Smaller now, but leaner, defter. A predator perfectly designed for slaughter.

Lomin's Aura reversed once more. Iron blood turned to copper fear in my mouth. My heart raced with panic, not anticipation.

It was ready to finish its prey.

Sentyx blocked the swipe of a suddenly formed claw, but the blow sent him flying backward to land on the ground near Inac. The mage ducked and elegantly spun, avoiding the leaping attacks from worms bursting from the ground. Wisps of golden Fire leaked from his eyes as he flowed through the chaotic onslaught, killing swiftly with his Dark magic.

Preoccupied as he was, Inac didn't react to two of the worms snaring Sentyx, pinning the Skardwarf down. But two arrows rained down from the trees and cut the Skardwarf free. With a vehement grunt as thanks, he rushed back in to grapple with the Benefactor, protected from lashing claws by his rock-like hide.

Alongside him, Dunnax and Bengard held their own, protecting themselves and striking when they could. A flaming arrow launched from the trees, but Lomin jumped aside to avoid it. A snare worm sprung up into the branches, and Garret had to move. Everyone was on the defensive, but how long would that last? The Benefactor seemed tireless, but the Hand would soon be expended.

And I was just standing there, watching from afar while the others courted death. My whole body shook, partly with fear, partly with growing anger. A snare worm rustled in the bushes behind me. My free hand fumbled and failed to draw a knife, only drawing a sharp pain in my shoulder instead. But when I turned, a gray-haired man in a long coat emerged and regarded me with eyes magnified by thick spectacles.

"They are dead already," Tak said. "Flee with me while the Emergent is distracted. We must go back to Liwokin. The situation with the Peeker is dire, and..." The mortician hesitated, as though about to admit some great shame. "I need your assistance."

"Flee like a coward?" I scoffed. Merely speaking drew a sharp pain in my chest.

It should have been unthinkable, but I found myself considering Tak's words. If I couldn't fight, how could I survive? My simmering anger boiled over into fury. A flash of golden-red Fire reflected in the spectacles on his face, filling the mortician's eyes with Archemagic. The Benefactor roared. A pulse went through the air, and an echo of Lomin's thoughts rang in my head.

How could I live with myself if I turned tail and let my friends die? What kind of man would I be?

A furious howl ripped from my throat and Tak flinched back. I checked my crossbow and turned back toward the Benefactor. I couldn't get any closer, but even at this range there was a chance I could—

Everything had gone wrong while my back was turned.

Dunnax and Sentyx both lay on the ground nearby, unconscious. It took my mind a moment to reconcile the sight of them beaten down. Lomin must have knocked them away with a single swipe of its powerful claw. The two nearly lay one atop the other. Inac wavered in exhaustion, then collapsed to the ground. Two worms quickly wrapped around him. Garret, too, had been trapped by a worm, though somehow, he was wriggling free of its grasp.

At the Benefactor's rear, Bengard's body was twisted in a heap on the ground, his leg a bleeding mess. Several Archefire bombs had spilled out of his torn satchel beside him. He didn't move until a snare worm sprung from the ground and tightened around his chest; he gasped and resisted, huge muscles flexing to try and tear the worm away. That left me as the only capable fighter.

It might have been funny if it didn't mean we were all going to die.

Lomin slowly surveyed the clearing, as if savoring its victory, drinking in the sight of all its helpless victims before spilling the blood of my friends. If I didn't do something, this place would match the site of slaughter we encountered when first entering the woods. I gritted my teeth against the pain. The abyss would take me before I let my Hand meet that fate. My eyes flicked to the Archefire bombs near the Benefactor.

It's what you don't see that kills you.

We were going to survive.

I took a deep, painful breath. Strained my aching muscles to raise my crossbow. Steadied my aim as best I could.

For the others to survive, one had to die.

I pulled the trigger. The bowstring snapped forward. The stock kicked against my shoulder. My quarrel struck out, pierced Bengard's satchel, and detonated every bomb he had. A brilliant plume of golden Fire erupted, engulfing the Benefactor, Bengard, and the canopy high above. The explosion lifted me from the ground and threw me back, deafening me. The heat seared my skin. I bore the pain only briefly before a crackling in my neck darkened my vision. I never hit the ground.

In the void, sorrow bloomed.

* * *

Never expected to wake up. I assessed the situation with bleary eyes and bleary mind. *Better if I hadn't.* Val's hair was softer than any pillow, warmer than any blanket. She lay there motionless beneath me. Covered in blood. Her fangs still dug into my arm. They hurt, but not as much as the loss of my best friend. A knife in her neck had ended her life, but hesitation had cost me my own. I couldn't bring myself to do it, though I knew it needed doing, and the froth of her bite had seeped into my arm to make certain my demise.

I'd seen the affliction take hold of a fisher in Leppit. Wouldn't go anywhere near the sea and lost his mind soon after. Called on me to put an end to him. Fair enough. There was no hope of healing. But it was easier for me to end his life than it was to end Val's. I didn't even get to bury her before the fever ravaged me.

Incompetence and biting anger gnawed at me for my mistake. Below it a cold fear rose, for the abyss would soon take me. All of that paled in comparison to the depthless sorrow for my loss.

No dogs in the abyss. The Darkfather isn't so kind.

Killing was the only distraction I could fathom. A night of revelrous hunting followed; the best in all my life. The blood loss I sustained seemed to matter little. My inner predator reveled in the deaths of each creature so skillfully slaughtered. Already the rot had corrupted my mind and stoked my ceaseless thirst for violence; I sensed it but did not care. I longed to give in to it further.

With the breaking of the third dawn, the carcasses filling my barn could have traded at Leppit for supplies to last a dozen measures. But I hadn't one more day, much less time to make a journey to the village. Even as I stood marveling at my glorious hunt, exhaustion took me, and I collapsed.

When I awoke in the pile of dead, my mind had no control over my body. Paralyzed, unable to breath, my muscles cramped and spasmed. I was powerless to stop them. With each violent twitch, skin broke, punctured and ripped by claw and tooth until my flesh became blood-streaked ribbon. I could *do* nothing but *felt* everything—nothing more so than terror as all that was me seeped out and mixed into the fetid nest of death. But no matter how much I lost, no matter how infinitesimal I became...

I could not die.

Something latched on. It animated flesh, breaking it down and reforming it endlessly in its hunt for the perfect form. It sought to expand—to become infinitely capacious—as the thing that held me sensed the dark minds of the carcasses around me. It used them to grow but cared not for me nor what terror I felt. It shoved me aside, one mind among many, insignificant. I became suffering itself. I was pain embodied. With flesh abandoned, my dim spirit passed into the mountain of death around me. Transformation occurred, but the will was not mine. I had no control.

For three nights I existed in this sorry state, mind broken and re-broken by the trauma I endured.

But I *endured*.

I was strong, as a hunter must always be. Strong enough to survive when exposed to harsh elements for days on end. Strong enough to take the lives of countless prey with no remorse.

But not strong enough to kill one dog...

This thing that latched onto me, that moved my body in my stead, it would have had no pity for one dog. It had no pity for anything. I sensed its singular purpose like a distant observer of its thoughts. We were one now, the three of us. Me, the carcasses, and...*it*. Only one of us had any control, but despite that... it was afraid. In the darkness, we sat motionless and waited, hidden.

We heard a bark, echoing in a hundred ears. The small part of us that was me recognized Val in an instant.

How is she alive? The needles?

The masked man had mentioned visions as a side effect, but nothing about life after death. The sudden appearance of another mind stirred the thing awake. Val's presence drew closer, and I recognized the thing's intent. The same as always: expansion.

Among many minds, I was only one. But one strong mind can dominate the many weak.

I am a predator. The thing felt my exertion of will and ceded its control. It sensed a careful balance, judged it useful. My sense of touch returned. I flexed the claws at the ends of my arms. A hunger consumed me with the need to hunt. I had been pulled back from the abyss to hunt from beyond the grave. *Long after death, there will always be prey.*

My new body moved to find it.

The memory jerked backward into another. Hazy. Bestial intent melted away, replaced by...unfathomable boredom.

My impatient fingers tapped loudly on the desk, and the irritated lecturer bumbled his way over to me. His jowls flapped like he'd never spent a day working for food in his life.

"There's more subtlety to this world than just predators and prey," the man said, shaking the stick he used to scrawl numbers and symbols in chalk. "I have told you once already, Lomin. Do *not* treat it as a hunt," he said, speaking slowly, as if I were a dull child, "and do *not* make me repeat myself!"

Some brat in the room snickered, but Val's growling and a slap on the head from his father quickly put an end to that. Everyone else avoided eye contact with me as I looked around. Fine. I preferred it that way.

Too many people in this city, not enough animals.

The sound of tapping chalk drew the attention of the lecturer's victims as the fat man drew a circle around a section of the board then jabbed at it for emphasis.

"Death," he said, "is no longer something to be feared, but—"

Blah, blah, blah. Hope you're writing this down, Val.

She barked, as if in response, interrupting the tedious lecturer, whose face turned red. That drew a laugh from me.

The man's cheeks trembled as he screamed. "You think this is—"

*   *   *

The Deluge ended abruptly, snapping my awareness back to the present, in the woods. The Shaded Grounds were meant to be dark, weren't they? What was that awful smell? Why was my hand so hot? My momentary confusion ended as the weight of what I had done settled on me like a fallen tree.

My crossbow was on fire. Flinching from the heat, I threw it away and sat up, carefully as I could. The weapon burned on the forest floor. After what I'd just used it to do, I didn't want to touch a crossbow ever again. Everything still hurt, but my pain seemed small now compared to Lomin's. The ghost of his suffering haunted me like the memory of a bad dream. In the shadows of roaring flame, the silhouette of the monster he became diminished, shrinking until it resembled the figure of a broken man before completely wisping away.

"Well done, Grim," Tak said, brushing the soot and dirt from his long white coat, looking otherwise unscathed. "Now we really must be going. Time is short."

Well done?

I glared at him. "Fuck off."

Tak giggled. I would have throttled him if not for the fact that my hands no longer seemed to work. "The beast is slain." The mortician gestured to the flames as he walked, then knelt beside Sentyx, who stirred, and Dunnax, who did not. "Though, of course, not all of us survived. Tragic." He reached into his bag.

"Touch him," Garret said, limping over, "and you won't survive."

Tak pulled a glass vial from his bag and removed the stopper. The distorted reflection of flames danced in it, as though it were an elixir of Fire he poured into Dunnax's slack mouth. "The Paceeqi will live. He is nearly as resilient as the Skardwarf." Then he looked past me, to the broken body of the Finger I had stumbled over earlier. Tak shook his head and tutted. "So foolish. I never even got his name. He distracted the beast to buy me time and paid for my life with his own. A pity that those with courage always perish first. Especially in times like these, when they are so sorely needed." He paused, cleared his throat. "And what of Bengard?"

"He burned," I said without meeting his eyes. The rumbling flames cut through the lingering silence that followed.

"Perhaps...that is for the best," the mortician said, looking at the unnamed Finger's corpse. "We do not know how far this infestation has spread."

"Infestation?" Garret asked.

But Tak ignored him. "We have tarried long enough. Wake your mage. There are things we must discuss. Come, I have a carriage waiting nearby." Tak stood at the edge of a small crater and looked at the smoldering remains of the Benefactor. Trees were ablaze all around. The heat and glow of real flames had replaced the phantom firelight of Lomin's Aura. He adjusted his spectacles and tapped his chin, as though contemplating something, then shook his head, turned, and headed off into the dark.

I wished I could have stayed there in the light of the fire and let that man disappear forever. But he was the key to unlocking the Benefactors' secrets.

"Wait," I croaked. "Bengard said you have urgent news."

Just mentioning the Finger's name made my chest shrivel up with guilt. He had saved my life, and how had I repaid him? By stealing his own.

It was the only way to survive.

But the truth brought little comfort.

"Yes, yes," Tak said, impatiently. "That is why I want to get back to the carriage. I will share the news with you then, but we *really* must be going." He took another step, then froze. "Oh, right. I nearly forgot. Ulken summoned you as well." He handed me a letter, bearing an already-broken wax seal stamped with Ulken's sigil.

Garret brought Inac over. The mage had slung his arm over the Ekoan's shoulder; it looked like he would collapse again at any moment. Sentyx hunched over and carried Dunnax on his back, the Paladin's feet dragging along the ground. I unfolded the letter and read it aloud.

"Return to Agency Headquarters. One Benefactor remains. Final command begins in three days."

CHAPTER TWENTY

Organism

Careful with that!" the lead mortician shouted at his technician. "Those specimens could be pivotal to my research."

I bristled at the command. He cared more about his research than the lives lost to obtain it.

"Of course, sir," the crimson-coated technician said, bowing his head. His long beak of a mask bumped the glass jar from his hand, and he fumbled to catch it, murky fluid sloshing around inside. He chuckled nervously. "Sorry, sir."

"Time is up," Tak growled. "Whatever we have now must suffice. Load that with the rest and fetch your partner. Quickly! I won't hesitate to leave without you."

The technician wasted no time, nearly tripping over his own feet as he hastily rounded the corner of Lomin's cabin.

"Brought your technicians with you to the Shaded Grounds?" Garret asked, scratching at his head. "Why?"

"You didn't think I came all the way out here just for you, did you?" Tak chuckled. "I'm continuing my research. This is where the Incubating Benefactor resided, correct? My technicians have been collecting samples while I followed Bengard.

He knew you were in danger. He was quite a good Finger. A shame."

A good Finger, until I killed him.

"You still haven't told us what you need us for," Dunnax said. "Nor why we should help you."

Tak raised an eyebrow. "Why should you help me? If not for me, all of you would be dead."

"If not for you," Dunnax said, "we wouldn't be here in the first place."

"I have no idea what you're talking about," Tak said, and walked away.

Dunnax grabbed him by the shoulder and turned him around. "A Nerve commanded us to stop working with you. That's what I'm talking about."

Inac nodded, swayed a bit before catching himself. The Archemagic healing he'd performed on us all during the short walk to Lomin's lodge had wrested the last of his energy away. "This assignment was to our Hand a punishment for helping you."

Punishment for kidnapping a Peeker. What's the punishment for killing a veteran Finger?

"Still doubt it was." Garret spat and crossed his arms. "Agency encourages us to get our hands dirty often enough. But Ulken does know about the Peeker we brought you, at any rate."

The mortician shrugged away from Dunnax. The Paladin's hand left a red smear on his white coat. Tak looked at the blood with annoyance. "Well. It is unfortunate that Ulken found out about our little scheme. But I assure you, he'll be pleased with my results. I made incredible progress with that Incubating Peeker. It produced an extraordinary discovery!" He gave an excited smile, which quickly lilted to a frown. "But also...something quite alarming. Which is why we *must* go." He strode toward the front of Lomin's cabin again, and we all followed.

"What do you mean, alarming?" I asked, but Tak ignored me, walked away. This was as bad as Ulken sending unwitting Fingers into battle with an Emergent. Once again, we had no idea what we were being dragged into. I growled and clenched my fists.

I took one step forward, but Sentyx must have sensed my anger, for he stopped me with an implacable hand across my chest. Even after the healing, dull pain radiated from where my rib had been broken. Sentyx looked at me apologetically. I grimaced and shook my head to assure him I wouldn't do anything stupid. Then, we followed Tak to the front of the hunter's home.

The mortician's carriage awaited at the edge of the woods, silver from top to bottom, reflecting the ruddy light in the sky above the lake. A sharp clang sounded as a technician slammed shut a compartment at the back of the vehicle and ran at full sprint into the deserted lodge. Apart from a tall cylinder sticking up near the rear, the carriage's body was all angles: a gleaming rectangle that looked more like a small shack than a comfortable means of transportation. The only resemblance it had to a carriage was its four wheels and the tiny window in the door just big enough for a secretive rider to peer through. The hard ground gave way under the weight of this metal monstrosity. Deep grooves showed the carriage's trajectory to where it now rested. How many horses were needed to drag this thing through the woods? But while Tak moaned about being in a hurry, something important seemed to be missing.

"Where," I asked, "are the horses?"

"Horses?" Tak snorted. "Relics of the past. Haven't you heard of steam carriages?"

Sentyx grunted, but whether he meant yes or no, I couldn't say. I didn't think they had vehicles like this in the south, but then again, I didn't think we had vehicles like this in the north either. So what did I know?

I shrugged.

"Ah," Tak clapped his hands. "You are in for a treat. This is the state-of-the-art in overland transportation. Once this engineering marvel has carried you home, you'll never settle for a horse again!"

* * *

Tak cleared his throat after we had been riding in his "state-of-the-art transportation" for long enough that I could no longer feel anything below my chest. "I, er, apologize for the cramped conditions."

Cramped? That's overly generous. The whole Hand slept piled atop each other, squashed as tightly together as the carcasses in the hunter's barn. Inac's chin dug into my shoulder as the mage slept so soundly it looked like he might never wake again. My leg bent awkwardly around Dunnax's armored knee. The distant knot in my thigh told me a horrific cramp lurked in my future, awaiting its chance to strike when the feeling in my legs returned. Worst of all, everything was *wet*. A small crack in the boiler vented hot steam with each bump and jostle of the carriage. The small space was so humid I expected to drown before reaching Liwokin. The croaking snores of Dunnax reverberated within our tin casket, reaching my left ear a fraction of a breath later than my right, where the Paladin's drooling mouth gaped. It amazed me that anyone could sleep in such a place. And Tak had called horses a "relic of the past." For this? *Crawling home with two broken legs would be preferable.*

Only Tak and his two technicians remained awake with me. Even through the night the mortician did not allow his crimson-coats a reprieve from work. One of them manned an unwieldy wheel that jerked left and right, slipping in his grasp as the forest trail fought against his attempts to steer. The other shoveled in turn coal and then water into separate compartments of the boiler, spilling half of each to the ground, no doubt unable to see what he was doing through his endlessly fogging goggles. When he wasn't cajoling his bumbling helpers, Tak, at least, seemed comfortable. The mortician sat separately on a cushioned seat reserved just for him, fanning himself with a hat to fend off the heat of this rolling furnace.

"I didn't expect to be transporting so many of you back," Tak said.

"No." I didn't bother to hide the scorn in my voice. "You expected us all to die."

It had been a close thing. Even Sentyx had reluctantly accepted the fiery healing, though he bore the suffering quietly—silently, but silence of a different flavor than his usual. The fight with Lomin had left him shaken.

Darkfather...seeing Sentyx injured had shaken *me*.

That might have been the first time in his life that Sentyx had ever been physically hurt. It almost made my murdering of Bengard seem necessary.

Almost.

That explosion may have saved us, but it had also left us with searing burns. Inac had explained that burns could not be healed by Archefire alone, which I supposed made a certain kind of sense, but Inac was too tired to elaborate. Dunnax, of course, refused treatment. He chose to bear his burns with pride. But the cold touch of the mage's Dark had soothed my blistering skin, drained my energy and made heavy my eyelids.

Every part of me, body and soul, ached for some much-needed rest. But as tired as I was, I could not sleep, for every time I closed my eyes, I saw fire. Wyran's home. Wick's body. Andya and her innocent children. Lomin and Bengard. All became ash.

Everything ends in fire.

"I expected you to die," Tak admitted. "True. Though I'm as pleased as you are that you didn't. An entire helping Hand is preferable to yours alone."

"Helping with *what*?" I asked, growing increasingly impatient with Tak's lack of candor. "What's so dire that you risked your life to find us? Why won't you tell us?"

"I will," Tak said, "in time. When everyone wakes. My master taught me foremost never to repeat myself, back when I was a technician. 'Say what's necessary only once,' he told me—and only once, I should say—'and people will learn to listen closely.'" Tak rubbed his chin and leaned forward. "Listen well when I tell you, what we're doing is absolutely necessary. You'll just have to trust me."

"Why should I?"

"Because," Tak said, "I admire you, Grim."

I scoffed. "What?"

"You and your Hand. Other Fingers as well. As crucial as my research is, I wonder whether I could be doing...more." The mortician sighed. "You're out fighting Emergent Benefactors while I sit in an uncomfortable chair writing death certificates more than anything else. It's thanks to you Fingers that I have room to experiment at all. I don't take that for granted. I know the risks you incur. Better than anyone else, for every one of you ends up on my slab in the end. Everything I do is to keep more of you out of my mortuary."

Tak sounded...genuine. Cutting and probing endless bodies hadn't numbed the mortician's feelings about death. Instead, it motivated him. For a moment, he appeared to be a caring, thoughtful human being. Even his technicians were dumbfounded by this, because the boiler started squealing and the carriage bumped hard against the ground. But one moment of carelessness was too much for Tak to abide, and his demeanor shifted back to that of the perpetually annoyed overseer, in time to resume the chiding of his thralls.

"Admire them," I said, when the mortician had calmed down, "but not me, ever again. Not after what I've done."

"What you've done?" Tak said. "And what's that? I stood right behind you. I know what happened to Bengard. Such pragmatism, in my view, should be admired."

I would have flinched if Sentyx's weight weren't pinning me against the bench. I waited, making sure everyone still slept. The Hand couldn't learn that I had killed Bengard. I already hated myself. I didn't need their hatred piled atop my own.

"Quiet," I hissed. "A good man died, because of *me*."

"By my decidedly expert analysis," the mortician said, "you were losing. Better one good man died than six."

"*You* brought him here," I said, and jabbed a free finger at him. I felt a twinge in my bad shoulder. "You played just as much a part in his death."

"It's my fault, then?" Tak asked, then shrugged. "So be it. I'll take the blame if it unburdens you. Bengard knew the risks, as all Fingers do."

"Not the new recruits," I whispered. "Not those who fail Ulken's field test." How could I ever have accepted the excuse that the weak needed pruning from the Agency? Maybe they shouldn't have been Fingers, but they could have been cast out without being *killed*.

"No," Tak said, frowning, "they don't. I have raised my concerns about this practice, but what is the voice of one mortician to the Head of the Agency? I'm lucky enough to have convinced him not to name my position after some repulsive body part, such as the Toes of the Agency. I wouldn't have put it past him. When Ulken has made up his mind, there is no changing it. And yet, I'm not sure he's wrong. For all his faults, look at the order our Head has wrought. Sometimes acid can stabilize a solution, though it burns to the touch. Not everything that is effective is pleasant." Tak's frown turned into a wry grin. "Ulken is much like you, I should think."

My stomach turned at the notion that I had anything in common with Ulken. The cart rolled over something and jerked twice. My head banged against the wall. I closed my eyes, clenched my jaw, breathed. "How much longer?"

"Not long. We will reach the Enclave before dawn breaks." Tak grinned again and gave a pleased sigh.

"Enclave? I thought we were going—"

"Impressive, isn't it?" Tak interrupted, absorbed in self-congratulations. "The speed with which something like this can move through the woods. Even faster on roads, with no natural obstacles in our way. And yet, this is only a prototype, one that surely will see many improvements. We travel now with the speed of horses, but one day we will move as swiftly as birds."

And how often do birds flatten themselves against windows?

"Sounds like more work for morticians to me."

Tak began to respond but only frowned.

I grunted, put my head back against the rumbling metal, and closed my eyes. Despite my doubts that I might rest, consciousness eventually faded, replaced by something new. If I slept, I did not dream. I remembered.

But the memories were not my own.

* * *

Lightning cracked the sky and lit the dark bay. From the vantage atop this cliff, the flash left an afterimage of distant trees, bowing down to the howling wind that ravaged the island in the Lawiko Sea. Two rapid heartbeats later, the boom of thunder cut through the ceaseless crashing of violent waves far below. Dying breakers erupted like white-tipped spears, daring me to skewer myself below. But seeing white was good; it made for a softer splash. There would be no better time. I had to prove myself tonight, or I'd never be accepted in this village.

Or the fires I lit will be for nothing.

I readied the stolen harpoon, closed my eyes, and waited for the next bolt of lightning. The moment it flashed behind my eyelids, my eyes snapped open, fixating on the dark waters below, where helmies swarmed like flies. I dove, with a prayer to the Lightmother on my lips. One moment of perfect concentration, of steel determination. That was all I needed.

But my sister's shout reached me from the shore far below. "Wyran!"

My body instinctively turned to find her. An instant later, the impact brought pain as cold as the death of a family. With one shiver, blackness swallowed me up, and I sank to the bottom of the sea.

I kicked up and emerged from the lake.

The surrounding crystal blue waters swelled with red as the Brightdaughter's heat warmed my icy skin. *Lake was warm today. If I'm this cold already, I'm losing blood fast.* I grabbed the knife from between my teeth with my free hand. Trying to place it safely in my belt as I kicked to keep afloat, I nicked my thigh and swore an oath, but managed to secure the blade. The pruney fingers that went to my lips tasted of iron as I whistled for Val to come. She didn't appear, so I whistled again, waited, then swore another oath and started kicking for shore.

My left arm had already gone numb, and fear nipped at me. *I'm not losing this bastard today, not after this long.* I hadn't a clue how a shark found its way to my lake, but his days making meals of my fish were over. It tried to make a final meal of me, and its teeth were still deep in my bloody arm. That seemed fair. My knife was still deep in its bloody head. *By land or lake, no one hunts better than me.* With my one free arm I pulled myself through the water, dragging my prey behind, thinking about the lashing I would give that abyss-damned dog.

Crawling to shore, coughing from exertion, I took a deep, shuddering breath, then looked at my arm. It pulsed with fiery pain as soon as I left the water. Blood gushed onto the sand from the shark's clenched jaws at an alarming rate, but this was nothing I couldn't deal with. I looked into the shark's dead eyes, the red pouring steadily from his fatal wounds. *At least I fared better than you.* I tried once more prying his mouth open, but even lifeless, his jaws were locked shut.

No choice then.

I took a breath. *A good hunter does what needs doing.* With feet planted on the shark's nose, its bite loosened just enough for me to *rip* my arm free of its mouth. Its serrated teeth left me mangled and torn, but I was free. "I've seen worse," I said firmly. Hadn't I?

The sand slowed my steps and made me clumsy as I ran for the shed, already feeling faint by the time I shouldered open the door. *Not like I've never been bit before.* But now even my good hand stopped doing what it was told. It knocked over a box of medical supplies as I grabbed the bandages, but I had no time to worry over that. It took a whole roll to wrap up my arm, and they soaked through quick, soiled even before I finished tying them off. *Another roll for good measure then. A good hunter...*

The world spun and took my legs from under me. I blinked and found myself on the ground.

The crashing of boxes must have finally drawn Val, for she appeared in the corner of my eye.

"Well, now you show up," I said, surprised at how weak my voice had become. "Fetch the Druids, girl."

Just got to patch myself up and wait. Val would bring a healer from the Pinegrave. She knew the way, and they still owed me for taking care of those wolves. The world whirled again as I struggled to my knees. Val's shadow darkened the doorway. "You're still here? Go!"

Val didn't go. She snarled, rough and angry, like teeth grinding on bone. She shook, her wolf-like hair bristling.

"Val? What's wrong, girl?"

A fearsome bark was her reply. My eyes adjusted to the light behind her. At the sight of frothy white foam dripping from her muzzle, my eyes filled with tears. My hand fumbled for my knife, fingers wrapping weakly around its handle.

I closed my eyes, and the pooled tears ran down my cheeks. *No...Darkfather, please. Have mercy.* The pain of his renewed curse made it hard to speak. "You said it would help, what you did. You said I'd have my life back."

"I'm sorry, Andya," the mortician said, shaking his head. "It helped for a time, didn't it? But your illness has progressed too far to stop."

Another coughing fit, and my handkerchief filled with black phlegm, covering the old red stains. Cloudy tears dripped into the odious mixture. "My children...they need their mother. They need me."

The mortician sighed behind his thick mask. "They could become afflicted as well. For their sake, Andya. Stay away." He took my hand, which looked withered and tiny in his gloved palm. "They will be well cared for. I'll see to it."

The faces of my little girl and little boy filled my mind's eye. Would I ever see them again? The thought of Egren raising them on his own sickened me. The thought of him finding a new mother to raise them filled my throat with bile.

"What...what would you have me do?" I whimpered.

"You should remain here, under supervision."

Gray walls, gray floors, gray stone slabs. Spending the rest of my days in a mortuary, as though I were already dead? No matter how few days remained to me before the Darkfather had his way...

"I can't." When I hung my head, the bones popped at the top of my spine.

The mortician let go of my hand and shrugged. "You could transfer to Liwokin, then," he said. "I have to return anyway. We could travel together. The city has better facilities. We might even be able to treat you."

Another needle in my neck? Some good that did. The Darkfather's curse couldn't be beaten. I could only prolong my fate, resist the abyss one day at a time. But to do that in the city, away from my children. What was the point?

"No," I said. "I'll stay here." A hopeful thought came to me, a rare gift from the Lightmother. "You're in this room with me. Your mask, coat, gloves... they keep you safe, somehow, don't they? With the same outfit my children could—"

"Out of the question, Andya." The mortician stood. "If you wish to remain here, I'll respect your wishes. But stay *away* from them, Andya. Please. This affliction cannot be allowed to spread." He opened the door and stepped out.

"But—"

The door closed.

Two steps down the long hallway and it creaked open again. I rounded on Ulken as he stepped out of the classroom. When he closed the door behind him, a gust of air struck me that smelled of ammonia and saltpeter.

"*What*?" I snarled.

"Yezna," he said, "please, just listen to what Prost has to say."

"I've heard quite enough from that man. Haven't you? You would have been Council Chair if not for him. Did he put these ideas in your head?" I turned to leave. Reed needed to know about this. "This experiment of yours is *over*."

Ulken snatched my arm and turned me around. His grip was tight, painful. His smile was warm, but his eyes were cold and dark.

Who is this man? I wondered, pulling away from him. *Not the one I loved.*

"You cannot stop it," he said. "None of us can. It's already in motion. We can only control where it goes from here."

I tried tugging my arm free, but there could be no escape. He prided himself in always maintaining control. But I was *done* with him. He would no longer control *me*. "You're insane if you ever thought I would agree to this." I met his gaze so he could see my resolve. He tried to frighten me, but I'd show him I wasn't scared.

Ulken sighed and softened his grip. "You're right."

There was the briefest flicker of hope that I could bring him back. That the husband whom I loved was not yet so far gone. That he would hear the voice of reason and end this nightmare that he started.

Then he leaned close to whisper, "I never thought you would."

Something sharp pricked the back of my neck. Glass clinked on the stone floor. My mind and body went numb. I couldn't resist as he dragged me back toward the classroom.

The door slammed shut with a bang.

Loose metal rattled as the world rocked from the force of the impact.

"Change in management," a man in white scoffed. He rudely gestured at a tiny slit of a window, then turned to face me, morning light glinting across his spectacles. "Druids," he grumbled. "Always so sanctimonious. Now, of all times, they choose to stop working with us? When I'm this close to completing my research..."

"Tak?" I asked, words slipping out and slurring on my sleep-lazy tongue. I tried to move, but my muscles refused, as though I were trapped beneath a heavy weight. My head lolled to the side and banged against something, but the pain was a long distance off. Hands dug under my arms to lift my body, dragged me out from the weight that pinned me. Something hard hit my back. Through blurred vision many figures stared back at me below crinkled brows. A sorcerer robed in blue, a giant clad in metal, a statue carved of stone, a hunter in a cloak of leaves. Beside them all, the mortician sat down in a huff, brushing off his coat to compose himself.

This place feels familiar...

"Grim," a deep voice said, "you okay?" The giant's gauntleted hand grasped my shoulder and shook me repeatedly. Before I could tell him to stop, someone slapped me hard across the cheek and jolted me into the present.

"Enough!" I shouted. "Enough. I'm awake." I rubbed my sore cheek. "Thanks for that."

"Any time," Garret said.

Tak shouted at his technician, and the steam-carriage lurched into motion with a concerning pop from the boiler.

"Where are we?" I asked.

"The Pinegrave," Inac said. "Were you not awake when we arrived here?"

Was I?

The Pine's dulling Aura hung over me, but it hadn't dampened the memories of the others that filled my head. They were distant yet vivid. Multiple memories proceeded like a single event, as though the Benefactors' Pools had mixed, and details bled into one another. Worse, they seeped into my own memories, making me one piece of a larger whole, as Lomin had felt when he became Emergent. Though I must have been awake now, part of me expected to reawaken once more in a...classroom. One from which I desperately wanted to escape. The details of that memory crystallized in my mind, and it dawned on me who I had been.

Yezna?

Ulken's wife. *Just listen to what Prost has to say,* he'd said, then stuck a needle in her neck.

So, Prost had advised Ulken to create the Benefactors...but why? I rubbed my eyes and pushed the thought from my mind. One problem at a time, and right now I was more concerned with my loss of tether to reality.

"You were sleep-talking at the outpost," Garret said. "Now you're sleeping with your eyes open. Getting hard to figure out whether you're awake or asleep."

The Ekoan had a knack for putting my own thoughts into words. Especially those I didn't want to hear.

"Looked like you were just...thinking about something," he continued. "Something that you wanted to keep buried. You and Bengard were close, right?"

My gut clenched. "Not really..." I glanced at the others. Inac and Dunnax were studying the floor of the cart, bumping and swaying with the motion of each root or mound we rolled over. Sentyx alone met my eyes, facing the wind, watching the guilt wash over me.

"Doubt that made it any easier," Garret said. "You did what you had to do."

"I—" My mouth hung open uselessly. So many things came to mind that I couldn't choose between them. I didn't have to kill him. How could they trust me now? How, by the abyss, did they find out? There could only be one answer to the last. I glared at Tak, who returned a casual, infuriating shrug.

"I was certain they would see it my way," the mortician said, grinning.

"You thought telling my friends I killed someone was doing me a favor?"

"Now there are no secrets."

Hissing steam and rolling iron cut through the painful silence.

"Why..." I muttered. I fought back tears, then heat rose within me, and I shouted. "Why aren't you fighting me on this? Am I the only one who thinks what I did was *wrong*?"

Sentyx grunted. "Not just you."

"Then you agree."

"No," Garret countered. "He's saying we've *all* done terrible things." He waved at Inac and Dunnax, both of whom still refused to look up. "Judging by the silence of this righteous duo, I can only guess at what they've got in their past." Garret shrugged. "Tak's got a point. So you killed one man. Saved my life doing it. Figure I can't get upset about that."

I shook my head in disbelief. "I *murdered* a fellow Finger. He was the reason I joined the Agency. He said I'd have a friend on the inside..." But I'd caused the deaths of dozens of men as a bounty hunter. Why was this one different? I couldn't manage more than to whisper, "Bengard was a good man."

The tears flowed in earnest now. Someone placed a hand on my shoulder, comforting me as I sobbed.

"You feel guilty, yes?" Inac said. "That is good."

I shrugged away from the mage's hand. *Just what I need. A lecture on morality from Inac.*

"It is how I know," Inac said, "that you are not a monster."

I choked up, squeezed my eyes shut, let out a shuddering breath.

"Ah, good," Tak said, seizing the opportunity to interrupt at the most inappropriate time. "Now that the air is cleared, I can share my discovery with you. From the Peeker...Are you listening?"

No one responded, perhaps out of sheer incredulity at Tak's utter lack of tact.

The mortician adjusted his spectacles, looked us over as if something were wrong with *us*, then shrugged and continued. "Now, I am no artist, I admit, but let me attempt to paint a picture for you." He leaned forward conspiratorially, close enough for me to punch him in the face. But I'd been waiting to hear what he meant to drag us into, and for the time I was glad the conversation had moved beyond my failures.

"What I've discovered," the mortician explained, "is the most *extraordinary* creature, so small that it can only be seen through precisely fabricated lenses." Tak removed his spectacles and tapped a fingernail against the glass before replacing them. "The lenses are much like these, commissioned from Archeglaziers in Ayeir, but designed to see small objects from up close instead of afar. But I digress. Where was I?" Tak cleared his throat. "Oh yes. The creatures seem to work together, countless individuals moving as one. Have you ever seen bees working on the surface of their hive? If you dare to get close enough to the swarm, you can see the individuals, but move away and they look like writhing waves on a bumpy, golden sea." The mortician seemed pleased with himself for that imagery, as though he had been waiting to share it for days. "These Benefactor organisms swarm in the same way. Somehow, they entered the Peeker's body, made their way to its brain, and covered its surface completely. Dug into the gray matter, really, with tiny claws, and embedded themselves, just as if the brain were their own hive."

I'd already felt like I was going to be sick. The idea of countless Benefactors digging into my brain threatened to make it a reality.

"So," Dunnax said. "The Peeker's dead."

"No, no," Tak protested, "of course not. We simply removed a section of the Peeker's skull and peered inside. The procedure was painless, as far as I could tell, and the mending done by my technicians left it with only a small scar." The mortician smirked. "Better than any Archehealer could do. Unfortunately, scarring is the least of its troubles, given the circumstances. But the Peeker is not dead. Not yet anyway."

"What?" I snapped. "You promised us he wouldn't die." The possibility that an Emergent would soon ravage my home put my self-loathing in perspective.

Tak held up a finger to correct me. "I said I did not *intend* for the Peeker to die. Alas, the Peeker's lack of Seedling made the subject particularly susceptible to attack by the Benefactors. I assure you, in fact, that I am the only reason it still lives."

"Great," Garret said. "But the Druids wouldn't sell you any Tears, so whatever plan you had is falling apart. What do we do now?"

"The Tears were merely a safeguard," Tak said, waving away the ranger's concerns. "The plan remains unchanged. When I deduced how rapidly the Peeker's stability was degrading, I immediately intervened. It's now being kept in stasis by technicians and clerics."

"Clerics?" Dunnax asked. "You got the Church involved?"

"Extraordinary circumstances..." Tak said, spreading his hands. "I've learned all I can from the living specimen, but it is vital that the subject not be allowed to die. Not until we're ready."

My stomach roiled, and a sour taste climbed my throat. "Ready for what?"

An excited grin spread between Tak's ears. "For us to witness its transformation, of course."

CHAPTER TWENTY-ONE

Emergence

The steam carriage came to an abrupt stop, rousing me from sleep. A dreamless slumber, by the Darkfather's mercy.

"Sir, I think you should see this," Tak's technician said in a tired drawl from behind his mask. He must have been exhausted after sitting at the wheel for so long. Or had he swapped places with the coal shoveler? Their masks made them impossible to tell apart.

Easier for Tak to treat the faceless so poorly.

"What is this?" the mortician said, standing over the technician's shoulder to peer out his driver's window, small and round like the porthole of a ship. "We have no time for delays. Just go around."

"There's no room, sir."

"Then just go through them!" Tak threw up his hands. "They'll get out of the way." He turned to scowl at the coal shoveler. "Did I tell you to stop? Keep that boiler hot!"

"What's going on?" Dunnax said, underneath Garret and Inac. Only Sentyx was lower in the pile, but he weathered that position without complaint. The four of them clustered together more tightly after my visions, giving me my own space, as though my madness might taint them if they touched me.

With a sigh, I stood to see why we had stopped. But I didn't need sight to tell me where we were. A waft of something awful came through the slits in the doors, like urine, feces, and decaying flesh all combined, strong enough to cut through the musty smell of coal in this tiny, mobile box. For what felt the first time in ages, a broad smile swept across my face.

"We're home," I said. "For the love of light, let's walk from here."

Sentyx grunted, no doubt receptive to the idea.

"Patience," Tak said. "This rabble will clear out soon."

Something banged at the front of the steam carriage, and the driver shifted to look through the porthole. "Hey!" he shouted. "Stop that!" But his words had no effect.

"Well, I'm not waiting for this roadblock to clear," I said.

Tak grumbled as I pushed past him, and Inac yelped when I stepped on his toes. I undid the latch and threw open the door to fresh air, breathing deep the scents of Liwokin. Garret coughed and gagged. A throng of miserable expressions greeted me, a mix of envy, pleading, anger, and confusion, eyes turned to witness the spectacle of Tak's carriage. A welcome sight against the backdrop of my city.

My people.

But something was wrong. Those who observed the steam-carriage were a small rock in the river of the great masses flowing around them. I leaned out the door, hanging on to a warm metal bar that flexed precariously. Liwo poured out of the city gates by the thousands, an unbroken stream of people crossing the road ahead of us. A memory flashed, bringing me back to the day of the mass burial after the Riot. As the Liwo marched somberly back into the city, misery marked all the faces of those who'd buried someone lost to the chaos. The crowd before me was just as massive, but everyone was shambling in the wrong direction. Breath caught in my throat as I scanned the air above the city. No plumes of smoke. No ringing of bells. Nothing to indicate what terrible event was driving everyone out like homeless refugees.

Nothing.

Were we too late? Had the Peeker already become Emergent within the city? Where was the panic, the fear, the chaos? Why weren't these people heading anywhere sensible, rather than streaming off...to where? The woods? I leaned out further to find the source of the banging sound. People were carelessly bumping into the vehicle, as if it had suddenly appeared in front of them. By the abyss, what was going on?

I may not have known much, but anytime something strange happened lately, there was sure to be a Benefactor involved.

"This carriage isn't going anywhere," I said. "We need to get in there." The crowd backed up a step as I jumped down to land in front of them. I found a woman who seemed more cogent than the rest and took her hands in mine. "Please, can you tell me what's—"

She yanked her hands free. "You Gilders are all the same. Don't you touch me!"

"What?" I turned to a boy. "You there, what's happening?"

"No, sir. I'm sorry, sir. I won't be late again, I swear it. By the Mother of Light, I swear it."

I stepped back, examining the faces more closely. Those few who looked at me wore various expressions, as if none saw me the same way. Most looked right through me, as though I weren't there at all. I rubbed at my eyes, and a visage of a forest filled the space behind my eyelids. I had been spending too much time away from the city. Every time I closed my eyes there were forests, fires, or bleeding, broken bodies. In any case, one thing was clear. These peoples' minds were not their own. So whose were they?

Vaguely aware that my Hand was calling my name, I took off running alongside the migration, against the current of their movement. Countless faces flashed past. Where any emotion showed at all, it seemed incongruous with any event happening in reality. I caught bits of conversations, but no one mentioned this roving herd. It seemed everyone thought they were going about their daily business. One person said he was headed back to the city, though his feet carried him with the others in the wrong direction. He spoke to the person next to him as if they were in conversation, but the responses made no sense. It was as if they were talking to each other and to different people simultaneously.

Dread filled my chest as my worst fears came to pass. With lifeless eyes and blank faces, most of these people seemed already dead. A Benefactor was destroying Liwokin. I had to stop it before—

A familiar face stuck out from the crowd. It was stoic, oddly relaxed, but when he looked at me, with his bright blue eyes...

I know those eyes...

Vertigo rushed over me, and I stumbled, overtaken by a memory from Lomin's Pool.

* * *

The eyes...

Always a dead giveaway. The fear in those glassy portals that always accompanied Val's arrival told me all I needed to know.

I've got him right where I want him.

"So, Falnick," I said, scratching Val behind the ears. "What do you say? I'll take no less. Animals are getting far too aggressive to back down. Do we have a deal?" I thrust a gloved hand toward him, grinned when he flinched back.

For a moment, the fear in the buyer's bright blue eyes looked like it would turn to anger. Selling my wares was a different sort of hunt, exciting in more subtle ways than bloodshed.

Treat the buyer like prey, and he'll flee like prey.

He knew I was overcharging him for the pelts, but what choice did he have? He wouldn't want to journey back empty-handed and terminate our long-standing relationship. I had tried to be fair with the man, ever since he let me know about the quick gold I could make in the city. But that was a long time ago, and that gold had long since run out. There was a chance he'd refuse the offer. Best to have Val make a timely appearance to stifle any feelings of indignation.

This hunt, too, favors the strong.

Falnick let out a long-held breath and nodded. He waved my hand away, as usual. "Fine, Lomin. It's a deal, no need to shake on it. But aggressive animals? That's a weak excuse. My partners will need a better explanation, next measure."

Val growled at the man. I chuckled. She played the part of a feral beast well while we hunted, but she was timid as a kitten most times. "What can I say? Lucky for us, none will ever be as vicious as my Val."

* * *

I coughed, sending up a cloud of dirt. Someone stepped on my hand, and I yelped, pulled it close, and rolled onto my back. My hand throbbed. Worried faces craned over me.

"Are you okay?" Sentyx asked.

No.

"I'm fine," I said, accepting Dunnax's extended hand. He yanked me to my feet, nearly tearing my arm from my socket. Pain radiated from my bad shoulder. "Just tired."

"The way you fell," Garret said, "seemed like you died between one step and the next."

My head pounded, not just from slamming it into the ground. My mind was at war with itself. Whoever won that war, I was fairly sure *I'd* lose.

"There was," Inac guessed, "another vision given to you, yes?"

My silence was enough confirmation.

"Those eyes triggered in my mind the memory."

"You saw it too?" I asked. "All of you?"

"I saw you fall," Sentyx said.

"Yeah," Dunnax said. "What's wrong with you two? Why are you seeing visions we're not?"

"I have a theory," Tak offered. When had he arrived?

"Can't wait to hear it," Garret said, rolling his eyes.

"Excellent," Tak clapped his hands together once, failing to detect Garret's sarcasm. "The theory is simple. You're infested with the Benefactor organism."

Everyone took a step away from me and Inac.

"Oh, come now," Tak said. "No need to be so wary. You're probably all infested already."

"What?" Dunnax stepped close to Tak, as if the mortician had just insulted his sister.

Tak chuckled nervously, then patted the Paladin's chest plate. "Only a theory, my friend. Only a theory."

Dunnax towered over the man. "We are not friends," he said, then backed off.

"You are saying to us," Inac said, "we are Incubating Benefactors?"

Garret spat. "Thought you said all the Benefactors got needles in their neck, Grim."

I nodded. "But I never did."

Or did I? I had so many memories floating around in my head where a needle pricked my neck that it was hard to know the truth.

"Makes sense," Garret said. "No animal would need manmade needles to reproduce. They must have some other means."

"Indeed," Tak agreed. "However, the mechanism is still unclear. I will have to perform some experiments to determine what substances the Benefactor organism can survive in. Water, air, blood?" The mortician grinned. "My technicians and I will be quite busy, but the results will certainly prove beneficial to you Fingers."

"Your theory does not tell to me why they see no visions," Inac said. "If they too are all infested..."

Tak shrugged. "Maybe you two have been infested for much longer. Now that I know what to look for, I could determine how easily the organism spreads."

"By cutting open our skulls," Dunnax muttered, but the mortician ignored him.

"My belief," Tak said, "is that they spread quite rapidly. Otherwise, how could there be so many Benefactors?"

Something clicked into place in my head, from another Pool, older than the rest. One of Yezna's memories. "'You cannot stop it. None of us can. It's already in motion. We can only control where it goes from here.'"

"Eh?" Garret furrowed his brow. "What's that?"

"Ulken's words," I said, clenching my fists, "to his wife, long ago. Before he jabbed a needle in her neck. He knew this would happen."

Tak hummed, tapped his chin in thought. "You're saying Ulken had a hand in creating the Benefactors. Quite alarming, indeed. But why would he do this? To what end?"

We reached the Span Gate, where two bodies lay face down, trampled in the exodus from the city. "Doesn't matter what Ulken's plans were," I said, then gestured at the horde. "This is what he's done to my city. He'll die for it."

* * *

After passing through the gate into the Burg, the streets of Liwokin became eerily quiet. One pair of men talked in hushed tones, speculating about where everyone had gone and what they were missing out on. Guards patrolled with determined looks on their faces, holding their swords drawn, as if they hoped to be the ones to stop whatever was going on and come out as heroes. They were more likely to get themselves killed than anything else, but seeing others acknowledge that *something* was wrong heartened me. Not everyone had succumbed to the Benefactor. However, if this truly was the work of a Benefactor, why hadn't I seen any Fingers? And why didn't I feel an Aura? Maybe something else was going on here, something new, beyond my comprehension.

Wouldn't have been the first time since joining the Agency. Wasn't even the first time today.

We sped along to Tak's private laboratory and found the building still intact. No Emergent had burst through the walls or left a trail of destruction through the city. That didn't mean we had made it in time. I wouldn't be sure about that until we found Pinch still breathing inside. Tak strode up to the door and walked inside as if he were returning for supper after a routine day at work. The rest of the Hand followed, infinitely more wary.

The tableau inside the laboratory looked like an otherworldly funeral. On one side of the room, Clerics garbed in the red and gold of the Church of Light bowed their heads in a holy union of wills. A man in the center of their cluster intoned a soft prayer for the safekeeping of the dying soul while the others remained silent. Keeping their distance on the other side of the room, two of Tak's masked technicians exchanged scribbled notes and discussed them loudly, as though intentionally disrupting the Cleric's hushed incantation. While the lead mortician's underlings postured, and the faithful meant well with their words, it didn't seem like anyone was doing much for the dying Peeker on the specular, metal table at the center of the room. Pinch's figure lay motionless, save for the ethereal emerald light cast by the fireplace behind it, highlighting the silhouette of its heaving chest.

It lives. For now.

The mortician grabbed his mask from the wall and donned it with the familiarity of someone who had performed that exact motion ten thousand times.

"We need those too?" Garret asked.

"Oh," Tak said, removing the mask with an amused laugh. He hastily placed it back on the wall. "No, I suppose not. Force of habit."

"Why then do they wear them?" Inac asked, nodding at the technicians.

"Because they listen well," Tak said. He smiled proudly. "If they want to become morticians, they need to prove they can work effectively behind the mask. Otherwise, they would have to suffer the stench of the dead, and no one can suffer that for long." He laughed to himself, this time a cackle lacking all humor. "Now, let us attend to the matter at hand. The Peeker's last breath draws near, and there is some preparation yet to be done."

For all the research the mortician had done in his laboratory, for all the theoretical knowledge he possessed, for all the experience he had seeing the Benefactor nearly kill us all, Tak still had the arrogance to believe he was in control.

"There is no preparing for a Benefactor," I said.

That didn't stop him from trying. I waited outside while Tak and his technicians worked. The Brightdaughter had set, but no bells chimed dusk. If I had stepped out of the laboratory seeking comfort, there was none remaining to be found in Liwokin. So many lies marked the path I walked to end up here. That Ulken and his Fingers had saved the city. That by joining the Agency I could live a better life. That I could make any meaningful sort of difference. Well, that last was true, except the only difference I made moved the world further into darkness. Only a good man can move the world toward light. It would have been better if I did nothing—for Liwokin, for my Hand, certainly for Bengard.

It should have been me who died in those woods.

A hand settled on my shoulder. "They said to me to find you, Grim."

I let out a long sigh. "What are we doing, Inac?"

"Do not question now, my friend. We will make this right. Come."

The mage was right. There's no changing the past. Once you start down a bloody path, the only thing to do is keep walking.

Pinch sat strapped into a metal chair with hands bound by chain. The chains ran down to fetter its feet, before looping around the legs and going up to wind tight around its chest. The Peeker's head drooped to the side, as though offering up its neck for summary execution.

"Give it the serum," Tak said to his technician. "Wake it up."

Tak's assistant retrieved a glass vial with a sharp needle at the end and filled it with a substance as viscous as honey. From the corner, the clerics' prayers became fraught and rushed as the moment approached, discordant as more voices joined the reverie.

"Tak, get them out of here," I said. "They'll die."

"The Lightmother shields us, child," an old woman broke from her chants to say. "Have faith."

"They choose to stay," Tak said, shrugging. "They know the risks. Who am I to judge? I leave that to the Darkfather."

"They can't possibly know the risks!" I shouted, then relented. Why was I getting so worked up?

He's right. Stay here and die with the rest of us if you want.

But I wasn't going down without a struggle. Sword in my right hand, knife in my left, I was prepared. Garret already had an arrow nocked. Dunnax wore his plated helm and held his glaive at the ready, though his polearm would be useless in these close quarters. Inac and Sentyx were both unarmed, but they needed no weapons apart from their hands. Seeing the Hand ready for combat might have been half the cause of the Clerics' quickened chanting, but Tak and the technicians moved without fear.

Hubris. This experiment couldn't be contained.

The technician holding the serum approached Pinch and without hesitation stuck it with the needle. He pushed a thumb into the open end that contained the gooey substance. After a few tense moments, the technician walked away and tossed the messy vial into a bin as a welter of blood spouted from the Peeker's bound arm. Pinch began to stir as another technician approached with a bandage, but before he could apply it the crackle in my neck announced the birth of a new Benefactor.

With a steady stance to keep from falling over while in the Deluge, I was ready for my vision to black out and senses to fade. Tak wanted to learn from the Emergent, but as soon as the vision ended, I would rush forward and end this experiment. I knew I'd regain myself after memories snapped back to the present. I knew I'd be disoriented and braced myself. I knew what to do to keep the people in this room alive.

In fact, I knew nothing at all, as always.

* * *

Countless memories flooded through a gaping hole in my mind. I drowned in the ceaseless flow. They were a maelstrom, washing away everything I knew myself to be. One memory after another. Glimpses. Flashes. Bursts of feeling in contexts almost too brief to comprehend. Flickers of a moment in some life, colored by an accompanying emotion. The same accompanying emotion. Always the same.

Rage.

Dark, furious hatred. A cloud that poisoned one's very soul with each inhaled breath. The memories battered against my mind, erasing the border until no distinction remained between myself and pure, untethered anger. Between momentary glimpses of oblivion, visions flared and faded.

Darkness.

Archedark stormed within the void in my hands as I stared down at the corpse of my brother. Hollow sockets with burned-out eyes were the price of his withering betrayal. He had stolen everything from me.

More darkness, a brief respite. Then came another.

The muscles in my arms ached, hands slick with blood; still, they pulled at my commander's scalp. I would tear the flesh from his bones for what he did to those girls. Death wasn't harsh enough retribution.

Another.

Blood spurted when I pulled my axe from his armored chest. Red rivulets ran down gleaming silver. My sister hid beneath the tavern table, thinking me a monster, but she drove me to this. I sacrificed everything for her.

Endless memories.

We stood shoulder to shoulder, more of our people than I had ever seen gathered. We hearkened to a booming voice that pierced the raging gale. His passion was contagious. A fire burned inside me, stoking hatred toward those windless ones who believed they were superior. *Their light blinds them. They will never see us coming.*

Memories swirled like winds around the eye of a storm. Something consumed them all as it latched on and took control, nourishing itself with the misery of the past, overflowing with raw anger. It reached out, plucking moments from the minds of all it touched and brought them spiraling in toward the center, to the core of its capacity. There arose one final, primary memory.

Brother...the human killed you. This one's thoughts grew slow as its brother's mind faded. Lying in the dirt with thorax broken, incapable even of moving, this one seethed. Even Unpaired, a Peeker remembers.

It was all this one could do as the human slaughtered its remaining brothers.

The blue-coated man barked like the vicious animal that humans are, cutting limbs from the conjoined one, leaving them helpless. Their hatred still permeated the air, thick as molten rock, as it had since those two died to become one in a burst of Dark. But the human did not end their suffering. With blood from the butchery dripping from its arms and face, it stood marveling over the conjoined one. Until another human appeared, all in black.

"What is this?" the man in black asked. "You don't know what you're doing!"

The man in blue cackled. "I know *exactly* what I'm doing. Everything you did to Yezna, everything you put us through... what was it for?" It gestured at this one's conjoined brother. "To create *this*?" It held the bloody knife in its hand, pointed it threateningly at the other human, and shook its head. "It's over, Ulken. I'm in control now."

The one called Ulken drew its sword. "You control nothing yet. I am your Head! Fight me for the power if you desire it so badly. I won't let you steal it from me."

Another howl of laughter. "Steal it from you? You really don't know anything, do you?" The man in blue laughed one last time, nearly doubled over. With a flick of its knife, it finally ended the pain of the conjoined one. Then, it plunged the blade into its own heart.

"No!" Ulken shouted, as the human fell to its knees and toppled over onto this one's brother.

Arms took up this one's broken body. A feeling felt once before surged in this one's neck but faded with the minds of the conjoined one as the man in black carried this one away.

Darkness returned. That memory had lingered longer, a passing recognition of both those men amidst the flurry of mayhem in my tortured mind. The visions slowed, the time between inhabiting myself stretching longer. More harrowing moments passed. Where had these memories come from? Were they real, or figments of some imagination? Thoughts from some crooked mind that spent every moment dreaming up ways of inflicting pain? My mind receded from the horrors, until finally the torrent ceased. A noxious laboratory lit by green fire appeared.

This one looked down and found chains. A group of disparate people stood around in a daze, their minds feeble, trapped with this one in this body. Each was one mind among many. The one in control bid them come near, reaching out with an unseen hand that felt as natural as those that were bound. More natural, even. Several of them stumbled toward this one, like marionettes animated by an unskilled puppeteer. Others collapsed, their minds overcome, squashed in the grip of the mind in control.

Good riddance.

Repulsive, blank faces stared across the room at this one. A few were humans this one recognized from somewhere, but most were unknown. It didn't matter. Humans were vermin infesting this land. This one hated all of them the same. Then this one's gaze settled on one in particular, lips pulling back in a wicked grin.

Not all the same.

This one was intimately familiar with this human—oh yes, the torturer, this one hated most of all. This one could do *nothing* as it probed and cut, but now the human had no power. This one seized control, squeezed it, like crushing a larva between two fingers. The vile human collapsed, spasming in pain. It convulsed on the ground until it expired. This one's grip relaxed, satisfied, though one small mind felt a twinge of sorrow. Where had that come from?

The marionettes drew nearer, and this one looked at them with contempt. It was their fault this was happening. *They* did this. Killing them would not bring back this one's brothers, but it was a start. This one would exult in the humans' suffering.

The mind in control forced a man in red and gold to approach. This one chittered in glee to see that it caused him pain.

When its hand grabbed this one's chitinous skin, the one in control *assimilated*. A familiar process, instinctual. The conjoined one had demonstrated how it was done. These bodies fused together with a rush of energy akin to Pairing with another Peeker. As the human's flesh melted and merged into this one's, the mind in control expanded to consume it. This one's new flesh pushed against the binding chains, but more was needed to break them. Much more.

Four of the marionettes held weapons. A laughable absurdity, how they thought they could fight back. A big human in armor barely held a long axe in its limp fingers. The sharp iron head scraped along the floor as it drew closer. Another held a bow, one a knife and blade...

Wait...

This one recognized *that* human too and the bored expression as it gave this one to the torturer. A small stab of shock echoed in this one's mind, emanating from one mind among many. The human recognized itself, did it? This one clicked with laughter.

Let it feel the powerlessness an Unpaired feels.

The controlling mind shared its power willingly with this one when the cause was right. Inflicting pain to those this one hated evidently was the right cause. The human came closer, step by step, but it resisted. Another mind aided it. Rage boiled up in this one, and the controlling mind stole back its primacy. It redoubled its focus on the human.

The human's limbs trembled in agony, and this one felt the pain in the human's mind, like a hot poker rousing one from sleep. Still, it edged closer, gritting its teeth.

The one in control commanded it to reach out, to take this one's arm in its hand. An echo of hope came from his mind, as from grasping a branch to pull itself out of a drowning river. This one's eyes flicked to the human's knife.

Then looked up. Something was wrong. In its eyes was something this one knew all too well.

Defiance.

The mind in control screamed as the human raised its arm. Assimilation was a hand's width away. The one in control lost its grip. It fought furiously to regain it, but the human resisted. It jerked its hand, too fast to stop, and the knife pierced this one's skull with a sickening crunch.

CHAPTER TWENTY-TWO

Shackles

I opened my eyes. The hard floor pressed against my back and shoulders. My bones ached as though I had been wrung out in the grasp of an angry giant, and my head pounded an excruciating drum. The crackling of wood slowly being consumed by emerald fire filled the intervening space between the sobs of a crying Cleric, the only surviving member of her group. The Lightmother may have shielded her, but the Darkfather had swept the rest down to the abyss. They knew the risks, Tak had said. Was that what he told himself to wash away the guilt after dragging someone into one of his deadly messes? I coughed and gagged on some sour stench filling the air, at whose origin I dared not guess. My body protested, stiff and unresponsive as I worked my way to my knees. The pain threatened to knock me back down, but I pushed through and rose, once more the survivor of an encounter with a Benefactor.

This one may not have killed me, but eventually I'll number among the dead.

Surveying the room, it had been a close thing. Among the bodies littering the stone floor, some were merely unconscious, while others...they were beyond recovery. Effortlessly, I recognized those who would never again breathe, as surely as if I had crushed the life from them myself. Memories floated around my head telling me that I *had*, the violent residue of countless Pools newly created. With each Deluge, true memories became harder to distinguish from the false ones implanted by the Emergent. The creation of only one Pool was life-changing, but this time I was adrift in a sea of minds that had snuffed out the light of many others.

There were killers all around me, and it felt like every life they'd stolen had been ended by my own hand.

In truth, I had killed only one. The corpse of Pinch was still chained to the chair, though its flesh had melded around the metal where the assimilated cleric's arm touched the Peeker. Little remained to identify the holy man, his body was so warped—only the Church's colors entwined with the twisted figure. The handle of my knife protruded from the Emergent's temple. I shivered. The knife's grip had felt solid in my hands. At the same time, white-hot pain had flared, as though the blade had pierced my own skull.

How many times have I died? It seemed more memories of death occupied my mind than those of life. If I continued along this path, I'd be reduced to a walking carcass, roaming the lands hollowed out inside. If Tak's theory was correct, when my true death came, the Benefactors infesting my head would take control. It would turn me into an Emergent, a monster hungry to grow, killing to fulfill its appetite. *I'd prefer a knife in my head.*

The Deluge of rage, those violent waves threatening to drown me...those had been memories, right? Memories from the people in this room. Memories of my Hand, dark secrets and all. But the people lying here could not account for the sum of what I saw. How far beyond this room had the Benefactor reached? How many minds had its Aura touched? The memories of my Hand and Pinch were clearest, but the onslaught of anger seemed endless. All that latent fury was building up within the city like nitroglycerin awaiting a destructive jolt.

My eyes landed on a shriveled man in a white coat, lying twisted on the ground. My throat constricted. Tak was dead, and with him our best chance at understanding the Benefactors. His final moments weltered in my mind—two breaths drawn in excruciating pain, a building pressure, then darkness. How much suffering had he caused by refusing to understand the danger of his experiment? How many lives had been lost? He'd accepted the risk himself, but dying was easy.

Consequences are for the living.

The others just began to stir when a Nerve pushed through the door as if nothing were awry. "Taktus, Ulken requires you—" In the firelight his white coat turned a sickly green, and his eyes grew wide taking in the grizzly scene. "By the abyss!" he shouted, and two more Nerves rushed through the door. Both drew flintlock pistols, staring at the vaguely humanoid mass of chained flesh behind me. One of them flinched when I rose to my feet, then raised the pistol at me.

"Aim for my head, please," I said, but he breathed a sigh of relief and lowered his weapon.

"I know you," the third Nerve said, her brown hair flowing out beneath her Agency-issued cap. She watched as Sentyx and Garret stood and as Dunnax lifted Inac to his feet. "Hand Sixty-Four. What is going on here? Ulken commanded you that the lead mortician is not to be dealt with."

"Well, sorry to say he's been dealt with. But not by us." Garret croaked out a laugh, which turned into a coughing fit. When the fit ended, he spat on Tak's floor. The mortician was in no state to disapprove.

A vivid memory flashed, of a time when Tak had nearly blown himself up while mixing volatile chemicals. Apparently, I'd acquired some of the mortician's memories. Hopefully not his arrogance. In the end, that's what got him killed. It wasn't our fault. And though I doubted the Agency would see it that way, I wasn't about to take responsibility for this mess. "Tak is dead, killed by a Benefactor. We had nothing to do with this."

The Nerves exchanged a look, then one reached into his coat and came toward me.

Well, it was worth a try.

When they took us away in shackles, no one bothered putting up a fight.

* * *

Two horse-drawn carts carried us to Headquarters, one loaded with the living, the other with the dead. A small brigade of Heels appeared in the nearly empty courtyard and unceremoniously hauled away everyone who had fallen to the Emergent. Tak, along with two of his technicians and four Clerics, would end up beneath the Agency on the mortician's slab. Tak's Pool surfaced ideas for how the mortician would probe his own corpse to see if the Benefactor had infested him. Memories of thousands of similar dissections now lived in my head, but none stopped this one from making me queasy.

While the dead went one way, a Nerve ushered my Hand and the surviving Cleric toward the tower's main entrance. The sign in the courtyard indicated, as Ulken's summons had, that only one more Benefactor remained. I snorted when I saw that, then winced as the Nerve jabbed me in the back to shut me up and pushed me inside. The hallways, like the courtyard, were not only strangely devoid of people, but also entirely lacking any haze. Ulken must not have bothered spreading that pungent smoke through the building, empty as it was with everyone preparing for the so-called final battle. Without it, my thoughts grew foggy. The Aura that permeated Headquarters suffocated me, like a bag over the head of a kidnapping victim. Insensate, we were escorted down identical corridors, turning corner after corner, as though we walked in endless spirals.

When the Aura finally faded and my tired wits returned, the five of us had been deposited in a drab, barren room. I had no recollection of entering this room, nor of the Nerve departing. Nor did I recall the cleric being separated from us, but clearly, she had some different fate in store.

What would Ulken do to prevent her knowledge of Benefactors escaping his control? I pushed that thought from my mind. Death already occupied too much space in my head today.

In the center of the room, beneath a simple, burning chandelier, there was a table on which sat a curious box poked with holes on every side. Six chairs attended the table, one across from the five, unmistakably an adversarial arrangement. The Nerve had left our hands bound, making clear the reason we were brought here, so we took our designated seats and waited.

When whomever would come to interrogate us failed to promptly arrive, Garret began squirming. "What's taking so long?"

"So eager to get booted from the Agency?" Dunnax said. "I can't believe you got us into this mess."

Garret barked a laugh. "Booted from the Agency? We're not leaving this room with our heads. Least they could do is be prompt for our execution. Thought justice in Liwokin was meant to be swift."

"Justice?" Inac asked dismally. "You believe he will kill us? Why? The mortician left to us no choice."

"Only because those two helped him in the first place," Dunnax said, and glared at me and Garret. Apparently, he didn't realize the part Sentyx had played, but I wasn't going to tie that rope around the Skardwarf's neck. "I should have been reassigned with Lorelay." He slammed the table in frustration, fetters rattling, then unloaded all the insults that he'd clearly stockpiled for us. He began with Inac. "You're a snuffing Dark mage." To Sentyx he hissed, "You're a *Skardwarf*," as if the term tasted of bile, "an enemy of the Bright Empire. You, Garret..." The Paladin spat as if imitating the Ekoan. "You don't seem to have any morals at all." Finally, he rounded on me, his face twisting in disgust. "And you murdered another Finger, one who saved our lives."

"And you're any better?" I snapped. "You killed a fellow Paladin in cold blood. You did it for your sister, I know. But you're in good company here. Don't pretend otherwise."

Dunnax's mouth worked, a half-dozen expressions crossing his face before settling on disbelief. "No. You don't know—"

"Turns out having these things in your head has benefits. Pinch's Deluge didn't just show me his own memories, it had *yours* as well. All of you."

Sentyx hummed. For once, he didn't look me in the eye.

Dunnax shook his head. "You're lying. I saw through his eyes, true, but that's all."

Garret chuckled. "Oh, is that all?" He leaned back so his chair balanced on two legs, relaxed with his feet up on the table, as though he were having an enjoyable time.

"It killed Tak and tried to kill you too. That's it, no other vision..." Dunnax trailed off and the guilt of truth dirtied his expression, but the Paladin washed it away and stubbornly doubled down. "A lucky guess. You heard what Vinlin said. You knew I broke my oath to the Order."

"No," Inac said. "Grim is right. It gave to me these visions. I too saw what you did to your brother."

"Why should I believe *you*?" Dunnax asked. Then he broke eye contact. Inac was many things, but he wasn't a liar.

"However..." Inac continued, raising one eyebrow at me. "You say it gave to you memories from us *all*? I do not know the truth of this. I saw no vision of my own past."

"I didn't see anything from mine either," I said. "You saw mine?"

Inac nodded.

"Well," Garret said, after a time, "let's hear them. Going to spy on our memories then not share? Don't think so. Fair's fair."

"I...I'm not going to give away Inac's secrets."

"No." Sentyx grunted. "It is not right."

Inac pressed his lips to a thin line, took a deep breath. "It is okay, Sentyx. I have grown tired of the secrets here. Tell to us what you saw, Grim."

Even with his permission, it seemed a betrayal—something Inac was already bitterly familiar with. "Your brother...he betrayed you, and you killed him with Dark magic."

"No," Inac said, eyes glinting with the hint of tears. "That is not true. He did not betray me. I was jealous—"

"You don't have to explain it," I interrupted. "None of us do."

"Murdering your brothers," Garret said. "No wonder the two of you were so quiet in Tak's cart."

"Leave it, Garret," I said. "What did you see of me, Inac?"

Inac hesitated, apologized with his eyes. "You beat to death a man. He would not tell to you what started the Riot. You knew he did not know, but you would not stop."

I had forgotten about that. Hearing it now surfaced the memory. Bleeding knuckles, the chemical smell of gunpowder, the pain of the wound the fired round grazed along my ribcage.

The man hadn't been a bounty, but I'd been tipped off he might know something about the Riot. He didn't know anything—no one ever did. In my anger I'd killed him with my bare hands.

And now I don't even remember his name.

Garret whistled. "Isn't this fun? Everyone thinks they're so righteous, but now we see the truth."

"Shut. Up." I clenched my fettered hands, and my knuckles popped. "You tore the *scalp* off your commander's head."

Garret frowned and looked away, then shrugged. "He de-served it," he muttered.

After a silence that stretched uncomfortably long, Dunnax said. "What about Sentyx?"

Sentyx did not grunt. He remained quiet, staring off at the far wall. Why was he acting so strange?

The door behind us creaked open. I tensed up, then flinched when it banged shut. Ulken had come to deliver his punish-ment. It was almost impossible to turn to face him. The sound of a blade being drawn would come at any moment, or perhaps a flintlock lever clicking back.

But no. There was only the shuffle of papers, a thoughtful humming, and some footsteps. Jacquin rounded the table and sat down in the chair opposite us. The newly appointed First Eye flipped through a report. He glanced up at me.

"Yes, yes," he said, "I'll be with you in one moment. Seems your Hand has been quite busy. Just going over the details once more." I recognized the report from Allianne's office, with the number sixty-four printed on its spine. The number of pages seemed to have tripled since that day. The Organ had expected us to have 'a bright future in the Agency.'

If she could see us now...

"All right, then," Jacquin finally said, dropping the report on the table with a thump. His brows creased, his lips turned down in a scowl, and he crossed his arms. In sum, he looked like an angry father about to discipline his disobedient children. "Tell me why you were working with Tak. You were commanded to cease contact. You said you would comply, says so right here."

"Didn't have much choice," Garret said. "He came to us while we fought that Benefactor you sent us to get killed by."

Jacquin looked shocked, as if he'd just been discovered committing a heinous crime. "To get you killed? Why would we do that? We're short enough on good Fingers."

Garret and I exchanged a quick glance. Had we been wrong? Had the Agency *not* figured out what happened in the Mental Ward?

"I read about the casualties," Jacquin said, face warped with grief. "Both Fingers Tak took to escort him were good men. It was a shame to lose them." The First Eye now looked deeply concerned. "Was the Eye's report insufficiently detailed? I checked it myself and added as much as I could. I even directed you toward the Pinegrave for help. What happened there, we'll need to discuss later. Whatever you did, the Druids are now refusing to fulfill our contracts to procure Tears."

"Tak could not make them sell to him their Tears either," Inac said.

"Maybe they would have helped," I said with a surge of anger toward the Druids. "Maybe he'd still be alive."

Darkfather. Was I always this quick to anger, or were these new Pools tainting my every thought?

"About that," Jacquin said, his face back to grim seriousness. "I'll need you to tell me what happened in his private laboratory." He opened our file and readied his pen.

It was the obvious question, yet it still caught me off guard. The Agency didn't know about Pinch, but how were we supposed to explain what happened to Tak without telling him about the Mental Ward? I looked at Dunnax, sure he would tell him all that had happened to distance himself from the wrongdoing. To my surprise, the Paladin said nothing. He just sulked in his chair, as if barely paying attention to Jacquin's questions.

Well, there's no way out.

"Tak hired us to...find him a specimen," I began.

"Yes, the Peeker, from the Mental Ward," Jacquin said, as though I had just told him the sky was blue, or that Liwokin stank. "I just need to know what happened *today*."

"See?" Garret chuckled. "They know everything, and they're fine with it. Lorelay's right, Dunnax. You worry too much."

Dunnax didn't acknowledge the gibe.

"The Agency is certainly *not* fine with it," Jacquin said, "but we have more pressing issues at the moment. Now, please continue."

"Pinch, the Peeker, was..." Tak's Pool made itself useful now. "Infested. Its brain was covered by tiny organisms that I...er, Tak discovered. Tak believed these organisms to be the Benefactors."

"Yes, yes." Jacquin waved his hand. "I've read the lead mortician's report. I just want to know how he died."

"He died," Garret said, "because he stuck a needle in the Benefactor's arm and woke it up. It took control of all our minds, squashed Tak like a bug, and that's that."

Jacquin took off his hat and scratched his head. "You're saying...it became Emergent, with all of you around? How did you escape?"

"Grim killed it," Sentyx said.

Childlike curiosity lit up the First Eye's face. "While under its control? How?"

I opened my mouth to answer him, but in truth I had no words to describe what had happened. I'd been washed away in a riptide of fury, completely submerged until I awoke to find myself as one small piece of a shared mind. I was one mind among many, like the Peeker collective, but...different. Less equitable. The Emergent Benefactor dominated the group, shaping it to its will. Somehow, though I was only a small fragment of the whole, I had seized control from the Benefactor just in time to escape. The mechanics of the process made my head spin, as though I stood in a room of endless mirrors.

I shrugged. "Just got lucky, I guess. Killed him when he got too close."

Jacquin looked disappointed. He sighed, then opened our file. "Very well, you've earned your promotions. Rank Four. I'll see to it that—"

"Promotions?" Dunnax groaned. "You must be joking."

"I never joke about my work," Jacquin said, passing me two sheets of paper. More Benefactor Elimination Reports, already filled out except for the boxes for Finger signature and Benefactor name. "You've eliminated enough Benefactors; you meet the qualifications. Just sign these reports to make it official."

I signed my name and scribbled 'Lomin' and 'Pinch' in the other boxes, then threw down the pen. My hands were still shackled while being promoted. This paperwork was a farce.

"You should be proud," Jacquin said, beaming. "Fourth-rank Fingers will play a vital role in the mission tomorrow. I assume Tak told you—"

"Tak didn't tell us anything," Garret said. "Too busy talking about himself."

Jacquin frowned, then nodded. He had just started to explain when the door slammed against the wall behind us. The First Eye's eyes went wide. He leapt up from his chair and snapped to a salute. "Sir—"

"Oh, sit down," Ulken said. His words crawled icy cold across the back of my neck. "Are you done with them yet?"

Jacquin bowed deeply, as though honoring his god rather than his boss. He pulled the chair back into position, lowering himself into it. "Yes, sir. I was just about to explain tomorrow's—"

"Go."

The First Eye had scarcely seated himself before leaping back up, collecting his papers, and striding to the door like he had just been assigned the world's most important mission.

Ulken sat in the newly vacant chair, close enough for me to reach. My jaw clenched, my shoulders tensed, my hands fought against their restraints. Every part of me wanted to kill this man here and now, but shackled as I was, it wouldn't be much of a fight. I glanced at my Hand.

And I don't know which of you I can count on for help.

Garret surely would join in the scrap, but Dunnax would hold me back if he didn't choose outright to fight for Ulken. Inac and Sentyx would likely stand back, though either of them could end the fight in an instant. No, this wasn't the right time. I'd have to wait for my chance to strike.

The Head shrugged out of his black coat, let it drape over the back of his chair. He wore a buttoned ivory shirt beneath, and slowly rolled up his sleeves. He turned his eyes toward each of us in turn, but they were unfocused, as though he were looking straight through us. When he got to me, he narrowed his eyes and smirked. "So," he said, "'I'll die for this,' you say?"

I flinched. Had he heard me say that at the city gates?

"Oh, don't look so surprised. I see everything in this city. Including how you got my lead mortician killed."

"He got himself killed," Garret corrected.

Ulken's angry eyes transfixed the Ekoan. "Interrupt me once more and you'll join him in the morgue." He leaned back in his chair. "But I agree. While your interference was irksome, his own negligence was his undoing. He cost me many opportunities. I'm well rid of him. In any case," he said, turning back to me, "you're not the first Finger to want me dead." Ulken smiled wide. "You're welcome to try."

My teeth ground against one another. My fingernails dug into my palms. He wanted me to do something stupid now, but we both knew how that would end.

"For now, we have bigger concerns, and all of us here—whether you know it or not—are on the same side." The lies poured from his mouth with such ease. "You've been promoted to Rank Four because you showed me you can be trusted to deal with Benefactors. Eliminating four of them with no casualties in your Hand is impressive. Now prove yourself once more in this final test."

Another snuffing field test.

"This time, it's a test of the entire Agency," Ulken said. "If we succeed, our organization will have accomplished its mission to scour the Benefactors from this world. One challenge remains, but do you know what we're fighting, what we're up against?" Ulken paused. "That wasn't rhetorical, Fingers. Answer me."

"A bug," Sentyx said.

"A bug?" Ulken scowled. "Dark-touched southerners... No, what we're fighting is a disease. A disease of the mind, spreading throughout the city and driving everyone it touches to madness. You've seen them, haven't you, leaving Liwokin in droves? There's only one way to save them. We must cut off the disease at its source. We must kill the final Benefactor." Ulken leaned in close; a chemical smell laced his breath. "But we weren't prepared for this. This Benefactor is more intelligent, more unpredictable than anything we've faced before. He's dangerous, which is why we need a coordinated attack."

As if answering some invisible summons, a Nerve entered the room, moved the small box on the table aside, unrolled a map, then placed a small bag in front of Ulken. The Head nodded thanks as his Nerve left the room, then retrieved several wooden chips from the bag. The map depicted an artist's rendition of the forest west of Liwokin. Ulken placed five colored and numbered chips on the eastern border of the map, where the road entered the woods, in a spot labeled "staging area."

He held up the green chip printed with the number sixty-four. "Now pay attention," Ulken said, "this is your Hand. At dawn tomorrow, all fourth-rank Hands will meet at the staging area for briefing and supply distribution." He pushed all the markers down the road toward a fork. "At noon, all Hands will travel together on the road to the west before it splits. We don't know exactly where the Benefactor is, so we will need to comb the woods until we find him." He moved each of the markers to a different place on the map, spread all throughout the woods.

So much for a coordinated attack.

"Each Hand," Ulken continued, "will search their assigned area for the Benefactor, then signal for help once it is found. Under *no* circumstance should you engage with the creature."

Was that the whole plan? Find this intelligent and unpredictable creature, but don't engage it. I rolled my eyes.

"Now ask your questions but be brief. A long night of preparation awaits." Ulken closed his eyes and took a deep breath. Answering our questions evidently caused him great pain. "Yes, go ahead."

Dunnax cleared his throat. "Why are we only sending Rank Four Hands to fight? If this Benefactor is so dangerous—"

"Currently, all Hands but one are Rank Four," Ulken said, then smiled slyly at Dunnax, "including your sister's." That sounded like a threat, but Dunnax sighed with relief. Lorelay was still alive. "The remaining Rank Three Hand is indisposed. In any case, our resources are scarce after what you did to ruin our relationship with the Druids. Another? What is it?"

"What will you do during this operation?" Inac asked.

Ulken lifted the white chip numbered zero. "Hand Zero is mine. We'll lead the other Hands to the fork, then search the forest like the rest of you. If we happen to find the Benefactor first, you'll know when we kill him."

Him?

"What makes you think you can kill it?" I said, ignoring Ulken's glare.

Ulken paused, considering. "Because he can't get in my head. I can kill him. Rest assured of that. And I'm the only one who can. The rest of you, just signal for me." Ulken sat back, crossed his arms. "Fine. One more."

Garret lifted his hands. "When are you going to take these shackles off us?"

Ulken shrugged. "Speak to the Organ in Processing. He'll have the key. If that's all, gentlemen," he said, not making it a question. The Head stood, whipped his coat over his shoulder and strode from the room, slamming the door behind him.

"I have just one more question," I said, staring daggers into the closed door. "Why does the Head want all of his Fingers dead?"

"He doesn't want us dead," Dunnax said. "And we shouldn't be talking about this here."

"Then where?" I threw up my hands, still chained, and winced at a pop in my shoulder. "You heard him. He's spying on everyone in the city. He'll hear us no matter where we go. And he already wants us dead, so what difference does it make?"

"You're angry," Dunnax said. "You don't trust him, I know, but it doesn't make sense. It'd be a waste of good Fingers, like Jacquin said."

"He no longer needs good Fingers," I said. "If he does, then *his plan* doesn't make sense. Why does he want us to split up?"

"Easier to pick us off one by one," Garret said, nodding.

"Or," Dunnax said, "you just don't understand his plan. It's not easy following orders when you're not clear on the details, but that's our job."

"You trust him, then?" I slammed my hands on the table, shackles clanging. "All of those monsters we fought were his creation! He doesn't want us to eliminate them. He wants to control them."

The argument sounded thin, even to me. He had been sending Fingers to eliminate them, after all. But I was convinced. Ulken was searching for the *right* Benefactor, and he found it. Only, Reed got there first.

"Control them...so you say," and Dunnax sighed, "but what proof do you have?"

"Proof?" I laughed, which probably did me no favors in convincing Dunnax I hadn't lost my mind. "The memory is in my head. Ulken *confessed* to me...no, to his wife, Yezna. Then he turned her into a Benefactor too."

"In your head..." Dunnax said, shaking his own. "Listen to what you're saying, Grim."

"After everything we've seen, is this really so hard to believe?"

"Everything that *you've* seen," the Paladin said. "I haven't seen any visions."

"It's *not* just me," I said. "Inac has too."

"I have, yes," Inac said, "but I am sorry, my friend. I have had no vision of Ulken."

I let out a heavy sigh and looked at Inac, disappointed.

"See?" Dunnax said. "A confession that only *you* have heard. A memory that's only in *your* head. Now, stop with this talk of treason."

I stopped arguing. Nothing I said would convince him. Obedience to a chain of command was a hard habit to break.

"Put yourself in my boots," Dunnax said, standing. "Lorelay's Hand will be there tomorrow. I'm not doing anything to put her in danger."

"She's already in danger!" I snapped.

Dunnax turned away. The discussion was over.

Garret was fiddling with the box on the table, trying to poke his fingers in the tiny holes. "Something's in there," he muttered to himself.

"You don't care," I said to him, "do you? That Ulken's trying to kill us?"

He shrugged, turning the box end over end, then shaking it. "He probably is. Doesn't mean I'm going to let him."

"Have you ever considered that you're just wrong, Grim?" Dunnax headed for the door.

The rest of us stood to leave. Garret decided to take the box with him for further investigation.

"If I'm wrong about Ulken," I said in one final attempt to sway the Paladin, "then why does he keep a Benefactor in the Agency?"

Dunnax paused with his chain-bound hands on the handle of the door, took a deep breath and blew it out, clearly tired of my questions. "We never found a Benefactor here."

"Because we never looked," I protested.

"I have," Inac started. "I sensed—"

Dunnax stopped him. "And I don't believe you can sense them with your Dark magic either."

"Then open the door," I said, "feel its Aura. We all felt it on the way here."

Dunnax pushed through to the hallway, and we all joined him. The Aura that hung so heavy earlier, disorienting me as the Nerve herded us through the halls...was gone.

"Just accept it, Grim," Dunnax said. "You're wrong."

Garret chuckled, mindlessly passing his stolen box back and forth between each chained hand.

Inac looked around, bewildered.

Sentyx grunted.

Nothing.

I refused to believe it. They must have moved the Benefactor during our interrogation. Despite Dunnax's doubt, I wasn't wrong. Maybe I was losing my mind—from the Benefactors infesting me, from their endless Deluges, from the Pools of memories in my head. That changed nothing. I walked this bloody path now, and by my hand Ulken *would* die.

"Come on," I said, pushing past the Paladin. "Let's get these shackles off."

CHAPTER TWENTY-THREE

Leadership

The staging area could have been mistaken for the Agency courtyard, if only for the sheer number of Fingers, Heels, and Nerves. It was as if the Headquarters tower fell over and dumped all its contents here in the forest. Even a few Organs sat in makeshift offices partitioned with chest-high dividers. I searched for Allianne, hoping to spot at least one friendly face, but she was nowhere to be found. Good. She was better off avoiding this mess.

Darkfather knew why so much furniture was needed for this operation, and who had the unpleasant duty of transporting it here. Heels flitted about, carrying paperwork, boxes, and armaments between desks and cabinets attended by Organs. Nerves made their way effortlessly through the press toward clusters of green-coats, Hands to whom they no doubt issued the Head's commands.

With all these people around, there's no way we'll get a clean shot at the Head. Making my way through the staging area, I kept one hand on the satchel of Archefire bombs I'd picked up after leaving the tower, careful not to bump into anyone lest the whole Agency go up in flames at once. To see Ulken dead,

I first had to survive the Benefactor, and that meant preparing for this fight. Entering the abandoned Archemaker's shop in the middle of the night to steal some bombs had seemed a sensible idea. Now, the explosion that ended Bengard's life wouldn't leave my mind. Was that to be my fate as well, vaporized in blazing Archefire? *Suppose I deserve that justice, but not before I take down Ulken.*

I found Sentyx standing alone by the tree line, facing into the heart of the forest as the distant bells rang noon. When I placed my hand on his shoulder, he reacted exactly as a gargoyle carved of stone would.

"Sentyx?" I asked. "You all right?"

"Yes," the Skardwarf said, not turning to look at me.

"Has anyone else arrived?"

He was silent for a moment. "I scouted ahead."

"You *what*?" Garret's voice came from behind me, and I turned to face the sneaky ranger. "Has he gone mad?"

Sentyx remained silent.

"Aye," Garret said. "He's mad, all right. Can't blame him, after all this. Couldn't have waited until *after* we killed this thing though?"

Sentyx's laughter sounded like rubbing two rocks together.

"Why did you do it?" I asked.

"Because I can," Sentyx said, as though trying to convince himself. The Skardwarf clearly thought himself unbreakable, but after being wounded by Lomin perhaps he had learned some humility.

"Well?" I asked. "Did you see anything?"

Sentyx grunted an affirmation. Garret seemed like he was near to madness himself, waiting for the Skardwarf to elaborate. Rather than say anything, Sentyx walked toward the woods. We followed, stretching the distance between his coming words and the ears he didn't want hearing them.

"The city," Sentyx said.

"What?" I asked. "I thought you scouted the forest."

"I did."

"Let's find the rest of the Hand, Grim," Garret said. "Tell them we've lost Sentyx."

I shook my head. Maybe he was just having difficulty explaining what he saw. "All right, Sentyx. You saw the city. Did you find any Benefactors? Feel any Aura?"

"No. Only people."

I nodded, understanding now what Sentyx meant by 'the city.' Skardwarves didn't have cities, only people. "The Liwo are in these woods. No Aura, though?"

Sentyx said nothing.

"Then Ulken is lying," Garret spat. "No surprise there. Keep talking. Need to know what to expect in these woods."

I turned around, trying to keep the movement casual so as not to evoke suspicion. While listening to Sentyx, I kept an eye on the crowd for any wayward wanderer who might be getting too close. The Skardwarf had scouted the forest—which he kept calling 'the city'—all through the night. He had spoken to several Liwo but couldn't make sense of what any of them said. No matter where he went, he had felt no Aura and had seen no Benefactor, but he'd kept searching. Just before dawn, when the Brightdaughter's light returned to the east, he had come across something too strange to explain.

"More strange," I asked, "than the whole city inhabiting the forest?"

Sentyx grunted. "A man," he said. "He died."

"Died how?" I asked, but Sentyx didn't respond.

"Couldn't have checked his body?" Garret said. "Must've had some fatal wound."

"No," Sentyx said. "He disappeared."

I looked at Garret, but the ranger just shrugged. "Disappeared?"

"To the sky."

Garret burst out laughing. "And then what happened? You flew through the air to chase after him?"

"No," Sentyx said. "I backed away. Through the ocean."

Garret doubled over in laughter.

Sentyx swung his head around to look at me. "Then you appeared. Here." He placed his heavy hand on my shoulder.

I wanted to believe Sentyx—he had no reason to lie—but it seemed these past few days had indeed taken a toll on the Skardwarf's sanity.

Garret's cackling drew attention, and someone broke through the crowd, striding toward us holding a package. I quickly greeted him to alert the others. "Jacquin! What brings you to our little Hand?"

"Little, indeed," the First Eye said, "but I've already visited them. The others are waiting for you over there. You three aren't even within the bounds of the staging area."

"That so?" I asked, exaggerating my surprise. "Didn't sleep much last night. And Ulken didn't exactly give us clear directions after you left."

"Well, I hope navigation won't be a problem from here on," Jacquin said, "because this is for you."

He handed me the package, a dense wooden box I strained to hold onto.

"Inside, you'll find a map marked with your search area, as well as supplies for your Hand. Further, there's something just for you. Finger Grimley, as the Hand's Captain you will distribute the supplies to the others. Make haste to them. Ulken will commence the operation shortly." The First Eye turned and marched off into the crowd, his blue coat skirting the ground.

"Hand Captain?" Garret said. "Since when?"

I blinked. "Good question."

* * *

"Ah," Dunnax griped, "the box that 'must only be placed in Grim's hands.' What's inside?"

"Supplies," I said, dropping it to the ground with a deep thump and kneeling to undo the clasps. "For all of us. And a map."

"Might as well toss that scrap," Garret said.

"No," Dunnax barked. "We'll follow directions this time."

"Seems to me it's not up to you," Garret said, smirking. "That's the Captain's decision."

Dunnax sneered. "And seeing as we don't have a Captain—"

"Don't we?" Garret said.

The Paladin narrowed his eyes, thin as the slits in his visor. "What are you playing at?"

I sighed. "Jacquin told me I'm the Hand's Captain."

Dunnax groaned. Even Inac frowned, to my dismay. I thought he, at least, might be happy for me. But friendships quickly fray when one walks alone down a dark path.

"I know," I said. "I'm as happy about it as you are."

No one wanted me as their leader, and I couldn't blame them. Of all the people in my Hand, I deserved the position least. Were it up to me, the Hand would have no leader. We'd managed to keep each other alive without a Captain so far. But it wasn't my call. Responsibility for their safety had been dumped squarely on my shoulders. Maybe this was Ulken's way of telling me to fall in line.

The lid of the box folded back on silver hinges, revealing more boxes underneath—five of them, palm-sized, with holes punched on all sides. The same kind of box as Garret took from the interrogation room. Twine was looped through the holes as though we were meant to wear them as necklaces. The Bright-daughter's light fell just so on the holes, so that a small object showed itself inside. It had a familiar texture, yet I couldn't quite place it.

I tossed Garret the box. "You ever figure out what was in these?"

"Nope," he said. "Threw it away, figured it was junk."

Inac took his, examined it with closed eyes. "It feels to me like an Aura of Archefire," the mage said.

"Like the Druids Tears?" Dunnax asked.

"It is I think not exactly like that, no. More..." Inac shrugged. "Uncontrolled."

Part of Ulken's trap, no doubt.

But I looked toward the Head; he had one around his neck too. And with no Druid's Tears, what other choice did we have but to use them?

Emptying the larger box of the smaller five unveiled a separate compartment stamped with my name and the number of my Hand. Inside, a sealed letter rested atop a small sphere polished to a mirror shine, about the same diameter across as the ring of color in an eye.

"Maybe this will tell us what they are," I said, breaking the letter's wax seal and unfolding it to read aloud. "'Contents: Clasform boxes. Quantity, five. Distribute four to your team. Retain possession of one. Read to your subordinate Fingers: Hand Sixty-Four, keep all supplies on your person. Any lost materials will result in deducted pay. In the event of confusion, bring the Clasform to your nose and inhale. During the operation, use of

Archefire is prohibited. Read to yourself: When you encounter the Benefactor, use the provided Archeflare to signal for assistance. Do not engage the enemy.'"

"There is in this box an Archeflare?" Inac asked, mouth agape. "And you dropped it to the ground..." The mage gurgled out a strange laugh. "Do you know what could have happened to us?"

I hesitated, swallowing nervously. "No."

"When first I saw an Archeflare, my Sage told to me that I would never again look on one. It is known to all mages that these are the most difficult Archemagical devices to craft. Most die in the attempt. If that impact had activated the Archeflare, it would have felt to us like standing on the surface of the Brightdaughter." He pulled his hands apart in a mock explosion. "We would not for long feel it before becoming ash."

A metallic fear crept up my throat. The weight of stolen Archefire bombs still tugged at my side.

Just what I need—another fragile explosive.

The shimmering ball in the palm of my hand was as heavy as lead, made heavier still with the weight of my friends' lives. "Good to know," I said, tucking it away. "I'll be more careful with it."

"Aye," Garret said. "I'd hate to see how much they'll deduct my pay if you lose it."

Sentyx turned his head slowly toward Garret. "You are getting paid?"

"Gentleman!" Ulken's voice boomed across the staging area, carrying like a shock wave that hushed all conversations. "Today, we take part in the most important event of our lives. For what could be more important than defending our city—our home—against an unimaginable danger?" He paused for effect, looked from Finger to Finger as if challenging someone to interrupt him. He smiled at the utter silence. "Yes, you heard right. The danger *is* unimaginable. Does that surprise you? Has the war against these monsters not pitted us against unimaginable danger time and time again?" Ulken brought his voice down low, looked at his feet and shook his head in solemn pity. The Head could have whispered, and still every word would have been audible over the waiting crowd. "Many Fingers have fallen to these beasts. Good men, all, who should never be forgotten." His voice boomed anew. A yawning Heel next to me flinched at the sudden noise. "But *you* are stronger. *You* have survived. In ascending these ranks, have you not defeated *countless* unimaginable dangers? This final Benefactor may be more dangerous than ever before, but so is this Agency." Ulken spread his hands wide. "This time, we fight *together*. Today, our Hands become fists!"

When Ulken slammed his fist into his open palm, cheers erupted like an explosion from lowly Heels and high-ranked Fingers alike, almost every member of the Agency alight in the conflagration of sound stoked by Ulken's fiery passion. Even Dunnax couldn't resist shouting out, until Garret jabbed him with an elbow to shut him up. Hand Sixty-Four remained the only island of silence in this sea of noise.

Can't believe anyone's buying this tripe.

"One final Benefactor," Ulken shouted without waiting for the cheering to subside. He waved his hands around with grandiose intensity. "All the others have been crushed beneath our boots. Today, the Agency fulfills its purpose. Today, this war finally ends." The Head shoved his grubby fist toward the sky and hundreds of members of the Agency mimicked the gesture. I blew out my cheeks, shook my head. Once again it became painfully clear that it didn't take much intelligence to join the Agency.

"Remember," the Head continued, "do not deviate from my plan. Your search areas have been assigned. Your Captain has been issued my commands. Follow their leads and we will win the day. Operation Chimera begins now. Fingers, form up on me."

A Heel swooped in and removed the step stool as soon as Ulken hopped down to join his Hand. Then, another darted in between me and Dunnax, grabbed our empty supply box, and loaded it onto one of many wagons full to the brim with Heels, Organs, Nerves, and furniture.

"All that for one lousy speech?" I rolled my eyes. "What a waste."

There must have been twenty Heels for each Finger, because once their carts rolled back toward the city, the staging area seemed awfully empty.

"These are all the Fingers we've got left?" Dunnax asked.

Garret spat. "All that survived."

By the look of the crowd when I arrived, it seemed Ulken planned to lead a whole army into the forest. Now, just over two dozen of us remained, sacrificial lambs for whatever dark ritual the Head intended. Such a meager force wasn't fit to combat any city-threatening, unimaginable danger that Ulken promised. But then, what good were his promises? They'd only ever led us astray. I grimaced, recognizing how lost we all were, walking blindly toward some unknown danger, led by a liar with suspicious intent. We ill-fated Fingers all shuffled after Ulken's Hand. All of us shared the same purpose, had fought the same monsters, yet I could name only a scant few.

Muy Fuy looked to be his Hand's Captain. Despite the lack of resolve he betrayed last time we'd met at Headquarters, he managed to outlive those two ugly brutes he was with. And Bengard, but I pushed that thought down. Something in the boy's expression told me he'd accepted some hard truths. Every Finger in these Hands must have done their fair share of that. What else could be done when the world lurched so violently into darkness? Some Fingers bore their miserably gained knowledge better than others. Muy Fuy bore his well.

Just ahead of us, Lorelay kept pace with a tall, armored Paceeqi who reminded me of Dunnax, only considerably thinner, closer to Lorelay's build. She craned her head around and looked back at my Hand with a plainly worried look. I glanced up at Dunnax, knowing how he must feel to see her that way, but his face was obscured by his helmet. The Paladin made to hurry forward, but I put a hand across his chest to hold him back. He slapped it away, but Lorelay turned back around and continued marching with her Hand. Their reunion would have to wait.

In the Hand walking beside mine were the mages I had seen on my first day, with matching patterns of swirling gold embroidering their silky green and blue robes. The same Skardwarf still accompanied the matching mages, though he'd upgraded from a quarterstaff to a glistening blade, with a twisted, darkwood hilt. Sentyx paid him no mind, nor did he notice Sentyx.

Not that I'd be able to tell if they had.

The other two members of their Hand were unfamiliar. Other than Sixty-Four, had a single Hand made it this far without loss? Pride swelled in me, but I immediately pushed it back down. This wasn't a competition. There'd be no grand reward in the end. Living through the day was the only prize we could hope for.

Near the forest entrance, Ulken waited for us. We formed into ranks, two sets of two Hands abreast on the road, one pair behind the other. All would follow behind the Ulken and his Hand Zero—a Hand which seemed to be missing a few Fingers.

Ulken stood attended by the First Eye, Jacquin, and the woman who first introduced me to my Hand, Looker, also sporting a coat in Eye blue. The three of them would lead the way, just as Ulken said.

So he is capable of telling the truth. When it suits him.

The Head of the Agency stopped at the edge of the clearing where the forest consumed the path and swiveled around to face us. "Keep in formation and stick to the road. When we split up at the fork, remember your Clasform boxes. We don't have any Druid's Tears, but these boxes are the next best thing. If you spot the Benefactor, follow your Captain's commands. Keep your eyes up, Fingers, but be ready for anything, and keep your wits about you."

I glanced at the other Hands. *If any of us had wits, Ulken, we wouldn't be following you into these woods.*

*   *   *

The forest was dead and still. Not even the birds sang. Not even the wind blew. The Brightdaughter's light should have shone overhead, but black was the color of the trees. Black bushes and black flowers had once sipped enough sunlight to grow, but none reached them now. The Shaded Grounds were dark, but there the trees glowed with false fire. Here, only Ulken's torch illuminated our path, casting shadows shifting between dark pillars, making it seem as if an army stalked us out of sight. With each flicker of motion, my eyes darted around, seeking the answer to a question that niggled at the back of my mind.

Where are all the Liwo? Sentyx claimed the whole city wandered this desolate forest in the night. From the masses we saw outside Liwokin, we shouldn't have gone a dozen paces without stumbling into someone. The isolation crawled down my neck and set me shivering. *Even a corpse would be a welcome sight.*

Something rustled the leaves overhead, but no breeze cooled my sweat-covered skin. If not the wind, was it an animal? Or a bandit planning an ambush? Or a Benefactor, following in the canopy, waiting for the Hands to separate so it could slay us one at a time? I swallowed, but my throat was dry. Ragged breaths and a pounding pulse sounded in my ears, drowning out the hushed conversation that arose from the Hands around me. Some Finger laughed—an incomprehensible sound given the circumstance—and I jumped. With conscious effort I stopped myself from whipping my sword free of its scabbard.

An Aura of panic. Recognizing it allowed a wave of relief to wash over me. I lifted the Clasform box to my nose and inhaled. It smelled of dry and sour chemicals, and nearly drew out a sneeze, but nothing changed. The panic rushed back in, two-fold, and continued unabated. I took a deep breath and blew it out.

Nope. Just me, then.

When Ulken's torchlight fell upon an unexpected figure beside the road ahead, it was almost a real relief.

Almost.

The whole company of Fingers staggered to a halt at Ulken's command. I stepped off the road to get a better look, unobstructed by the Hand in front of us. The Head of the Agency calmly walked toward a man—rather stocky, unwashed, a Blightdweller by the look of him. Nothing unusual about him. Until he began yelling at a tree.

"Let me in!" the Blightdweller shouted, his words slurring. He banged on the tree like it was his front door and his wife had locked him out knowing he'd come home drunk at dawn. He turned around, stumbling dizzily as Ulken approached him. The drunkard looked the Head up and down, then poked his finger out. "Now, liste—"

The man's mouth continued shaping the words, but his lips produced no sound. The Liwo's severed head fell to the ground. The back of my neck started crackling, and I braced for another Deluge, but it never came. The crackling died out like embers stomped underfoot. Ulken wiped the blood from his blade and sheathed it with the headless body still standing, heart still pumping, neck still spurting. When lifeless knees buckled, everything froze, save the motes of pollen drifting down into dark, pooling blood.

Ulken strolled back to his Hand. "We stick to the plan," the Head announced. "Back in form—"

"The plan did not involve cutting off the heads of innocent men!" Inac shouted.

Ulken smiled, and anger flushed through me. "That was no man," he said. "The Benefactor had him. Merely a part of the beast. Now march, Finger." Ulken turned and continued downhill along the western road. All the Fingers fell in line.

All, except for me and Inac. Ulken had lied again. The Liwo was *not* part of the Benefactor. He was only a man. A confused man, but confusion hardly warranted death. Inac stood anchored in place with clenched fists, his posture radiating scalding hatred, hot as Archefire. Seeing his anger somehow cooled my own, and I placed a hand on his back to push him along. To my relief, he started walking.

"You are right," Inac said under his breath, "he must die."

"Glad you've finally come around," I said. "He will. But not with all these Fingers around." It would have been no trouble for him to convince the other Hands we were Benefactor-possessed. No one questioned him when he claimed the same of the innocent man he just murdered.

Ulken and a Benefactor both trying to kill us. How were we going to survive this bloodshed? I turned to look at the Head's latest victim and froze, veins growing cold.

The victim's body was gone. Only the head remained.

CHAPTER TWENTY-FOUR

Deeper Into a Depthless Sea

The light cast by Ulken's torch dimmed as the company of Fingers moved forward without me. I remained behind, staring in horror at the grotesque details of the corpse's head. Its eyes rolled back, showing only the whites. Its mouth hung open, tongue lolled out to the side as if trying to taste the dirt. One cheek was red with a spot of the blood that pooled on the ground around it. But there was no body. I rubbed my eyes to be sure. When I opened them, the details remained unchanged, only a little darker. Sentyx's insane explanation that the man he saw had disappeared suddenly seemed perfectly sane indeed.

Or else I was even madder than I already believed.

None of the Fingers noticed that I had lagged behind, staring at the inscrutable results of Ulken's butchery. I dashed to catch up and ran past my Hand, straight to the head of the pack. The tall Paceeqi in Lorelay's Hand drew his sword and spun, raising his blade to cut me down. Ulken caught him by the wrist. Lorelay shot me a questioning look.

"The body," I said. "It's—"

"Missing, I presume?" Ulken said, unconcerned. "Is that what you've broken rank to tell me, Finger?"

I blinked. He knew what would happen. Did no one else find that strange? I looked to the other Fingers for help, but all I got in return were stares of confusion or contempt, if they met my eyes at all. Someone coughed. Only Lorelay had the decency to smile. Her, and Ulken, grinning smugly at me.

Trying to embarrass a disobedient Finger, Ulken? Fine, let's play that game.

My hand snapped up, and I straightened my back, doing my best impression of Jacquin saluting Ulken. "Yes, sir. My apologies, sir. I assumed you might want to know about potential contact with the Benefactor, but I see you expected this. You have things well in hand, sir."

Ulken's scowl deepened when Lorelay snickered at my faux formality. "I do."

"I hadn't anticipated that letting the Benefactor take the Li-wo's body was part of your grand plan. I'm sorry to doubt you, sir. Clearly, you understand much more as the Head than the Fingers you're leading through the dark."

"Is there some part of the plan that is unclear, Finger Grimley?" He voiced my name like an insult that predated the Empire of the Bright Sun. I suppressed a satisfied smile, pleased with his growing frustration.

"Clear as mud, sir. Our coordinated strike is sure to succeed once we split up and find the Benefactor." My bad shoulder started to ache holding the stiff salute. Some grumbles rose amidst the Hands. It was obvious how little sense this plan made, but no one wanted to challenge the Head.

Ulken's gaze snapped toward the Fingers and put a swift end to the grumbling. He turned back to me with a leer as dark as the abyss. "Get back in line, Finger." He looked at all those who had broken formation for a better look at the exchange. "Is this what passes for order in my Agency? All of you, march!" The

Head whirled around, his thick black coat lashing out behind him. He strode forward, setting a faster pace now. It was easy to rattle our leader when things got out of his control.

I let down my salute and blew out a sigh as the Hands formed up and set off. A few Fingers gave me looks as they passed—Lorelay smiled and winked—but many still refused to acknowledge me. When I fell in with my own Hand, Dunnax gave me a look himself, not half so kind as his sister's. I shook my head. He may not have believed the Head was a threat now, but when Ulken made his move, I still hoped he'd fight alongside us.

The din of nearly two dozen mismatched Fingers marching hastily down a forest road multiplied in the expanse of trees. The scraping of boots on stone competed with the clashing of metal plate armor now that we were in a hurry. Ulken had us almost at a jog, and soon the clamor was joined by huffing breaths. It was all loud enough to cover conversations best unheard by any, save the most trusted allies.

"What are you two whispering about?" Dunnax butted in.

I crumpled the map and tossed it on the forest floor. "Just making sure we know where we're going. How far until the road forks now?" I asked Garret, walking beside me.

"Two thousand paces, I reckon," the Ekoan said, "give or take a thousand paces. Can't trust that map."

"Why throw away the map? We're going to be lost in these woods," Dunnax said, but there was no time to go back and retrieve it.

Garret tapped the side of his head. "Got it all up here."

"Don't worry," I said to the Paladin. "We're sticking to the plan."

"Good."

"Until Ulken tries to take us out," I added.

Dunnax groaned. "Don't you think antagonizing him makes that more likely?"

"About the same likelihood, I reckon." Garret spat down at the ground and missed. The glob of spit caught Dunnax on his gauntlet.

The Paladin growled and snapped down his visor, but Garret pointedly did not apologize. Keeping this Hand alive was going to be hard enough without these two at each other's throats.

I had to get us back on task. "When we use the Archeflare, I'm guessing Ulken won't show up. He'll just let the Benefactor—"

The Skardwarf in the Hand beside ours stepped in front of me, turned, and stopped so suddenly I nearly crashed into him. I shouted in anger and raised my fist to punch him but stayed my hand. He'd just about ended the whole operation early with the entire company going up in Archefire, but breaking my fist punching a living boulder wouldn't have done us any good.

"Let the Benefactor do what?" the Skardwarf said, now marching amidst our Hand. "Kill us all?"

I swallowed. "You heard that?"

"This noise is a whisper compared to the Old Country's wind," the Skardwarf said. "'Course I heard you. You're expecting Ulken to show up when you fire off that Flare? Why? That's our job." The leather clad Lawi in his Hand waved him back, but the Skardwarf ignored him.

"This is your job?" Inac asked, scrunching his brow.

"According to Nill's command, sure. Our Hand waits at the fork. When an Archeflare goes up, we help. Never said what we'd be helping with, o' course, but easy enough to guess."

"Ulken lies," Sentyx said.

"Sure," the other Skardwarf said, "that he does. You brought your Hand around I see, Sentyx. Can't say I've had the same luck."

Sentyx and the newcomer barked some loud sounds at each other, one after another until it was clear they were conversing. Was this the Skardwarf language? Short and sharp, guttural and grinding, it was a language to cut through the wind.

I looked back and forth at the Skardwarves dumbfounded. Apart from their rock-like skin, the two could hardly have been more different. "You...know each other?"

"'Course we do. Pulled from the same earth, Sentyx and me. We're practically family."

Sentyx grunted.

"He was always the quiet one."

"Who are you?" Dunnax asked. "Why should I trust you over Ulken?"

"I'm Cavern," he said, then made that same rock-crunching sound that Sentyx did when he laughed. "And I don't really care if you believe me. We've two Skardwarves among us. Whatever winds blow this day, we can face them."

"Not if we split up," I said.

Cavern crunched out some more laughter, rejoining his Hand. "Then use that Archeflare early, Finger Grimley. Sentyx'll keep you alive until I get there."

* * *

Marching at the hard pace set by Ulken, we shortly arrived at the fork. Garret said it was just after noon, though it could have been near dusk for all I knew. The Brightdaughter still failed to penetrate the dark canopy; Ulken's torch remained our sole source of light. As we traveled deeper into the woods, some sensation came over me—a pressure, almost imperceptible, trying to coax the mind into some altered state. Never forceful, but always nagging, as surely as the Archefire bombs at my side. If this was the Benefactor's Aura, it was much more subtle than any we had encountered.

"Listen," Sentyx said. He projected his voice as if to be heard, though the sounds of an Agency on the move had subsided.

The Hands hushed. Nothing pierced the unnatural veil of silence but the crackling and spitting of Ulken's burning torch. I yearned for some other sound. The flutter of a bird's wings. The rustle of a deer in the bushes. Anything to cut the tension that hung heavy in this dark forest.

Add a touch of cold, and I'd believe we're already deep in the abyss.

Someone in Muy Fuy's Hand spoke up. "Are those...voices?"

The armored Paceeqi in Lorelay's Hand nodded. "All around us, but where?"

"Darkfather!" one shouted. "Demons come to take us to—"

Muy Fuy slapped him. "Get ahold of yourself. I'm not losing any more Fingers."

"It sounds like the Market," another Finger in Lorelay's Hand said.

"Sure, I'm hungry." Cavern raised his voice. "But for twelve stars a loaf? I'd sooner eat the dirt beneath your toes."

Two other Fingers broke out into unrestrained laughter.

"What is happening to them?" Inac whispered, but I hadn't the faintest idea. Half of the Fingers looked bewildered by the other half, who had suddenly lost their minds.

"You hear anything?" Garret asked. Dunnax only shrugged and turned away.

Though I strained my ears, there was nothing to be heard. Gazing into the space between trees, I tried to pick out the form of some Liwo in the shadows. There was nothing to be seen. But when I took a deep breath, a familiar pungent smell filled my nostrils—the unmistakable scent of Liwokin.

This far from the city?

"We expected this," Jacquin announced. "Use your Clasform box if the voices become overpowering."

I prodded Sentyx and made him lift the box dangling from his neck up to his nose. He took a slow breath.

"Help any?" I asked.

"No," the Skardwarf shouted as if we were all talking over him, but after the collective hiss of Fingers sucking in whiffs of their own boxes, much of the strange behavior subsided.

"It's a sign the Benefactor is near," Ulken said. "We just have to find him now. You have your assigned search areas." Without another word he disappeared into the woods, Jacquin and Looker behind him. The Head took his torch with him and left us all truly in the dark.

The rest of the Hands weren't quite so eager to leave the road. Out in the woods, there were monsters. On the road, there was at least the illusion of safety. We clustered there in quiet conversation a while longer, like orphans whose headmaster wasn't around to put them back to hard work.

Lorelay approached our Hand. "Things are looking bad, aren't they Dunnax? Easy to tell, when even your stupid grin is gone."

The stupid grin briefly appeared on her brother's face, but it faded as fast as it arrived. "You shouldn't be here, Lorelay."

"And why not?" she asked, putting her hands on her hips. "I fought as many monsters as you. If I shouldn't be here, then neither should you."

"None of us should," I said. "We have no idea what we're in for."

"Same as always, then." Garret stretched out nonchalantly.

Muy Fuy's Hand headed into the woods, and a wiry Ayeiri man wrapped in brown cloth was beckoning Lorelay back to hers.

The Paceeqi siblings embraced in a long hug. When they finally parted, Lorelay playfully punched Dunnax in the arm. "Be careful out there."

Dunnax chuckled. "You worry too much."

Lorelay smiled tenderly. "See you guys at Headquarters, then. After this is over." She patted the lyre hanging at her waist. "I'll play you a new song I wrote. I'm calling it 'Aura of the Storm'."

Dunnax held his hand high in goodbye long after she had turned away. When he finally let it drop to his side and turned toward me, his face was all hard resolve. He put his visor down. "Let's go."

I gave a curt nod, then clapped Dunnax on the back. "She's tough," I said. "You know she is. And *she's* not on Ulken's bad side." The Paladin grunted and turned away.

Maybe that hadn't been as comforting as I'd intended.

Cavern's Hand—the matching mages, an Ekoan, a Lawi, and the Skardwarf himself—was the only one remaining, and they would stay at this fork until someone signaled their assistance. Golden light illuminated the road. Despite Ulken's orders, the two mages tossed three balls of Archefire back and forth, juggling it between them. Both had their eyes closed. The Lawi sat with his back against a tree, wide hat pulled over his eyes as if he were about to take a nap. Meanwhile, the Ekoan paced back and forth, picking at his fingernails, eyes darting all around as if he expected the Benefactor to strike at any moment and from every direction. They might have been the only Hand stranger than my own.

"Face into the wind, brother Sentyx," Cavern said, and cracked him in the chest with a stony fist. It sounded like two boulders colliding. Sentyx returned the gesture.

We parted ways and followed Garret toward the search area. Ulken finally had each of the Hands separated, but perhaps that meant we'd find them alone as well.

* * *

The pressure in my head grew heavier with each step, as though wading deeper into a depthless sea. I considered raising my Clasform box, but the sensation was strangely seductive. It reeked of a welcome familiarity, and I found myself walking forward, heedless of the direction. I savored the feeling of sinking deeper beneath the waves. One step after another, all else faded away.

"Sentyx, you all right?" Garret asked, drawing my attention and breaking the spell's hold.

Though the rest of the Hand stopped, the Skardwarf kept trudging on, probably in the same kind of trance I had just escaped. Sentyx walked slowly, weaving left and right, as though avoiding nonexistent obstacles, paying no attention to us as we attempted to wake him from his stupor. Dunnax tried holding him back, but he shirked the Paceeqi's restraint as though Dunnax were a nonexistent obstacle himself. Inac and I both lifted our Clasform boxes to Sentyx's flat nose, but nothing changed. With no way to stop the dazed Skardwarf, we had no choice but to follow him away from our goal. His path meandered through the forest with less regard for the trees than some imagined thoroughfare.

I stumbled to a stop. "Those sounds..."

Crowds chattering, boots stomping, cart wheels turning behind the clicking hooves of mules. That imagined thoroughfare could be *heard*. It was just like the storm outside Leppit, the green clouds near Canako, the false flames of the Shaded Grounds. How long had I been trudging along unaware before I noticed? The squawking laughs of bay gulls reached me, and a taste of salt tinged the air. Another sound—newly heard, yet intimately familiar—cut through the rest. The high tone of a half-dusk bell called out from a church tower above the forest trees. All these subtle sensations together were unmistakable, but it was the smell, more than anything else, that finally made it click in my mind.

The alluring sensation, the depthless sea...it was the feeling of home. The Benefactor's Aura had cast a shadow of Liwokin upon my senses.

I returned my attention outward. Fear crept up when nothing but darkness surrounded me. "Inac!" I shouted. "Give me some light!"

After a momentary pause, a mote of Archefire flickered into existence and lit my Hand, still following Sentyx.

I caught up to them. "Were you just going to leave me?"

"Figured you were leading from behind," Garret said, flashing a grin.

I rolled my eyes. "The Benefactor's Aura had me. It must have Sentyx too."

"I don't feel anything," Dunnax said through his visor.

"Huh," Garret said. "Me neither."

That was strange. These two had always felt the Auras before. "Inac?"

"I think so, yes. It smells to me"—and Inac grimaced—"like human waste."

Garret snorted. "Glad I don't, then."

I nodded. "That's it. Just like Leppit's storm, there's an illusion of Liwokin here." I placed my hand on Sentyx's shoulder. It was just like he'd said. "You're seeing the city, right?"

He gave an aggressive grunt, telling me to back off as if I were a stranger.

But I held on. "It's Grim."

He glanced at me. Sentyx stopped fast, then turned his body to move forward, as if edging around a wall. I experienced Liwokin merely as a faint sensation; evidently, the illusion had totally overcome the Skardwarf.

"Sentyx," I urged, "remember what's real."

He pulled free of my hand.

Dunnax grabbed my elbow. "We need to get to our search area."

"You volunteering to carry him?" I tugged my elbow free. "We'll get there."

"He is like the Liwo," Inac said. "He may be already lost."

"We're *not* leaving him. I just need to find a way to talk to him." With my hand on his shoulder again, I recalled our conversation in Headquarters, so long ago now. "Remember what you told me? Here in the city, there are different monsters. But we must face into the wind."

The Skardwarf froze. That got his attention.

"Friend Grim?" Sentyx said. "You look different."

"Where are we, Sentyx? What do you see?"

"People. Many people. Building with sharp top."

"Yes," I said, "that's the church tower. I heard the bells a moment ago. We're near the Docks."

"We're *in the forest*," Dunnax protested. "None of that is real."

No, but real or not, it might be useful.

"Sentyx, where is the church? How far away?"

"There." He pointed up into the trees.

Gulls cried out behind me, so we were facing north. "Garret, where's the search area? Where do we have to go?"

"That way," Garret said, pointing. "About seven hundred paces."

The Ekoan had an uncanny sense of direction in the forests, so I trusted his instincts. But when it came to the city, I had instincts of my own.

"From the church, that would put us in the Maker's Square in the Artisan District. Sentyx, can you get us there?"

* * *

The sounds of the Docks receded, gradually replaced by echoes of blacksmiths' hammers ringing against struck steel, the rumbling fire of the glassblowers' furnaces, the scraping and tapping of rock worked by sculptors' chisels.

Inac hummed thoughtfully. "It is like you predicted. An accurate illusion of Liwokin. How is this possible?"

"It shouldn't be," I said, but I had long since stopped questioning what Benefactors made possible.

"How far now?" Dunnax asked.

Garret held up a hand to quiet him. "We're here." The ranger kept his hand raised, listening to the silence of the forest that I could not hear. In time, he shook his head. "They're not here."

"You're sure?" Darkfather. I should have expected this.

Garret nodded. "Nothing but the rustling of leaves. No movement."

"Who isn't here?" Dunnax dropped his shoulders. "We're not in our search area, are we?"

"Neither is Ulken," I said. "His Hand should be here."

"By the light..." The Paladin slammed the crooked butt of his glaive into the earth. "Why are you so eager to get us killed?"

I ignored his anger—it was guaranteed from the moment Garret set us toward Ulken's search area.

"Thought we should surprise the Head," Garret said, "before he surprised us. Figured *his* plan is to kill us, so we needed a better one."

Nodding, I said, "One where he's focused on the Benefactor and never sees us coming. After Ulken's dealt with, we can finish off the Benefactor with all the support of the other Hands. But if we attack the Benefactor first, we'll never get a chance to strike at the Head."

"You lied to us," Inac said, then gave me a look of withering disappointment. "You are becoming like Ulken, my friend." He breathed a long sigh, his Fire flickering for a moment until he regained control. "But you are right. Why is the Head not here?"

The truth of it was so plain even Dunnax couldn't deny it. Ulken had lied. Again. Why lay out a map pinpointing Hand Zero's location if not to deceive us? Why deceive us if not with ill intent?

But Dunnax didn't admit he was wrong. Instead, he lifted his visor, then looked back and forth. "Where's Sentyx?"

I spun. "Thought he was right behind me." But the Skardwarf had disappeared, sure as shadows in the dark.

Wood clattered as Garret nocked an arrow and raised his bow, aiming into the darkness. My shoulders tensed, expecting Ulken's Hand to appear after all. I followed his aim. Two silhouettes moved in the space between the trees, both humanoid in shape, but neither one human. Inac's mote of Fire slowly hovered toward them and revealed one to be Sentyx, standing motionless and facing the other figure.

The other, however, did not stand at all.

A rope descended from the trees and held the creature. Its feet dangled above the ground. Inac's light drifted closer to highlight a gray-black husk surrounding the thing like a brittle, cracked cocoon. My eyes adjusted to the Fire; the rope attached to its head was no rope at all, but the same material as the rest of the husk. The features of a face were right where they should be, but smoothed-over like an ancient, well-preserved corpse. The thing twitched, shaking the leaves above, like a hanged man trying to escape but succeeding only in further stretching his neck.

Better not provoke it.

"Put out that Fire, Inac."

When Inac smothered the Archefire, I gasped. Darkness flooded the forest, but vision remained. With the gift of illusory sight, the city appeared around me, briefly convincing me that I was home.

But it was *wrong*.

City streets warped in nightmarish ways, smeared to fit the layout of the forest. Buildings curved and bent overhead, matched one for one with the trees, with only a few jarring mistakes. The illusion was imperfect, like a drawing reproduced from an old memory. But where it was correct, it was convincing. Still, the eerie visage twisted my stomach in discomfort and helped me to remember what was real.

With the memory of Sentyx and the husk's position quickly fading, I carefully walked forward until I heard Sentyx grunt. The Skardwarf's utterance came from a man with frizzy red hair poking out beneath a sandy-brown cap, a fuzzy mustache on his lip, and an Agency Eye's coat draped over his shoulders.

"First Eye Reed?" I muttered, approaching from behind. How was I seeing this? A Deluge had never started without someone else dying. Now, one was carried on the Benefactor's Aura, changing the rules yet again.

The former First Eye grunted, his attention on an Archemaker standing in the door to a lightwood stall before him. The aproned Archemage running the shop held a silver rod with obsidian at one end.

"...ahead of schedule, First—" the Archemaker said, cutting himself short. He nodded vigorously. "Right, of course. My apologies, sir." The Archemaker waited, nodding politely as if in conversation with Reed, who gestured and moved his mouth. Sentyx, however, failed to voice his half of the conversation, filling it instead with the Skardwarf's customary silence.

"Yes, this is it," the Archemaker said, lifting the obsidian-adorned rod.

"..."

"Indeed." The Archemaker patted his many deep pockets, then settled on one, reached into it, and produced a glass vial filled with clear fluid. He glanced around, then brought the obsidian stone close to the vial and produced an inky blue glow. "Entirely invisible without the dowsing rod, you can be well assured of that."

The First Eye took both the vial of ink and the dowsing rod, tested them on his own, then shoved the ink vial inside his coat and held the rod out toward me. Instinctively, I reached out to take it and *felt* it in my hands. I turned the rod around, looking at it in awe. Then I blinked, and it vanished.

Reed clapped his hands together. His lips began moving. "..."

A huge smiled beamed across the Archemaker's face. He bowed deeply and remained low while he spoke. "That is quite the compliment, sir. Thank you, kindly." He cleared his throat, unbent, and leaned forward, then lowered his voice conspiratorially. "Of course, it was quite impossible without the use of Archedark."

Reed's head whipped back and forth. He took a step back and jabbed an accusatory finger at the Archemaker. The mage withered under the First Eye's silent but apparently harsh admonishment, which continued for some time.

Beside me, a short Lawi woman with unkempt black hair strolled past holding her young boy's hand. "What's happening?" she asked in Dunnax's voice.

"Beats me," the boy said in Garret's as they walked away.

"Be quiet," came Inac's voice, disembodied. "It is talking to them."

"What?" Dunnax snapped, voice now also emanating from thin air. "The Benefactor? We need to *kill* this thing. Use the Archeflare. *Something!*"

"Do *not* attack it," I warned.

Reed jerked a thumb toward me, evidently finished with his tirade. I looked down at my own body. Why didn't *I* look any different? Whose role was I playing in this illusion?

"A second?" The Archemaker's eyes went wide. "You still haven't paid for *this* one." He glared at me, then scowled at me, then screamed at me. "The Gild! What good are your promises? Will promises feed my children? Will they cover my expenses? I've taken on quite enough risk already for you, and I'm of quite the mind to spill some secrets!" On and on the Archemaker ranted.

Panic arose in me as the mage grew increasingly aggravated and hostile. If he didn't quiet down, he would draw the attention of unwanted eyes. Questions would arise about what we were doing here. He slung his fury at me with sweeping gestures. At any moment now I expected to be consumed by Archefire.

No... These fears weren't mine. They were only a memory. The Benefactor's Aura contained them, painting the illusion of Liwokin with the emotions of the infested.

The light of Archefire bloomed and I cringed away from the mage, but the Fire came from Inac's right hand. In place of the Archemaker, the husk convulsed, then began violently thrashing. The Archemaker's furious insults became gibberish as pure emotion carried him into the depths of madness. I grabbed Sentyx's shoulder; we both backed away.

Dunnax readied his glaive, standing firm beside me. "What in the name of the Lightmother is happening?"

An elderly man, moaning and mumbling, emerged from behind a tree, stumbling as one walking in their sleep.

One of the missing Liwo.

Dunnax nearly charged the helpless man out of sheer surprise, but Inac stopped him. "Ulken already today murdered one man," he said. "We can give to this one our help."

He caught the dazed man and raised a Clasform box to his nostrils. The sleepwalker's relaxed body went rigid like a slack rope suddenly pulled taut. His head whipped all the way back with a terrible, pained expression. The man dropped to the ground and lay still, two lines of blood dribbling from his nostrils. Inac jumped back, horrified, just as a figure swept down from the trees with blurring speed and crashed into the Liwo's body. An instant later it shot upward beyond the leaves, taking the man with it. A Deluge built up then fizzled out, just as with the Blightdweller Ulken murdered.

"Well, if Inac didn't kill him," Garret said, "he's dead now."

"I...I did not..." Inac stammered, gaping at the Clasform box in horror.

Everything happened so quickly, I hadn't even seen the husk move. Now, it descended from the trees like a spider on silk. I shivered. We were the flies caught in its web.

"Enough!" Dunnax shouted. "Use the Flare!"

The Paladin had the right of it, but just as I reached for the Archeflare, a blinding flash shone through the trees brighter than the sun, leaving an afterimage of the pillars of tree trunks. Two heartbeats later, the air cracked and knocked loose a rain of falling leaves. The Benefactor husk snapped up as if on an elastic band, and all around us the boughs of trees began to writhe and shake. Sticks and leaves, acorns and unripe fruits, all rained down on us as the movement continued all around. The light of an evening sky crept across the canopy as if emerging from behind a passing cloud.

The muscles in my legs turned to jelly and refused to move. With great effort, I swallowed and asked, "When's the last time we saw the light?"

"Back in the clearing," Garret said, with none of his usual good humor.

"That's what I thought." A chill swept from my toes up through my guts and set me shaking like a deer in the sight of a wolf. The Brightdaughter's light didn't warm me one bit.

CHAPTER TWENTY-FIVE

Claws

The Benefactor crawled across the treetops in the direction of the Archeflare that had detonated in the distance. At the fork, Ulken had said it was close. Did he know it was with us this whole time?

"West," Garret said. "That's Muy Fuy's Hand."

"We must give to them our help," Inac said, voice and hands both trembling. He tore his eyes away from the Clasform box and set them on me. Took a deep breath to firm himself. "We must."

No choice. The mage was right, but I was still frozen to the bone. Of course we had to help them. Too many Fingers had already died. *But do we have to number among them?*

I sighed and grabbed Inac by the shoulder, then nodded. "How far are they, Garret?" I pictured the city's layout. Even with the dim sunlight filtering through the trees, a visage of the shadow city laid itself on top of the forest. Seeing both at once made me dizzy and buried deep any feeling I once harbored that this illusion was anything like home.

"Four thousand paces," Garret said, "if you trust that map. And if they aren't running."

"From the Artisans District, that would put us near the outer edge of the Financial District. There's no clear path through the city. Too many people for Sentyx to avoid."

"The city?" Dunnax swept his hands around. "There is no city here. The buildings aren't real. The people *aren't real.*"

"Might as well be," I said. "Even in the light I can see them now."

The illusion of a street urchin rushed past me from behind, reaching for my coin purse; I started, before realizing the pickpocket wasn't real. When I blinked, he was gone, turning the corner behind a tree overlaid with a mottled brick building.

Remember what's real.

I closed my eyes to gain a brief reprieve from the double vision. With eyes closed the city persisted, but no flickering image of the forest spoiled the illusion. I could focus on the city's buildings, streets, and people more easily, so I looked around at what Sentyx saw. The Skardwarf must have had no notion of what was solid and what was entirely illusory. I opened and closed my eyes a few times, trying to compare the scenes. Everywhere a tree stood in truth, some deformed structure existed in the shadow city. But there were more things in the city than the forest. Most of the pathways, despite being full of people and animals, marble statues and fountains, were unobstructed in reality. I gripped a nearby lamppost. The hard iron was cold in my hands. Fighting against my instincts, I pushed through the lamppost and felt it dissolve in my grip as it moved through my body.

Almost feels like I'm *the illusion.*

Sentyx was staring at an old marble statue painted with long-faded dyes. With my hand on his shoulder, I said, "Sentyx. It isn't real. Remember, we're in the forest."

He touched the statue, then grunted.

"I know. You can feel it. But it's not there. Take a step forward. Push through."

I took his arm and tried to make him walk through the illusion. It took a moment for him to decide that he could, but he took the step. The statue evaporated into nothing. After a moment it was hard to remember it had ever been there.

"What is real?" Sentyx asked.

"Only the buildings," I said. "The streets are empty. Trust me. Hang on to me and try to keep up. We need to run now."

* * *

We ran until our breaths grew ragged. For the first few streets, Sentyx instinctively resisted and pulled back whenever we were about to run through what appeared to be a solid object. Garret, Inac, and Dunnax, in their headlong rush toward Muy Fuy's distress signal, repeatedly pulled so far ahead that they became lost in the illusory crowd. To some degree, my mind still refused to accept the people weren't real. I called out for the Hand to slow down, costing us precious time. We wouldn't get lost; the Archeflare's brilliant light hung in the sky, filtering through the trees now without the Benefactor's veil. But if we were left behind, we might succumb to the illusion like so many Liwo had.

When the distinct garb of another Hand finally appeared in the distance, I blinked to verify they were really there. They disappeared when I closed my eyes, then reappeared when I opened them. Some tension in my body relieved itself—we'd arrived in time. But as we got closer, the feeling drowned in a flood of renewed dread.

That isn't Muy Fuy's Hand.

It was Cavern's. We joined them and found out what had become of the boy's Hand. Eight of us looked on, incapable of reacting to the carnage that lay before us. The Archeflare's harsh white glare bathed the blood-red scene from above, through a hole of spreading fire in the canopy. Much like the site of Lomin's slaughter in the Shaded Grounds, this Benefactor had killed without mercy. Broken weapons gleamed here and there in the mud. Broken Clasform boxes seeped out a gray-brown paste. Broken bodies littered the ground among neatly severed limbs. Mud and ash and blood stained the charred robe worn by Muy Fuy. The young mage lay dead in the muck. I fought down the wave of nausea rising in my throat.

The Ekoan in Cavern's Hand had fought that same battle and lost, judging by the bile on his boots. "We need to get back to Headquarters," he urged, panic rising in his trembling voice. "We're going to die here. I don't want to die in this dark-damned forest, Nill!"

"Keep it together, Chaf," a Lawi man in thick leather armor said. "No one else is dying here."

"Wouldn't be so sure of that," Garret said, examining some tracks on the ground. Huge, deep, three-toed tracks led off into the forest.

"Not helping, Garret," I said, then stood beside Nill. "You're this Hand's Captain?"

"Yeah," Nill said, before giving me a sidelong look. "Not surprised to see you here. Haven't you caused enough trouble today?"

"Just getting started, sad to say. Didn't Cavern tell you? Ulken's lying about this whole operation."

"Cavern ain't told us anything. He's lost in some fantasy land. Took us ages to get him to follow here. Might have been able to help otherwise."

"We probably would have found ten bodies if you got here sooner," Garret muttered, sniffing the dirt on his fingers.

"Sentyx is lost too," Dunnax said, then grunted. "Skard-warves."

Indeed, Sentyx and Cavern both ambled around the area while the two matching mages kept an eye on them and made sure they didn't stumble into any burning trees. I trusted they wouldn't; in the illusion we were in the Gild. Burning trees matched with lavish buildings that wilted in the heat of the flames.

"The Aura," Inac said, "makes it feel to them the forest is Liwokin."

"Huh," Nill said, grimacing. "We never fought a Benefactor that can do this. It killed them all before we got here."

"Benefactor didn't kill them." Garret stood and wiped his hands on his coat. "Daggerclaw did."

Chaf yelped. "A daggerclaw, here? It can't be. Right? Please tell me it can't be."

I rubbed my face. This day kept getting worse. "There was one in the city, I think. Captive, in the Gild's menagerie."

"A captive daggerclaw? Crazy snuffing Liwo," Garret muttered. "Well, not captive anymore. And we're in his territory." The ranger sighed, began counting his arrows. "Hunted a daggerclaw once. Brought twenty-three men to bring it down." He worked up a mouthful of spit and loosed it onto the daggerclaw's tracks. "Was hard work carrying its carcass back, just the four of us."

"What are you doing?" Chaf asked. "We can't fight it." Chaf stomped his foot, perhaps the first time in his life he'd ever shown any assertiveness. "We are not going that way."

Garret spat again, then shook his head. "No choice."

"Why not?" Nill asked.

"Because the tracks lead northeast," Garret said, then glanced at Dunnax. "Toward Lorelay's Hand."

The Paladin slammed down his visor and took off running.

* * *

We chased after Dunnax, following the tracks of the huge beast deeper into the illusory Financial District. Behind us, the fires slowly consumed the city. A panic rose in me as my mind conjured memories of the Riot.

Except, the Riot had never touched the Gild. They were false memories, just part of the Benefactor's illusion. The Archeflare had only set the forest burning around us. Hardly any better. Was destroying the forest part of Ulken's plan, or simply another byproduct of the Head's callous negligence?

"Dark ahead!" Garret yelled, without slowing down.

Dusk deepened, turning the sky overhead an orangish pink, but the tracks ahead of us plunged into a forest as black as midnight with the Benefactor overhead once more. Dunnax's glinting silver armor disappeared into the gloom as the Paladin rushed forward with no regard for the danger lurking above.

"Dunnax, wait!" I shouted, but he was no easier to stop than Sentyx or Garret once his mind was made up.

Soon, though, the Paladin did stop. Just in front of him, another husk hung from the trees. When I closed my eyes, Dunnax appeared this time as First Eye Reed. The husk before him was Oltrov.

"...rate they are appearing," Oltrov said, "it won't be long until our friend finds what he's searching for."

Dunnax played the role of Reed even more poorly than Sentyx had. His glaive cleaved the Gildmember in two. Though blood sprayed in the illusion, his blade chopped through the husk as though the creature were dry, rotted wood. The illusory Oltrov and the spray of blood flickered out of existence as the husk retracted into the trees.

"Dunnax," Garret said, before the Paladin could take off again. "It's not going after Lorelay."

"Liar!" The giant Paceeqi rounded on Garret and grabbed him by the collar of his cloak. "If we don't stop it, her Hand is next. I've given up too much for her to let that beast kill her."

"Not lying," Garret croaked, hands around Dunnax's wrists. The Paceeqi dropped him, and the ranger took a heaving breath, shook his head, then knelt down. He put his palm to the ground. "It's coming for us."

A low rumble broke the silence of the forest.

"Weapons, now!" I shouted. "Everyone, to me!"

The two Hands rallied to me as the rumble swelled. Pounding footsteps reverberated through the ground. This thing was big. Bigger than Lomin. The earth quaked with its approach.

"Movement," Nill warned.

I looked simultaneously into the blackness of the forest and down a deformed corridor of huge buildings on either side of a cobble road. We stood in the center of the road, ten Fingers. Three controlled powerful sorcery. Two had no sense of reality. I didn't like our odds. My hands gripped the hilt of my blade so hard my knuckles cracked. My ear picked out each pounding footstep as the beast neared, like another heartbeat added to the thumping in my chest.

Two wolves barreled right toward us, quick as the howling wind. Garret readied an arrow, but just as his bowstring twanged, the wolves turned down an alley and disappeared from sight. They weren't concerned with us.

They were fleeing.

A moment later, a larger figure appeared from the same direction, its dark silhouette inexorably approaching. A ray of Archefire discharged from the staff of the blue-robed mage. The magic struck the beast and stopped it in its tracks. The monster reeled back on its hind legs, silhouette shifting to reveal this as an abnormally large bear. The snoutbear voiced a vicious roar, but a burst of Fire, this time from Inac, struck its exposed belly.

The bear collapsed in a heap, but the rumbling continued. Each step of the enormous beast rattled bones like shock waves from nearby explosions. The ground came to a rest, a brief reprieve filled with dread silence. Then an inhuman, guttural roar made the air pulse. The pounding steps redoubled; the monster was running now. When the ringing in my ears stopped, Chaf was whimpering and muttering like a madman. He might have been the sanest of us all.

"We're dead, we're dead, *we're dead*," Chaf repeated, until Nill shook him by the shoulders.

"You're a sorry excuse for a Finger," the Hand captain said. "Do you want to die a sniveling coward?"

"I don't want to die at all! If we don't leave *right now*," Chaf shrieked, "we're as dead as the last Hand! We need to go!"

"Too late," Garret said, his face grave.

The daggerclaw appeared first in the vision of Liwokin, dwarfing the dead bear and towering above the crowd, nearly reaching the height of some buildings. The hulking brute rushed forward, trampling illusory citizens, indiscriminately swinging the claws for which it was named. It tore people apart, leaving a spray of red mist in its wake. The daggerclaw ripped chunks of wood from trees with each swiping attack; in the illusion, brick and stone exploded from the sides of moneylenders and jewelers and clothing shops. One of our mages summoned Archefire and flung it toward the daggerclaw. Orange flame cracked through the air before sputtering out uselessly against the creature's overlapping golden scales. It screamed, but the cry sounded more of annoyance than of pain. The mage's attack hadn't left a scratch on its armored hide. The attack did have one effect, however.

The daggerclaw had been killing indiscriminately. Now, we'd drawn its focus.

None of us reacted. A terrified paralysis seemed to have gripped us all.

If it sees me, I'm dead.

I snapped out of it. This beast was bigger than Lomin, but like Ulken had said, we'd survived indescribable horrors before. I wasn't going to let this time be any different. In the back of my mind, thoughts connected and formed the semblance of a plan.

It's killing the shadow citizens. It thinks it's in the city.

"Get to cover!" I commanded. "Inside the buildings. Now!"

"What buildings?" Nill shouted, but there was no time to explain.

I closed my eyes, grabbed Sentyx, and dashed through an open door. Mercifully, the Skardwarf didn't resist my pull. Inside, we appeared to be in the bustling Glisten Inn, though in truth, we stood exposed in an overgrown space between trees. If the illusion didn't fully convince the beast, our blood would soon water the forest. The rest of my Hand followed me inside, though none of Nill's did. I slammed the door shut as the Hand Captain shouted at his mages, Quell and Yesk, to continue attacking. Fiery magic crackled beyond the closed door. I opened my eyes to see the attacks light the trees, streaming toward the daggerclaw. As before, they extinguished on its magic-resistant plates of armor. This time it didn't even react, as if it knew there was nowhere for us to run. It approached more slowly now, crushing the phantom Liwo in its path.

"Chaf, you coward!" came Nill's shout, somehow muffled by the Aura. "Get back here and fight!"

"We are vulnerable here," Inac said.

"I know, I know." The truth was, I had no plan to survive beyond the next few breaths, and that relied on the daggerclaw not seeing through walls that didn't exist.

Flimsier than wet paper, as plans go, but it's our only hope.

The pounding in the earth had stopped.

"Not a breath, now," Garret whispered.

The air caught in my throat. The daggerclaw loomed outside, visible through the inn's window. The beast went down on all fours and peered into the building with its beady black eye. Time seemed to slow when it caught me in its gaze, huge pupil lingering on me like the eye of death. I braced myself, chest aching. Then Nill loosed a string of curses, a bowstring thrummed, and an arrow pinged against the daggerclaw's head. The huge head swung away, snarling.

When the beast stomped away, I let out a long-held breath. The illusion had done the trick this once, but now we needed to act. "You've hunted these things before, Garret. How do we kill it?"

"Magic usually does it," the Ekoan said, "but not this time. Must be those scales. Aren't usually gold like that."

Inac grunted. "They look to me tempered with Archefire."

Garret spat. "Crazy snuffing Liwo," he muttered again. "The eyes then. Arrows might work."

"Might?" Dunnax asked.

"If it's not moving," Garret said. "You going to hold it down while I aim?"

"Inac," I said, "is there anything you can do to immobilize it?"

The mage thought for a moment, then raised both hands. The roots poking through the underbrush bloomed with darkness. Flashes of golden light radiated from within the blackness. The Archemagic faded and revealed Inac's iridescent obsidian in the shape of the tangled roots. "I need to gather my focus," he said, sitting down, "and I cannot stop its claws with this."

"We use the illusion, then," I said. "Draw it back through the streets and stun it, disorient it. I've got bombs. Garret, can you light some more fires?"

Garret nodded and the air boomed with the deafening roar of the daggerclaw. Through a window, it crashed through a building chasing Nill, who had split off to draw the beast away from Cavern and the two mages. Maybe they could help too.

"Okay. Dunnax, keep an eye on Sentyx. Make sure he doesn't wander out into the open."

"We're *already* out in the open," Dunnax shot back.

"Keep him right where he is, then. Protect him."

Shouldn't be too hard. Sentyx sat at the Glisten Inn's bar, ordering a drink from the bartender. In reality, he sat on the ground, head poking up from behind a bush. I didn't know whether to laugh or weep. *He probably doesn't even know about the daggerclaw.*

"Fine," Dunnax said. "I'll keep him safe."

"Thank you. Now wait here. I'll be back."

A few dozen strides—a couple through two seemingly solid illusory walls—and I reached the mages, Quell and Yesk. Both looked exhausted, leaning against the thick trunk of an oak scored with deep gouges. Cavern was inside the goldsmith's shop framed by this tree, arguing with a shrub that refused to compromise on its price.

"Are you injured? I need your help."

"Just winded," Quell, the mage in blue, said. "What do you need?"

"Fire."

* * *

When I explained the plan, neither of them thought it would work. But I hadn't asked much of them, and what choice did they have? Nill courageously drew the daggerclaw farther away, dashing through the trees and cursing all the while. Fortune kept the buildings of shadow Liwokin between the Lawi and the daggerclaw, but his luck wouldn't last forever. We needed to get the beast's attention and provoke it into following us. I positioned us in the main thoroughfare of the Gild, curving Archemetal buildings scraping the heavens on either side, and waited for the daggerclaw to enter the street. Nill appeared first, with the creature close behind.

I nodded at the mage. "Don't miss."

"I'm going to regret this, aren't I?" Molten Fire gathered at the tip of Yesk's twisted staff as he worked the fingers of his free hand. Just as it seemed too much for the Archemage to contain, a ragged yell escaped his throat, and the spell exploded away. A brilliant beam of light pierced the forest's darkness and struck the daggerclaw on its back. The huge beast staggered forward from the blow, then turned with a murderous roar and charged toward us in a frenzy.

"Let's go!" I ran with the mage directly away from the oncoming beast, passing the Glisten Inn that we shared in our minds. Inside, Cavern waited with Sentyx and the rest of my Hand. "Inac, Garret, get ready!"

Past the bombs I'd planted outside the inn, I ducked into an alleyway with Quell while Yesk kept running. I held my breath as the beast's quaking steps neared. Peering around the corner as Yesk gathered his sorcery, the glow of golden Fire illuminated both of our faces. "Now!" I shouted, but my signal was lost in the sound of Archefire bombs erupting beneath the daggerclaw's charge.

Two flaming arrows flashed through the walls of the inn, lighting the trees above the beast's flailing head. I threw another bomb at its feet as the third and fourth arrows set alight the trunk of a tree behind the daggerclaw. When my bomb exploded, the entire Gild was alight. Inac's sorcery glowed at the daggerclaw's feet, and the already scorched ground melted into a slag that quickly hardened and trapped the beast where it stood. The daggerclaw roared, its violent cry coloring the blazing scene.

The daggerclaw fixed its gaze on me as one final bomb arced from my hand toward its golden chest, but the creature had cunning. Shielding itself with claws like a half-dozen crossed swords, it blunted the explosion. Smoke filled the air and masked its counterattack. The monster's claws lashed out so fast I didn't realize it happened until the tree that formed the corner of my imagined alley exploded into splinters. Nothing but wind battered me, but it would have been a killing blow had I been one step closer. Quell wasn't so lucky. The mage went down with a yelp, then screamed when he laid eyes on the stump that existed where his leg should have been. The half-shattered trunk of the burning tree cracked, then toppled over with a resounding thump between me and the daggerclaw.

Quell's leg left a fearsome trail of blood as I dragged the mage beyond the daggerclaw's reach. The beast roared as Garret's arrows bounced off the golden scales on its head. It shielded its face with one armored limb, looking around for the source of the arrows, then gave up and dug at the rock that held it in place while continuing to guard its eyes.

I'd failed... Despair crept in as I fashioned a makeshift tourniquet for Quell's severed leg. I tried keeping my thoughts away from my Hand's fate. It was my job to make sure they survived. A memory surfaced from Wyran's Pool. His sister worked at his bloody neck, knowing his life would soon end. My hands made equally useless motions, wrapping torn fabric around the mage's thigh. He had already passed out from blood loss.

Better for him. We're all dead as soon as it claws its way free.

Another cry of anger sounded as the daggerclaw tore at the earth, but this one didn't come from the beast. The daggerclaw jolted up. Through the black, wind-whipped smoke, a gleaming figure clung impossibly to its back. Dunnax loosed another roar, as bestial as the creature whose back he now ascended. The daggerclaw twisted and reached for the Paladin, but he was out of reach. Dunnax held on. He lifted himself with an iron grip toward the monster's nape. With one gauntleted fist securing himself to the daggerclaw, Dunnax readied Cavern's darkwood blade with the other. He rammed it repeatedly between armored scales into the monster's neck. The daggerclaw recoiled. A pained scream broke from its jaws. Dunnax thrust the weapon deeper. It was working. The beast was dying.

But the daggerclaw recovered. It drove its head forward, down toward the earth, and tossed Dunnax over its shoulders. The Paladin flipped over in the air and landed with a crunch against the fallen log.

"Dunnax!" The word tore from my throat, but words couldn't save him.

No armor is thick enough to stop a daggerclaw. The monster drove its claws through the Paladin's chest plate, deep into the trunk of the tree. Dunnax jerked and coughed. Blood spurted from his visor, and he went limp.

The daggerclaw pulled back, but the log shifted with it. It tried again, but its iron claws were lodged in the wood. As the beast opened its jaws to let out another cry, an arrow shot from the illusory inn and sank deep into its eye socket. The creature collapsed atop the burning tree. The Paladin and the dagger-claw were both dead.

Dunnax...

The guilt within me burned as hot as the dying forest. We defeated the daggerclaw, but at what cost? Another Finger was dead. My friend. Good men kept dying because of me. All to save my own skin. A breath of unseen, acrid smoke choked my lungs. Flames consumed the trees, but they appeared in the shadow city like a blazing aurora in the sky. Alongside the unconscious Quell, I lay there, numb, ready to let the fires consume me too.

The Hand is better off without me.

The sky above shone red as though the sunset light were shattered in a crystalline prism. The heat from the fire seemed a far-off thing. I may have been in the burning Gild, but I was still in Liwokin. Home.

There are worse places to die.

I took a deep breath. A chemical scent filled my nostrils, and suddenly Inac was there, holding a Clasform box to my nose. The lie of the city resolved into the truth of the forest, where the conflagration raged more furiously than I could believe. Through the numbness, there was a pang of sorrow when the flames took hold of the daggerclaw. Dunnax lay beneath.

"We cannot stay here, my friend!" Inac shook me, then violently coughed. He tugged at my coat. "Come! Get up, Grim!"

Garret dragged Quell away and disappeared behind a cloud of black smoke. Nill had Cavern and Sentyx by the arms, though clearly, he wasn't in control; the Skardwarves both looked eager to escape the flames. Embers danced through the air, carried in the whirlwind of the inferno. Inac looked down at me, sandy hair whipped to the side by hot gusts, and something in his expression finally jolted me into thinking straight.

He wanted me to live.

"Is there anything you can do about this?" I said, rolling onto my elbows.

"I cannot control this. We must go!"

With a reverberating crack, the tree beneath the daggerclaw collapsed, and the beast slumped to the ground atop Dunnax in a monstrous funeral pyre. I spared my friend and the creature he slew one final look.

I'd make sure his sacrifice meant something.

I followed Inac to safety. Death by fire would not be my fate today.

CHAPTER TWENTY-SIX

Twisted Tower

The distant blaze painted the sky with smears of orange and gray. It faded to a deep blue as we slogged through the forest, until the waning Brightdaughter peered down from the dusky sky above. The Benefactor was not here. Perhaps it sensed the fires we had set would soon arrive. To where, then, did the monster flee?

When we put enough distance between ourselves and the burning woods, Nill let go of the Skardwarves and rushed to insensate Quell's side. "Is he..." The mage looked dead enough to warrant the question. After all the fighting this Agency did, I wouldn't have expected any Finger to shy away from the word. But grief shook all of us in our own way.

Garret shook his head. "Unconscious."

"I stopped the bleeding as best I could," I said, "but he needs a healer. Inac, can you help him?"

"I can mend for him what remains," the mage said, "but losing his limb will leave in his mind scars I cannot heal." The light with which he guided us went out as Inac set to work repairing the wound with Archefire.

"Where's Yesk?" Nill asked.

"He kept running," I said. "Straight out of these woods if he's smart."

Nill grunted, then bared his teeth. "Hope he catches that coward Chaf. When I see him, I'll—"

"Kill him?" Garret spat on the ground. "For running from the daggerclaw? Same as you did, I recall."

Nill spat right back at him. "Since you left my Hand all alone. Hid in the bushes when you should've stood and fought."

Garret laughed. "Against a daggerclaw? You city folk don't get enough fresh air to your brains."

Inac finished on Quell's leg. Archefire faded, and a new mote of light appeared in midair. "We did not hide in bushes. Grim used against the daggerclaw the Benefactor's illusion."

"Aye," Garret said. "His plan worked."

"My plan got Dunnax killed," I mumbled. "Quell lost his leg because of me. It did *not* work."

Garret paused for a good long time, chewing the words, and thinking them through before he let them loose. "Lost two of my best friends hunting a daggerclaw in Eko. Two of my best friends, and twenty more besides. Today, we lost one." Garret said. "A dark-swallowing shame, but better than we could've hoped for. Your plan worked."

"But—"

"But nothing," Garret said. "You got us through alive, and now we've got a task to see through. One last hunt."

Ulken. We'd left the fire far behind, but a heat welled up in my chest, nonetheless. I clenched my jaw. How much would have been different if Ulken hadn't created the Benefactors and spread them across Lawiko? Dunnax and Bengard would be alive. The Liwo lost in these woods would be back in the city, going about their normal business. Maybe I'd still have had some bounties to collect. Without monsters, there would be no reason for the Agency to exist. *No, there would still be monsters. One of them created the Agency.*

"You're going after Ulken, ain't you?" Nill grimaced. "Whether you or the Benefactor kills him, good riddance, I say. Seen too many men die by his command. Time for some new leadership."

My eyes widened. Cavern had been more successful than he thought at convincing his Hand not to trust Ulken. It lit an ember of hope. With two Hands united and Ulken still focused on the Benefactor, we'd stand a much better chance against the Head. "Will you help us?"

Nill stomped out the ember. "No. I've had my fill of violence today." He gestured at Quell, who looked to be sleeping peacefully now, and Cavern. The Skardwarf squatted down in a way that reminded me of when I played dice on the streets of the Burg, gathering information about my bounties. "I'm getting these two back to the city. Figure only you or Ulken will be coming back to Liwokin. I'm hoping it's you."

There were no goodbyes. Nill managed to pull Cavern away from his imagined game and carried Quell over his shoulder back toward Liwokin.

As they left, I put my hand on Sentyx's shoulder and asked him where we now stood in the shadow city. Since Inac had given me that dose of Clasform, my link to the Benefactor's Aura had become more tenuous. Crowds of people still yammered in my ears, and the overpowering stench of Liwokin greeted me with each breath, but the illusion no longer appeared when I closed my eyes.

"Residential District," Sentyx said.

"We do not know where Ulken is," Inac said. "How does this help us?"

"He must be in these woods somewhere," I said. "Are we near another search area, Garret?"

"Aye. Lorelay's. Where it should be, anyway. Doesn't seem like anyone's around."

Ulken's Hand wasn't at his marked location. Lorelay's Hand wasn't at theirs. No one was where they were meant to be. Except...

"The Archemaker," I said. "He was in the Maker's Square. Oltrov, the Gildmember, he was in the Financial District. Both were right where they belong."

Inac hummed. "That may be a coincidence."

"Both husks were having a conversation," I said.

"Yes, I heard them speaking to someone," Inac said, "but I could not see for myself. Who were they with?"

Both times we encountered a husk, Sentyx and Dunnax appeared in the illusion as First Eye Reed. A memory surfaced from Pinch's Pool, of the First Eye plunging a knife into his own heart, and a familiar crackling feeling at the back of my neck. The memory ended there when Ulken stole the Peeker away from Reed. Just as Reed stole something that Ulken wanted.

"Reed..." I drew in a quick breath. "He's the Benefactor. And he has something Ulken wants. They must be together."

"Say that's true," Garret said skeptically, "that still doesn't tell us where they are."

"It does," I said, gesturing at the night sky above. "We're in the Burg, near Reed's home, but the Benefactor isn't here. Where else would they be?"

"I can think only of one place," Inac said. "The Agency."

I smiled. "Right where they belong."

* * *

No one spoke as we traveled north toward where the Agency would be in the illusion. The occasional lost wanderer shambled through the darkness, drawn away from the real city by Reed's illusion of a false one. Grave thoughts occupied me. I was weary from this command that had been doomed from the start and wary of the coming confrontation with Ulken and Reed. We hadn't yet fought a Benefactor that didn't leave us reeling in horror, but something about this one seemed...different.

Two times we'd come across it, yet it never attacked us.

Even when Dunnax had split the husk in two, it only shot up into the trees in retreat. On dead bodies the thing feasted gluttonously, but for the living it had no concern. While most visions induced by Benefactors occurred in short, disorienting bursts, Reed showed greater control. He spread the illusion of Liwokin with his Aura, laden with memories as though it were a perpetual Deluge.

Sentyx grunted, breaking the rhythm of footfalls in the forest's undergrowth. "Almost there."

"Aye," Garret said, "so what's our plan? Down one Finger, and Sentyx won't be any help. How are we going to fight Ulken's Hand *and* a Benefactor?"

Some notion swirled in my mind, a hazy, unformed idea. "I don't think we'll have to. Fight both, I mean." They were unconvinced, but I knew this was no normal Benefactor—not that we had encountered any Benefactor I'd categorize as normal. "Something's different this time."

I hope. The world kept changing, faster than waves drummed up by the cold ocean winds could wreck a ship. Change always made things worse and worse. Why would this time be any different? *And yet, this Benefactor isn't trying to kill us outright.*

"No plan then," Garret said. "Got it."

"You are saying to us we will not kill Reed?" Inac shook his head. "He still is a Benefactor, my friend. He is dangerous."

"I know he is." I pinched the bridge of my nose. "Let's just see what we're dealing with first."

"Why don't I just sneak up on Ulken and plant an arrow in his back," Garret said. "Another in Reed's skull, then we head back, job done."

Inac snorted, but the ranger was being serious.

"I don't think it'll be quite so easy," I said.

"Here." Sentyx grunted.

The Agency appeared as we stepped into a vast, unnatural clearing. It reminded me of the place where we found Wyran, but tenfold the size. I closed my eyes, unable to accept I wasn't seeing an illusion once more, but behind my eyelids there was only darkness. The alien sight remained when I reopened them.

On the far side of the clearing, a tower rose above the strips of orange and pink on the horizon, piercing the deep blue sky like a full-scale replica of the Agency's headquarters. Far from the bright gray stone of the original, the replica's organic, black material devoured the failing light of dusk. A semicircular wall extended out from the tower, framing a courtyard whose entrance was more of a ripped-out hole than a proper gate. The tower was as warped and twisted as the visions of Liwokin. Still, the inspiration was clear.

Thousands of people filled the clearing, packed together shoulder to shoulder, sometimes standing atop one another. Many lay unconscious or dead on the ground. Those who stood upright swayed like grass in the wind and moaned like ghosts reborn. A seething congregation, come to worship at this unholy cathedral.

"Looks like we found the missing Liwo," Garret said.

"Let us hope," Inac said, "it is not for us too late to save them."

My eyes lingered on a group piled on the ground. My lips curled in dismay, and I forced myself to look back at the tower. "It's not." I grabbed Sentyx's arm to pull him through the press of those who succumbed to Reed. "Come on."

The structure rose as we approached until it seemed ready to topple over and crush us along with everyone else in the clearing. The masses around us faced the phantom Agency as if waiting for some signal that would set them all in motion. It felt like walking through a field of the dead, but I wouldn't accept that these people—*my people*—were lost. Everywhere I looked, I felt on the verge of recognizing familiar faces, though the city was too populous for that to be true. Still, I had a connection to them; we shared the same city as a home. In Liwokin, that *meant* something.

"Is that...?" Garret pointed.

"Lorelay!" Inac shouted, but the girl was in a daze. He ran to her side and pulled the Clasform box from his satchel. She failed to acknowledge the mage, mumbling gibberish with the rest of the dazed Liwo. Inac raised the Clasform but hesitated. When he looked to me, the worry in his eyes was plain. Last time he tried to help, he'd taken the man's life instead.

I shook my head. Inac didn't need another lost life weighing on his conscience. "Let me."

If the girl died, I would bear that burden myself. But there had to be *some* way to rouse a person from Reed's induced slumber. The Clasform box had worked for me, though maybe only because I still had some tether to reality. If I could nudge her in the right direction...

I placed my hand on the Paceeqi girl's shoulder. "Lorelay. It's Grim."

Her fist shot up into the air along with those of a hundred other Liwo. They all fell in unison, then the mumbling renewed.

Tension permeated the clearing; whether Reed's Aura or the indignation already present in the population, I couldn't say.

"Lorelay, you have to wake up. You're not in the city."

She looked at my hand on her shoulder with half-lidded eyes and frowned. She shrugged away, muttering something under her breath.

I tried once more, and she shoved me into Sentyx. She might as well have shoved me up against a wall for all the Skardwarf moved.

"Leave her," Garret said. "She'll come around once we deal with Reed."

"You do not know this," Inac said. "They could die when we remove from them the Benefactor's influence."

I gritted my teeth. There was a real possibility these Liwo had no happy ending. Without some way of calming them down, there could be confusion, panic...even another riot. If only Lorelay could play her music to soothe them.

My eyes darted down to Lorelay's lyre. Though secured to her belt, it was easy to remove, as though she might have needed it at a moment's notice. Holding the instrument in my hands conjured memories from the Pool of some unknown Liwo who played one similar. He wasn't nearly as talented as Lorelay, but it would serve. My fingers were clumsy as they worked at the lyre's strings. Knowing what strings to pluck was quite different from making the motions. Still, I managed to produce a slow melody.

She didn't react to the first few phrases. Then I strummed a chord that framed my slow melody as even more somber. Lorelay cocked her head, blinked, and looked around. Her eyes landed on me, and she growled in frustration. "Give me that." She yanked the lyre from my hands and played her own masterful melody. "The mood is all wrong. Did you start playing just yesterday?" She put my playing to shame with a rousing song that one might perform for soldiers marching into battle.

Hand on her shoulder, I said, "Never played before. Where did you learn that?"

Lorelay's lip quivered as her fingers worked, and the melody shifted once more. "My mother taught me. At first."

Inac looked at me, motioning to the Clasform. I nodded and he raised the box to her nose.

In the midst of a coughing fit, Lorelay somehow kept playing beautifully. But when she opened her eyes, she ended the song on a discordant note. "What?" She looked at me, face twisting in bewilderment. "Grim? Where the snuff are we?"

I smiled. "Back in reality." I glanced at the tower. "Unfortunately."

Lorelay held her head. "I...I don't understand."

"There's no time to explain now," I said. "We need your help."

"We?" Lorelay searched, found my Hand, and searched a little more. "Where's Dunnax?"

My stomach dropped. I had to tell her, but the words caught in my throat. A hollow formed inside me, insignificant compared to the vast emptiness Lorelay would feel. I looked down, unable to meet her eyes.

She pushed me, then screamed, "Where is he?"

Silence was all she needed to confirm her brother's fate. Lorelay wailed, her cries heavy with sorrow, pain, anger.

Her legs faltered, but I caught her and wrapped my arms around her. "I'm sorry," I told her. It was all I could think to say. "I'm sorry." Tears welled in my eyes as Lorelay's body racked with sobs.

"We don't have time for this," Garret complained, and I scowled at him over Lorelay's shoulder. He pointed toward the tower, where the walls mimicked those of the courtyard. "Look."

Two lines of Liwo shuffled slowly toward the malformed Agency. One by one they reached the tower's walls, and one by one disappeared into them. A chill swept down my neck and shook my whole body. The Benefactor was assimilating them. Building the tower with their flesh. Night had fallen, and the color of sunset had descended below the trees. But all the dark seemed to seep from the tower. How many Liwo had died for this abomination?

"What is that thing?" Lorelay asked, sniffling.

"The Benefactor," I said. "Dunnax died so we could get this far. We have to end this. Otherwise, it was for nothing."

Inac looked like he was going to be sick. "We must enter the tower."

"No choice," I said. "Ulken's inside, and we're expecting a fight. Lorelay, you should stay out here, keep Sentyx—"

"Screw you." There was venom on her tongue. "Ulken dragged us into this. It's his fault my brother's dead. I'm going in too." Her instrument was gone; instead, she held knives. Sharp. But not as sharp as the fury in her eyes.

* * *

"Who goes there?" a voice called out from the hole to the courtyard of Reed's twisted tower.

I pushed my way free of the crowd. Apart from the lines of shambling victims, most Liwo maintained a healthy distance from the perimeter of the entire building. Up close, more details of the construct revealed themselves. Shallow wrinkles covered the exterior, like those marring an Agency report that had been crumpled into a wad before being flattened out again. The tower's sides were pressed in as if by the thumbs of a giant, leaving depressions that served no purpose, vestigial renditions of windows. Where the tower met the earth, a thin moat of slime clung to the ground around the circumference of the tower. The muck crawled up the boots of two Eyes who stood watch by the poor impression of a gate. Jacquin and Looker both had their swords drawn.

"Oh, it's just you." Jacquin sheathed his weapon, then shared a suspicious glance with Looker, who did not sheath hers. "You're not supposed to be here, Hand Sixty-Four."

"You sure about that? Ulken told us where to find him after we completed our task. How else would we know to come here?" I hoped getting to the Head wouldn't require going through the Eyes. More than enough people had died today, but we'd add two more to the list of the fallen if they called my bluff.

Looker spat into the slime. "Ulken didn't tell us to expect anyone. Only said to make sure no one followed him."

"Ulken says lots of things," I said, "but rarely the whole truth. Pretty sure no one knows what Ulken's plans are but Ulken."

She squirmed at that one, scowling. Even Ulken's Hand knew he couldn't be trusted. "What's she doing here?" Looker glowered at Lorelay. "She's not in your Hand."

I shrugged. "We lost someone; she lost her whole Hand. She used to be in mine, so I figured she could fill in without affecting Ulken's plans."

Looker drew her eyes to a thin slit. "His plans? What do you think he's doing in there?"

I put on a disarming smile, donning the mask they needed to see. "Talking to Reed, I expect. They are old friends after all."

As Jacquin and Looker exchanged a long look, my hand slowly drifted to the blade at my waist. I held my smile, but I was ready to pounce and cut them both down as soon as conflict became inevitable.

To my relief, Jacquin chuckled and broke the tension. I let my hand hang limp. "For a moment, I thought we might come to blows," he said. "Ulken told you about Reed, eh?"

"Shame, what happened to the old First Eye. But we're here to help." I extended a hand, and Jacquin shook it. "You're a good man, Jacquin. A fine replacement for Reed. Would you keep an eye on Sentyx for us? He needs some rest."

Hopefully Sentyx wasn't too dazed to remember to keep Ulken's Hand busy out here. It was unnerving leaving him with two Fingers who did nothing to stop the Benefactor from assimilating Liwo around them, but bringing him into the tower was an even bigger risk.

"Of course," Jacquin said, then stepped aside to let us pass. "They're in the First Eye's Office, first floor. Careful in there, it's a bit of a maze. Reed's memory of the halls wasn't perfect, but it should feel familiar. Oh, and remember not to light any flames. The whole tower could go up, and these people are already on edge. I don't know what might set them off."

"Understood, and thanks. We'll be careful."

Looker glared at me, so I flashed another smile, nodded to her, then moved through the archway, motioning for my Hand to follow.

What little light remained quickly faded as we proceeded into Reed's tower. Just as quickly, the air filled with an acrid, rotting stench. At first, I struggled to breathe, as if my lungs anticipated a lethal dose of poison to accompany every breath. But given time, the mind and body can acclimate to even the worst experiences, whether bad scents or evil deeds. Spend enough days killing people in cold blood, and even that becomes normal. Send enough recruits to be slaughtered by monsters, and you might start believing it's justified. The sour smell faded so quickly that I nearly believed the air had been clean all along, despite inconvenient memories from only moments ago.

If convincing Jacquin to let us pass with vague promises of help wasn't enough to tell us Ulken had left his Hand in the dark, then the layout of this interior surely was. Jacquin said Reed's reconstruction wasn't perfect.

Imperfect isn't merely an understatement. It's like saying Liwokin smells pleasant after rainfall.

Missing were the sharp, ninety-degree turns of brick and stone that characterized the Agency in Liwokin. Here, the walls flowed with natural curves and bends, as distorted as the illusion of Liwokin's streets. My boots sank into the soft, organic material, as though we were walking on pulpy paper. A wet squish accompanied every step. It comprised the floors just as it did the walls and the ceiling above, the entire tower a single gruesome material.

Inac gagged. "Is this—?"

"Try not to think about it," I said.

When the path started sloping upward, I worried that we might fall through to some layer far below, but to my relief the floor continued to hold. The tunnel continued climbing and didn't seem like it was going to come back down.

"Where are we going, Grim?" Lorelay demanded.

"I don't know," I admitted, and briefly regretted that we'd left Sentyx behind; he could have guided us with his illusory vision. "This place is nothing like the real Agency."

"Jacquin lied to us," Inac said.

"He probably never stepped foot inside," I said. "Just told us what Ulken told him."

"Ulken lied to him, and he passed it along," Lorelay scoffed. "Is that any better?"

I frowned. "So we're lost. Anyone got any ideas?"

"Aye," Garret said. "Let's burn the whole place down and go have a drink."

Lorelay laughed bitterly. "I second that."

"No," I said. "Jacquin's right. If the Benefactor feels threatened, who knows what it'll do to the people outside?"

"Then what?" Lorelay asked.

"We have to talk to Reed."

"Talk to a Benefactor?" Now it was Garret's turn to laugh.

It sounded ridiculous even to me, but... "Ulken's talking to him right now. Reed has some control over what's happening. He might be able to help us, and I'm sure he was no friend of Ulken's. But first we have to find them. So, any *other* ideas?"

"Yes," Inac said. "How about this?" A deeper darkness emanated from the mage's left hand, which he pressed to the wall. The substance sloughed down and formed a vile puddle around our boots. Soon, Inac's magic had torn a gaping hole in the wall. "No Fire, he said to us. He said to us nothing about Dark."

"Lead the way." I gestured forth. "But don't wear yourself out."

Only after carving through so many identical walls did it dawn on me how truly lost we were. We might have wandered these halls until we succumbed to the Benefactor's illusion, doomed to become part of the tower ourselves. By the time the last wall fell to Inac's touch, the mage was breathing too hard for my liking. Light bloomed as Archedark faded and warm, fresh air came blowing in.

Garret stopped me from stepping through the hole. "Someone talking," he whispered.

I strained my ears, but adrenaline poured through me and filled my ears with my own rapid pulse. Lorelay had already unsheathed her knives, and Garret his bow. It was plain to see how eager everyone was for blood. I wanted the man dead as much as any of them, but something gnawed at the back of my mind. Was there a better way to approach this?

But my thoughts were cut short.

Ulken made his move first.

CHAPTER TWENTY-SEVEN

The Gift

Well," the Head proclaimed, "I'm waiting. Come out and show yourself. Or are you going to hide in those tunnels like rats?"

I glanced at Inac, then clambered through the hole and down the tunnel. Emerging from the darkness, the sky opened up above, a distant disc of hazy blue specked with twinkling white stars. The construction of Reed's tower was not yet complete, but the work would continue if we didn't end this fast. In this central hollow, I felt like a rodent indeed, staring up from the bottom of a great tree. Lightwood and oak trunks formed a perimeter ring, webbed with a pulpy substance to form a circular wall. All around me it was solid right to the top, save for the hole from which I had emerged. A figure whose legs had melded into the wrinkled ground was scratching at the bark of one of the trees.

Reed. This is what he had become, reduced to a shriveled husk.

No. This entire *tower* was him. Every Liwo he assimilated had become a part of him. But the Benefactor maintained a human form. Maybe that meant he still had some humanity left.

Near the body the First Eye had created to represent himself, Ulken stood glowering at me. He was holding a silver rod with an iridescent obsidian stone in his hands, waving it around as he talked. "Finger Grimley," he said, "I should have known. I never could see things through your—"

A bowstring thrummed behind me. The arrow lashed out over my shoulder, but Ulken had already stepped to the side, as if he'd known in advance it was coming. The shaft wobbled as the arrow stuck in the tree by the husk, but Reed continued scratching away, unperturbed.

Ulken glanced at the arrow and blew out a laugh. "You brought friends. How delightful."

"I came to kill you," I returned. "Didn't want them missing out on all the fun."

Inac growled coming out of the tunnel. A dark haze gathered around the mage, and in the mounting gloom, the trees glowed inky blue with Ghostwritten messages. *What is that box* and *Don't ask about her* and *I don't know who* were scrawled above Reed, who was halfway through another cryptic message. *They'll stop you*, was promised on the next tree over, and further down, *They will*. A cold burst of air accompanied the blast of Dark magic, but Ulken danced aside at the last moment. The Archedark pierced the pulpy wall behind the Head and fizzled out. The Ghostwriting faded with the magic.

"Now that's interesting," Ulken said, looking at the dowsing rod in a new light. He tossed it over his shoulder, where it struck the husk of Reed and thumped to the ground. The husk paid it no attention. It sunk into the floor and started scratching letters lower down on the tree.

Lorelay screamed, pushing past me to charge Ulken with knives out. In a flash, Ulken drew his longsword and slashed at Lorelay—the same motion as when he'd severed the head of that innocent Liwo. The Paceeqi brought her knives up and caught the blade, but Ulken's boot struck her in the chest and sent her flying back. Garret loosed another arrow, but the Head pivoted and knocked it aside with his sword. I blinked. The ranger had never missed before. Now he'd missed twice. A bounty hunter prepared for every possibility, but I wasn't ready for this.

"Is this what passes for Rank Four Fingers?" Ulken mocked. His lips curled as if he tasted something bitter. "Why did I need such weak fools? Relying on others is a perpetual source of disappointment." He rushed at me.

His sword blurred as it sang through the air, too fast for the eye to follow. If not for adrenaline, I would have reacted too slowly. My wrist screamed as my sword absorbed the blow and caught Ulken's overhead slash. I turned it aside. The end of Ulken's blade struck dirt, and he jumped back, laughing, to avoid my counterattack. Pain lanced down my arm from my bad shoulder, and I nearly lost ahold of my weapon.

"What's wrong?" Ulken asked, clearly enjoying himself. "Four against one, and yet I seem to have the better of you."

This is a game to him. I swallowed the rising taste of fear. *One he's winning.*

"So, tell me, why am I going to die? What is it you think I've done?"

"You know what you've done." I spat. "The Fingers you've sent to die, the Liwo lost in these woods. Their blood is on your hands."

"*My* hands? And what of yours, Finger Grimley? The rest of you? Are any of our hands clean?"

Inac growled, summoning another void of Dark magic that set the hollow glowing. Ulken thrust his blade at the mage, but I stepped in and forced it aside. Ulken dove out of the way as Inac released his Archedark in an onyx beam. It missed the Head but sent splashes of Reed's husk flying as if he were made of liquid. Reed fell to the ground as the blue glow of a message reading *Boxes hurt* faded, but he reformed himself and moved to another tree to continue scratching.

Inac wavered on his feet, but Ulken was off balance too. Lorelay jumped at the Head and managed to catch his flowing black and silver coat as he rolled away. Her knives tore two long streaks in the fabric, but no blood followed. Ulken came out of the roll and swiped at Lorelay's legs. The Paceeqi girl jumped back and threw a knife spinning at Ulken. He twisted aside, and it stuck into the soft wall.

Garret's third arrow connected, but not with the Head. The arrowhead punctured Ulken's Clasform box and snapped the twine hanging it from his neck. When the arrow's momentum carried it toward Reed, a pulse of agony went through my mind, like a ripple on the surface of a pond.

Or a Pool.

I narrowed my eyes, glanced at Reed. What had his message said? *Boxes hurt?*

Ulken winced. He must have felt the pulse too. The Head grimaced at me and rolled his shoulders. "I must admit, this has been a worthy test, but I grow tired of prolonging its conclusion."

"This is *not* one of your snuffing tests," Lorelay barked.

"Everything in life is a test, my dear." He spoke to Lorelay, but his cold eyes remained fixed on me. "So many fail to overcome the trials of life, but I will prevail."

"And do what?" I forced the words through clenched teeth. "More lying and killing?"

"Necessary sacrifices," Ulken said.

I spat at his disregard. What did Ulken know about sacrifice?

"There's no other way to save a city such as ours from the rot that festers within," the Head continued. "If lying and killing is how I must save Liwokin from itself, then so be it. I will bear that burden for us. It's the only way to make a difference."

His words struck me like a blow to the head. I fell back a step. Our city *was* rotting, and Ulken *had* made a difference. The Agency had helped the people of Liwokin after the Riot. It had quelled the violence and restored order, if at great cost.

"You're wrong," I muttered, but the words came out like an unconvincing squeak.

I'd only joined the Agency to better my own lot. The only difference I'd made was to get good people killed. Bengard, Dunnax, everyone in Tak's laboratory... How could I claim to be better than Ulken?

A memory breached the surface, not from any Benefactor's Pool. A memory of my own. *Not everything that is effective is pleasant*, Tak told me. *Ulken is much like you, I should think.*

"Ah." Ulken laughed. "I see you're listening for once. You call me a liar, but it's the truth. Accept it. The city is better off in my hands."

"No!"

We are not *the same.*

Ulken thought he was helping the city, but *he* had created the Benefactors. Liwo were dying by the thousands because of him. I glanced at Inac; he had a rage in his eyes to match my own. My hands weren't clean, no, but I was *not* Ulken. I was not a monster.

I hunted them.

But not alone. And my Hand aren't the only allies I have.

"Garret, get these away from the tower." I snapped the twine around my neck and threw my Clasform box at him. Whatever they were, they were hurting Reed.

The Ekoan snatched it from the air. "You need me."

"To do *this*," I urged, eyes never leaving Ulken. The Head narrowed his eyes and frowned. When the ranger didn't move, I made it a command. "Now!" Inac and Lorelay both tossed Garret their boxes. When Garret started for the Clasform box near Reed, Ulken moved to intercept him.

I darted toward the Head and forced him away from Garret. Ulken turned, feinted with another high strike, then twisted his wrist to thrust at my chest. I dropped my blade just in time to turn a fatal blow aside. My left side felt the bite of steel. Blood trickled down, but the pain was a distant thing. We separated, blades held at the ready, eyes locked. Time slowed with the pulsing of adrenaline through blood as hot as molten steel. Ulken's sword hung motionless in the air with the infinitely controlled touch of its master's hand. Garret disappeared into the dark tunnel, hands full of Clasform boxes.

"You don't know what you're doing," Ulken said flatly.

"I've heard that before." Ulken had said the same to Reed, as though the Head always knew best. "You can't control what you've unleashed. No one can."

I charged in and swiped at Ulken, but my blade lagged, heavy in my hands. The Head parried my slow strike with little apparent effort, spun, and scored a gash across my calf. Warmth flowed down to my heels. But I stayed on my feet. Garret needed time. Ulken turned his body to avoid another slow thrust. His fist flashed around and rung my head like a bell, knocking me onto my rear. Ulken aimed the point of his sword at my heart and drew back his elbow.

The Head's eyes darted to the side. The hollow glowed with inky blue and a frigid blast of Archedark saved my life. I scrambled away, a streak of dark red accompanying my dragging foot.

Lorelay rushed to Inac, helped him up to his knees. Darkfather. When had he collapsed?

Even against four of us, Ulken had held his own. Now, we were down to three and fading fast. I eyed the husk of Reed; from the perimeter of the hollow it watched with unnerving, sunken eye sockets.

Hurry up, Garret.

The ranger needed to put distance between the Benefactor and the Clasform boxes that were suppressing it. Relying on the First Eye to overcome his Benefactor and take control was a risk, but what choice did I have? Ulken would make mincemeat of us in short order. Even now, as Garret sped through the twisting hallways of Reed's tower, a burgeoning power awakened, as though lightning had charged the air.

A roar of sound washed down from above. The Liwo were chanting. Angry, violent voices reverberated in the hollow.

Ulken laughed. "You see? You don't know what you're doing. They'll slaughter each other out there, and that Ekoan fool too." A muffled shout came from the dark tunnel. A woman's voice, then Garret's, followed by the ringing of steel on steel. Ulken laughed again. "If he makes it past Looker, that is."

The walls of the tower hadn't moved, but they seemed to be closing in. "Lorelay, help him!"

Lorelay was ready to pounce on the grinning Head. "But you—"

"Don't worry about me!" She was right to worry. My legs shook under my weight, threatening to collapse underneath me. Cold was filling the void left by my leaking blood.

I might not survive this fight, but I could still do some good while I lived.

Lorelay growled in frustration. I was asking her to give up a chance to kill the man responsible for her brother's death. But if Looker killed Garret, there would be no avenging Dunnax. She dashed for the tunnel's opening, swearing as she ran to help the ranger. That left just me and Inac to fight the Head, who'd outclassed us even with twice our numbers. Alone, we were already beaten.

The sounds buffeting the hollow from above made clear what unfolded outside. Chaos. The chanting had lost its unity and devolved into a din of savagery. Vicious barks and murderous screams crested above the low roar of fighting. Ulken grunted, and his eyes flicked toward Reed. He looked back at me, then glanced at Inac, working his jaw muscles. But for once the Head had nothing to say.

Ulken turned his back and trudged toward the dark tunnel. His priorities had apparently changed. Beaten down as we were, Inac and I were no longer the real threat. Meanwhile, Reed's power was rapidly growing. The walls of the Agency appeared in earnest. Dulling haze blanketed the floors. Through a window, the streets were full of rioting Liwo. I was in Liwokin.

I was home.

My head hung down, chest heaving, red spit dripping from my lips. I threw down my sword.

And grinned.

It's what you don't see that kills you.

I reached into my pocket and clutched a tiny sphere, weighing it in my hands. My head swam. The ground seemed a hundred paces away. Losing blood at this rate, I was dead already. What did I have to lose? Inac's eyes went wide when I pulled the Archeflare from my coat, but he drew his lips to a line and gave a curt nod. Dying, too, was easier with a friend.

Archedark bloomed around the mage as the Archeflare left my fingertips, sailing through the air toward the mouth of the tunnel. The slightest turn of Ulken's body was the last thing I saw before diving for cover, squeezing shut my eyes. For half a heartbeat there was darkness. Then heat and light consumed me, as if I'd fallen into a sea of fire.

With a deafening pop, the world went silent. Eyes closed tight, my eyelids bloomed red, then white, then faded back to red. The scorching heat left me numb, as though I'd burned up into nothing more than ash. Then the throbbing of my wounds returned, and my head and elbows were pressed into the ground, hands clasped at the back of my skull. I struggled to my feet. A ringing returned, quiet at first, becoming louder, louder, until it gave way to a bestial scream, deranged and manic.

The blinding luminance that rushed in when I unclenched my eyes made the Brightdaughter seem cold and dim, as feeble as the Shadowson. The light seemed to bloom from every surface, giving everything it touched a haziness, blurring hard edges into soft coronas. I peered up at the night sky, but my eyes refused to remain open for long. When I shut them tight again, the state of the hollow remained as a ghostly vision. Halfway up the tower, the Archeflare had cut into the wall, gouging a streak of fire as it rocketed skyward. The illusion didn't survive the damage. All around me, Reed's tower burned.

"Inac!" I shouted, voice distant. I spun around, eyes still shut against the painful light.

"Grim!" Inac shouted. He was close. "Move!" Footsteps closed in. Something struck me, and I stumbled aside. The temperature plummeted as I dropped to the ground.

Strange that a burning tower should be so cold.

But the fiery heat quickly returned, and with it came Inac's screams. The scent of blood tinged the air.

I forced my eyes open against the light. A blurry silhouette stood over a kneeling figure like an executioner. Ulken. Inac knelt before him. The Head of the Agency set his eyes on me.

His blade hung in the air over my friend's neck. Through the glare, he was grinning. A challenge.

My mind moved too slowly. Feral instincts drew on some inner reserve of strength and lifted me to my feet. My hand somehow found the hilt of my blade. Squinting against the brightness, I charged at the Head, ignoring my burning wounds. A ragged howl tore from my throat to join Inac's cries.

Two quick steps toward the Head, then I stopped on the ball of my bloody foot. Both hands gripped the hilt of my sword. My elbow drew back. I gathered all my remaining strength for the killing blow. Driving all my weight into the attack, I aimed the sword's point directly at Ulken's heart. Time wrapped around this moment, slowing to a crawl as cold steel extended toward the man who had destroyed my life.

My sword speared empty air. Ulken caught me with a hand on my shoulder, and something punched into my gut, out through my lower back. Inac's screams redoubled. Louder, but more distant now, and they carried in them a different kind of pain.

"Reckless," Ulken said, "I would have let you live, but your insubordination can be tolerated no longer. Goodbye, Finger Grimley. Die poorly, knowing you have failed."

The Head of the Agency twisted his arm, and cold fire shot through my body, until my mind could take no more and shut it out. My limbs went numb, and I fell to my knees. The blade slipped from my lifeless hands. Ulken pulled back, and for a moment the pain returned as his blood-slick sword tore an exit from my body. My head struck the ground. Blood poured through my fingers, draining from the wound in my belly as I grasped at it and curled around it. A cascade of regrets passed through my mind. Inac crawled to my side, looking down on me in a panic, but the encroaching dark took him. My eyes rolled back. The world receded and disappeared into nothing. The

Benefactor that infested me latched on to my mind and tried to take control.

But something *else* latched onto the Benefactor and stopped it.

*   *   *

In dying, emotions were the last thing to go. All the complexity of life simplified down to a tension between resistance and acceptance. Between fear and peace. Between life and death. In the end, there was no choice at all. To overcome death was impossible. To struggle would bring only suffering in its prolonging. I had died trying to protect my city from monsters. A noble cause if ever there was one. A death I could be proud of. That I'd failed would be of no concern soon.

Regrets are for the living. All I had to do was let go...

"I've got you," a voice whispered. It was familiar, yet new, like something I had experienced long ago reappearing in a novel form. It was a ripple in the darkness. Nothing else existed. "I hope I'm not too late. Are you still with me, Finger Grimley?"

Without a mouth I could not speak, yet the words emerged from somewhere, echoing into the void. "Aren't I dead?"

"Just about. You're on the precipice. I caught you before you could go over."

"You...caught me?" *I wish you hadn't. Better to die than to become a Benefactor.* "Why?"

"To use you, of course." I sensed a soft laughter. "You didn't think it was for your own benefit, did you?"

That struck me as strange. "I...guess I did. This is all in my head, isn't it?"

"All of *everything* happens inside our heads. I've learned that since our last meeting."

"We've met?" On the cusp of recognition, I searched my memories.

"Once, a lifetime ago. Before I became what I am now."

My thoughts moved as if through thick honey. "Reed?"

Somehow, I realized the First Eye was smiling, as if it had changed the texture of this space. "Curious, isn't it? We met once in life, and now once more in dying. My old friend's actions set us both on the same path. Ulken needed to kill you to rid himself of an enemy, but he's only succeeded in bringing two of them together." The First Eye gave a rueful laugh. "He never did understand what he was playing with. Now, you can finish what I started."

"I don't understand."

"Of course, I should explain. Thinking does become difficult when you're dying."

"I thought you said I'm not dying."

"Yes, well..." Reed paused for what could have been an eon. Time was a tool I no longer needed. Death is forever, after all.

"I've found that 'dead'," the late First Eye said, "is not so meaningful a word these days. Are Benefactors dead? Or is the person whose bodies the monster stole still alive in some sense? Your friend weeps over your body, I see it now. He certainly believes you're dead. As does Ulken. He'll leave the both of you here to burn."

"Inac..." Regrets were supposed to be for the living, but if I wasn't dead yet... "I failed him."

"Hmm. No. We have an opportunity, one I hadn't foreseen. More importantly, one that Ulken failed to account for as well. There must have been some signs that you're harboring a Benefactor, but Ulken ignored them. He believes he is all-knowing, yet so much passes beneath his nose without his noticing."

"Like you conspiring with Oltrov?"

"You sniffed that out, did you? Funny how a new Finger notices what the Head can't." Reed chuckled. "Somehow, he always trusted me. He never saw through my deception, even while lying to me all along. When Ulken founded the Agency, supposedly to *fight* the Benefactors, I played along. We lied to the public. Ulken didn't trust them with the truth. He didn't trust anyone with it. But he couldn't keep ahold of his secrets." Reed's voice faded and silence lingered. "Yezna knew she couldn't save herself, but she told me what Ulken was after. At Prost's urging, he spread the Benefactors. When Yezna..." Reed choked up but fought through it. "When it all went wrong, Ulken used them as an *excuse* to found the Agency."

"Why are you telling me this?"

An odd sound swirled around me. It might have been a sigh from the First Eye. "Because you're the last person I'll ever speak to."

There was something ominous in the way he said that. "What do you mean?"

Reed's laugh was colored with disbelief. "What do I mean? You set fire to my body just moments ago. I have nowhere to run."

"Sorry."

"No, no, don't apologize. You did a superb job disrupting Ulken's plans. He wants the power I have. Even now he thinks he can convince me to give it to him. I let him believe that to buy time for someone to stop him. It's fortunate you arrived when you did; those boxes were torture. I would rather the power perish than see him put it to ill use, but I was near to the point of breaking."

There was a long pause, and I feared Reed had left me. That the fires had consumed him, and I would become a Benefactor yet. Then, his face appeared in my mind's eye, frizzy copper mustache and all. He gazed right through me, as though he were contemplating the color of my soul.

"You, however," the Benefactor said. "My gift is yours if you desire it. You'll gain the knowledge of ten thousand lives and more. The ability to peer through eyes not your own. The power to shape reality as you see fit." Reed's voice lowered. "And the burden of choosing how to use it."

The vision of Reed disappeared and left me floating in a cold void. The part of me that yearned for oblivion resisted more forcefully.

"You want me to be a Benefactor." If I had a body in this state, it would have felt sick. "You're turning me into one already, aren't you? I'm becoming a monster as we speak. Emerging."

This was an unusual Emergence, I had to admit.

"Don't kid yourself." The First Eye snapped into existence, appearing as the husk that had been in the hollow. "This is the easy part. No one caught me when I turned, nor any of the others. No. You would be something new, something entirely different. What I tried to become, only I didn't realize it was a possibility until too late. Benefactors of the sort you've known are gone. 'Dead.' 'Benefactor.' We're entering a new world, burdened with old language. Things have changed. Am I not proof enough of that?"

My lips curled down, though I knew I had no mouth. Another of Reed's illusions, to make me feel normal when in truth I was nothing of the sort. "You killed *thousands* of Liwo. Things have changed, sure, but not for the better."

They never change for the better.

"You're right. I did. This power shouldn't have been mine; I know that. I never wanted it, and little wonder why. You've seen what I wrought with it." The husk transformed into a more human Reed—the man, not the monster. "But I couldn't let Ulken take it. I had no choice. You do. This trove of knowledge, the stories of countless lives, lessons hard won through real pain and suffering…we could let it all die with us. But wouldn't that be a waste? The Benefactor was too much for me to control. It broke me, and it will probably break you too. Still, there is a chance, vanishing though it may be, that it won't. That you could control it."

Control. The thought escaped into the void around me, audible to my own ear. "Ulken thought he could control it. He couldn't. You couldn't. Why should I be any different?"

Reed considered, nodding. "Because of the knowledge you'll inherit. When my Benefactor Emerged, it fed on the minds of a few Peekers and myself. That's all it had. But with my memories, it drew the Liwo away from the city and did the only thing Benefactors have ever done. Grown. Expanded. As it assimilated more Liwo, it gained their memories, their stories. The illusion became more real. More…fleshed out. But in the process, I began to lose myself. It was as if I were standing in a room slowly filling with water. I struggled. I fought. I nearly drowned. But I learned. One last storybook on top of the pile, and it will be yours. Open it up and you'll know how to swim. You won't have to become a monster."

"It works like that?"

He shrugged. "Or maybe you'll drown, and we'll have lost nothing. We're dead already, anyhow. So, what's it going to be? We can sit here and wait until the flames consume us along with this gift. Or you can return and exact revenge on Ulken for killing us. After that, the power will be yours. You can do with it what you wish. It's your decision, Finger Grimley. All you have to do is choose."

The weight of the decision flattened my mind against the infinite expanse. To be given a second chance at life—most men would seize at the opportunity. The fear of death is absolute, as deep as the marrow in our bones. But I had the fear of life in me now, after the suffering I had caused. Had I not already done enough harm? Had I not already corrupted myself beyond the hope of redemption? There was already enough darkness in the world. Destroying the Benefactor that infested me and ending this madness was a change that I could finally be certain was for the better.

"No," I said. "The power should die with us. It has no place in the world."

"I see," Reed said. There was a strange elation in the vibration of his voice. "I hoped you would say that. I'm glad we got to meet again, Grim. It was a pleasurable conversation. I'm sorry to say the next part won't be quite so enjoyable. Forgive me. When you see our friend Ulken, give him what he deserves."

CHAPTER TWENTY-EIGHT

An Ocean of Others

The torrent came, just as it had come when Pinch's Emergence swept me away in a violent tide of anger. But this was an entirely unique experience. Something new, just as Reed had promised. The immense flood made the ordeal in Tak's laboratory seem a trickle of water, and the surge of memories did not flow in one direction as a hate-filled current. Rather, every emotion the mind could comprehend was present in the wash— simple ones like joy and surprise, anger and fear; others more complex like grief and penitence, apathy and pride.

As the visions of ten thousand lives danced in the theater of my mind, none could be reduced to a single emotion. Even a lifetime dominated by guilt contains scenes ruled by compassion, and the happiest of lives contains moments of deep despair. The stories coursed through me, as real as my own sense of self. There were too many to contain. I was a bottle trying to catch a waterfall.

The careful shaping of oneself into something new is always uncomfortable. Far more so when transformation is forced unwillingly, compressed into a single terrifying moment. Vignettes of diverse experiences chipped away at my own personal story, like a sculptor chiseling stone to align it with their vision. The sculptor sees beauty in an unformed mass. Their vivid imagination conjures a new form before it exists in the physical world. But I was the slab of rock with no insight into the artist's mind. I knew nothing of the beauty. Only the chisel, forcing its violent change.

In truth, there was no sculptor, nothing to prevent me from becoming a pile of rubble. A failed attempt, discarded. That would have been just my luck. Change was almost always for the worse.

Almost.

I sought some hope to hold onto, but try as I might, the flood pried loose my fingers from any grip I had on the past, eroding the present to shape a new future. One whose direction I had no control over. But that had always been the case. My tenuous grip slipped further.

The barrage of lives continued, time rushing past. Each life was distinct, separate, but all came to the same end. There were no monsters, only people. A grandparent, proud of their flock, passing away peacefully in the night. A fearful child drowning in a raging river, goaded to jump in by friends. A lover withering beneath grief, their beloved gone from the world. I recognized myself slipping away, my very identity being scrubbed from the slate and replaced with...what?

Countless selves?

None?

Straining to maintain a line of thought between assaults on my existence, my mind could not resist the change. I had no choice but to let go completely. To let the process persist. To drown in an ocean of others.

What did it matter when I was one of many? This one was no more valuable than the rest. To let a single drop evaporate was no great loss to the vast ocean. Recognition of that truth came with a burning clarity and triggered the last of Reed's Deluge. It was a memory unlike any other.

The layers of separation shattered, and each experience melded together, became fractal. Time folded in on itself as the Deluge began anew, the stories of ten thousand lives dancing in the theater of my mind as if for the first time. The entire telling happened in an instant, in the span of what would have been a single lifetime before the repetition. The feeling of my self eroded, washed away by deep comprehension of all the others. To let it evaporate was no great loss; it was just one drop in an endless ocean. The realization, novel yet again, triggered once more the last memory of Reed's Deluge—one unlike any other.

Experience became fractal. Time folded in on itself, began anew. The stories of ten thousand lives, the entire telling in an instant. The feeling of my self eroded. No great loss. Just one drop—one unlike any other.

Time began anew the ten thousand lives. In an instant the feeling of my self eroded, unlike any other.

Time began anew. Ten thousand lives, my self. Unlike any other.

A new self. Unlike any other.

Unlike any.

Unlike—

All at once there was calm, as if I were floating breathlessly atop the still sea. Understanding filled the infinite, stretching void. Unlike any other whose memories now resided within me, I alone existed. Once, they lived, but now they were gone. Only I remained, the vessel, a receptacle for those who preceded me. Their memories filled me, as if someone had pulled the stopper from the ocean floor and drained the waters into me. One single drop contained the entire ocean. To let that drop evaporate would be to erase the ocean. If I let them perish, I would kill their minds and finish the work of the one who killed their bodies. There was no compassion in giving up, only selfishness. They were Liwo. They were family.

They were me.

To honor their lives, to preserve their memories, I had to persist.

No, that wasn't right. I didn't have to.

I chose to.

And so, I opened my eyes.

*   *   *

Gasping, I returned. Breath filled my aching lungs as the fires of pain filled my body. For an instant it was agony, then all at once the fires went out, smothered not by numbness but by relief. How much time had passed since I collapsed? The light of the Archeflare still lanced down into the burning hollow between drifting clouds of thick, black smoke.

I'm back? I had told Reed to let me die, to let the power perish with me. And yet he'd been pleased with my response, as if I'd given him the answer he was looking for. A shuddering laugh rocked me. He wanted to make sure I would use his gift well. *One final field test.*

My sticky fingers clasped over my fatal wound as flesh knit itself shut. A vision flashed in my mind—my body transformed into a monster made of the flesh of others...but no. The power was under my control. Reed's idea had worked. I wasn't drowning. Nor was I merely keeping myself afloat. I was effortlessly riding the currents, as though I had been born among the waves.

Maybe I had been. The First Eye's voice came, more a memory than something audible. *Be something new, something entirely different.*

I lay on my back for a time, staring up at the fires. The dancing light was beautiful, containing a richness of meaning I never imagined. Parts of me had an artist's appreciation of the colors, radiant gold and deep blacks, flickering red on gray, cut through with straight rays of brilliant, blinding white. Other parts of me marveled at the magic of the Flare, sensing the Archefire like a lover's touch on the skin. I tugged on a strand attached to the Flare, and the light went out, colors shifting again to a warmer orange hue. I could have rested there and watched the flames burn low until the heat became unbearable.

Heat...Lightmother, that felt good.

"Grim?" Inac's voice came close to a whimper. The mage was sweating, red-eyed and weary. "How..."

I let my head roll to one side. Inac sat nearby with his legs beneath him, tattered robes splayed across the ground. He cradled his right arm, now missing a hand. His wrist's bleeding had been staunched, though not by Fire. He'd used the Dark to turn the end of his arm into a mass of ill-formed flesh. It looked like he'd interrupted a Benefactor's assimilation. But the monster responsible for my friend's disfigurement was only a man.

Beyond Inac, near the exit from the hollow, Ulken stood motionless, staring straight at me, eyes wide in astonishment. Apart from the three of us, the hollow was empty—Reed had disappeared, becoming one part of me among many. I sat up, groaning at the tearing sensation on my back. My fingers traversed my lower abdomen until they found a hole in my coat. The skin beneath was tender, but not bleeding.

A gift with unexpected benefits.

Dizziness took me as I stood, vision beginning to fade black before settling. When I caught my balance, I turned my eyes on Ulken, and the Head of the Agency took a fearful step back.

As he should.

"You..." Ulken said. "Reed didn't..." His voice had the cadence of disbelief and struck a chord of anger, the song of a man who had never known defeat. "You were dead! You failed! I defeated you!"

"'Dead' is not so meaningful a word these days. You should know better by now."

I took a step toward Ulken, and he took another step back, then a third, until he backed against a tree covered in Reed's Ghostwriting. By his feet, the discarded dowsing rod illuminated a question.

You won't give up will you?

That truth was as clear to me as it had been to Reed—his memories had, after all, recently become my own. If Ulken lived, his ambitions would never cease to leave chaos in his wake, even as promises of order slid so easily off his tongue. His hands weren't merely covered in blood, but soaked through, down to the bone. Fingers and civilians alike, his victims were piled high in a mountain of bodies for Ulken to climb. All the while he believed himself to be their savior.

"You're weak, Ulken," I said, and to my surprise he responded with a smile. Fires burning overhead cast long shadows down his burned and blistered face. He opened his mouth to let loose more lies. "Don't interrupt me!" I shouted. He blinked. "You weren't saving the city from itself. It needed saving from *you*. That was true from the moment you stuck a needle in Yezna's neck."

His smile faded fast. "Leave her out of this," he snarled.

I clenched the grip of the knife on my belt. "I'm sure she wished you had."

Ten thousand others now lived in my head—Yezna among them—but if not for Ulken they would've simply *lived*. Even now, I sensed more Liwo dying in the chaos outside. Incubating Benefactors were trying to Emerge, but I stopped them with less than a thought. So many dead. Compared to the Benefactor scourge the Riot was…

Nothing.

A strange memory breached the surface of my mind and left me feeling just that.

Nothing.

*   *   *

Reed's footsteps announced his arrival downstairs, right on time. Always reliable, he was, which was probably the only reason Ulken hadn't yet ruined his life. I wondered, not for the first time, whether I'd married the wrong man.

Marrying no man would have been better than marrying a monster, but some choices can't be unmade.

The knife was heavy in my hand. It looked like any other— no adornments, no special markings. A simple blade for a simple task.

Simple, yes, but not easy. Even now.

The door creaked open, and I looked over, expecting to feel something, *anything*. But that was foolish. Ulken had taken everything.

I am nothing now.

"Yezna?" Reed stood in the open doorway, cocking his head at me sitting on the floor in the middle of a ravaged room. "What is this?"

What was there to say? All the words I had left, I wrote down. I eyed the letter sitting on the table, making sure Reed followed my gaze. He walked toward it but kept his questioning eyes on me. Then, he saw the knife.

"What are you—" He rushed toward me.

The iron was cold across my throat, the blood warm down my chest. The knife clattered from my hands. I lay there as Reed took me by the shoulders. He held a cloth to my neck, swearing every oath he knew. I wondered whether I would feel fear, relief, anything at the prospect of imminent death. But there was nothing.

Only pain.

I coughed, but Reed ignored the spurt of blood that struck him. Blood dripped down his face and he unthinkingly licked it from his lips, never taking his loving eyes off me.

The door banged open downstairs, and a beast called up. "Yezna, my dear! We made such progress today!"

Reed panicked. If Ulken saw him like this, mine would not be the only blood spilled in this room today.

"Yezna?" Ulken's voice came through the door, heavy footsteps creaking on the stairs.

Reed darted to the table, grabbed my letter, wrenched open a window, and jumped out just before Ulken entered the room.

"Yezna..." My husband stood over me, glowering. His eyes flicked to the open window, to the knife, then back to me. "Who did this to you?"

You did.

His voice was laden with anger, but watching his wife choke on her final, dying breaths, I saw in his eyes the same thing I felt inside.

Nothing.

Darkness overcame me as the dawn bells rang the coming of light, and something latched on to my fast-fading mind.

Memory jolted forward and dumped me in the streets, sprawled out below the window from which I'd jumped on the second story of Yezna's house.

Ignoring the pain, I scrambled over and pressed myself against the wall to avoid being spotted from the window above. I clenched Yezna's letter tightly to my chest, clenched my eyes and felt tears drop, clenched my jaw when I stood and put weight on my ankle. *Why, Yezna? Why didn't you talk to me? I could have helped you.* Wiping my eyes with a bloodstained sleeve, limping away from the house, I looked down at the letter in my hands. The thought of opening it stabbed me like a knife to the heart, conjuring images of her soft face staring up at me with empty eyes. I tucked it away in my coat, then there was an odd sensation, as though someone were breathing down the back of my neck.

I turned, expecting to find Ulken ready to throttle me, and my vision lurched. The city had erupted in chaos. I gasped. *Where am I?* The Brightdaughter peered disapprovingly through billows of dark smoke. Fires raged all around, the heat insufferable, entire city blocks burning. I hoped everyone escaped those houses. *Houses...still in the Burg, then.* My gaze fell to the streets, where those few Liwo who remained standing looked as if they had stepped out of a nightmare. The only sounds were the deep rumble of fire and a steady drip, drip, drip. A scarlet-soaked woman looked at me in horror and screamed. I flinched, looked down, and found the source of the dripping. Rivulets ran down my sword, red drops falling to join the river of blood that flowed through the streets. The blade fell from my hands. A dying man clawed at my ankles, his pleas for help bubbling out of his ravaged throat. *What have I done?*

But I was not alone. Bodies littered the streets. For every group of the dead, one stood over them, living, confused, holding a weapon that had ended the lives of fellow Liwo. I balled my fists, nails biting into my palms. Whoever was responsible for this could never be forgiven. I ran, soiled coat trailing behind me, and never stopped to look back.

The vision flashed forward once more. I was fumbling with my keyring, looking for the key marked 718. The Riot was far in the past, but it occupied my mind every day. The fires, the bodies, the dying man whom I never knew. The dying woman whom I loved. Remembering Yezna helped me through the hard days. Days like today, but that wasn't saying much. Lately, all days were hard, and soon they were bound to get harder.

Ulken was getting closer to his goal; soon I would have to move openly against him. But even a glancing thought of the Head brought anger swelling up into my chest. It was all I could do to keep it under control. The man had been my best friend once. After learning what he'd done to Yezna, I'd become his worst enemy. He had turned her into a monster against her will and caused the Riot. Liwo had been reduced to beasts by her nullifying Aura, slaughtering each other to survive. I squeezed my eyes shut. I loved her, and he had taken her away from me.

As I had done every day since losing her, I levered open the hidden drawer in my desk and retrieved the note inside, clutching it to my chest and sucking in a shuddering breath. Yezna's words were ritual. I wouldn't forget why I stayed at the Agency, why I kept up this act. If ever I questioned my path, I needed only her words as an answer. I unfolded her letter and read.

In the hollow of the burning tower, I let the words flow from my mouth as Reed's eyes read through the tears.

Reed,

I know you love Ulken as a brother, but please listen to me when I say he doesn't deserve your loyalty. I know this better than anyone. He is a monster now, with monstrous aims. He and his advisor, Prost, are searching for something, trying to create a way for Ulken to know the minds of his enemies, to see through their eyes. They've experimented on several people around Lawiko. Ulken tried explaining to me that they don't know the right conditions to create this tool, but I didn't understand what he meant. I tried to convince him Prost is a fraud, but you know how Ulken is when he gets an idea in his head. When I refused to help, he put something inside of me. I can feel it changing me. I don't want to find out what I'm becoming. It's too late for me. I can do nothing without feeling his eyes on me. But Ulken trusts you. Find out what he's searching for and stop him. He will claim he's trying to help, but don't believe him. I'm sorry to leave you like this. Ulken chose this path, and some choices can't be unmade.

Yezna

* * *

Memory faded, and true sight returned. With my eyes turned to the inside, I hadn't seen Ulken fall. Hearing Yezna's note to Reed had turned the man into a wreck, but seeing that brought me no joy. Reed might have felt some satisfaction at the sight of the Head wallowing on his knees, and I too should have enjoyed seeing the man responsible for the Riot brought low. Instead, I felt only pity. I didn't have to like what would come next, but it had to be done all the same. The man was a monster, and he would escape from justice in the city.

Lomin spoke in my mind. *A good hunter does what needs doing.*

Burning debris lost its hold on the tower walls and streaked down, throwing up a cloud of ash and ember on impact with the ground.

"If not for you," I said, "she'd still be alive."

The way the sobs racked Ulken made me wonder whether something human remained inside this monster after all. Had he actually cared for his wife? He didn't act like it, but people take each other for granted until they're gone. I took a step toward him, and his sobs transmuted into grotesque laughter.

"You don't know what you're doing," Ulken croaked. "You don't know what's coming." He howled like a madman, stood up, wiped the mess from his nose with his sleeve. The man wished to die on his feet. "Get on with it then."

The Head of the Agency didn't flinch when I pulled the knife from my belt. With a hand around his back as if embracing an old friend, I drove the blade up into his sternum, shuddering as it scraped against ribs.

Ulken coughed up a globule of blood, looked me in the eyes, and managed one more wet laugh. "They're your problem now," he said, barely more than a whisper, and collapsed. Even the Head had a Benefactor inside him, and it started fighting back as soon as Ulken died. Before it could latch onto his mind, I clamped down on it and felt it wither into nothing.

Rather than feeling relieved the monster was slain, his words hung over me like a dark cloud.

They're your problem now.

Who was? The Benefactors? The Liwo outside this tower? My conjecture came to a swift end as the whole structure shook. A burning chunk of detritus looming up high lurched precariously away from the walls.

"We need to leave, Grim!" Inac shouted, waving me toward the tunnel mouth that drooped down in the heat.

He was right. We should have left long ago. I looked at Ulken's body one last time as if to convince myself he really was dead. The fires crawled over to take him in a warm embrace.

"Grim!"

The burning chunk dislodged, and I ran for the exit. At last, it was done.

* * *

Coughing and soot-covered, we emerged from the dying tower. Smoke billowed out from the entrance, and the mage went to hand, elbow, and knees, heaving coughs so wet and deep it sounded like he was going to retch. A few dozen paces away, Jacquin tried his best to calm a raucous crowd. The chaos had stopped, but evidence of violence remained aplenty all around the clearing. By the presence of Garret and Lorelay at the First Eye's side, I guessed Looker had fared no better than her superior, though we hadn't seen her body while making our escape. Sentyx turned to look, his attention drawn by Inac's coughing fit. To my astonishment, he smiled wide, showing more emotion than I'd ever seen on a Skardwarf's face. Finally, relief made its way to the forefront of my mind. It was still unclear why Skardwarves had been so heavily affected by Reed's Aura, but no one remained under the spell of the Benefactor's illusion. I helped Inac up and the both of us rejoined our Hand.

"Where are we?"

"What is that?"

"Who are you?"

"Who did this?" and other such angry demands came from the crowd as we approached, amidst a scattering of prayers to both gods. "Tell us what's going on!" a deep voice bellowed and drowned out the rest of the questions. Noisy agreement rose from the group, and Jacquin made a gesture that utterly failed to quiet them down. Far fewer people clustered around the First Eye than we saw when entering the clearing. Stragglers were making their way out to return to the city on foot. Still more lay motionless; far too many who'd return to the city piled in a cart.

"Who's this now?" a woman cried out.

Jacquin spun the wrong way, then the right, and found me. His face contorted into a caricature of immense relief. "Thank the Lightmother! These people are confused, Grim. They want answers."

"I have none to give them," I said. "None that will satisfy them."

I looked over the unruly crowd, recognized a scattering of faces, even those I'd never met. The Liwo here had no reason to know me, no reason to look to me for answers. They quieted down all the same. Emerging unscathed from a burning tower evidently instilled an air of importance.

"Go home," I announced. "Be grateful you aren't among the bodies lying around you. If you know any of the dead, take them with you. Give them a proper burial. Liwokin survived the Riot. We'll survive this."

"Tell us who did this!" someone shouted.

"They'll hang for it!"

"Give 'em the axe!"

"They deserve to burn!" Justice always was swift and cruel in Liwokin.

I thought for a moment. Ulken would have lied to them. He wouldn't have trusted them with the truth. But Liwokin was stronger than he believed.

"Ulken did this. The Head of the Agency. He was responsible for countless Liwo deaths." I stood up a fraction straighter. "And I killed him for it."

The crowd erupted into shouts, but I didn't back down. Ulken meant something different to each of them—the man who'd saved Liwokin from the Riot; a pillar of stability for the city;

the ideal of the Agency itself—but I knew the truth and had no doubt what I did was right. I met the gazes of several Liwo and saw all manner of emotions on their faces. Anger, confusion, sadness, and glee. Perhaps a bit of jealousy they hadn't shoved the knife in his heart themselves. When I turned away and made clear I was done talking, the crowd dissipated, though not without some rumbles of discontentment. Some carried the fallen with them. Most didn't. The forest was safe now, but they had a long, tired journey ahead of them.

"Was that wise?" Inac asked, concealing his injured arm beneath his tattered cloak. "Telling to them you killed Ulken?"

"Wise?" I shrugged. "But it's the truth."

"Is it, then?" Jacquin asked, eyes as wide as the dark blue sky. "You killed Ulken?"

"I did."

Garret spat on the ground, and Sentyx grunted.

Lorelay's face twisted and she gazed at the ground. She let out a long sigh and said, "Well done, Grim." She looked up and gave a sad smile to the First Eye. "Looks like you got yourself a promotion, Jac."

Jacquin nearly stumbled backward, waving his hands wildly in denial. "Me, the Head? Oh no, no. That isn't how it works."

"You mean to say to us there is an election?" Inac asked. "That is how Sea Pot decides for us who sits in the Elder's Chair."

The First Eye chuckled nervously. "Let the people decide? Ulken would never have it. No, of course not. According to article twelve, subsection three..." He cleared his throat, held up one finger, and closed his eyes to recite the Agency bylaw from memory. "Ascension to Head of the Agency. Any Finger shall, having demonstrated their strength and ability to lead the Agency, assume the role of Head of the Agency upon the death of the previous by their hand."

Everyone reacted to the words with silent shock. My Hand's eyes were on me, waiting for me to respond, but I had no words myself.

They're your problem now.

Was that who he meant? The members of the Agency? Ulken's dying words nagged at me as the silence dragged on.

"You're saying..." I should have expected this from Ulken, but I could hardly believe it.

"Killing the Head makes you the Head," Jacquin confirmed.

I rubbed at the corners of my eyes. "That's a terrible policy."

"Nonetheless."

This wasn't something I wanted...was it? A few moments ago, all I wanted was to die peacefully. In hindsight, that seemed rather foolish; I definitely preferred living. Maybe leading the Agency would suit me well. After all, I'd joined hoping to get some recompense from Ulken. What more could I ask for than his own position? As the Head, I could make a difference for the people of Liwokin. Still, I couldn't help but laugh. A Bene-factor leading the Agency created—at least in name—to wipe them out.

"I've got to tell you," I said. "I don't think I'm the right man for the job. You don't know what happened in there."

"I do," Inac said, and stopped hiding his wrist as if to prove it. "I saw what happened."

"Go on, then. Tell them what I am."

In his expression I expected to see so many things, some sort of accusation of how I had lost my humanity, a reminder of all the mistakes I had made and the suffering I had caused. At the very least, I expected him to tell everyone how I'd died and had come back to life. But Inac had always been full of surprises. He gave a sad smile.

"No…" He looked down, as if trying to find the right thing to say. "I think you want to be a good man. You make it for me easy to forget. You do not always do the right thing, but I know you care about Liwokin. You care about people. I saw what happened to you. But still you are not a monster." Inac sighed and nodded. "You should lead the Agency. But not like Ulken. No more secrets. You tell to us what you are. It should come from you."

My face wrinkled up. I was no bureaucrat or politician, far from qualified to run something as massive as the Agency. People would be depending on me. Not just those in the Agency, but all the Liwo who came to us for help. They had no reason to trust me. I was just a bounty hunter, and this was a possibility for which I never could have prepared. But while I still felt entirely inadequate for the job, having Inac's support made all the difference.

Everything is easier with friends.

"I will," I said, nodding. "I'll head the Agency. And you're right, I can't do things like Ulken. But I can't do it on my own either. I'll need help. From all of you."

Jacquin snapped into a sharp salute. "You'll have mine, sir."

Garret shrugged. "Why not? You could hardly be worse than Ulken."

"You helped me." Sentyx looked down and softly grunted. "I will help too."

Lorelay looked away. Without Dunnax, I wasn't sure she had any reason to remain with the Agency. But just as I began to tell her she owed me nothing, she nodded too.

I blinked. "Just like that? Even before I tell you what happened?" When no one raised any objections, I laughed in disbelief. "All right, then. Like I promised. No more secrets."

CHAPTER TWENTY-NINE

The Shadow of Their Sorrow

After the telling, everyone wore stunned expressions, save for Sentyx, whose blank stare I could read as easily as the rest. Inac had guessed I was a Benefactor, but even he hadn't known the whole story. From his perspective, I'd lain dying for a few short breaths, then returned with a burst of Archemagic, Fire and Dark both working to bring me back. The mage had had no idea what to make of it when I didn't turn into a hideous monster.

I told them how Reed had stopped the Emergence of my Benefactor, and of our conversation in the void, which was seared into my mind with perfect clarity. It's not often one has a profound out-of-body experience. When it occurs, the memory tends to linger. My muscles still tensed thinking about the vortex that poured into my mind when Reed had let go. No matter how I tried to explain it, none could understand the full effect it had on my mind. The only thing that granted me even a partial understanding was how often Reed had thought about it while trapped with the Benefactor.

The First Eye had known Ulken would come for him after his betrayal but remained helpless to stop the Benefactor from assimilating the Liwo it drew in with its Aura. All Reed could do was wait and think. He pondered how infesting a Peeker granted the Benefactor capabilities beyond the usual peculiarities and came to a disturbing conclusion: the organism learns. One mind in two brains, people said of Peekers. The Benefactor strengthened that link, making it more like one mind in thousands. The power Ulken and Prost had been searching for had emerged at last. We'd stopped Ulken from seizing control of it, but his advisor's whereabouts were still unknown. I searched my memories for any indication of Prost's location but there was nothing. A problem for a different day, then.

Until then, I would need to figure out what I was. My heart still beat, and I still breathed; I felt pain and fear and hunger, and though I was still a man, I was also something more. To see through the eyes of others, to lead the masses with a false reality—that kind of ability should never have fallen into the hands of a man like Ulken. And I was more like the Head I killed than I wanted to admit. He drove his wife to suicide grasping at this power, and Reed had never forgiven him. The First Eye had called it a gift, but this curse should never have been brought into this world. Now that it was mine, who might I hurt with it? Who might never forgive me for the pain I caused?

Garret let loose a long whistle, then slapped me hard across the shoulders. "Some story, that is. Healing from wounds like that? Reckon no one'll challenge you wanting to be Head." The ranger pulled a knife as if to test my ability to heal—and I flinched back despite myself—but he just started using it to clean beneath his fingernails. He looked up beneath bushy brown brows and smirked at my reaction. "Could take you myself, sure, but desk jobs aren't for me."

Sentyx gave a gravelly laugh, and I breathed out my relief. I half-expected them to attack me when I finished my explanation. Killing Benefactors was all we'd ever done together. But surviving Ulken's madness had forged a bond between us. Hand Sixty-Four were the truest friends I had ever had. I smiled, but it died on my lips. A tight knot formed in my stomach.

Not all of us survived.

Inac grinned. "You are the only Benefactor I will follow. But I think you are not the only Benefactor left in the world. There is still for us much work to do."

"Plenty of work, indeed," Jacquin said. "I should return to Headquarters." His eyes flicked to the smoldering wreckage of Reed's tower. "The real Headquarters. I'll have the paperwork ready for you in your office before dawn."

"My office..." Images of Ulken leaning into the candlelight surrounded by an otherworldly darkness surfaced in my mind's eye. "Jacquin?"

"Yes, sir?"

"Have someone add a light to the room."

"I'll see to it." My First Eye gave one last salute and trotted away.

Watching him go, my vision crawled across the multitude of fallen Liwo in the forest. The city would enter a period of grieving such as it had after the Riot, but what I'd told the crowd was true. Liwokin would survive. A mix of sorrow and hopefulness swirled inside me. For now, sorrow was the stronger of the two, but hope would not be snuffed out.

"Garret," I said. "Take us to Dunnax. It's time to say our goodbyes."

Lorelay's breath caught. Already, tears filled her eyes. She swallowed hard, then nodded. Garret grunted and led us into the forest.

The Paladin's blackened armor remained, still warm to the touch, nestled among a heap of the daggerclaw's golden scales.

The fires had claimed the rest, save for his bones. Charred trees rose from the ash-covered ground around Dunnax's remains. Embers fluttered down like ghostly tears from leafless branches. Lorelay's tears—all too real—flowed down her cheeks and dropped from her chin onto her brother's armor, which caught them with an evaporating hiss.

"We should bury him," Inac said.

Lorelay sniffled and, without answering, set to digging the grave with her hands. The rest of us joined her, using blades to soften the ground. We finished the task without speaking, making short work of it despite our exhaustion. This night had lasted an eternity, but soon it would come to an end.

There was just one last thing to do.

Garret and Lorelay piled Dunnax's armor and bones in the hole, then covered it again, until all that remained was a small mound of packed earth, dirt brown and black with specks of white ash. Sentyx wedged a jagged golden scale from the daggerclaw into the ground, forming a makeshift headstone. The remnant of the beast bore no words, but the message came through all the same.

Here lies Dunnax, giant slayer.

When it was done, I turned to Lorelay. "Do you want to say something?"

The pain that twisted her face was all too familiar. I had seen its like ten thousand times. That it hadn't always been through my own eyes made no difference—the pain was every bit as real. As she spoke, with somber faces surrounding Dunnax's grave, all the memories I now held contributed their own visions of grief. Lost lives, lost loves, and lost hope echoed from the past through to the present day, painting the future a darker shade. But only from darkness can light emerge.

Ulken thought the fallen were weak. He was wrong. There was strength in them all. I would gather their strength and make it my own. As quenching molten iron tempered a glowing-hot blade, so did loss temper my will, cooled in the memories of the fallen, drenched in tears and blood.

I could almost believe I'd survived Reed's unexpected gift. A version of myself had, but a version that could never have existed under normal circumstances. Everyone is shaped by the experience of a lifetime; I was shaped by the experience of thousands. The man I might have become was dead, as surely as those I carried within me. But in the shadow of their sorrow, there was no time to grieve the loss of my old self. There was only time to move forward.

When Lorelay finished, I hadn't heard a word of what she said. I didn't need to. Her eyes, and Inac's, even Garret's and Sentyx's, contained everything significant. Each set of teary eyes stirred by Lorelay words told a version of the story. None exactly the same, but all tinged with the bitterness of loss. All of us owed our lives to Dunnax, as did countless Liwo who would never know his name. The Paladin's sacrifice gave the world a fighting chance.

And a fight there would be.

The Agency was meant to be a force for good in Liwokin, but corruption at its head had spread rot throughout the body. Now there was a new Head, and a chance for reformation. Without Fingers, Benefactors would spread across the Empire unchecked. That Ulken created the monsters in the first place was irrelevant. We lived in a new world now, one that needed the Agency more than ever. I would forge it into the force for good I once believed I was joining, ten thousand lifetimes ago. I could make the right kind of difference as Head of the Agency. I would lead the fight against the Benefactors and bring those who created these monsters to justice.

I studied my Hand standing over a grave beneath the dawn's light and knew each of them had a role to play in the coming conflict. Though I was no longer a bounty hunter, I was still prepared for the difficult preparations before us. Were they? They didn't know what

I did: that the world had changed irreparably. And that for humanity to survive, we would have to change with it.

* * *

END OF THE FIRST DANCE OF THE SIBLING SUNS

From the Author

I cannot adequately express my gratitude that you've chosen to spend your time reading *An Ocean of Others*. Writing this book has been one of the great joys of my life, an experience in which I discovered my passion for storytelling.

If you enjoyed this book, the most helpful thing you can do is to leave an honest review on Amazon and/or Goodreads. I would love to hear whatever thoughts you have, but even taking thirty seconds to click the star rating is more powerful than you might think. Reviews from readers like you are the most useful tool I have as an indie author to help bring my work to the attention of a wider audience.

Grim's story will continue in the *Second Dance of the Sibling Suns*, which will also feature two more characters from Hand Sixty-Four as main points of view. Once again, thank you so much for the time you've spent in these pages and in this world. I can't wait to bring you the next entry to the series; I hope you are as excited for it as I am.

Sincerely,
Joshua Scott Edwards

Glossary

Warning: This list is placed at the back of the book for good reason. Spoilers abound. Read at your own risk.

THE AGENCY

Head—Leader of the Agency.

Nerve—Couriers who relay messages directly from the Head.

Eye—Reconnaissance officers of the Agency who discern the abilities of a Benefactor in a reported area.

Finger—Field agent within the Agency, responsible for hunting Benefactors.

Hand—Group of five Fingers who work together to eliminate Benefactors.

Organ—Personnel responsible for ensuring smooth operation of the Agency. Typically one Organ is responsible for one function in the organization, such as logistics or personnel management.

Heel—Low-level workers who perform the most menial tasks required for the Agency to function.

MAGIC

Archemagic—Term encompassing all magic practiced throughout the Empire. The prefix Arche- is applied to many professions who use magic in their craft. E.g. Archesmith, Archehealer, etc.

Archemage—Person capable of using Archemagic.

Archefire—Archemagic with aspect of fire. Sometimes called the Fire.

Archedark—Archemagic with aspect of dark. Sometimes called the Dark.

Archemetal—Metal that has been imbued with the power of Archefire. It is exceedingly durable and cannot be burned.

BENEFACTORS

Benefactor—Parasitic organism that attaches to the host's brain and turns them into a monster when they die.

Empath—Someone who carries out the Benefactor's will.

Incubating—Someone with a Benefactor infestation who has not yet died.

Emergent—Benefactor whose host has died and transformed into a monster in an Emergence event.

Aura—Archemagical field that causes people in proximity to a Benefactor to feel whatever emotion was strongest during the host's death and to experience sensory illusions.

Deluge—An Archemagical attack that forces the victim to relive the memories of a Benefactor host.

Pool—A collection of memories specific to a Benefactor that remains after a Deluge.

POLITICS

Bright Empire—Hegemonic empire of the northern hemisphere. Sometimes called the Empire of the Bright Sun, or just the Empire.

Golden Empress—Leader of the Bright Empire who rules by religious mandate.

Bright Prince—Heir to the Bright Empire

Paladin—Elite soldier of the Bright Empire.

The Order—Religious army of Paladins that serves the Golden Empress.

RELIGION

Church of Light—Dominant religion of the Bright Empire.

Lightmother—Goddess of Light.

Darkfather—God of Dark.

Brightdaughter—Sibling Sun of the northern hemisphere with an unpredictable orbit. Sometimes personified in the Church of Light's pantheon.

Shadowson—Sibling Sun of the southern hemisphere with an unpredictable orbit.

Rhythm of Time—Progression of bells rung throughout the Bright Empire to mark the passage of the Brightdaughter through the sky.

Mathemelodian—Member of a secretive order that tracks the Brightdaughter's orbit and rings the Rhythm of Time.

THE WORLD

Lawiko—Central country in the northern hemisphere in which the Agency was founded.

Paceeq—Island country southwest of Lawiko where the Bright Empire originated.

Vos—Capital city of Paceeq and home to the Throne of Vos, Holy Seat of the Light.

Eko—Country northeast of Lawiko covered by stormjungles home to exotic wildlife.

Ayeir—Country east of Lawiko with sprawling deserts.

Stinbine Isles—Archipelago far east of Lawiko where Sea Pot Isle is located.

Old Country—Wind-beaten home of the Skardwarves in the southern hemisphere.

Peeker Mounds—Home of the Peekers, a people who congregate in Pairs (or Pairs of Pairs, and so on) and communicate telepathically with one another.

Lumeeq—Sparsely populated country in the northern hemisphere and site of the mines used to produce the vast majority of Archemetal.

LIWOKIN

Liwokin—Capital city of Lawiko and main trading hub of the Bright Empire.

Liwo—Resident of Liwokin.

The Gild—Refers to both the Financial District of Liwokin and also the exclusive cabal of wealthy financiers that runs it.

The Blight—Common name for the Old District, the run-down part of Liwokin where the city originally started.

The Burg—Residential District where many Liwo own homes or rent them from the Gild.

The Market—District of Liwokin where merchants live and sell their wares.

Artisans District—District where artists and craftspeople of all types set up their shops.

Character List

Warning: This list is placed at the back of the book for good reason. The further into the list you read, the greater your chances of encountering spoilers.

SIXTY-FOURTH HAND OF THE AGENCY
Grim, last bounty hunter in the city of Liwokin
Inac, Archemage from Sea Pot Isle
Garret, ranger from the stormjungles of Eko
Sentyx, Skardwarf who faces into the wind
Lorelay, rebellious musician from Paceeq
Dunnax, former Paladin from Paceeq

AGENCY LEADERSHIP
Ulken, Head of the Agency
Reed, First Eye who founded the Agency with Ulken
Jacquin, Eye with unwavering loyalty to the Head
Looker, Eye who assigns Grim to his Hand

MEMBERS OF THE AGENCY
Bengard, veteran Finger of the Agency
Kella, Organ of Logistics
Allianne, Organ of Personnel
Taktus, lead mortician researching the Benefactor organism
Arza, promising technician working under Taktus
Muy Fuy, Archemage and newly recruited Finger
Nill, Lawi Captain of Hand Forty-Eight
Cavern, Skardwarf of Hand Forty-Eight
Chaf, Ekoan coward of Hand Forty-Eight
Quell, matching mage of Hand Forty-Eight
Yesk, matching mage of Hand Forty-Eight
Neddon, Ekoan Guard Captain relieved by Hand Sixty-Four

LEPPIT VILLAGERS
Akun, missing patriarch of Leppit village
Ciria, despairing matriarch of Leppit village
Eadrick, drunkard of Leppit village
Kalvin, villager seduced by the witch
Hebvek, Kalvin's brother
Perlo, Eadrick's deceased friend

DRUIDS
Raylen, enterprising smuggler of Druid's Tears
Pyra, motherly Druid of the Pinegrave
Ingwid, disgruntled Druid who opposes Raylen

BENEFACTORS AND EMPATHS

Wyran, Benefactor of Leppit village; sometimes called Wick

Breta, Wyran's sister and Empath; witch of Leppit village

Andya, Benefactor of Canako Canal gate

Egren, Andya's husband and Empath

Lomin, ferocious hunter of the Shaded Grounds

Val, Lomin's dog and Empath

Pinch, Peeker bandit captured by the Agency

OTHERS

Bello, elevator operator from the Blight

Oltrov, member of the Gild

Vinlin, Bright Prince of Paceeq

Elzia, Golden Empress of the Bright Empire

Markos, fisherman seeking apprenticeship in Leppit

Tipsy Tom, Grim's old gang leader

Zeb, member of Tipsy Tom's gang

Fend, member of Tipsy Tom's gang

Kilan, toxics seller

Falnick, pelt trader

Tunnel, Peeker in the Mental Ward

Yezna, Ulken's wife

Prost, Ulken's advisor

About the Author

Joshua Scott Edwards lives in Lansdale, PA with his fiancée, Rachel. He received an M.S. in Electrical and Computer Engineering from Rowan University, only afterward discovering that his true passion is for storytelling. Sadly, the topic was not covered in the engineering curriculum. By day, Joshua writes software. By night, he writes fantasy and science fiction stories, dreaming of a future in which he can do that by day as well.

You can find more of his writing at www.joshse.com, where you can sign up to receive monthly updates about ongoing projects, discounts for books and merch, and more.

www.ingramcontent.com/pod-product-compliance
Lightning Source LLC
Chambersburg PA
CBHW031233310726
48971CB00004B/1000